ALL THAT CONSUMES US

ALSO BY ERICA WATERS

ALL THAT CONSUMES US

ERICA WATERS

An Imprint of HarperCollins*Publishers*

HarperTeen is an imprint of HarperCollins Publishers.

Library of Congress Control Number: 2022952316
ISBN 978-0-06-311596-5
Typography by Corina Lupp
23 24 25 26 27 LBC 5 4 3 2 1
First Edition

For those on lonely paths

ALL THAT CONSUMES US

This is it, the last time you'll kiss me. I want to burn it into my heart, inscribe every touch so that later, in that dark place, I'll be able to run my fingers over the memory, feel the worn grooves of it against my skin. A spell for not forgetting, a spell for not disappearing.

It's midnight, and the moon is a pale sliver in the black velvet sky, less luminous than your eyes. The long fragrant branches of a weeping willow reach and sway, forming a lover's canopy around us, so that I can almost forget the others who circle us with their burning candles, their chanting voices. You reach out a too-warm hand to cup my cheek. My breath hitches.

Your lips touch mine, your tears wet against my cheeks. It's a soft, gentle kiss, already grieving for this memory, this time, the two of us.

Then, too soon, there's the knife and the pain and the ground opening up beneath me.

I'm alone in the dark.

ONE

There are two Corbin Colleges. During the day, Corbin is all autumn leaves and fluttering scarves—a postcard-perfect campus. But as I rush down this dimly lit, deserted sidewalk, I'm in the grip of nighttime Corbin, a different creature altogether. Just a few hours after sunset, Corbin has become a place of shadows and whispers, millions of trees creaking in the dark. Fog drifts up from the ground, muffling every sound except those nearest. The green hills of Appalachia seem to loom and lean, closing me in.

But it's not the dark or anything it might hold that I'm afraid of. Public failure is a far more frightening specter, one I'll be facing the second I walk into the lit club's reading to share my work for the first time. I'm already five minutes late, and I haven't even written the story's ending yet, so I break into a run when I see the English building. It's a stately, red-bricked thing, with perfectly symmetrical windows full of light, inviting me in from the dark and the cold—as if I'm not safer out here in the fog, far from the threat of public humiliation.

I jog up the stairs and through the heavy front doors, making my way down the hall to the largest of the classrooms, a lecture hall built like a small auditorium. I slip inside, trying to make as little noise as possible as I hurry down the aisle. But I needn't have bothered. They haven't started yet. Students mill around, sipping sodas and laughing at jokes like they aren't the least bit nervous about the lit club's flash fiction reading. They're mostly English majors, but they look like all the Corbin students do: well-dressed and self-assured, a sea of wealthy private school kids whose parents have ensured they will never have to know the cost of their education, let alone pay for it.

As soon as I find my seat, I yank out my unfinished story and start scribbling. I only had a half hour to write it while I scarfed down lunch between classes. It's basically *Jane Eyre* fan fiction, and it's got that gangly first-draft energy, all awkward sentences and overblown exposition. It's also the most cringey self-insert garbage I've ever written, and I know it. A young writer who has to teach high school English to pay off her college debt? It's a painfully obvious look at my future, and everyone will see straight through it.

But that can't be helped now. I jot down a final line and skim the pages quickly, looking for anything I can improve in the next thirty seconds. The opening is weak. I scratch it out and add a sentence to the top: *I sat by the window in the train, watching the dusty moors sweep by.* It's a little better, but not much. I find a few unnecessary adverbs and cross them out, fix a dangling modifier, cut the passive voice.

Finally, too disgusted to look at my own words any longer and desperate for a distraction, I scan the room for someone to talk to. I recognize the twenty or so other English majors from the orientation meeting the department held six weeks ago. They all seem to have brought friends—more people to watch me totally bomb my first reading. Even still, I wish I'd had someone to ask along for moral support. The room buzzes with warmth and energy, but I feel outside of it, left out in the cold. I've been so busy with work and trying to keep up with classes that I haven't really had time to go to the mixers. Still, there must be someone here I know. I brace myself and study the crowd again.

Britney Prins, a creative writing major with unnervingly perfect eyebrows and an obsession with Sally Rooney, sees me looking at her group and gives me a polite smile. Was it an invitation to join them? I wait to see if she'll catch my eye again, but she doesn't. It's always so hard to read the students at Corbin. Back home if someone didn't like you, there was nothing subtle about it. But here, there's a whole system of slights and innuendos that I always seem to read incorrectly.

I still haven't decided whether to go over when someone touches my elbow.

"Tara, right?" Dr. Coraline asks. He's the lit club's faculty sponsor. He's handsome in a late-forties kind of way, with sandy hair falling across his forehead.

I nod, summoning up a weak smile.

"There's a problem with the mic, so we're not going to start for a few more minutes. Feel free to mingle." He nods toward the group of English majors I'd been watching. "If I remember correctly from your orientation survey, you and Britney are both fans of Rilke."

"Oh," I say, a blush starting at my neck. "Okay, sure." I

did mention Rilke in that survey, but I suspect this is more about my pathetic social skills than literary kinship. I walk mechanically toward the group, already feeling my shoulders rolling in, arms wrapping protectively around my middle.

When I join Britney's circle, everyone goes silent.

"Hi," I say.

More silence. I've broken into the flow of their conversation.

"I'm Tara?" My voice goes up at the end, turning my name into a question.

They look at me expectantly, as if waiting for me deliver news. As the silence drags on, I start to panic.

"Dr. Coraline wanted me to let people know the mic isn't working, so we won't start for a while," I say, desperately seizing onto the lie. "Sorry to interrupt." The blush goes all the way up my face, and I know they can see it.

"Thanks, Theresa," Britney says with a big pitying smile. She starts to say something to the others.

"Oh, it's Tara actually," I say.

"Right, sorry." Britney grimaces at me. "We were talking about how much we love Evelyn Waugh."

"Oh, I've always wanted to read her," I say.

Britney raises her spectacular eyebrows, her mouth opening slightly. Someone else laughs.

"Evelyn Waugh was a man," Britney's boyfriend, Bobby, says, a smirk on his lips. He fiddles with a small ivory inlaid box that I think is a cigarette case. "*Brideshead Revisited*? *A Handful of Dust*?"

I close my eyes, embarrassment washing over me. I'd

mixed up Evelyn Waugh and Edith Wharton. "Of course. I meant—"

"You know, *Brideshead Revisited* has made me consider doing that study abroad program at Oxford," Britney says to Bobby. She angles her body away from me, toward the others. I want to flee back to my seat, but I make myself stand there, nodding and smiling like an automaton without comprehending a word that anyone says. Dr. Coraline catches my eye and shoots me a thumbs-up, clearly proud of himself for drawing me out of my isolation.

I glance at my watch and wonder if I ought to just bail on the reading. It's already been a long day, I'm tired, and I'm wasting precious time here. I still have homework to do before my janitorial shift tonight. I'll be lucky if I get to bed by two before I'm up again at seven to shelve library books. But if I don't make myself participate in these lit club readings, I'll never get any better at my writing. And then what's the point of coming to a school like this?

"Look," Britney says, the tone of her voice changing.

It jogs me out of my spiraling thoughts. The others turn, and I do too, just as a trio of freshmen from Magni Viri walk in. Two girls and a guy, deep in conversation. They're as well-dressed and self-assured as all the other students, but they look slightly hungover, their eyes red-rimmed, their clothes wrinkled like they slept in them. I only know one of them, a girl with waist-length curly red hair and pale ivory skin, dressed all in black except for the checkered laces in her Doc Martens. Meredith Brown, the English department's fastest rising star.

I bet *she* knows who Evelyn Waugh is.

"What do you think that's about?" Britney asks the others.

She means the argument the MV kids are clearly having. Meredith's eyebrows are drawn together in a scowl, her lips moving fast. The boy is shaking his head vehemently. It looks like a pretty serious disagreement, but given Magni Viri's reputation, it's probably an intellectual debate we mere mortals cannot comprehend.

I strain to catch their words, but their voices are hushed.

"Probably deciding whose turn it is to sacrifice a virgin," Bobby says in a low voice.

"What?" I look away from the MV kids. "What are you talking about?"

"Haven't you heard the rumors?" Britney asks, apparently more willing to talk to my uncultured self now that there's gossip to be had.

"You mean about them being a cult?" I've heard that rumor plenty of times, and it's not completely unwarranted. Magni Viri students rarely hang out with anyone outside their academic society. They live only with each other, study only with each other, date only each other. Even their dorm building, Denfeld Hall, is completely inaccessible to the rest of us. Legend has it that no one outside of Magni Viri has ever set foot inside. Denfeld is perched at the very edge of campus, looming from its hillside like a dark angel surveying the graveyard below. It's one of the few original buildings on campus still standing, a stone mansion like something out of a Gothic romance.

"They're not just a cult. They're a secret society," Bobby says.

"How can they be a secret society if we know about them?" I ask. It comes out snarkier than I intended. "I mean, they're not like Yale's Skull and Bones. They're a registered academic society that anyone can apply to. *I* applied."

Magni Viri is clearly too rarefied for someone like me, but of course I wanted a chance at free tuition, free room and board, and incredible connections.

"The academic society is just Magni Viri's public face. But they have a whole dark underbelly," Bobby says, lowering his voice, his eyes lighting up with lurid interest. "My dad went here, and when he was a student, he saw them perform a satanic ritual under a full moon."

"A satanic ritual?" I ask. This boy is such a tool.

"I'm serious. They're super creepy. My dad had wanted to join Magni Viri, but after what he saw, he was glad he got rejected. He said even if I'd been accepted, he wouldn't let me join."

I nearly roll my eyes. Of course two generations of entitled rich people will choose to believe that an academic society is some nefarious underground organization rather than accept their own mediocrity.

"Sure," I say.

"Believe what you want," Bobby says indignantly. "But I'm glad those creepy fucks keep to themselves." He ties his scarf more securely, as if the thought of Magni Viri gave him a chill.

I shoot a final surreptitious glance at the Magni Viri kids, who have settled into seats near the back of the auditorium. They don't look creepy to me. They look like the luckiest people alive. Full scholarships, academic support, connections I can only dream of. And best of all, a built-in friend group. Every time I see a group of them, their lives knitted so tight together, I feel my loneliness like a broken rib, an ache spreading through my entire body. I'm just as jealous as Bobby and every other Magni Viri reject at Corbin College. Though at least I'm more honest about it.

I can't help but imagine what my life would be like if I'd been accepted to Magni Viri. I could have majored in creative writing instead of the more practical English-for-teachers track. I'd have time to write. I wouldn't need to work two campus jobs to make ends meet. I wouldn't be drowning in loneliness as just another face in freshman housing.

But Magni Viri didn't want me. They wanted Meredith Brown.

If I'm honest, sometimes I feel like she's living the life I should have had.

By the time they get the mic working, it's seven thirty. I ask Dr. Coraline if he can make sure I'm in an early slot since I have to work tonight.

"Just not first," I say, and he laughs and puts me down for second place.

I go back to reading over my story, already hating every word of it. I only look up when the overhead lights go down. Dr. Coraline hurries to the mic to introduce the first student . . . Meredith Brown. I immediately regret having to go second.

Meredith stands tall at the front of the dim room, long

curly red hair blazing in the single light trained on her. Her alabaster skin seems to glow, as if it has swallowed up all the other light in the room.

"This story is called 'Incubus,'" she says in a slow, steady voice, the barest trace of a wealthy Southern accent softening her vowels. She holds a few printed pages in her hand, but she doesn't even glance at them. Head tilted up, green eyes on the audience, she recites her story from memory—or perhaps she creates it on the spot, drawing the words up from some secret well inside her.

After her first few sentences, everyone around me has stopped breathing. It might be because Meredith is one of the most beautiful people any of us has ever seen, or it might be because her words have woven a spell around us that we're afraid to break. I suspect it's a bit of both. No one shifts in their chair, clears their throat, leans over to whisper to a friend like they usually do at these readings. Most college-aged writers haven't exactly mastered the art of commanding a room.

But Meredith has. She speaks, and we listen. She does not fidget, play with her hair, adjust the cuffs of her blazer, or pull at the neck of her shirt. She doesn't look down, sweat, shake with nerves. Her voice is as steady and even as her gaze. She tells us her story. She holds us in thrall.

It's a strange, surreal story, like a waking nightmare. All sly allusion, evasive as a dream you can't remember, but it builds a slow dread inside your chest. I'm not even sure what the story is about, but I'm shivering by the time she's finished, my heart pounding and my eyes darting to the shadowy corners of the room, my arms squeezed tight over my chest. My breath comes short.

"Thank you," Meredith says, with a simple nod, as if she hasn't undone an entire roomful of people with her words.

The audience erupts into applause. I clap too, torn between envy and awe as I watch her step down from the stage in her tailored clothing and stride confidently down the aisle to sit with her friends.

Dr. Coraline takes Meredith's place at the mic. "Thank you, Mer. That was . . . brilliant. Truly brilliant." He shakes his head in wonder. "Next up is"—he glances at his clipboard—"Tara Boone."

I close my eyes for a moment and consider getting out of my chair and leaving the room. It isn't fair to make me follow that, to make me follow her.

"Tara?" Dr. Coraline asks, peering out into the lecture hall, his blond eyebrows raised hopefully behind his glasses. "Tara Boone? Are you still here?"

I shove to my feet with a squeak of protest from the chair and walk doggedly to the front of the room, my notebook gripped in one sweating hand. I can imagine what everyone sees when they look at me—the exact opposite of Meredith. I tug self-consciously at my fuzzy brown sweater, hating the way it sticks to my clammy skin. Once at the front, I push my shoulder-length dirty-blond hair behind both ears and squint at the audience. It isn't such a big crowd, only about forty people altogether. But it's forty more people than I've ever read my work to.

My hands tremble as I open the notebook. I swallow,

loudly, audibly, into the microphone. People in the audience start to whisper to one another, already losing interest in anything I might have to say. I feel Meredith's cool gaze on me from the back of the auditorium, and once again I consider walking out of this room, dropping out of college, and never returning to the state of Tennessee as long as I live.

"This story is called 'The Lady on the Train,'" I say, hating how my voice shakes. "It's—it's a work in progress." I read the story quickly, with terrible inflection, stumbling over the words. I never lift my eyes from the page. I can hear the hollow way the words fall in the room, clumsy and entirely without force. I might as well be rattling off the weather report for all the impact my story makes.

The dull sound of my own voice, the tremor of my hands holding the notebook, the awkward silence of the room around me all builds a slow, smoldering anger inside me as I read, until I'm practically spitting the words. If I didn't have to work two campus jobs to survive, I might have more time to write. If I didn't have to take the English department's secondary education track so I'd have a chance of a job after I leave college, I might get to develop my writing craft. If I'd been accepted to Magni Viri like Meredith was, I wouldn't have any of these problems. I could be just as good a writer as she is. I wouldn't have to worry about how to pay for my tuition. I wouldn't already be stressing about the student debt I'm going to have. I wouldn't be exhausted and barely keeping my head above water. I'd be holding this room captive just like she did.

Instead, I'm failing in every possible way.

After I read the last words of the story, I don't bother to

thank the audience or wait for their applause. I stalk from the stage, snatch up my backpack, and head for the door. I know it's rude of me, but I can't stand to sit here and listen to a dozen stories that are so much better than mine.

When I pass by Meredith, surrounded by her group of friends, her eyes meet mine for an electric, fleeting second. I expect to see mockery there, but instead she gives me a searching glance that seems to see straight through my skin and bones to what's underneath. I shiver and look away, wanting nothing more than to get out of this room, as far from perfect Meredith Brown as possible.

TWO

The moment I step inside my dorm room, I wish I'd gone to the library instead to study before my janitorial shift. My roommate, Helena, is here. She looks up from her laptop and blinks at me for a few seconds before turning back to her work. Helena is a business major from Connecticut whose pale blond hair lives in a permanently sleek ponytail, whose skin has the poreless sheen of porcelain, whose words are clipped and precise. Her side of the room looks like an interior designer put it together. She decided after one conversation with me on move-in day that I wasn't worth her time and has barely said another word to me since. I hardly mind since she did little more than grill me about my career plans and call my accent "sweet." When she does bother to talk to me, she's polite in a waspish way, but I overheard her on the phone with her mom once saying she expected a "higher caliber" student body. It was pretty clear she meant me.

So I do my best to ignore her right back. I toss my things onto my bed and then collapse there too. I lie still, staring at the ceiling, the horrible reading running over and over again in my head. I listen to Helena's fingers tap-tap-tapping on the keys and feel hot tears forming at the corners of my eyes.

Is every year at Corbin going to be this hard, this grueling, this lonely? I think I made a mistake coming here. I think I overshot. I should have gone to community college or at least a state school. I don't know why I thought I could do this. Why I thought my life could be different, could be more. When I got waitlisted, my mom told me a college like this wasn't for people like us, that I should set my sights closer to home. If she were still talking to me, I might call her up and tell her she was right.

But I was so sure of myself back then, so convinced I was going to get everything I dreamed of. High school had been easy. The teachers didn't expect much from a bunch of kids whose parents mined potash, waited tables, drew unemployment. There was nothing for me there, so I took as many online dual-enrollment courses as I could and graduated a year early, a month before my seventeenth birthday. I just wanted to get out of there, be someone else. Start my life. My *real* life.

I shouldn't have been in such a rush. Because back home, I might have been the weird, nearly friendless smart girl who read at pep rallies and always knew the answers in class. But here—here I'm not even that.

Instead, I am . . . no one. Nothing. Unremarkable. Another face in the crowd. A girl who writes half-finished stories that no one will ever like or remember.

The loneliness washes over me so powerfully that I almost can't stand it. I pull out my phone and scroll through Instagram to distract myself. I pause on a photo of Robin, my best friend from home. She smiles at the camera with her face pressed against her boyfriend Charlie's. They're both in band uniforms. She looks happy.

I click on her profile and scroll through all her recent photos. It's mostly her and Charlie, or her and other kids from band. There aren't any recent ones of me, which was more or less my own doing. After I started taking online classes, Robin and I drifted. She got busy with band, and I was always at work, trying to save up for a car to get me to college.

I have to scroll a long way to get to a photo of her and me. We're at the river, both in bathing suits, and I'm holding her up out of the water like she's a giant baby. We're both laughing. Right after the photo was taken, she dunked me under the water. I smile at the memory and wipe a few tears off my face.

I comment "Miss you" on the photo, then click the button to send her a private message. But my thumbs hover over the screen. Why should I break into her happiness with my problems? I've barely talked to her since I got here—we barely spoke before I left. And it's not like she can help me anyway.

I sigh and turn my phone over onto my chest. I need to stop this pity fest and get my essay that's due tomorrow done before I head to work.

I consider staying and writing my paper in bed, but the silence coming from Helena's side of the room feels so heavy I'm afraid I might collapse under it, sink through the floor and into the earth.

I hardly make a sound as I slip out of the room to find another place to haunt.

Back outside, on the foggy sidewalks of nighttime Corbin, I walk slowly and tiredly to the library, my one refuge on campus. Like Denfeld Hall and the chapel, the library is a pre-1900s building, one of the few that Corbin hasn't had to tear down or renovate into modern oblivion. Tonight it looks deliciously Gothic, hulking in the shadows like a gargoyle.

I push open the nearest of the two sets of heavy oak doors and walk beneath the arching stone doorway, my angry, dejected mood already starting to give way to the romance of the place. It's as silent as a tomb tonight, and Foster, the senior philosophy major who works the circulation desk at night, doesn't even look up when I pass by, earbuds in and his glazed eyes locked on a copy of Derrida's *Of Grammatology*.

Just as I reach the bank of carrels at the back of the first floor, my phone rings, startling me. I thought I'd silenced it before the reading. I yank it out of my back pocket and quickly reject the call, not even bothering to see who it is. I flick on the silent setting. Immediately, another call starts coming in again, mutely lighting up the screen. My phone never rings, so I can't help but wonder if it might be something important. But there's no number listed. It reads "Unknown Caller." My mind starts to spin through scenarios. Maybe there's a problem with my financial aid. Maybe Mom was in an accident. Maybe—

I shake my head. It will probably be a scam about my nonexistent car warranty. Still, I feel compelled to answer. I swipe the green phone icon.

"Hello?" I whisper.

The woman on the other end says something unintelligible.

"I'm sorry?" I whisper, a little louder. "This is Tara Boone. Who is this?"

A student working on a laptop at the nearest carrel turns her head sharply and scowls at me. I make an apologetic face and turn away from her.

"Hello?" I try again.

Sounds come from the other end, barely discernable: the rasp of cicadas, nails scraping on wood. I glance at the screen as if it can explain what's happening. The call duration reads 3:01. Three minutes. Has this gone on for three minutes already, or is my crappy refurbished iPhone on the fritz? It must be.

"Hello?" I try one last time. More weird noises, and then the call disconnects. My skin has broken out in goose bumps, the hair at the nape of my neck prickling unpleasantly, as if charged with static electricity. I drop the phone into my back-pack and shake out my hands, and the strange feeling passes.

I reach the stairs and start up the three narrow, claustro-phobic flights to the reading room on the fourth floor. The ancient stairs creak, and the fluorescent lights overhead flicker and shiver, casting strange patterns on the walls. When I finally make it up to the top, I breathe a sigh of relief. The reading room is the best spot in the library, especially during daytime, when light streams in through the huge, soaring windows and sparkles over the green and gold vines painted on the ceiling. It's what I always imagined when I thought of college.

But tonight, after Meredith's eerie story and the creepy phone call, even this comforting space feels weirdly unset-tling. The windows are dark, reflecting the room back at itself, everything vaguely warped and distorted. Shadows lurk in the corners, filling my imagination with unseen figures. The long rows of battered oak tables are mostly empty, only a few students typing tiredly on their laptops beneath the ghostly glow of green-shaded lamps, their faces shadowed and haggard.

Ignoring the shiver that runs up my spine, I settle into my favorite spot by the wall, nearest the long row of windows, and take a deep breath. I close my eyes, blocking out all the unnerving visuals my mind won't stop conjuring. Instead, I let the ever-present smells of the library fill my senses: must, dust, old paper, stale coffee. Familiar, comforting, speaking of long years of thought, research, art, creation. The tightness in my chest eases. *This* is why I'm here, I remind myself. This is what I imagined college would be. A place to dream, write, *become*.

With that thought, I try to banish the events of the night—the disastrous reading, Helena, and the weird, creepy phone call—and take out my laptop to get to work.

I'm two pages into an essay for Literature of the Ancient Near East about the goddess Inanna's descent to the underworld when someone lets out an ear-piercing scream that rips me from my work. I shoot to my feet.

The handful of other students in the reading room look around, their eyes wide. Everyone is frozen, unsure what to do. My first thought is that there is a shooter in the building, but then I realize I've heard no gunshots.

"Should we . . . ?" a white guy in an argyle sweater, sitting a few tables away from me, asks the room, his arms crossed protectively over his chest.

But no one answers and no one moves.

The scream comes again—weaker this time, laced with horror. My body moves toward the sound, as if of its own accord. Across the long room and down the stairs, my heart pounding in rhythm with my boots as I thunder down the steps. I never have been able to resist answering someone's cry for help, I think wryly. I almost didn't make it out of my hometown because of it.

I vaguely sense people following behind me as I break onto the third floor and hear a woman's voice, muffled by the rows of books. She's weeping, moaning, whispering frantic words. I hurry toward her as quietly as I can down the long aisle, peeking around each row.

On the very last one, a white woman with messy, shoulder-length gray hair stands with her back to me, eyes on the shadowy corner.

"Are you—are you okay?" I ask. The woman cries out and spins toward me, her hand clutching the collar of her blouse, a shawl unraveling around her shoulders. She's my professor for Intro to Gothic Lit. Behind her oversize glasses, her face is pale and distorted by fright, so different from how she looks in class. She's usually smiling, lit up from within by her own enthusiasm for the subject. But now she looks shattered.

"Dr. Hendrix?" I ask. "Has anything happened?"

She turns away from me and gestures at the corner. "I found—I found her. Is she—is she . . . ?" The professor lets out another moan and claps her hand over her mouth.

I take a step forward and peer around her. The fluorescent light overhead stutters and hums, barely casting its light onto the body that lies on the floor. Still, there's enough illumination for me to see everything I need to know. Masses of long red hair, a pale face, green eyes open and staring.

My breath catches in my throat and lodges there, leaving my lungs burning for air. But like someone in a trance, I stumble forward and kneel beside the girl. I feel for a pulse at her neck. Her skin is cold. Her heart isn't beating.

Meredith Brown is dead.

THREE

Just a few hours ago, Meredith Brown stood in front of a roomful of people and mesmerized them with only the sound of her voice. How can she now be lying here on the floor of the stacks, all the life gone from her body? I kneel over her, trying not to think of the surge of jealousy I felt watching her stand on that stage. Of how badly I wanted what she had. Of how much I resented her for it. Now, in the face of such emptiness, my feelings seem hateful, almost cruel.

I put my ear over her chest to listen for the sound of breathing. There's no movement in her lungs, but I inhale a sweet floral perfume, potent enough that I can taste it. I feel the place at her wrist where a pulse should beat. It's completely still, her skin like ice.

"She's gone," I say to Dr. Hendrix, shaking my head. I look beyond the professor, to where a small number of students have gathered. "Can someone call nine-one-one?"

A girl whips out her phone and dials.

"Should we do CPR?" the guy from the reading room asks, biting his nails.

I cup Meredith's cheek and look into her eyes. "There's no point," I say. "She's long, long gone. I think she's been here for a while." I feel numb, unreal. I feel like I'm watching myself from a distance.

"What happened to her?" someone asks.

"I don't know," I murmur. There are no marks on her body. No blood, no bruises. Her face reveals nothing, no signs of fear or anger or despair. Only—

I tilt my head. There are tear tracks on her cheeks, long since dried.

What does a girl like Meredith Brown have to cry about?

The light overhead flickers again, and the student who called 911 lets out a squeak and hurries away. The other students back away too, but Dr. Hendrix stands frozen, staring, apparently unable to comprehend what has happened.

"Did you know Meredith?" I ask gently.

Dr. Hendrix blinks at me for a moment before she nods. "She was so gifted. I've never had a student produce work like hers."

"She was in Magni Viri," I say, thinking of how she walked with her friends earlier this evening, how they moved together like a single organism, even while arguing. Dr. Hendrix's face darkens, but she doesn't say anything else.

I sit back on my heels, my mind stuttering like the fluorescent light overhead. I don't understand how Meredith can be lying here dead without a mark on her body. A heart attack? A drug overdose? I can't imagine a single scenario that makes sense.

A few minutes later, the campus security officer arrives and shoos us away from the body. I go back upstairs and get my things, then wait with Dr. Hendrix for the police to come.

We sit on the floor, a bookshelf between us and Meredith's body. We don't say anything. The professor's hands tremble so badly that I reach out and lay my fingers over hers. With a convulsive movement, she grabs my hand and clings to it, her eyes still staring straight ahead. This is the most human contact I've had in months. It makes my skin prickle, makes all the hair on my arms stand on end.

The last person who really touched me was Mom, on the day I left home, my car already packed with everything I owned. Mom's grip was more desperate than Dr. Hendrix's is now. She clung to me, weeping, begging me not to go. Begging me not to leave her.

I told my mom I loved her and kissed her cheek, then I got into my car and drove away. Her tears turned to screams, and she swore at me until my car pulled out of the parking lot of our apartment complex.

We haven't spoken since. Every time I've tried to call and check on her, she lets it go to voice mail. She never calls me back.

I'd like to believe that weird call from earlier was her. A broken, muffled voice whose words never reached me.

But I know it wasn't Mom. She holds a grudge for too long to have given in already.

So who was it? *What* was it?

It's a foolish thought, but here in the gloom of the stacks with a body lying on the other side of the bookshelf, I can't help but wonder: What if the call was from Meredith Brown? Her spirit reaching out in the moment of death, desperate for someone to hear?

I shake my head. Putting the sheer bizarreness of the thought aside, why would she call me, a girl she doesn't even know? I'm no one and nothing, a person so lonely I'm imagining a dead girl reaching out to me.

The police don't have many questions for me, so as the EMTs roll Meredith out on the stretcher, her body covered from curious eyes, I follow behind them, a mourning train of one. I can't help but picture Meredith's ghost walking beside me, trailing her spent body in shock and confusion. She couldn't have known when she woke up this morning that today would be her last day, could she? She couldn't have known as she walked arm in arm with her friends that her skin would be cold in a few hours. She was bright and vibrant and alive in a way I've never been. She took up space in the world; she drew our eyes. How could she have guessed she'd leave Corbin College swathed in fabric like furniture in an empty house?

Just as we exit the front doors of the library, the two Magni Viri students I saw Meredith with at the reading come running up, their chests heaving as if they ran all the way from Denfeld Hall.

"Is that Meredith?" the girl calls. "Is that Meredith Brown?" She looks frightened and pale, the flashing red lights cutting across her tawny skin and glinting in her dark brown eyes. I didn't recognize her before, but now I remember she was in my history class for a week before she dropped it. Her name is Azar, which I remember only because I watched her write it in all caps, then slash a horizontal line through the *z* in a decisive, precise way I found intimidating.

The EMTs ignore her, working together to load the stretcher into the back of the ambulance. One of Meredith's hands slips out, as pale as the sheet that covers her, except for the dark beds of her nails, painted the color of a twilight sky.

The boy, white and artsy-looking in that wealthy, careless way you see all the time at Corbin, rushes forward and grasps the sheet at Meredith's feet. "I need to see if it's her," he gasps out. The EMTs try to push him away, but he manages to yank the sheet off Meredith's feet, revealing shiny black Doc Martens with checkered laces.

"That's Meredith!" Azar yells, her voice shot through with agony. She clutches the collar of her shirt, the same way Dr. Hendrix did earlier in the library. "No, no, no, no, no."

"She's dead?" the boy asks, disbelieving. "She's really dead?"

One of the EMTs, a burly man, pushes him gently away with a murmured apology.

"Neil," Azar calls, but then she doesn't say anything else.

Now apparently drained of life, the boy—Neil—stands there gaping as the EMTs climb into the rig and slam the doors closed. Azar trails over and grips his arm, and together they watch the ambulance roll away into the foggy night, the siren off but the red lights still flashing a warning to anyone who might obstruct the vehicle's path.

"What the fuck?" Neil says. "What the fuck?"

Tears roll down his cheeks. He turns and catches me staring. "What the fuck are you looking at?" he spits.

Azar stares at me, her eyes wide with shock and grief.

"I—I'm sorry." I feel like I've been caught watching them

undress, stolen away the privacy of their pain. "I was there when—when we found her."

Azar flinches but doesn't say anything. Neil just stares at me. I keep talking, barely aware of what I'm saying.

"You're her friends, right? From Magni Viri? The police are still up there on the third floor, where she . . . They—they'd probably want to talk to you. Since you're her friends and . . ." I swallow. I don't say the rest of my thought—that they might be the last people who ever spoke to her.

"What happened to her?" Azar whispers.

"I don't know," I say. "There wasn't a mark on her. She looked fine, except . . . except she was . . ." I trail off, not wanting to say the word *dead*.

Neil glares at me, tears running down his sharp cheekbones.

"I'm really sorry," I say, ducking my head. "I'm sorry about your friend." I hurry away into the darkness, clutching the straps of my backpack. I could swear that someone is walking beside me, keeping pace, but there's no one except me, alone in the cool air and the moonlight. A shiver runs over my skin.

My mind reels. I can't believe what just happened. I pull out my phone, wanting to tell someone, to talk to someone. I call Robin, and it rings twice before clicking over to voice mail, as if she rejected the call. I hang up without leaving a message, hurt washing through me.

A text comes in: *With Charlie. Sorry, can't talk now!*

My phone trembles in my hands. I know I shouldn't, but I dial my mom's number. It rings and rings and rings until her recorded voice comes on.

"Hey, this is Beth. Leave a message if you want to."

I squeeze my eyes shut at the sound of my mom's voice. When the tone beeps for me to leave a message, I hang up and shove my phone into my back pocket.

Beneath the ache of her rejection is relief. If she'd answered, she wouldn't have comforted me. She wouldn't have helped. She would have listened for thirty seconds before she launched into a description of her asshole boss or how she was afraid her boyfriend was going to break up with her. After Dad left, that's how it always was with us. Me putting her first, trying to be whatever she needed. That's how I let it be. Because she was my mom, and we were all each other had.

I walk aimlessly for a long time, seeing nothing, aware of nothing, lost in the memory of Meredith's body on the floor, before I realize I forgot to go to work. I forgot that I was supposed to be mopping floors tonight. I check the time on my phone. It's eleven thirty, which means I'm an hour and a half late for my three-hour shift. I have two missed calls from my supervisor, Mr. Hanks.

Shit.

When I look away from the screen, I realize I'm not sure where I even am. I seem to be standing in an overgrown garden of some kind, very dark, lit only by moonlight. There are stone angels half-covered in ivy, moss, and lichen, their clasped hands raised to heaven in supplication. A tall wrought iron fence rises above me, and I'm directly in front of a locked gate. I peer through the bars, but it's too dark to see anything.

"What the hell?" I whisper. I spin in a circle, trying to orient myself. The green hills rise up ahead of me, which means I'm on the north end of campus, the oldest part of Corbin

College. This side of campus is heavily wooded and nearly always in shadow. I glance up and catch sight of Denfeld Hall on a slight rise, its dark, moody face bared to the moon. Suddenly, I know where I am. It's the campus cemetery, which is off-limits to students.

An owl calls out from somewhere close, startling me so badly I drop my phone. It smashes onto the uneven stone path with a sickening crunch. When I pick it up, the screen glows, revealing splintering cracks running along the glass.

I swear. I can't afford to replace this phone. And I'm probably about to lose my job. Mr. Hanks has a zero-tolerance policy for . . . well, everything. He will be deeply pissed off that I missed work, and "I found a dead body in the library" might not even be enough to sway him. I don't particularly enjoy mopping floors, cleaning toilets, and scraping gum off the undersides of tables, but it's work I need if I want to stay here.

I pull up my call log and tap his number, already cringing. But when the call connects, there's no angry Tennessean on the line. Instead, there's the same strange mix of sounds from earlier: nails on wood, buzzing cicadas. Maybe I messed up my phone more than I thought—it was already an old wreck before I dropped it. But when I end the call, the cicadas continue to buzz all around me in the darkness. I close my eyes and take a deep breath to steady my nerves.

This has been a weird day, but it must all be a bizarre string of coincidences. My brain is overloaded. I'm stressed and probably a little traumatized on account of the dead body. But I can handle this. I just have to go find Mr. Hanks and explain myself. Tomorrow, things will be normal again. I'll work and go to class and write my papers. I'll disappear into my hectic schedule once more. There will be no dead girls or cemeteries in moonlight, only a cracked phone and an angry boss and a slew of deadlines staring me down.

At this thought I nod firmly and turn back to go the way I came, my shoes scraping along the stone path. It's actually quite beautiful out here, I realize. Quiet, undisturbed, less like a college campus than a private park. The woods are dark, huddled against the green hills. The air smells of dead leaves and old stone. Cicadas hum in the canopy, and owls call out, now close, now distant, their voices warm, deep vibrations, almost a purr.

I follow the woodland path, the trees on my left and the open green that slopes up toward Denfeld Hall on my right. I'm shivering in my cotton sweater, my backpack increasingly heavy. All I want is my warm bed and pajamas. I'm considering whether I should save my confrontation with Mr. Hanks until tomorrow when voices ring out across the green. I freeze, listening.

"Isabella!" a man bellows.

"Isabella!" a girl calls.

Then more voices, all layered over one another, calling out for Isabella. For a moment, I wonder if they are calling for a missing dog. Maybe Denfeld Hall has a pet that's run off.

Then I realize they probably aren't calling out a name at all. They're saying something in another language, maybe Italian or Latin. The voices call out to one another, echoing back and forth in an eerie litany. Goose bumps break out over my skin. Is this some strange ceremony for grieving a lost member of Magni Viri? Is this for Meredith?

I can't tell.

But I do know I don't belong here. I'm not a part of this. I definitely don't want to be caught loitering here in the dark, spying on them.

I hurry faster along the path, breathing a sigh of relief when the lights of campus twinkle in the distance. I walked much, much farther than I imagined. I leave the echoing voices of Magni Viri behind, exiting their ivy-covered grounds like a sleepwalker awakening from a dream. The newer red-brick buildings at the heart of campus, warm and ordinary, draw me on.

I head straight for Facilities Management, a small, squat building that houses Mr. Hanks's office. The closer I get, the faster I walk, until I start to run, my backpack banging painfully against my back. Mr. Hanks is standing at his door, locking it, when I come racing down the hall. He turns, startled, the deep furrows in his forehead bunching together. His eyes widen as I approach.

"Girl, you're white as a sheet," he drawls. "What the hell happened to you?"

I open my mouth to explain, but then my vision goes spotty and I sway. Mr. Hanks catches me before the weight of my backpack can slam me into the ground. He lowers me gently to the cold tile, his jaw clenched tight and his eyes inscrutable.

"Don't think fainting's going to get you out of trouble now," he says, but his gruff voice has a soft edge of gentleness to it. He kneels next to me and eases my backpack off my shoulders. "Hold on, I'll get you a cup of water."

He disappears down the hall and then returns with a triangular white cup filled to the brim with water from the cooler. I take small sips, waiting for my heartbeat to slow. The water makes me feel even colder inside, but it wakes me up too, brings me back to myself.

"This have anything to do with that ambulance?" He emphasizes the first syllable of the word and draws out the last, rendering the word like "AM-bu-laaance."

I've heard other students laugh at Mr. Hanks's accent, but I like it. It reminds me of how my grandpa from North Carolina used to talk. It's soothing, frightened as I am.

I nod and take another gulp of water. "A girl died in the library. I was the one who—" *Found her* dies on my lips, and my voice skips. "I touched her skin, and it was so cold." I shiver. I feel more frightened and repulsed now than I did in the moment.

Mr. Hanks shakes his head. "You're all right now. Don't worry about that missed shift. You can make the hours up later this week if you want. We've got to spiff up the chapel for some big shot speaker they're dragging out here for convocation."

"Who?" I ask absently.

Mr. Hanks snorts. "Hell if I know or care. Come on now and let's get you off this floor before you catch cold and miss another shift. Then I *will* fire you."

I smile weakly. This is the longest Mr. Hanks has talked to me since I started this job, his gruff nature softening for the first time into something warmer. Maybe he isn't quite as unyielding and terrifying as he makes himself out to be. He helps me to my feet and walks me to the front of the building. I watch him lock the front door and get into his little green Nissan truck and drive away. Only once the taillights of his truck have disappeared do I turn and head back to my dorm.

I realize I'm shivering so hard my teeth are rattling. I wrap my arms around myself and walk faster. I'm colder than I have ever been. I might be from Florida and experiencing my first true autumn, but even I know this cold isn't normal. It can't be less than fifty degrees out, not nearly cold enough for this hollow feeling that has settled in my bones.

It must be delayed shock, I decide. From finding Meredith's body. That's why I wandered over to Magni Viri's corner of campus. Why I felt so afraid. My body was reacting to everything even if my mind couldn't take it all in.

Still, when my phone rings in my pocket, I ignore it. I'm afraid that if I answer it, I might hear the cicadas again, afraid I might feel Meredith's ghost walking beside me in the moonlight.

I don't think I'm lonely enough to want a dead girl for company.

Not yet anyway.

FOUR

The rest of the week passes normally—or as close to normal as I can get after finding a dead body in the library. I shelve books and go to class and mop floors in the evening. When my phone rings, it's bot scams, not nails on wood and screaming cicadas. The feeling of a phantom person walking at my side has disappeared. I'm ashamed to admit to myself that I miss her.

I think constantly about Meredith, the electric way she looked at me at the reading, then the way her eyes looked through me in the library, empty of life. I think about her more than I should, I know that. She even shows up in my dreams—sometimes alive and talking to me, sometimes touching my face, kissing me. Other times, she is dead—an Ophelia floating in a lake, surrounded by flowers; a rotting corpse in a casket, worms crawling through her eye sockets. In the worst of the dreams, it is my face on her dead body, my face surrounded by her long red hair, my eyes green like hers, open and staring at the library ceiling.

By now, news of Meredith's death has spread all over campus, and people whisper about her in hallways and in the cafeteria, speculating on how she might have died. Even

Foster in the library puts down his Derrida to ask me what I think happened to her. I almost mention the tears on her cheeks, but it feels vulgar somehow, like revealing what color underwear she had on.

I already feel strangely guilty about her death, as if my wanting what she had somehow contributed to it. I wanted her life so badly, and now she doesn't have it either.

On Friday afternoon, the school holds a memorial service for her in the chapel. There are lit candles everywhere, white roses surrounding a picture of her. She looks softer in the picture than I remember her—nicer, happier, a girl excited to start college, beaming at her imagined future. She's even wearing a Corbin College sweatshirt, the black swan of the logo stamped onto spotless white. She doesn't look like someone who belongs in moody and secretive Magni Viri.

The contrast is especially remarkable with every single member of Magni Viri in attendance, all of them grouped on one side of the chapel. They don't wear any special uniform, but you can tell they belong together all the same. They feel like a complete organism somehow, a thing set apart.

Meredith's class—the remaining five of them—sit in the front row, their eyes red-rimmed, circled with sleepless purple. Azar and Neil sit close to each other while the chaplain speaks, Neil's arm around Azar, her head on his shoulder. I get only glimpses of the others: a Black boy with a serious face; a pale, tousle-haired person who might be a girl or a boy or neither, and a girl with long hair whose face I can't see from where I'm sitting. I imagine Meredith in the row with them, burning like a candle flame in their midst. It seems impossible that a girl like that could be so easily extinguished by death.

When the chaplain finishes speaking, she cedes the stage to a short, slight white man with a gently lined face, who introduces himself as Dr. Theodore O'Connor, the director of Magni Viri. I recognize him from his photo on the school's website. Everyone sits up a little straighter as he approaches the microphone, riveted by this rare appearance. So little is known of Magni Viri that, in students' minds, the academic society is a fragile tissue of speculation and suspicion. Students are always hungry to know more.

"Meredith Brown was a rising star," Dr. O'Connor says without preamble, his voice quiet but radiating deep feeling and authority. It's a surprising voice for so small a person. "At only eighteen, already she was a novelist producing some of the finest writing of any living writer today. Had we not lost her, I have no doubt that she would have taken her rightful place in the ranks of our most admired authors. She would be another Pulitzer or Nobel Prize winner for Corbin College to boast of. More important, she would have been a voice for your generation, someone to elucidate the peculiar struggles and values of your cohort. We have not only lost a precious human being in Meredith's passing; we have also lost literature the likes of which the world will never see again. We mourn the loss of Meredith's life, but we also mourn the loss of her genius, the loss of her contribution to the world. Meredith was the epitome of what we in Magni Viri strive for: brilliance, excellence, and achievement."

Dr. O'Connor's eyes land on me. "So I ask all of you to do what Meredith cannot: give your gifts to the world. Do not squander your talent, your energy, your genius. Whatever you have inside you, make the most of it, offer it up. Become someone truly *great*."

I am frozen under his gaze, which is steely and demanding but also complacent, as if he has no doubt that we will all rise up to obey.

When he looks away from me, my breath comes flooding back into my chest, my skin tingling. That is what I want, more than anything. I want to be great, someone who matters in the world—the next Daphne du Maurier, Shirley Jackson, Sarah Waters. Someone who writes the way Meredith did, someone whose books are still read long after she's dead. It seems impossible though. I'm not sure I can ever be more than a small, lonely creature grasping at the edges of dreams too big for me.

The chaplain returns to the stage to ask if anyone would like to say a few words about Meredith, but no one moves. The only people who truly knew her are the members of Magni Viri, and it's clear they won't share something so intimate outside their own group. The chaplain closes the service with a prayer, and everyone files out in a stunned silence, moved by the loss of someone our own age, or perhaps by the forceful words of Dr. O'Connor.

When I break into the cool air outside, I feel like I've been released from a spell.

"Can you believe that shit?" someone behind me whispers. "Meredith Brown was not a fucking genius."

I glance back and catch sight of my roommate and her eternal sidekick, another Connecticut snob, named Korey.

"Absolutely not," Helena says. "She was in my Quantitative

Reasoning class, and I swear the girl could barely do basic math. Like, I get it, math isn't everyone's strong suit, but she needed, like, remedial lessons."

"Well, she was in my Freshman Seminar, and her writing was okay, but it wasn't winning any Pulitzers," the other girl says with a laugh. "Magni Viri is so obsessed with itself."

Helena laughs too. "More like Mediocre Viri."

I shake my head and walk faster, to put some distance between us. Helena talks a big game, but I know Magni Viri is why she came to Corbin College, same as me. It wasn't that she needed the money; she wanted the prestige. Some girl boss Elon Musk type she's obsessed with is an alum, and Helena was sure she'd be chosen for Magni Viri just like her hero. Even after the semester had started and it was clear she'd never set foot in Denfeld Hall, she was constantly trying to make friends with the Magni Viri kids, who of course shunned her like only MV members can. I'm surprised she didn't launch herself at Dr. O'Connor after the service to beg for Meredith's open spot.

No matter how fast I try to walk, Helena and Korey outpace me with apparently zero effort. I hear every word of their horrible conversation, and as they pass me, Helena shoots a simpering smile my way and says to Korey, "College isn't for everyone, you know? I mean, no shame. It takes all kinds to keep the world turning."

I bite my lip, hating Helena even more than I thought possible. I'm still seething at her retreating back when someone taps me on the shoulder. I spin, startled.

It's an upperclassman from Magni Viri I recognize, a

redheaded, freckle-faced boy with the beginnings of a beard. He looks like a mashup between a Victorian dandy and a banjo player in a folk band. There's a trans pride flag pinned to his suspenders.

"Tara?" he asks, lifting his eyebrows—also red—and smiling expectantly.

I nod, flustered.

"Sorry, I should introduce myself. I'm Quigg," he says, sticking out a freckled hand for me to shake. "Well, Seamus Quigg, but everyone calls me Quigg."

"Oh, Seamus like the poet?" I say stupidly, off-balance at being approached like this.

But Quigg smiles, blushing kind of sweetly. "Yes, exactly. My namesake. He's my favorite poet."

"I loved his translation of *Beowulf*," I say. "Sorry, did you want something?"

"Oh, yes! Um. Dr. O'Connor wanted to see you?" he says, the end of the sentence turning up like a question.

I squint at him. "The head of Magni Viri?"

"O Captain! our Captain himself." He smiles wryly. "Can you come—back to the chapel? Do you have time?"

I nod and follow him mutely, unable to imagine why the head of Magni Viri could want to talk to me. Is it because I was there when Meredith was found? Does he think I have more information? That must be it.

Quigg keeps up an easy patter of mostly one-sided conversation as we walk back to the chapel. He's nothing like I imagined a member of Magi Viri to be. He's not snobbish or secretive. He seems . . . normal. Nice.

"Do you like Magni Viri?" I ask.

Quigg blinks at me for a beat and then laughs. "Of course! Magni Viri is the best."

I feel a little pang of jealousy. "What's it . . . what's it like?" I ask, trying to keep the wistfulness from my voice.

He shrugs. "Oh, you know, like a big family. We have fun and fight and party and study and do pretty much everything together. You're never by yourself if you don't want to be."

"That sounds nice," I say, longing opening up in my chest, vast as an ocean.

"It is. I love it. I mean, there's a lot of pressure and competition too. All those type A overachievers all in one house, you know?" He laughs. "But it's good motivation."

"What are you studying?" I ask, suddenly wanting to change the subject. It hurts to hear about what I can't have.

Quigg's eyes light up. "Theater."

"Oh! I think I've seen you on the posters for *Macbeth*!"

"Yeah, that's right," he says proudly.

He's got the lead role of Macbeth himself, I realize. I would have figured Quigg for a comedy actor based on his easygoing personality and eccentric style. It's a big deal for a trans boy to land a role like Macbeth at a school like this. He must be an incredible actor. I think I can see it in the way he carries himself, the sense of pride in his voice and bearing.

I want to ask more about the play, but we're already at the door of the chapel. Everyone has cleared out after Meredith's memorial.

"He's waiting for you in there," Quigg says, nodding at the intricately carved door of the chapel. "It was really nice to meet you, Tara. I hope to see you again soon." He gives me a little wave and saunters off with his hands in his pockets.

I swallow and pull open the heavy oak door. My footsteps echo across the foyer and into the nave. At the sound of my steps, Dr. O'Connor stands from a pew in front, waiting for me with his hands clasped behind his back, a pleasant, neutral expression on his face. Meredith's picture still smiles at the room from behind him, so I feel like I'm walking toward the both of them.

A strong floral smell surrounds me, both familiar and strange. It must be coming from the white roses at the front of the room. My head swims, and my stomach aches.

"Tara," Dr. O'Connor says when I'm only a few yards away. "Thank you so much for taking time to speak with me." I expect him to offer a handshake like Quigg did, but he keeps his hands clasped behind his back.

"Hello," I say, trying and failing to smile at him. He's a small man, but even off the high stage, he's still imposing somehow, exuding a crackling, brilliant energy.

"Please, have a seat," Dr. O'Connor says, gesturing at the first pew. He sits down a few feet away on the same bench, so we're both facing toward the front, where Meredith watches us with bright, happy eyes. It's deeply unnerving. Did he choose this location on purpose? Did he hope to rattle me? If so, he's succeeding.

As if he's read my thoughts, he says, "I apologize for the strange meeting place. I have another engagement on this side of campus in a few minutes. It was merely convenient to meet here, though perhaps in poor taste."

He glances at Meredith, and a sad look passes over his placid expression. "You must be wondering why I wanted to speak with you," he says.

I clear my throat. "I assume you want to know more about the night I found Meredith in the library," I say.

"Well . . . no, actually. That was a strange coincidence—a *very* strange coincidence," he amends. "Your finding her and what I'm about to tell you aren't connected at all."

I stare at him, too puzzled to venture a guess.

"Tara, I'd like to offer you a place in Magni Viri," he says abruptly.

"Excuse me?" I'm so shocked I nearly laugh. I squelch the urge, but my lips turn up into an incredulous smile despite my efforts.

He chuckles. "You were originally in the running for a spot. It was practically a coin toss between you and Meredith."

"Are you serious?" I ask, my throat nearly closing up. I think about how he described Meredith as a potential Pulitzer Prize winner, the voice of a generation. I think about the effortless way she performed her story at the reading. How could there be a coin toss between a girl like that and me?

He nods. "Oh yes. It was a very narrow thing."

What if the coin had landed on heads instead of tails? My first semester of college would have been so different. No Helena, no janitorial shifts, no lonely meals in the cafeteria. I would have had friends, stability, a place to belong. Just like Meredith had before—

But it wasn't a coin toss. It was a choice that Magni Viri made.

"Why Meredith, then?" I ask through the tightness in my throat, flushing with shame as the question escapes me. She's dead and yet I'm still jealous of her.

He cocks his head at me, apparently surprised that this is what I'm curious about. He smiles. "Let's not get caught up in comparisons. It doesn't matter. What matters is that you have a place in Magni Viri if you want it. You can move into Denfeld Hall on Monday if you like."

I open my mouth and close it again. I don't know what to say. This is the last thing in the world I expected to happen to me today. Somehow I don't trust it.

A dim and distant part of my brain is screaming at me that this is everything I have wanted since I first learned of the existence of Corbin College, that I need to stop dawdling and give the man an answer. But Meredith is staring at me from her photograph, and I can't help but think of the last time I saw her, dead on the library floor.

"What happened to Meredith?" is what finally comes out of my mouth.

"She had a brain aneurysm," he says quietly. "It ruptured."

I nod. That makes sense, I think. It explains her appearance. But it doesn't explain the tear tracks on her cheeks.

"Was she happy in Magni Viri?" I ask.

"No," Dr. O'Connor says. "No, I don't believe she was."

I meet his eyes, surprised by his candor.

"I do not believe Meredith Brown would have been happy anywhere, in any circumstances," he adds. "You see that sometimes in people of genius."

"I'm not a genius," I say quietly. "I'm the first person in

my family to go to college. I—I'm struggling here."

"I know," Dr. O'Connor says, his voice kind. "That's why you belong in Magni Viri. We need you, and you need us. We can help you achieve your potential. You won't have to work on the janitorial staff anymore. You won't have to worry about where the money's going to come from. You will have the support you need, the structure, the community." He pauses. "You have no idea what you are capable of becoming, Tara, but we have a pretty good idea. That's why we're offering you a spot. We see greatness in you. We want to help you achieve it."

"It sounds too good to be true," I say, still too shocked to feel anything approaching happiness or gratitude.

"Well, you will have to work very hard. You will have to meet and exceed grueling standards. Magni Viri is no walk in the park," Dr. O'Connor says.

"But you think I can handle it?" I ask.

"Of course."

"Why?" I don't know why I'm fighting this, why I'm not grabbing this opportunity with both hands and screaming my acceptance. But a part of me isn't convinced. A part of me needs to *know*. "My grades in high school were very good, but it's not like I went to a prestigious school. My test scores were high in verbal but average in math. I haven't won awards or published stories in important magazines. I'm like a hundred other students at Corbin."

He chuckles again. "I thought you might need some convincing. A surprising number of our students are unable to see their own potential." He turns toward me on the bench and meets my eyes again. "Tara, the things you see as weaknesses are the very reasons we want you. I read your application essays. I know what you've been through. I know how hard you've had to fight. And I know how badly you want to achieve your dreams—how badly you *need* to achieve them."

My cheeks heat up, remembering what I wrote about my mother in the personal essay. I've often wondered if I was too open and that's why I didn't get into Magni Viri, that maybe they thought I was too trashy for the program. I talked about my mom's temperamental boyfriends, the evictions, the constant, unrelenting weight of responsibility I felt for her. After I'd pressed Submit on my application, I felt immediate shame and wished I hadn't been so transparent. And Dr. O'Connor read all that.

I can't help it, I put my burning face into my hands.

He pauses, and I feel his eyes on me. "What's your deepest, most audacious dream, Tara, the one you are embarrassed to say aloud? You don't have to tell me, but at least think it to yourself."

I sigh, but the dream appears instantaneously, a thing so potent I can almost taste it. I look up at him again. "I want to be a novelist," I say quietly, "a successful one, the kind that can make a good living from writing. But that's not practical for—"

He holds up a hand, shakes his head. "So many of the people who achieve success in this world only do so because of who their parents are, because they are privileged, because the world expects them to be successful. Then there are ones like you. You claw your way up to places where others have been lifted.

"Now we want to make that climb easier for you. We want to see how high you can go when there isn't a hundred-pound pack on your back weighing you down. Let us do it." His eyes are earnest, intense. "There is this spark in you, a spark that the world would callously stamp out without realizing what it had lost. But we want to fan that spark into flames, into a wildfire. We want to watch you burn."

For the first time during our conversation, I fully understand that I'm being offered the spot in Magni Viri that I started dreaming of the moment I learned about the program. The spot I was denied. Whether Dr. O'Connor is deluded about my abilities or not, I would be beyond foolish to pass up a place in Magni Viri. It would solve every single problem I have.

And beyond the practicalities, I *want it*, and badly. I want to walk the corridors of Denfeld Hall, to go arm in arm with this school's brightest, most ambitious students. I want to be chosen, to be special, to be part of something great.

"I understand if you need time to think about it," Dr. O'Connor says.

"Yes," I say, my gaze drawn to Meredith's picture in its frame of white roses. It's hard not to feel like he's offering me something that still belongs to her. Her green eyes seem to bore into mine, accusing. But it's not enough to dissuade me, not with a prize like Magni Viri on the table. With a shudder, I turn away from her and focus on Dr. O'Connor once more. "I mean, no, I don't need time to think. I accept." I make myself smile at him. "Of course I do."

"Wonderful! I'm so glad you're going to join us," he says,

his eyes twinkling with genuine pleasure. "I had hoped you would agree, so I came ready with your paperwork. You can give that to the RD when you move into Denfeld on Monday." He passes me a manila folder, which I accept and open with numb fingers. On top is an acceptance letter on Magni Viri letterhead, welcoming me to the program and detailing the financial arrangements.

"Oh," I breathe, shocked by the numbers on the page. Magni Viri will cover everything my grants and scholarships don't, and there's even a small stipend for books and personal expenses. No more need for loans. No more worries about debt.

Dr. O'Connor stands and steps into the aisle, making room for me to exit too. When we leave the solemn atmosphere of the chapel and break into the evening air, he reaches out to shake my hand. "I promise, Tara, Magni Viri is going to change your life."

To my shock, after a lifetime of wariness and pessimism, I find I actually believe him. A thrill runs through me, a hot bright ribbon of pure elation. Even Meredith's staring green eyes can't subdue it.

I'm going to be a member of Magni Viri. I'm going to get a true shot at my dreams.

"Thank you," I answer. "I think so too."

But I don't feel like my life is changing. I feel like it's finally beginning. Like all this time I've been waiting for Magni Viri to come calling.

FIVE

I drift back to my dorm in a dreamy haze, barely aware of the other people on the sidewalk. I picture myself walking this same path with the Magni Viri first-years, a little world unto ourselves, talking about books and films, having inside jokes—no job to hurry off to, no lonely meals in the cafeteria.

When I get to my dorm, the room is mercifully empty. I sit on my bed and stare at the gray concrete walls, the modular furniture. I wonder what my room in Denfeld Hall will look like. Surely more interesting than this. Everything about my new life is going to be more interesting—my environment, the people. But what about me? For the first time, doubt worms through my bright daydream, wriggling unpleasantly beneath my skin. Will I be interesting enough for the rest of them? Will I be smart enough, talented enough, sophisticated enough?

There's still a chance that Dr. O'Connor is wrong about me. That he has made a terrible mistake. That I'll show up at Denfeld and be nothing but a disappointment to him and everyone else. A disappointment to myself. Or that the other students won't like me, that they'll resent me for replacing Meredith.

Is this a mistake? Am I overshooting again? What if this

is like when I tried to join the LGBTQ+ club during my first week and everyone was utterly alien to me, a bunch of rich queer kids cracking jokes about the locals they saw on their drive to campus—caricaturing them as trailer trash meth heads with bad teeth. Of course, they didn't know that I used to live in a trailer park. They didn't know that I never show my teeth in photos because they're crooked and chipped. I got up and left the room, and no one noticed me go.

But if the Magni Viri students are like that, I won't be able to just get up and leave. I'll have to sit quiet and bear it or fight back and make enemies.

What if, what if, what if—my thoughts spiral, and soon Magni Viri has transformed in my mind from the answer to all my prayers into a dark menace waiting to devour me. I pull out my phone, wishing I had an adult to call, someone I could talk to and ask for advice. But even if Mom was willing to talk to me, she wouldn't understand. *I* was the adult in our home. I was the one who gave advice, the one who talked Mom down when she was losing control.

Out of habit, I scroll to Robin's name in my contacts. After she rejected my call the other night, she never tried to reach out again. That dismissive text saying she was busy with Charlie was the last I heard from her. My finger hovers over her name, but I can't bring myself to call her again, not after a brush-off like that.

I'm on my own.

That's the whole point of joining Magni Viri, isn't it? So I won't be on my own? So I'll have someone to call next time I feel this way?

That thought sends me up off the bed and to my feet.

No. I refuse to get in my own head this way. I'm joining Magni Viri on Monday morning, and that's that. I'm taking the rare opportunity that has fallen into my lap, and I'm going to make the most of it. Stuff like this never happens to people like me. I'm sure as hell not going to be the one to waste it.

With that, I launch myself into packing. I yank the oversize suitcase out from beneath my bed and start pulling clothes out of the closet. I could wait and do this over the weekend, but I want to do it now, before I lose my nerve. I want to make it clear to myself that this part of my life is ending and another is beginning.

My closet is halfway empty when Helena bursts into the room, looking harried. She stops in the doorway, her eyes on my suitcase. Her face registers surprise and then some emotion I can't read—relief? Vindication?

"What's going on, Tara?" she asks sweetly, schooling her expression into one of concern. She had been in a hurry, but now she walks slowly to her desk and drops her backpack into the chair.

I don't say anything, keeping my back resolutely turned away from her. I fold the same shirt three times.

"Oh, Tara," she says in a comforting voice, as if I told her I'm failing all my classes. "Well, college isn't for everyone, I guess. Maybe you can try community college and work your way back up. Or, you know, there are lots of decent paying jobs that don't require a degree."

"I'm not leaving Corbin," I say. "I'm just leaving this room."

"Oh," she says, puzzled, trying to work it out. "The dorms are expensive, huh?"

I spin around to face her, fed up with her passive-aggressive bullshit. "I'm moving into Denfeld Hall."

Her face is blank with incomprehension for about three seconds. Then her eyebrows knit together. "How did you get a room in Denfeld? That's only for Magni Viri."

I cock my head, raise my eyebrows expectantly, and wait for her to figure it out.

Her confusion turns to disbelief and then to anger. "You're lying."

"I start Monday," I say simply.

"Yeah right." She smirks openly now, completely dropping her faux-sweet persona.

I pick up the manila folder O'Connor handed me earlier. I hold my acceptance letter out so she can see the Magni Viri logo at the top. Her mouth falls open, and she reaches for the letter, a hunger in her eyes. I snatch the page away before she can touch it.

"How? What? Why?" she sputters.

"I met with Dr. O'Connor today. He offered me a place. Apparently, I was in the running with the girl who died. Now her spot is open." Despite my vindication, I still wince, hating that my chance at a new life depended on another girl's death.

Helena shakes her head, stunned into silence. But then her mouth twists into an ugly expression. "Why *you*?" There's no mistaking what she means.

I laugh, unable to stop my joy at her shock; the way this news upends her solid views of the world. "Who knows,

Helena? Maybe they like 'low caliber' students in Magni Viri."
With that, I turn away from her and keep packing, my heart
beating hard and fast, my cheeks warm with the pleasure of
finally getting the upper hand.

Helena stands still behind me for a moment, silently fum-
ing, then opens and slams a few drawers before storming back
out, leaving the textbook she needs for class behind on her
desktop.

I let out another stunned little laugh. At least Helena
finally showed her true colors, revealing the poison behind
her waspish politeness. I know she'll invent a perfect narrative
to satisfy her jealousy and dislike of me, but that moment of
seeing her realize that I had what she wanted so badly . . . It's
hard not feel a sick little thrill of satisfaction.

I had worried that her reaction might make me doubt
my place in Magni Viri, but it didn't. If anything, I feel surer
now than I did before. It's the right decision. I deserve a room
in Denfeld Hall just as much as Meredith Brown did. I've
worked harder for it than Helena ever would. I pack up the
rest of my stuff with sure, confident movements.

Only a few more days.

I spend the last of my free hours on Friday night going over
the paperwork Dr. O'Connor gave me. Most of it is standard
stuff, but when I reach the code of conduct I'm expected to
sign, there's plenty to surprise me.

The first rule is that I'm not allowed to hold a job, either
on or off campus, during my enrolled terms in order to focus
on my studies. I guess that's why they provide a stipend for

personal expenses. I sigh. I'd hoped to keep my library job so I could build up a little savings. But it's a small sacrifice to make for everything I'm gaining.

The second is that I am not to invite anyone outside of Magni Viri, whether student or family member or otherwise, into Denfeld Hall or its grounds. The only reason given is "to respect the privacy of Magni Viri members and to maintain an atmosphere conducive to academic and personal excellence."

"Wow," I whisper. So the legend about no one outside of Magni Viri seeing the inside of Denfeld Hall is true. No wonder Magni Viri students are so secretive and insular. It's literally in the code of conduct to keep others out. That rumor about the MV kids being a weird satanic cult passes through my thoughts again, ruffling my sense of certainty. But of course they aren't. What I overheard on Denfeld's grounds on the night Meredith died was a little strange, but it wasn't evil. Magni Viri is just a stuck-up academic society obsessed with its own exclusivity, I remind myself before I keep reading. It's no wonder they've inspired some jealousy-fueled rumors.

The last surprise—aside from the fact that there's nothing in here about abstaining from drugs or alcohol—is that I'm expected to participate weekly in Magni Viri social events, both organized and spontaneous.

Am I contractually obligated to go to parties? That's unexpected, but I guess organizations like Magni Viri are about networking and forming lifelong connections as much as they're about academic achievement. This is what I wanted, isn't it—to be knitted into a group like this? I release a shaky breath, skim the last of the page, and sign my name at the bottom before I can lose my courage.

It's done. At least on paper, I am a member of Magni Viri.

My face breaks into a huge smile, and I'm still smiling as I change into my rattiest clothes and then hurry to the chapel for my last janitorial shift. Even though I'm dressed in a bleach-stained sweatshirt and holey jeans, I walk with a new sureness in my step, my head held high.

When I enter the chapel, I'm relieved to see that Meredith's picture is gone, along with the smell of her funeral flowers. I wonder if someone from Magni Viri took the picture, if I'll find her staring at me the second I walk into Denfeld. God, I hope not. I already feel weird enough about taking her place.

Empty of people, the chapel is solemn and echoing but deeply peaceful. The stained glass windows are shadowed and strange in the electric lights, their blues deep indigo, their reds like spilled blood. The religious scenes they depict seem more imbued with meaning at night without the sun shining upon them. Jesus and his disciples. Mary and her little Christ. Lifted cups, lifted faces, lifted hands. I pass the marble memorials set into the walls, each inscribed with the names of the dead: Smith, Bauer, George, Sanders, Snow. I trace the grooves of their names and wonder who they were.

Probably all rich men who paid to be remembered in this way, whose money ensured their names would live on long after their bodies rotted in the earth. When I die, will anyone run their fingers over the grooves of my carved name? Will anyone wonder who I was?

I find Mr. Hanks in a room behind the altar, wheeling out cleaning supplies. He gives me a few quiet instructions and then we get to work. Once we finish the floors, Mr. Hanks climbs up on a ladder to wash the windows while I wipe down the pews with furniture polish. He is his usual gruff self, though I sense a softer edge to him now. He hums quietly while he works, a Johnny Cash song my grandpa used to sing all the time. I find myself humming along, enjoying the easy partnership we somehow developed without my noticing. I don't know how I ever thought he was mean.

But maybe I'm feeling nostalgic because this is the last time I'll be cleaning up behind the students of Corbin College. I won't miss the gum under the desks, the urine on the toilet lids, the mud ground into the entryway mats.

But I might miss this—this sense of quiet, when the buildings of Corbin College lie in wait, and—

Nope. Not going to get romantic about cleaning. Not even a little bit.

When Mr. Hanks climbs down from the ladder, I can't put it off any longer. I approach him, nervously wringing my hands. He takes one look at me and laughs.

"You're quitting, then?"

"How did you know?"

"I've been here a long time."

"I was offered a place in Magni Viri," I say.

He frowns, and I hurry to explain. "One of the rules is that I'm not allowed to have a job, so I can focus solely on my studies. I'm sorry to—"

He shakes his head. "Don't be sorry."

"Okay," I say. "I won't, then." I laugh.

He almost smiles, though there's an unreadable expression

on his weathered brow. "Old Magni Viri, huh? That's a strange bunch."

"So I hear. You have any stories about them?" I ask, hoping he says no. I don't want to be talked out of joining, or to walk into Denfeld more nervous than I already am.

He pauses, chewing the inside of his cheek, but then he shakes his head and shrugs. "They clean their own damn house, so they're all right by me." He squints at me. "What, you afraid they got vampires up there?"

"More afraid I won't fit in," I admit.

He snorts. "Don't worry about whether they're going to like you. Worry about whether or not you like yourself. That's the secret."

"Well, you don't like anybody," I say.

He lets out a short, surprised laugh. "Solitude has its virtues," he says, lifting a dusty finger in mock admonishment.

"I'll try to remember that."

He surveys the chapel. "I think we're done here. All ship and shiny. You did good work."

"Thanks," I say, touched. That's the first compliment he's ever given me. I look around at the equipment we've used. "Do you want help getting anything back?" I find myself strangely hesitant to part from this surly, taciturn man. He's been the most solid presence in my life at Corbin, and I didn't even realize it until now.

"Nah, go write your papers," he says. "Good luck, girl." Then he turns and walks back up the aisle before I can say anything.

"Good night," I say, and head out of the chapel, promising

myself I'll go back to visit him sometime.

Campus is dark, fog rolling along the ground, but the sky is clear, a million stars glinting overhead. I look to the north side of campus, where Denfeld Hall and the cemetery lie swathed in the shadow of the hills. Only a few more sleeps and that will be my new home.

I peer into the dark distance, as if I could see across all that space and blackness and into the new life I want so badly. I just hope it wants me too.

SIX

Quigg shows up at my door on Monday morning. On Friday he was jolly and radiating energy, but today he's morose and exhausted, maybe a bit hungover. "You ready?" he asks, trying for a bright smile and only half succeeding.

I open the door to let him in. Helena sits hunched over her laptop, hitting the keys so hard and fast I'm fairly certain she's typing gibberish just to seem busy. Quigg gives me a quizzical look, and I barely manage to contain a laugh. I shake my head.

"This is everything," I say, pointing at my suitcase, backpack, and a single box.

"This is everything you own?" he asks skeptically. "A minimalist, huh? Well, you're making my job much easier. We'll only need to make one trip." He throws my backpack on, which looks rattier than ever against the impeccable brown tweed of his vintage blazer. He stoops to pick up the box of my meager possessions before making me a gentlemanly bow and exiting the room.

"Shall we?" he calls when I don't follow.

Quigg's already in the hallway, but I keep looking at Helena, wondering how on earth to end such a relationship. If the tables were turned and it was her leaving to take a spot in Magni Viri, I don't think I could stand it. I almost want to apologize to her, but then I remember how big an asshole she's always been to me.

"Bye," I say. "It's been . . . Well, bye."

She doesn't respond.

I give my old room one last glance around before shutting the door behind me forever. I only lived here a month and a half, but already it felt like the entirety of my lonely little world.

I feel horribly conspicuous as Quigg and I walk across campus together, as if every person we pass can tell what's happening—that I'm moving into Denfeld Hall, becoming a part of Magni Viri. I'm sure I don't look the part in my second-hand sweater and well-worn boots. I shrink into myself, focusing on the sound of Quigg's oxfords clicking on the side-walk, the steady dull roll of my suitcase's wheels. As the redbrick buildings fade behind us and Denfeld Hall looms up, dark and Gothic as an English cathedral, nothing but miles of green hills at its back, I feel like I'm transferring out of Corbin College and into the University of Magni Viri.

But there on the lawn is Corbin's emblem in the form of a fountain—a black swan with lifted head, water pouring from its beak into a low, dark pool. The sight of it doesn't reassure me though. It speaks of wealth and grace and sophistication, all qualities I so obviously lack.

"Would you mind switching and taking this box for a bit? My arms are tired," Quigg says, stopping beside the fountain. He looks like a stiff wind would blow him over, and his face is pale beneath all that coifed red hair.

"Of course. Give me the backpack too," I say. "No offense, but you look awful."

He chuckles weakly. "We go a little hard on Sunday nights, just to warn you. But you'll see," he adds hurriedly before I can ask questions.

I peer down at the cemetery on my right, but I can't see much through the gloom of the thick trees that shadow it. Black wrought iron fence, old gravestones, a small building that must be a mausoleum.

I turn my attention back to Denfeld as we approach the house, which is even bigger than I had expected. It's made of dark stone, or perhaps a lighter stone weathered over the years to a grim gray color. There are architectural features I don't have the language to describe—parts that look like they belong on a castle, a tall pointing spire, and over the heavy wooden doors, an enormous stained glass window like you'd see on a church. The entire effect is very grand and cold and foreboding. I feel like Jane Eyre at the door of Thornfield.

Quigg must see the fear in my eyes because he turns me to face him and puts his hands on my shoulders. "Look, whatever you think about yourself, however unworthy you feel, it doesn't matter. The second you go through these doors, you're one of us. It's that simple. We take care of our own."

I nod, too overwhelmed to speak.

Quigg pulls the heavy iron door handle. A cascade of smells rushes across my senses: beeswax candles, wood polish, old books, cold stone, and black tea. The entryway to the house is breathtaking, the stone walls covered in blue-tinged light from the stained glass window far overhead. There is an ancient-looking Persian rug underfoot and a stone staircase leading up toward another, smaller stained glass window, this one in the shape of an arch. Here the stairs split, leading up toward opposite ends of the building.

I expected the inside of the hall to be dark, fussy, morbidly Victorian. But it feels open and airy, the ceiling arching up, up, up and filled with light the same way a cathedral is. Dust motes float in the air, and piano music drifts in from some distant room.

To my surprise, tears stand in my eyes.

Quigg leaves my suitcase beside the stairs and takes the box from my arms and sets it down too. I barely notice, my senses overwhelmed by the eerie, almost holy effect of the foyer.

"You'll get used to it," Quigg says, seeing my awestruck expression. "You'll always love it, but it will get easier to bear."

I nod. Then my eyes catch on a huge, faded oil painting of two young white men, each of them no older than thirty. They stand side by side, shoulders nearly touching, heads lifted, eyes on the viewer. They are dressed in suits, one of them expensive-looking and the other more modest, one bare-faced and the other boasting a dark beard. The bare-faced one has a dreamy, gentle look about him. The bearded one's gaze is more steely and determined. They make an interesting pair.

I squint to read the small lettering engraved on a tarnished brass plate beneath:

Walter Weymouth George and Fr. John Bauer,
November 1900

"Who are they?" I ask.

"The founders of Magni Viri," Quigg says. "They were both professors here. WWG was a pianist, and Bauer taught theology and metaphysics."

I start to make a joke about rich white dudes and academic societies, but it dies on my lips under John Bauer's unflinching gaze. I'm still staring at the painting when Quigg nudges my arm. "So do you want a tour, or should I take you to your room?"

"Tour," I say quickly, pulling my eyes away from the painting. "I want to see *everything*."

"Okay," he says, "pretty much the entire ground floor is shared property: the kitchen, the library, the common rooms, and greenhouse." He proceeds to walk me through the rooms, hardly pausing to let me take each one in before moving on to the next.

The kitchen is enormous, clearly a post-1900s renovation. And it's a mess—dishes piled in the sink, orange peels on the counter, empty liquor bottles sticking out of the trash. A tall, gaunt student in a brocaded dressing gown leans against the counter with his eyes closed, eating a bowl of Froot Loops. I stare at him a moment longer than is polite, shocked by how ill he looks, his sallow skin and sharp cheekbones casting him more wraith than human in the pale light, but he never opens his eyes anyway. Then my attention is caught by a disheveled-looking girl who's rummaging frantically in one of the fridges and inhaling a cup of coffee, clearly running late.

Neither of the students notices Quigg and me walk through, and we continue on to the dining room, which is ornate and formal and totally empty. A faint smell of burning permeates the space, and my eyes catch on the curtains, which are blackened and filled with holes, as if they've recently been set on fire.

"What happened here?"

Quigg sighs. "Bernard Cottingham. That was the fellow in the kitchen who looked like a disgraced nineteenth-century noble. He says he's an experiential artist, but he's honestly just a pyro. Stay away from him if you can. Thankfully he's graduating this year."

"Jesus," I say under my breath, but Quigg has already moved on. I hurry to catch up.

The library immediately banishes Bernard and the burned curtains from my mind. It is rounded in shape, huge and gorgeous with yet more stained glass windows and arched shelves filled with old, leather-bound books. Green velvet furniture and bronze reading lamps dot the space. I stand so long gaping that Quigg has to come back and physically guide me out of the room to continue our tour.

He glances at his watch. "I actually have class soon, so I will let you explore the rest on your own. If our RD is here, she can give you a key to your room and everything." He leads me to a closed door, which he raps on.

"Come in," a distracted-sounding voice says. Quigg opens the door to reveal a messy study, books piled on every surface, loose papers drifting from desk to floor. Most of them are covered in what looks like Greek.

"Hey, Laini," Quigg says. "Tara is here. Can I hand her over to you?"

A head slowly peers out from around the biggest stack of books. I make out a pretty, heart-shaped face, most of which is taken up by enormous glasses, a small rosebud mouth, and a shaggy black bobbed haircut. She blinks at me for a moment, as if coming out of a trance. Her eyes are ringed with an exhausted-looking shade of purple that stands out glaringly against her faded-gold skin tone.

"Hello," I say uncertainly, unnerved by how run-down every member of Magni Viri I've seen today looks. I guess they all partied way too hard last night. I dig in my backpack for my folder of paperwork.

"I gotta go, see you both later," Quigg says, dashing out of the room and leaving me standing amid the books and papers. I glance out the window at the back of the study, which looks out on a maple tree with vibrant orange leaves. There is a row of dusty-looking teacups in the windowsill, some of them ringed with mold.

"Sorry, I, um, where were we?" Laini asks, as if we'd been mid conversation. She scratches her forehead.

"I'm Tara Boone. I'm supposed to move in today," I prompt her. I cross the room and hand her the manila folder.

"Oh!" she says, as if realizing for the first time who I am. "Yes, of course, hello." She stands suddenly from her chair. "I'm Laini Moore. I'm the resident director. I'm, um, a Magni Viri alum. I graduated two years ago, and I stayed on to continue work on my translation." She pushes her glasses up her nose.

"What are you translating?"

She waves her hand lazily over the piles of books and papers. "Oh, um, it's a new translation of Sappho?"

"Oh, wow, that's really cool. I read Anne Carson's over the summer."

She blinks and looks like she's about to launch into a passionate opinion on the matter, but then stops herself. "I'm guessing you have other things to do today besides talk Greek translations, so let's get you moved in, all right?" She rummages in her desk and then hands me a spiral-bound notebook and a key with a tag that reads "#11." "Those are the house rules. Please read them and let me know if you have questions. You're in room eleven with Wren."

"Oh. I have a roommate?" The feeling in my stomach is less like butterflies than a swarm of angry yellow jackets. What if this will be like rooming with Helena all over again?

"Yes, but don't worry—it's not Meredith's room. We thought it would be hard for Azar after losing Meredith. So Wren volunteered to share. They aren't— Oh, and Wren's pronouns are they/them, by the way. Anyway, Wren is hardly ever in the room. They practically sleep at the piano."

"They're a music major?"

Laini nods. "A composer. Really brilliant. You might have heard them playing when you came in, though I think Wren has knocked off now. Do you like classical music?"

I shrug. "I don't *not* like it. I guess I haven't ever really listened to much."

"Well, you will listen to quite a lot from here on out," Laini says with a laugh. "Let's head up to your room. Wren might be there, and you two can meet."

We grab my stuff and head up the left-hand wing of stairs to the second floor. Laini points at various doors and tells me who resides behind them. I do a double take when she points out Azar's room, since that's where Meredith used to live. But then Laini stops at a door halfway down the hall, overlooking the foyer.

"Here we are." She knocks lightly, and after a moment the door opens and Wren blinks at us sleepily.

They are white and have very pale skin, a mop of wavy brown hair, and dark brown eyes with purple smudges beneath. They look very young, hardly more than fifteen. Is it possible I won't be the youngest one here?

"Welcome, welcome," Wren says. They take the box from my arms and set it on an empty desk. I drop my backpack on the floor, and Laini heaves my suitcase onto the unmade bed.

Wren turns back to me. "So, uh, I'm Wren Norwood. My pronouns are they/them."

"It's nice to meet you," I say, feeling awkwardly formal. "I'm Tara Boone. She/her. Thanks for sharing your room."

"Right—well, I'll let you two get acquainted," Laini says. "I'll be in my office all day if you need me, Tara. Welcome to Denfeld!" With that, she hurries away down the hall, clearly eager to get back to her Greek.

Wren smiles at me, studying me with interest. I busy myself looking around the place that will be my new home for the next four years.

This room is nothing like the cement block I lived in with Helena. The walls are covered in green patterned wallpaper, and a window with heavy drapes pulled back throws light into the room. The floors are bare wood, the boards warped and splintered in places. The beds are old-fashioned, made of worn brass gone shiny on the top of each post. The effect is surprisingly homey.

"I'm a bit of a slob," Wren says genially. "I hope you don't mind. That's why I originally asked for my own room, so I wouldn't be a burden to anyone. But considering the circumstances . . ." They trail off.

Wren's side of the room is indeed messy, with clothes thrown over furniture and books piled up in corners. Their trash can is overflowing with balled-up paper. Wren themself is messy too—untidy hair, wrinkled polka-dot pajamas, mismatched socks. They fidget uncomfortably, waiting for my judgment. I feel an immediate and intense fondness for them and this room.

"Oh, I don't mind a mess," I say, smiling. "Thank you for letting me stay. It would have been awkward to take Meredith's bed and everything."

"Yeah," Wren says. "Poor Mer." Their face falls.

"Were you friends?" I ask gently.

Wren shrugs. "Yes and no. We weren't close, not like she was with Azar and Neil. But friendship is sort of built in here. We're always together. It's kind of like family, you know? Like, you didn't get to pick them and you don't always necessarily like them, but you all sort of belong to each other?"

"Sure," I say, though Wren's words leave a hollow feeling in my stomach. Mom and I belonged to each other, but I chose to leave her. Just like Dad did. Guilt gnaws at me, even though I know I don't deserve it. I push thoughts of my family away. "Who in the house are you close to?"

Wren wrinkles their nose. "Jordan, I guess. He's one of my

favorite people I've ever met."

"High praise," I say with a smile. Mentally, I run through the row of first-year students I saw at the memorial. Jordan must be the serious-looking boy who sat next to Wren. I only got a glimpse of him: very short hair, a deep brown complexion, a crisp dress shirt and blazer.

"You'll see," Wren says. "You'll love him. And Penny, of course. She's a gem."

"She's in our year too? I don't think I know of her."

"Penny Dabrovsky—she's in the room next to ours. Long hair. Very dapper, walks with a cane sometimes."

"So it's Neil, Azar, you, Penny, Jordan, and . . . me?"

"Yep, and the other years have six each too. And Laini keeps us all in line. So that's twenty-five total in our house."

"How—how old are you?" I finally ask.

Wren laughs. "I just turned seventeen last month. I know I look young. To be fair, I'm the youngest in our year. But I'm used to taking care of myself. The others like to baby me sometimes, and it's honestly pretty annoying. It's not like they're much older than me."

I blush, annoyed at myself for prying. "I'm seventeen too," I say. "I graduated a year early. So is the house pretty divided up by year, or do you hang out with, like, the juniors and seniors too?"

They hesitate. "Sometimes. They tend to be pretty . . . wrapped up in their research. But Quigg and I are pals. He's a junior. Oh, and he's O'Connor's assistant, but I guess you already know that."

I nod and open the notebook Laini gave me. I turn the

pages, but the words run over each other, not forming into any coherent meaning.

"You look overwhelmed," Wren says.

"It's a lot of new people," I admit. "I've been pretty much on my own since I got to Corbin. I think I may have forgotten how to, like, hold a proper conversation." I don't mention that the house's state of exhaustion and disarray has made me nervous for what my future in Magni Viri holds. I don't think I've seen one person without dark circles under their eyes.

"I'm not sure I ever knew how to hold a proper conversation," Wren says with a laugh. "But let's give you some practice, eh? Tell me about yourself. Like, where are you from? What's your major?"

For a moment I'm tempted to lie. To invent a fabulous backstory that's so much better than the reality, like Richard Papen did in *The Secret History*—a book I read over the summer hoping for clues of what life at a liberal arts college would be like. But Wren looks earnest and interested, and so I tell them the truth. And despite my worries, I don't *want* to lie. This is supposed to be a fresh start for me—I don't want to do it as someone else. Maybe that's why I tell them a lot more than I mean to. About leaving rural Florida and my mom, about my horrible roommate, all the jobs I've been working, how hard college is. How badly I want to write and how impossible it seems. The words keep pouring out, as if they've been dammed up inside me for months, waiting for a chance to get out. Waiting for someone who cared enough to listen.

Wren does listen, nodding in all the right places and letting me finish my story before saying anything. To my relief, there's no pity in their response, only a frankness as they reply. "You know, Jordan and Penny are both first-gen students too," they say. "You'd be surprised how many people in Magni Viri are."

"Really? I haven't met anyone else at Corbin who is."

"Well, it doesn't sound like you've met many people at all," Wren says with a teasing laugh, though it's not a mean one.

I laugh too. It's easier now that my old life is behind me. "True. So is your family full of musicians?"

"Oh, God no. My parents have the most boring jobs imaginable. My dad works in tech security, and my mom is an attorney. They hardly knew what to do with me."

I ignore the pang of jealousy I always feel when people at Corbin talk about their parents. I don't want to think about my mom, don't want to wonder if she's going to work, paying her bills, staying away from that scary ex like she promised she would. She's not my job anymore. I keep telling myself this.

"Do you have any performances coming up?" I ask after we've both been silent for too long. "I'd love to hear you play."

Wren's eyes light up. "Come on. I'll play for you now." They leap off their bed, pulling me with them from the room. I have to jog to keep up with them as they hurtle down the stairs and into the music room, which Quigg didn't show me earlier. There's an enormous grand piano in front of a huge window.

"I'll play you the new piece I'm working on," Wren says. They sit at the piano and launch right into a very complicated-sounding song full of minor chords. It reminds me of watching a thunderstorm roll in from miles away, the way you can in Florida. After a while, the tempo gets fast and then even faster, until Wren's fingers are flying over the keys. I find a chair against the wall and settle in, mesmerized.

I don't know anything about classical music, but I can tell that Wren is brilliant, that they are making something profound and important. Wren plays for five minutes and then ten and then fifteen.

The music moves through me like a river, wrenching loose anything that isn't tied down. Memories, emotions, fears, secret dreams. I feel like the blood is humming in my veins, like every particle of me vibrates with the notes that pour from Wren's fingers, pushing me to my feet with the indiscernible need to do *something*.

I'm at the base of the stairs before I realize what I'm doing, where I'm going. But I don't stop. I drift up the stairs and down the hall, Wren's music loosening its hold on me as it softens into the background. When I reach the door to the room I know was Meredith's, I pause, trying to fight down the urge.

But the door is ajar, and when I rap on it, it pushes open still farther, releasing a whiff of lily of the valley perfume. The smell unaccountably makes all the hairs on my arms stand on end, brings me out of the dreamy state of mind that Wren's music had evoked, like a splash of cold water in my face.

"Hello?" I call, sticking my head inside. But the room is empty, and I can only hear the faint notes of Wren's music, still playing, in the distance. I realize how weird it would be if Azar found me here. I'm about to turn away when I catch sight of Meredith Brown's pale face staring at me. I startle, nearly bolting from the room before I realize it's a blown-up canvas print of her and the other Magni Viri freshmen.

Without thinking, I step deeper into the room, drawn irresistibly to the photograph. The six of them are bunched close together, Meredith at the center, staring down the camera with a defiant, smoky gaze while Neil kisses her cheek. The others seem to radiate out from her, as if she's the sun and they're planets rotating around her powerful gravitational pull.

With effort, I pull my eyes away from her and look around the room. All of Meredith's belongings are still here, as if she's expected back at any moment. The walls are hung with modern art, mostly abstract blocks of color. Her bed is made with a black-and-gold duvet. A green cardigan hangs on the back of her chair. A neat stack of notebooks rests next to her laptop. I pick up a heavy black pen from the desktop, rolling it between my fingers. I wonder if her hands were the last to touch it; if something of her essence remains on everything she owned, the way her perfume lingers in the room. That's what made my skin break out in goose bumps when I entered the room, I realize—lily of the valley was the same fragrance that surrounded Meredith's dead body when I bent to listen for her breath in the library. Didn't I smell it in the chapel too?

She's still here, I think—wildly, nonsensically. *She's watching me.*

I spin around, my heart in my throat, my hand over my mouth, fully expecting to see Meredith at the door, demanding to know why I'm touching her things.

But there's no one there.

My hair stirs at the back of my neck, as if someone has blown on my skin. I whip back around, my heart racing, and meet Meredith's eyes in the photograph again.

I can feel her here. I can feel her beside me. The same way I felt her the night she died, keeping pace with me behind the stretcher that carried her body away.

My breaths come fast and shallow. Hysteria rises up in my chest, threatening to choke me. "Meredith?" I whisper.

My phone rings, and I scream, barely managing to muffle the sound with my hands. I yank it from my pocket and answer the call, bringing the phone up to my ear. I fully expect to hear Meredith's voice on the other end, that same soft, liquid voice that entranced the entire room at the lit club reading. Instead, cicadas scream in my ear. Wind moans through naked treetops. Fingernails scrape on wood. Beneath it all, a strange, garbled music plays—the kind you hear late at night when you've woken from a deep sleep and the house is full of faraway noises.

I squeeze my eyes shut, terror filling every particle of me.

"Tara?" a girl's voice says, distant, almost inaudible, as if heard from underwater.

A hand squeezes my forearm, the fingers soft and warm. If I had any breath to spare, I would scream. Instead, I stagger back, opening my eyes.

There's a girl beside me, nearly six feet tall. I have to tilt my head back to meet her eyes.

"It *is* Tara, isn't it?" She looks as startled as I am. "I didn't mean to scare you. I called your name. Are you okay? Did you get a bad phone call?"

For a moment, all I can do is stare at her. She's white and has long honey-brown hair braided along one side and pulled up into a loose bun at the back of her head. She's dressed in gray wool slacks, a striped button-down, and a corduroy vest. She has a beautiful cane that looks like an antique. The cane is what finally clears my confusion.

"You must be Penny," I finally say.

"Yeah, and you're Tara, right?"

I nod.

Penny, not Meredith. Meredith isn't here. Meredith is dead. I'm just freaking myself out.

Wordlessly, I sink to Meredith's bed, struggling to get a breath into my burning lungs. My phone's screen has gone blank and dead.

"Wow, did I scare you that badly?" Penny says, sitting beside me. She sets an APA guide with Azar's name on the cover down on the bed. She must have borrowed it and come in here to return it. She's probably wondering what I'm doing in here.

As my panic fades, embarrassment takes its place. My face flushes hot and is most likely bright red. "Sorry," I whisper, rubbing my cheek. My lips feel numb. I really let my imagination get to me this time.

"Strong startle response, huh?" Penny asks, forehead creased with concern.

I shake my head. "It's nothing. I got distracted thinking about Meredith, I guess. You surprised me."

Penny looks away from me and around the room. "It's so strange that she's gone. Every time I pop in to see Azar, I expect to see Meredith at the desk, typing away at one of her stories." She laughs, a bit sadly. "The girl never stopped writing."

"Why is all her stuff still here?" I ask carefully. "Didn't her parents want it?"

Penny meets my eyes again. "Mer's parents aren't really the sentimental kind."

"Oh," I say, unsure how to respond. My mom always held on to my childhood things, squirreling away old report cards, honors day awards, science fair trophies. She even kept my newborn blanket and baby teeth. If I died, I think she'd want everything that was mine—at least, before I left home she would have. I'm not sure how she'd feel now. Maybe I'm already dead to her.

Penny sighs. "We're going to box it all up eventually, but . . . we all kind of agreed to let it stay for a while. Like, we want Meredith to know that she's still ours, I guess. We didn't know her that long, but she was ours. She always will be."

I nod, averting my face so Penny doesn't see how her words have affected me. Even dead, Meredith is more a member of Magni Viri than I am. Even if her ghost isn't here, her memory is.

"Hey," Penny says, tugging my sleeve to make me look at her. "Don't worry. We've got space here for you too." She smiles, and I realize she's got beautiful lips, slightly ridged as if they're chapped, and a little dimple on one side when she smiles.

The longer I look at her, the harder it is to stop. She has high cheekbones and lightly tanned skin. Her eyes are hazel, spaced farther apart than most people's and fringed with long lashes.

"So were you looking for Azar?" Penny asks, cocking her head.

I realize she must think I came in here to snoop. Which I guess I did, though I'm still not sure why. It's almost as if the eerie force of Wren's music carried me here. Or maybe just my own morbid curiosity.

I blush again at being caught out. "Wren was showing me their music, but then I think they forgot I was there. I was just coming up here and passed by . . ." I trail off helplessly. I'm too flustered to think of a lie.

But Penny only smiles. "Wren gets really caught up in their music. They'll play for six, seven hours without stopping, and I'm not exaggerating about that. We literally have to pull them from the bench sometimes to make them eat and go to class," Penny says.

"Are you serious? That sounds . . ." I trail off again, not wanting to say what I'm thinking.

"Unhealthy and obsessive?" Penny offers.

"Intense," I finally say.

"Everyone here is like that to some degree, but Wren is the worst. Maybe since you're their roommate, you can keep an eye on them?" she asks.

"Yeah, of course. We'll keep an eye on each other," I say, remembering what Wren said about not liking being babied by the others. "Wren seems like they're going to be a good roommate."

"Better than your last?" Penny's lips quirk.

I cock my head. "How did you . . . ?"

"Quigg texted all of us. He's a terrible gossip, just so you know. Don't tell him anything you don't want all of Magni Viri hearing about." She laughs, a husky, throaty sound.

"Not that it's really possible to keep secrets around here. The walls have ears," she says, a little bitterly. I can't help but look around the room at her words—as if I'll spot someone hiding in the curtains.

"What do you mean?" I ask.

Penny shrugs. "Nothing. It's just a lot people all thrown together in one house, you know?" she says, a little too casually. "Want to get out of here, maybe take a walk?" she adds.

I seize on the idea, suddenly desperate to get as far as possible from Meredith's room, maybe even out of her house. "Sure, I've got a few hours until class. My first of the day was canceled." I grimace as I think of poor Dr. Hendrix, who still hasn't recovered from finding Meredith's body. An involuntary shiver runs through me.

"Let me just grab a jacket," I say, and then stop when I realize I can still hear Wren's music. "Should we tell Wren where we're going?"

Penny shakes her head, half smiling. "Chances are they haven't even noticed you left. They'll be playing for a while yet, don't worry."

It's only when I'm back in my own bedroom that I realize I'm still gripping Meredith's expensive black pen in one hand. I ought to take it back to her room, but I don't. I slide it guiltily into my desk drawer, a little piece of brilliant, beautiful Meredith Brown for my own.

SEVEN

When Penny and I exit Denfeld Hall, it's midmorning and the sky is a brilliant, unreal blue. I gulp down air as if I haven't taken a proper breath in hours.

Penny laughs, apparently picking up on my discomfort if not its cause. "If you think it's claustrophobic now, just wait," she says. "Thank God for the woods. Have you hiked any of the trails around campus?"

"Not yet," I say.

"Good, I'll be your trail guide," she says with a quick smile.

I follow her down a gravel path away from the house, nearly losing my footing a few times on the steep incline. Then the path turns from gravel to dust and we're in the woods.

Cicadas rattle and scream, and the wind moans in the treetops, making branches rub together. It sounds exactly like that weird call I got the day Meredith died. The call I got when I was in her room too.

I shiver for the second time this morning, but I keep going.

Penny and I walk in a surprisingly comfortable silence for several minutes before she speaks. "I love the woods here," she says. "They remind me of home."

"Where are you from?"

"Pennsylvania. It looks a lot like this. Green hills and forests. Penn's woods." She smiles. "It's how I got my name. My dad works in forestry. He wanted to name me Penn, but my mom insisted on adding the *y*." She laughs. "He calls me Penn anyway."

"So you're super outdoorsy?" I venture. She doesn't quite fit the bill with her wool and corduroy. I'm not sure what to make of her. Out here in direct sunlight I can see her clothes are well-worn, fraying in places. She might be dapper, but she isn't rich. Plus, Wren said Penny was a first-gen student like me.

"I grew up hiking with my parents, camping in the woods with my friends. It's all there was to do there really, out in the middle of nowhere, three hours from an actual city."

"I've never been camping," I admit. "I'm kind of scared of nature."

"Ah, nature is the least of our problems," Penny says, "and we're its worst nightmare."

"I don't know," I say. "I'm from Florida. You should see the size of our roaches."

Penny laughs.

After a few quiet moments, she pauses on the trail and uses the end of her cane to point something out on a nearby tree. It's a small brown bug, desiccated-looking.

"Cicada exoskeleton," she explains.

"Isn't it late in the year for them to still be making such a racket?" I ask, looking up at the trees, as if I could spot the cicadas in the branches.

"It is," she agrees. "But this was a brood year, and there

were just so many of them. Plus, the weather hasn't been too cold yet. It's going to turn soon though, and then they'll all be gone. The woods will be so quiet."

"It's strange how they stay underground for so long," I say. "All this life under our feet, waiting for some signal from the universe to come out and live."

"Nothing stays buried forever," Penny murmurs.

I shiver yet again, though I can't put my finger on why. I decide to change the subject. "What are you studying?" I ask. "I feel like everyone in Magni Viri is in the humanities."

"You'd be surprised. Jordan is a biology major; he's interested in cancer research. Azar is into robotics. Me, I came here to study bats."

"Bats?" I ask with a delighted laugh. It's about the last thing in the world I thought she'd say.

"Yeah, I came for Dr. Coppola. She was doing some of the most important bat research in the US. But she died over the summer. Heart attack."

"Oh my gosh," I say. "I'm so sorry."

Penny shrugs. "It was too late to change schools, at least for this year. I would transfer somewhere else, but Magni Viri . . . Well, I won't get another financial aid deal like this. So I'm going to have to make the best of it."

I'm about to ask how she got into bats, but then she sighs. "I'm tired today, so we'd better head back."

"Sure, that's all right," I say. Suddenly, I can see the weariness all over her—the tightness at her eyes, the ginger way she moves. It's not the same kind of tiredness I've seen in the other MV students today. I think she's in pain.

"I hear Magni Viri parties hard on Sunday nights," I say, unsure of what to focus on.

She flinches. "Yeah, it's a wild night." She bites her lip and doesn't say anything else for a while. Then she suddenly brightens. "There's a bat cave nearby. I kept seeing them all come whooshing over the tops of the trees, so I hunted it down. They're the ones Dr. Coppola studied. Brown bats. Really cute little guys. Remind me to bring you back to show you another day."

I'm not sure I want to go near a bat cave, but I say I will. Penny lapses into a moody silence, and I don't mind the quiet. This has been one of the most overwhelming days of my life. I feel like I'm full to the brim with sensations. What I need is a quiet room and a pen in my hand, to get some of these thoughts out of my head and onto paper. I feel a thin flicker of excitement run through me. For the first time since I got to Corbin, I actually have time for that.

But when we make it back to campus, it's already lunchtime. Penny and I collect Wren, who is still going hard at the piano, and wait for them to go change into proper clothes. Then the three of us walk to the cafeteria. Jordan, Azar, and Neil are already at a table in the corner, deep in conversation. They stop talking as soon as I set my tray down, and I'm reminded forcefully of my recent disastrous attempt at conversation with Britney and Bobby at the lit club reading.

But Wren comes to my rescue. "Everyone, this is Tara," they say proudly, as if I'm a project they made in art class.

"Hi," I say, my cheeks flaming as the three of them stare at me. I can't help but think about the last time I came face-to-face with Azar and Neil. How angry he was at me, as if I were somehow to blame for Meredith's death. How distraught they both were. And now I'm taking their friend's seat at the table. It's excruciating.

I want to run, but I force myself to act normally. I remind myself that it's not my fault that Meredith died. It's not my fault that I'm here and she isn't. Dr. O'Connor said I deserve to be here. If things had gone differently, I might have been sitting at this table all along.

Jordan gives me a small, kind smile, his dark brown eyes radiating warmth. "Welcome to Magni Viri. I'm Jordan Flanagan."

"Thanks," I say, deeply relieved. I slide into the seat across from him, next to Azar.

Azar nods at me. "Nice to officially meet you, Tara. I'm Azar Davani. This is Neil Byrd."

Across the table, Neil glowers at me. Azar must kick him in the shin because he winces and lets out a begrudging hello before returning morosely to his roasted chicken.

"Nice to meet all of you," I say. I don't know whether I should clear the air about Meredith or pretend she never existed and make mundane conversation. I decide to do neither, tucking into my bowl of potato soup instead.

I half expect them to grill me about myself, but instead Jordan tells us all about a study on jumping spiders that he read in an old issue of *Science*, and he and Penny start going back and forth about the problem-solving abilities of invertebrates. Azar cuts in with a cryptic remark about slime mold solving mazes, and soon they're arguing forcefully about nonhuman intelligence. I follow the conversation but only barely. When I look over at Wren, they're totally zoned out, staring at the ceiling, their own bowl of soup forgotten.

I nudge Wren's shoulder. "Aren't you hungry?"

They startle. "Oh. Yes. Thank you." Wren eats the rest of the soup quickly, as if afraid to get distracted again before their belly is full. "It's good today," they say around a mouthful.

"Want some ice cream?" I ask. "I'm getting some."

"Ooh," Wren says, letting their spoon clatter in the bowl. I laugh as they drag me off to the soft-serve machines. When we return with sprinkle-covered swirled cones, Penny gives me an approving smile. This is what she meant about being a good roommate to Wren, I realize. Making sure Wren eats and spends some occasional time in the world the rest of us inhabit. I like the idea of having someone to care for. A quiet part of me does wonder if I just miss taking care of Mom, or maybe I miss being needed.

But I feel like Wren is someone who will take care of me too. They've already gone out of their way to make me feel welcome here, and they let me prattle on for ages about my experiences at Corbin without interrupting or downplaying my feelings. It won't be like it was with Mom, always one-sided and exhausting. Quigg said Magni Viri takes care of its own. So far that seems to be true, even if Neil has been sullenly avoiding my gaze since I sat down.

"So Quigg told me y'all party pretty hard on Sunday nights, which kind of surprised me," I say, my curiosity to know more about Magni Viri finally winning out over my shyness.

Azar laughs and exchanges a loaded look with Jordan. "You thought we'd all be a bunch of school-obsessed nerds?"

I laugh too. "Yeah, I guess so."

"Well, I mean you weren't wrong, but Magni Viri can be pretty high pressure. Even the biggest nerds need to let off steam," Azar says carefully. "So that's what the Sunday night parties are for . . . at least in part."

Neil huffs out a laugh. "You'd make a good diplomat, Azar."

"Why's that?" I ask, looking between them.

But Neil only raises his eyebrows at Azar, some silent conversation happening between them. Azar shakes her head at him.

"If I'm honest, I expected you all to be a little scarier," I admit, when it's clear she won't be answering my last question.

"What do you mean?" Penny asks with a laugh.

"Well, you know the rumors about Magni Viri. Students think you're all, like, Satan worshippers performing blood sacrifices under the full moon. People say that Magni Viri is more secret society than academic society."

The entire table goes wide-eyed and silent. My smile dies.

"Sorry, I didn't mean . . ." I trail off uncertainly as the others eye one another.

Are they mad? Surprised? Did they really not know what people say about Magni Viri?

"It's not like that," Azar finally says, her voice brusque.

"I know—of course—it's just . . ."

I look helplessly at Wren, who is biting their lip and staring off into space. Penny meets my eyes, but her expression is conflicted.

"Sorry, I shouldn't have brought up stupid rumors. Forget it," I finally say, weirded out by everyone's reactions. I'd expected them to laugh it off or joke about it. But this intense quiet is unnerving.

Jordan clears his throat and is about to say something when Neil interrupts. "So, Tara, O'Connor told us you're a writer," he says, his attention fully on me for the first time.

"I want to be, yeah," I say cautiously, unsure why he's deigning to speak to me now, especially after I made things so awkward. Does he remember me from the lit club reading? I hope he has no memory of my disastrous performance, but that's probably too much to wish for.

Neil leans toward Azar and mutters something too low for me to hear. Is he telling her about my shitty flash fiction piece?

"Neil," Azar says warningly.

"What is it?" I ask, confused and wary.

Neil smiles waspishly, reminding me suddenly and horribly of Helena. "I said O'Connor couldn't have chosen a more perfect member."

"What's that supposed to mean?"

"Nothing, he means nothing," Azar says, shooting eye daggers at Neil. Everyone else looks uncomfortable and embarrassed, afraid to say anything. Heat rushes to my cheeks.

"What have you written?" Neil asks me, eyebrows raised in mock interest.

I shift uneasily in my seat. "A few short stories. Part of a novel." I decide not to share about how I lost my confidence a quarter of the way through the novel and gave up. That was over the summer, before I came here.

"I suppose you have a really important perspective as a . . . what are you? A Floridian? Though something tells me you'll be writing like Flannery O'Connor in no time."

"Neil," Jordan says, an angry edge to his voice.

"Give it a rest," Penny says, sounding weary.

I look around the table, unable to understand what's happening. What Neil is trying to say. Why everyone else is suddenly acting so cagey and on edge. Like there's something they all know but won't say to me. Even Wren looks like a deer caught in headlights. I open my mouth and then close it again. I feel sure I'm the butt of a joke somehow. And I'm not going to sit here and endure it any longer.

"I've got work to do," I say, standing up from the table. "It was really nice to meet all of you. Thanks for the warm welcome." I walk away, still holding my ice cream cone, which has started to drip over my fingers. My face burns with anger and embarrassment, and tears stand in my eyes.

I toss my ice cream in the trash can outside the dining hall and wipe my sticky fingers on my jeans. I almost take the path back toward my old dorm but remember at the last second that I live in Denfeld now and veer off toward the north side of campus. It's a long walk, and I have class in an hour, so I hurry.

Gradually, I become aware of someone calling my name. I turn, expecting Wren or Penny, but it's Azar. She jogs behind me, her shoulder-length hair swaying around her chin, her form like a runner's, even in high-rise trousers and an oxford shirt buttoned to the throat.

"Hey," she says, "thanks for stopping. I wanted to say I'm

sorry about Neil. He can be kind of an asshole sometimes. But he's worse now because of Meredith. He was in love with her, you know. It's really hard to see you here in her place."

"I'm not trying to take her place," I say tightly.

"But you are," Azar says. "You have to take her place; I get that. I'm just saying that it's hard for Neil. It's hard for me too. I loved her too. She was . . ." Azar shakes her head. "Meredith was mesmerizing, magnetic. It's almost impossible to believe she's really gone."

"I'm sorry," I say. "I really am. Meredith was— I didn't know her, but I know what you mean. She *was* kind of mesmerizing. And really talented."

"Give Neil some time. He'll come around to you, I promise," Azar says.

"I'm not sure I want him to. He seems like a snob."

"Oh, he's a horrible snob," Azar says with a laugh. "But he's a good friend. He's very loyal . . . even after you're . . . well . . ." The word *dead* hangs in the air a moment, unspoken. But then Azar cocks her head at me. "Look, you're going to encounter a lot of strong personalities in Denfeld. Magni Viri is basically the House of the Self-Absorbed. We're all tortured and misunderstood wannabe geniuses." She grins. "Try not to take it personally, okay? I swear it's not about you."

"Feels like it is," I say, still off-kilter. "Feels like dealing with my roommate all over again."

"That bitch Helena? We will literally go jump her for you. You get that, right?"

I laugh, shocked. But then I shake my head. "I feel like he was trying to tell me I'm some redneck idiot who doesn't deserve to be in Magni Viri. Is it because of what I said about the rumors? I didn't actually believe them."

Azar's brow crinkles with surprise. "What? No way. He didn't mean it like that. I swear. He wasn't really even talking about you. It was . . . something else."

When I give her a skeptical look, she keeps talking.

"I know you've had a hard time since you got to Corbin. But we're all dealing with shit. We've all got things that put us at a disadvantage, that make life harder. Like, I'm Persian, okay? I was born in the US; my parents were raised in the US. But the way some of these people act when they find out I'm Iranian American." She shakes her head and laughs. "*And* I'm a lesbian!"

"I figured," I say with a small smile. I gesture at her paisley-patterned button-down.

She squints at my cuffed jeans and boots. "Bisexual?"

This time I laugh outright. "Yeah."

She grins. "See, you can drop the chip on your shoulder when you're with us. And I mean that in the nicest possible way."

"Neil really wasn't ragging on me for being poor or something?"

"No, not at all."

I put my face in my hands, embarrassed to have misjudged the situation so badly. "I feel so lost all the time," I admit. "Like everyone else knows how everything works, what everything means, and I'm always struggling to catch up. And now I have to figure out Magni Viri on top of it. Not that I'm not thrilled to be here," I add.

"Jordan feels like that about college too," Azar says. "I'll tell you what I tell him. Just ask me and don't be embarrassed. My parents are both academics, so I know this culture inside and out. I'm happy to help."

"Thanks," I say.

"Anytime," Azar says. "And I'll talk to Neil. He'll be nicer next time, I promise."

"Okay. I gotta go get my stuff and head to class," I say. "See you at dinner?"

"You bet," Azar says.

I hurry away, thinking over what she said. Can I truly let my defenses down with them? Will they really accept me? Azar said everyone in Magni Viri has something that makes college harder. Maybe that's why the students are so close, why they stick together. Because they understand vulnerability and the need to belong.

But even if I misread what Neil was saying, there's definitely something they're all hiding from me. They all looked so freaked when I mentioned the rumors about Magni Viri.

And it seemed like Neil was trying to tell me something no one else wanted him to say. Maybe I'll eventually be fully a part of their world, but I'm not yet.

Magni Viri is still keeping its secrets.

EIGHT

By ten o'clock, I'm exhausted. My first day as a member of Magni Viri was . . . incredible, overwhelming, bewildering, terrifying. I almost cry with relief when I realize I can go to bed early since I don't have a janitorial shift. My mind can't take in anything more.

I've already been asleep for several hours when I wake suddenly from a hazy, confusing dream. Meredith was there, her fingers tangled in my hair, nails sharp against my scalp, her heady perfume surrounding me. After a moment, the dream fades and I hear the thing that woke me: the sound of something scraping across my bedroom door. I startle, sitting up fast, my heart racing. I hold still, listening with my entire being. Wren sleeps on, oblivious.

I decide I must have imagined the sound or that it was part of my dream. I'm about to lie back down when a floorboard outside my door creaks, long and loud. Someone's definitely out there.

I shiver, imagining Meredith's ghost crouched outside the door, peering into the keyhole. Maybe she wants her pen back. Or maybe she wants me out of Denfeld Hall so she can be Magni Viri's sixth freshman forever. I squeeze my eyes tight, praying Wren locked the door when they came to bed.

There's a rustling sound, and then a whisper. All I can think about is how I felt Meredith's presence in her room earlier, surrounding me. The way those nearly inaudible whispers coming through my phone's tinny speaker sounded.

This time the whisper is clear. "Tara," the person says in an ethereal voice. "Tara, open your door."

I let out an involuntary whimper. But since the problem clearly isn't going to go away, I throw my legs over the side of the bed and pull a sweater on over my pajamas, shaking as I do it. The moon shines in through the open curtains, just past full, surprisingly bright. There's a strange, irregular knock at the door, followed by a low, muffled laugh that makes the fine hairs on the back of my neck stand on end. I think of Rochester's wife wandering the halls of Thornfield, setting people on fire in their beds, and then I remember the burned curtains in the dining room. What if it's the fire-obsessed Bernard out there?

"Wren," I whisper, shaking their shoulder. "Wren, wake up."

Wren opens their eyes groggily. "Wha?" they mumble.

"Someone's at the door," I whisper.

"So open it," Wren says, snuggling down into their blankets again.

I'm not sure what else to do, so I walk over to the door and, after a long moment of silence, open it a crack. I peer out into the gloom of the hallway, and a face peers back at me, inches from my own. I scream and stumble back. Behind me, there's a loud thump and a groan. When I turn, Wren is on the ground, struggling to free themself from the blankets.

The person at my door chuckles, and I finally recognize them. It's Quigg. And he's very drunk. He tumbles into the room, a few others on his heels.

"Oh, shit, did we scare you? It's initiationnnn night!" he sings.

"What?" I cross my arms over my chest, acutely aware that I'm not wearing a bra under my sweater. "You scared the shit out of me."

"Time to become one of us!" he trills.

"One of us! One of us!" the others chant, laughing. It's Penny and Azar, now joined by Wren, who has finally extricated themself from the bedcovers and is wearing their quilt like a cloak. The three of them grin at me.

"You missed initiation night, so we're hosting one just for you," Quigg says. "You've got five minutes to get dressed if you want to." With that, he and Penny and Azar go laughing out of the room.

Wren throws an oversize denim trucker jacket on over their pajamas and pulls on some bright yellow rain boots before leaving with the others, and I'm left standing in the middle of the room in a pool of moonlight, swaying with sleepiness and confusion. Initiation ceremony?

I go to the window and look down. Groups of people are walking away from Denfeld, heading in the direction of the cemetery. So the entirety of Magni Viri is apparently going to be present at my initiation. *Shit.* Now my heart is racing for a totally different reason.

I scramble to get dressed, nearly falling over as I pull on

my jeans. I flip on the light right before I'm ready to leave and stare at myself in the mirror for a long moment. The stubborn freckles across the bridge of my nose are the same. My eyebrows have the same straight, serious set to them. My mouth is still a little smaller than I would like. Nothing about me has changed, yet I barely recognize the girl who stares back. She is bright-eyed and alive, as excited as she is afraid. I shake my head at her before dashing out of the room and toward the staircase. The others are waiting there for me.

"One of us! One of us!" they start chanting again as they hurry me down the stairs.

Penny takes a little longer, coming down carefully, though still chanting with the others. I laugh and cover my face as they sweep me along. What the hell have I gotten myself into?

Once we're outside, Quigg puts a finger to his mouth. "Shhh! Let's not wake the entire campus."

Azar grabs my hand. "Come on!" she whispers, and takes off running, giggling maniacally.

Wren runs after us, and Quigg and Penny come more slowly from behind, their heads together in conversation.

"What—is—this?" I gasp as we run through the cold night air. "Some sort of . . . hazing?"

When we pass people, they call out to us or let out little whoops of encouragement.

I really hope they aren't going to try to make me drink beer through a funnel or something. But then I remember the rumors about Magni Viri's satanic rituals and decide a little binge drinking sounds pretty tame in comparison.

Azar laughs. "It's tradition," she says, not at all out of

breath. "We all did it together, but you didn't get your chance. You're not a true member of Magni Viri without it. Don't worry, it's painless—well, mostly."

We burst through the gate of the cemetery, which someone has unlocked, passing under the dark archway and into the shelter of the pines. It's darker here, and colder, tucked up as it is against the side of a hill. Azar finally stops running. I slump forward, hands braced against my knees, dragging in ice-cold breaths. My lungs burn, and my skin tingles. But I feel alive, alive, alive.

In the dark, the cicadas rasp and the trees sway, moaning in their canopies. An owl hoots from somewhere very near. There are voices too, two dozen of them whispering and laughing beneath the cover of night. Azar puts her arm through mine and guides me down the cemetery path, which winds around trees, headstones, and statuary. Azar's flashlight catches here on a lichen-crusted obelisk, there on a mossy cross. The headstones look old, weathered and crumbling. Stone angels loom up out of the darkness, their faces covered in ivy.

I shiver and shiver and shiver, my sweat cooling on my skin, my temperature plummeting the longer we walk.

Someone starts up a song, an eerie tenor floating out of the dark, the words in Latin. Others catch it and harmonize, and soon I'm surrounded by voices I can't see. Lights begin to bloom in the darkness, candle flame spreading. Azar puts a candle into my hands and lights it. Her face leaps out at me from the black night: enormous, glinting eyes and white teeth.

Then I feel Wren on my other side. They have a candle too, which flickers over their features, rendering them in shadows. Wren puts their arm in mine.

"Don't be scared," they whisper.

But suddenly, strangely, I'm not scared. I'm exhilarated. My heart beats loud and fast, and my skin tingles. The song the others sing finds its way inside me, the same way Wren's composition did. I feel it running through me like a current of electricity.

Without realizing it, I've started singing too, my mouth shaping Latin words whose meaning I don't know. But I *feel* the song, as if it comes from some wordless place inside me. It feels cosmic, charged, containing me and them and something bigger than us too, something like God or spirit or existence itself.

For the first time since arriving at Corbin, or maybe for the first time ever, I don't feel alone. I feel tethered to these people, these strangers, as if they were my own kin—closer even than my own mother.

We sway and sing through the cemetery, our candle flames flickering and bobbing in the darkness as our voices rise and fall, surrounding us. The flames start to move all over instead of in a straight line, until they form a large circle. We stand singing amid the gravestones, beneath the trees. The clouds overhead move aside, and the moon shines down bright and pearlescent. I see Quigg and all the first-years, even Neil, whose face is blank and serene.

Next to me, Wren's usually abstracted expression is instead fixed and rapt, almost ecstatic, as they sing. This ought to feel weird, silly, outlandish—standing out here in a cemetery singing Latin chants—but it doesn't. There's no room for self-consciousness here. We sing and sing, and the candles flicker, and the cicadas scream, our own Greek chorus. It must go on a long time because the moon slowly changes position in the sky, so that the cemetery grows darker, the air chillier. Soon, I can't see any faces except the ones nearest me, cast in strange, flickering shadow.

Goose bumps break out on my skin, spreading from the nape of my neck down to my legs. Something is changing; something is going to happen.

Every candle in the circle goes out at once, blown dark in one fell swoop. At the same moment, our song stops, as if the breath in our lungs has been snatched away like the candle flames. The smell of smoke drifts on the air.

Darkness and silence descend. Even the cicadas are quiet. The only sound now is the wind in the treetops.

I wait, trembling and swaying, an ache opening up inside me.

Somewhere far across the circle, light blooms. A candle relit. The flame is handed off on one side and then another until it spreads toward me through the circle. Wren relights my candle, their expression still awed and rapt. The purple smudges beneath their eyes seem deeper and darker than ever.

Someone steps out of the circle and walks toward me, their candle flame bobbing and weaving through the gravestones. I'm surprised to realize that it's Laini. I didn't expect our resident director to be out on this excursion. The candle reflects off her glasses, giving her two flames for eyes.

"Tara," she says, once she's standing in front of me. "We, the body of Magni Viri, welcome you. We wish to accept you as one of our own." Her face is as solemn as a priest's performing last rites.

"Thank you," I say, unsure whether I'm meant to respond.

"Since our founding in 1900, we have carried on the traditions of our great visionaries, Walter Weymouth George and John Bauer, seeking to expand the limits of the human mind and to make immortal contributions to human knowledge and human flourishing." Laini speaks in the cadence of ritual, tradition, words well honed, passed like heirlooms through the decades. "If you will accept your place as a link in a strong and unbreakable chain, let us hear your promise, here in the heart of Magni Viri, where every soul listens and waits to receive you."

She hands me a small slip of paper, printed in a clear, strong hand. "These are your vows," she whispers. "When you're ready, please read them aloud."

The flame illuminates the words, which seem to each spring forth from the darkness, like bread crumbs leading to another world, another life. I clear my throat and read. "I, Tara Boone, accept my place in the distinguished ranks of Magni Viri. I come to you able, deserving, and willing. I promise to be a vessel for genius, for the profundity of the human mind, for the sacred act of creation. To Magni Viri I lend four years of my life, my faculties, my spirit. I will not waver; I will not fail. I belong to you, and you belong to me. Let my body, my heart, and my mind nourish you. Accept this offering and make us one."

"Hold out your hand," Laini says quietly. Quickly, without warning, she stabs a sewing needle into the pad of my first finger. A bead of blood wells and rolls. She turns my hand over and presses my skin to make the blood fall to the earth.

Before I can react, Laini wraps me in a hug, the heady jasmine scent of her shampoo enveloping me. "Good job," she whispers, and then raises her voice for the others to hear. "Tara, we, the body of Magni Viri, receive you. We accept you as one of our own. With blood and spirit, we are bound—past and present and future, now and always."

An enormous, raucous cheer goes up around the circle, breaking the strange, solemn mood of the initiation. The vows had bewildered and unsettled me for a moment, but now I laugh, relieved and happy. Everyone surges toward me to welcome and congratulate me. I am hugged and patted and smiled at, both by those I've met and those who are still strangers.

But they don't feel like strangers. They feel like a part of me. They feel like home.

We go arm in arm back to Denfeld, laughing and talking and singing ordinary songs. I am warm and safe and happy, among friends. I feel like I'll never be alone again.

NINE

I wake with the final shivery remnants of last night still clinging to my skin—the moonlight, the music, the feeling of something shifting, like I was emerging out of the darkness into my true form.

I rub the sore spot on my finger where Laini pricked me with the needle. It was a strange night, a strange initiation. The cemetery, the oath, the blood, the ring of candles. I see now where the rumors about Magni Viri's satanic rituals come from. Bobby's dad must have actually witnessed an MV initiation ceremony. I'll admit it must have looked pretty creepy from the outside.

But it didn't feel creepy. It felt like warmth and welcome. It felt like shedding my old life and joining theirs.

Because now I belong with them and *to* them, and they belong to me. There's no going back.

I am truly, irrevocably, a part of Magni Viri.

I shower and dress in the glow of my new status, not giving a single thought to my usual worries. I even decide I'm not going to fret about what happened in Meredith's room yesterday, not going to dwell on what I felt in there. I just have too powerful of an imagination, and I'm creeping myself out. I've read one too many Gothic novels. As I head downstairs for coffee, I shove Meredith out of my mind. I smile at everyone I pass, and they smile back. That ever-present ache of loneliness inside me is gone, as if banished by my initiation.

Dr. O'Connor asked me to meet with him at 8:00 a.m. sharp, so I don't have long to linger in Denfeld. I have to go face the reality of what it means to be part of Magni Viri. I hurry out the front door, my scarf trailing untidily behind me, feeling like I'm leaving a home behind instead of the imposing darkness of a haunted mansion like yesterday.

O'Connor's office is in the main part of campus, on the top floor of a cozy redbrick building that houses the social sciences department. It's surprising to find him someplace so ordinary. I suppose I'd forgotten that he's also a professor, as well as the head of Magni Viri, even if he only teaches a class or two every semester.

I take a deep breath and then knock on his half-open door. He waves me in, barely even glancing up from his computer. His office is large, with a huge window that overlooks campus. Vintage black-and-white photographs of people and build-ings decorate the walls. My gaze briefly catches on a photo of a woman posed at the front door of Denfeld Hall before I'm distracted by everything else in the office. The shelves are bursting with books, and there are trinkets Dr. O'Connor has clearly collected from many travels, all of them beautiful and expensive-looking.

I pull my eyes away from a little golden fountain that makes delicate chiming noises as I settle into the chair across from him. He leans back, smiling neutrally. He reminds me of a cat, I realize, that same patient, inscrutable gaze, that same lurking possibility that he might pounce at any moment.

"Well, how are you finding Magni Viri so far?"

I can't help but smile. "Really good," I say.

"Everyone's been welcoming?"

I bite my lip. Everyone except Neil. "Of course," I lie.

But he reads my hesitation. "I imagine some of your peers are still struggling with Meredith's death."

"Yes."

He smiles sympathetically. "They'll come around. They are a resilient bunch of people, as are you."

I nod, my eyes alighting on an antique typewriter at the end of his L-shaped desk. It's beautiful, with a shiny black body and silver keys. I bet he uses it to write correspondence.

"Well, then," Dr. O'Connor says, leaning forward and lightly tapping his hands against the desk to regain my attention. "Let's talk about your course schedule." He must have it pulled up on his computer because he reads off a list of my classes: Quantitative Reasoning, Literature of the Ancient Near East, Gothic Literature, American History I, and Freshman Seminar. "Why did you select these courses?"

"Well, I have to take Quant Reasoning and Freshman Seminar," I say. "They're core curriculum. And a history elective is required."

"Sure, but why American history pre-Reconstruction? How does that fit with the literature courses you've selected? And why those courses?"

I blink at him for a moment. My academic adviser didn't ask me any of this. She simply made sure I was taking three required courses and two courses for my major. That was all. And I never considered the classes' connections. So I tell Dr. O'Connor the truth. "I picked the literature classes that sounded most interesting to me. And American history fit with the rest of my schedule."

He nods. "And why aren't you taking a writing course?"

"I'm an English major on the teaching track, not a creative writing major."

He raises his eyebrows at me. "Do you not wish to be a writer? Is that not the dream you have for yourself?"

I squirm, uncomfortable under his scrutiny. "The English-for-secondary-education track sounded more practical. I had planned to teach when I graduate, maybe do Teach for America to pay off my loans quicker."

His eyebrows, impossibly, rise still farther. "Do you wish to be a high school English teacher?"

"Well, no, but I got rejected from Magni Viri, didn't I? I had to be practical."

"Are you going to change your major now?"

My cheeks burn. "I don't know. I haven't had a chance to think about it. But I mean, I will have to make a living when I leave here, even if I won't have loans to repay," I say, hedging.

Dr. O'Connor levels a burning gaze on me. "You are a scholar of Magni Viri now, Tara. We chose you because we believe you can be exceptional. But you have to act like it. Do not choose a life for yourself like lukewarm tea."

I clench my jaw, suddenly angry. What does this privileged man in his fancy office know of my life, my dreams, my potential?

"What do you want me to do?" I ask, annoyed to find tears burning in my eyes. I look away, pretending to study the typewriter again while I blink the tears away.

"I want you to take control over your life and your education," he says, leaning forward, drawing my eyes back to him. "Choose your course of study with purpose. Choose your future with purpose."

"Drop/add is already long over," I say. "I can't change my schedule even if I wanted to."

He waves the concern away. "You will drop one class and take an independent course with me instead."

"I'm not interested in the social sciences," I say carefully.

He laughs. "It will be coded as an honors tutorial. It will be your required project for Magni Viri this year, which I will oversee with the help of one outside faculty member whose expertise is relevant."

"What kind of project?"

"You will write a work of fiction. A novel or a collection of short stories."

I shrink into my seat. "Oh."

He cocks his head at me. "Tara, why on earth does that surprise you? I didn't choose you for this program for your ability to teach other people's literature. I chose you for your ability to write your own."

His gaze is implacable. He is leaving me no room for self-doubt, no room for hesitation. He's going to force me to become the writer I've always wanted to be. I ought to be happy, but I feel instead like I'm being strong-armed into something. Like my path is once again being decided for me.

"All right. Which class will I drop?" I ask, my mouth gone dry.

He keeps staring at me, scowling now. He wants me to make my own decisions, take control of my education. But only in the way he wants me to do it, that much I can see. I pause, considering my options. There's no point in dropping my required courses. I'll have to take them eventually. That leaves history and the two lit courses.

"Can I think about it and get back to you?"

"By the end of the week," he says. "No later. In the meantime, start writing. I expect to see pages when we meet again in one week."

"Fine," I say, pushing back my chair more forcefully than I mean to.

When I reach the door of his office, he calls my name. I turn.

"Stay angry. Let yourself feel. You've been like a bit of flotsam drifting through the sea since you got here. That all changes now. Now you are a ship on the waves, captaining your own destiny."

I nod. "Goodbye," I say, hating the way my voice shakes. I walk quickly out of the building and stop on the steps to drag in big lungfuls of the cold, crisp October air. My throat burns with the tears I was holding back, so now I let them run warm down my cheeks.

I sink down onto the steps and put my head on my knees, all the anger leaving me, as if in defiance of Dr. O'Connor's command to stay angry. I feel overwhelmed and vaguely ashamed, as if I've just proven to him how lost and unremarkable I am. As if I've shown him how little I understand about this education I'm trying to get. No wonder the senior MV students look so exhausted—they've been putting up with O'Connor for years.

"Tara?" someone asks.

I look up, surreptitiously wiping my eyes. It's Penny, standing in the sunshine, her hair loose around her shoulders.

"Hey, you all right?" she asks. She sets down her leather backpack on the steps and then sits next to me, bracing her knee as she lowers herself to the step. She doesn't have her cane today. She's dressed more casually than I've seen her yet, in an oversize cream-colored fisherman's sweater and faded jeans. "First meeting with O'Connor, huh? He can be such a hard-ass."

I sniff and laugh. "He really pissed me off actually."

Penny smiles. "You're an angry crier, aren't you? My little sister is like that."

"I'm an everything crier. Sad, angry, frustrated—you will find me crying about it." I laugh again, wiping the last traces of my tears away. "Honestly, he made me feel like an idiot."

"You're definitely not an idiot." She bumps her shoulder against mine. I get a whiff of her shampoo, which is not the usual fruity ones in the women's hair care aisle. It smells like cedarwood and cardamom, like a forest in autumn. I have to stop myself from leaning forward to breathe it in.

"I have to drop a class to take a tutorial with him."

She nods. "All the first years do a yearlong tutorial with him. It's really just to give us time to work on our own projects. He mostly makes sure we're staying on track and getting any help we might need."

"What's your project?"

She grins. "O'Connor managed to get hold of Dr. Coppola's research for me, so I'm learning as much as I can from it. She was working on ways to combat white-nose syndrome, which is a disease caused by a fungus bats pick up during hibernation. It has been wiping out bat populations all over the US."

"Oh wow, that sounds complicated," I say. "All I have to do is write some fiction."

"That's all?" Penny says in a teasing voice. "Invent people and places and stories from thin air?"

I put my face in my hands and groan.

"Come on," Penny says, pulling me by the arm. "Forget O'Connor. Let's go hang out. I want to get to know you better."

"Don't you have class?" I ask, refusing to get up. But I do finally look at her; she's smiling mischievously.

"Nah, I was just heading to the library. You know, if I had my cane, I'd whack you with it. Better be glad." She compromises by gently kicking the sides of my legs.

I laugh and finally get to my feet. "Where to?"

"Have you seen the conservatory yet?"

"I think Quigg mentioned a greenhouse, but it wasn't on the tour."

"Come on," Penny says. "You'll love it." We walk back to Denfeld in companionable silence until my phone rings in my pocket. The sound of it is like an ice bath: it takes me right back to that moment in Meredith's room yesterday, to the certainty I felt that she was going to speak to me. That all this time, she's been trying to reach me. I take a few deep breaths, hoping whoever's calling will just give up, but the phone keeps ringing.

"Aren't you going to get that?" Penny asks.

"It's car warranty scams," I say, pulling it out.

The screen reads "Unknown Number." There's no way I'm going to answer it. That creepy cicada soundtrack is the last thing I need today. I turn off the phone and shove it deep into my bag, turning my attention back to Penny.

When she opens the door to the conservatory, I nearly gasp. It's a riot of green—plants soaring to the glass ceiling, climbing the walls, spreading across the floor. Penny leads the way through confidently, weaving around plants until she finds a shelf. She pulls a blanket down from it and spreads it out on the floor beneath a whole section of orchids.

"On days I can't go to the woods I like to come here," she says. She sits on the blanket and pats the space next to her.

"It's beautiful," I murmur as I take a seat. I crane my neck, looking up through the plants to where the sunlight pours in. "Who takes care of it?"

"We've almost always got a botanist in the ranks here. Right now, it's Dennis, have you met him yet? Third year, built like a Viking? He's really into archaeobotany."

"Archaeobotany?" I ask, sounding out the word.

"Oh, yeah, like, he studies ancient plants, especially poisonous ones. There's an entire section of poisonous plants over there," she adds, pointing toward a distant part of the greenhouse. "Nightshade, stuff like that. And a lot rarer ones too."

"Should that be in a college garden?" I ask, immediately uneasy at the thought. Denfeld already has a resident pyromaniac; does it need a potential poisoner too?

Penny shrugs. "It's all carefully labeled. There's, like, a skull-and-crossbones sign." She lies down and clasps her hands over her stomach. I lie down too, and for a while we stare up at the little makeshift jungle. Slowly, calm spreads over me, as if all these plants are releasing tranquilizers into the air.

"I could have really used this place all semester," I say, turning my head toward Penny. "I would have hidden out in here permanently. Magni Viri kids have all the luck."

Penny's face clouds, and something like regret passes over her features, but then she smiles. "Good thing you're one of us now," she says.

Memories of last night's ceremony flash through my mind—the music, the candles blowing out in one fell swoop, the immediate feeling that I had bound myself to the others. I wonder if my initiation was the reason everyone got weird at lunch when I mentioned the rumors about satanic rituals. They were already planning my initiation, maybe worried what I'd think about it, or afraid of spoiling the surprise of it.

"So the initiation . . . ," I say, "it was indescribable. I've never felt anything like that."

Penny nods. "Yeah, I remember feeling the same way."

"It made me feel like . . ." I grasp for the words. "Like you were really welcoming me in. Giving me a place."

"We were," Penny says. "But it's a really old tradition. I know it's a little dramatic with the Latin chanting and everything, but that's sort of par for the course for Bauer and Weymouth George."

"The founders?" I ask, thinking of the antique oil painting in the foyer. Two young men standing shoulder to shoulder against the world.

Penny nods. "Yeah, they were kind of over-the-top. Made everything a spectacle. Supposedly they were best friends, really devoted to each other. Weymouth George died shortly after Magni Viri was founded, and Bauer never got over the loss. He built that huge mausoleum in the cemetery for him."

"God, that's so sad. And . . . intense. Maybe kind of gay?"

Penny laughs. "Yeah, maybe."

"It's cool to belong to something old, something passed on, you know? Like you're another link in a really long chain," I say, "and there will be others after you."

Penny's eyebrows scrunch together in a serious expression, but then she smirks and shakes her head. "You're as dreamy and dramatic as they were." She pokes me in the arm. "What else do I need to know about you? What kind of books do you like?"

I pause, caught off guard by the abrupt change of conversation. "Gothic," I finally say. "Mysteries. *Jane Eyre* is an old favorite. *Rebecca*. Um, a few books by Sarah Waters. We're reading *Carmilla* in my Gothic lit class right now, which is kind of blowing my mind actually."

"So you like creepy books with women's names for titles?"

I laugh, self-consciously pushing my hair behind one ear. "I suppose so."

Penny's eyes track the movement. "You're one of those beauty-in-terror types, aren't you?" she says, raising an eyebrow knowingly.

"That's a type?"

"Oh, big time." Penny gives me a slow smile, her eyes crinkling at the corners.

I'm silent for a while, thinking about it, and then I lean forward and whisper into her ear.

Penny sits up fast. "You did not just quote *The Secret History* to me."

Now I grin, glad to be the perceptive one. "It's your favorite book, isn't it?"

Her mouth drops open in shock. "How did you know?"

"Your beauty-in-terror quip. Plus, your outfits gave you away."

Penny falls back to the floor, covers her face, and lets out a shriek of laughter, half embarrassed, half delighted. She peeks at me from between her fingers. "I was worried about coming to college, so I found, like, every book I could set in college and read them all. I don't know how much useful information I actually got out of them, but I really loved *The Secret History*. As soon as I finished it, I started it over again."

"I did the same thing," I say, surprised. "Read all the books, I mean."

"Really?" Penny sits up again, leaning toward me, her expression open, excited.

I stare at her a moment, caught off guard by the feeling

of kinship. This is the deepest connection I've felt to someone in a long time. And judging by how Penny is looking at me, I think she feels it too.

I clear my throat, flustered. "Does Magni Viri feel like the Greek class to you? A little private world unto itself?"

"A little," Penny admits. "But I like us better." She smiles at me in a new way, and my insides seem to glow.

We talk for a while longer, about our classes and the ones we hope to take next semester. Penny is a good listener: quiet, patient, sometimes teasing. After a while, I pull her wrist toward me to check the time on her watch, my cheeks automatically warming at the feel of her skin.

"I'd better get to class," I say.

"Okay," Penny says, smiling at my hand where it touches her wrist. "See you at lunch maybe?"

"All right. Thanks for this."

"Anytime," Penny says, then rolls onto her back and gazes up at the ceiling. She looks beautiful here, at home, surrounded by all this green and growing life. Rays of sunlight fall through the canopy overhead and illuminate here a downy cheek, there a thin ribbon of red in her honey-brown hair.

"Don't fall asleep and miss lunch," I say as I turn to weave my way out of the jungle of the conservatory.

"Wouldn't dream of it," she says sleepily.

I smile all the way back to my room. Penny didn't help me solve my O'Connor problem, but she did make me feel better about it. And she reminded me that I do know what I like and what I want, who I am.

Magni Viri isn't meant to change me, I remind myself.

It's meant to help me become wholly and fully myself. I don't need to be Meredith Brown, just the best possible version of Tara Boone.

That's a truth I need to hold on to if I'm going to survive four years in this place.

TEN

I wake suddenly in the night with a feeling as if I've been thrown from my bed. I lurch up, gasping, still beneath my covers. I was dreaming. Confused images leap out at me, as if from the corners of my nightmares. Masses of writhing cicadas, tangles of copper hair, bats exploding from an underground cave, the trees in the cemetery swaying and creaking. I gasp in air, trying to recall what exactly I dreamed, but the images fade too quickly, leaving only a shivery unease in their wake.

I peer over at Wren's bed in the darkness, but they're not here. Their quilt is still covered in books and papers and clothes. They never came to bed. I glance at the glowing blue of the clock on their side of the room. It's 3:43 in the morning. The room is cold. I get up and put a sweater on over my pj's and pad out of the room in my socks. As soon as I open the door, I hear it: piano music.

I sigh and make my way downstairs, trying not to look at the shadows in every corner. I try not to think of Meredith Brown. I try not to imagine her walking beside me through the sleeping house, red hair like flames against the dark.

I go to the kitchen first and make two cups of chamomile tea. Then I head to the music room. Wren is at the piano, lost to the music, which pours like a trickling stream, sad and lonesome. They look exhausted. Their hair is a rat's nest of matted curls, and the purple rings under their eyes are nearly black.

"Wren," I say from a yard away, but they don't notice.

"Wren!" I say louder, but get no response. I set a cup of tea on some sheet music that lies scattered on top of the piano. With my free hand, I touch their shoulder. They don't respond right away, so I shake it.

Wren reels back from me, striking random keys, a look of pure terror on their face. I almost spill my tea. My hand hovers in the air, and I'm not sure what to do in the face of their shock.

"Sorry, but did you know it's nearly four in the morning?" I say, keeping my voice low and soft, once we've both recovered.

Wren blinks at me. "Is it?"

"Here, I made you a cup of tea," I say, nudging the steaming mug toward them.

Wren takes a sip. "Thanks."

"What are you working on?"

Wren shakes their head. "Huh? Oh, I don't know. Is it really almost four?"

"Yeah," I say, ill at ease with how out of it Wren seems. "Why don't you drink your tea and come to bed?"

Wren nods and tries to get up from the piano bench. But they are clearly stiff and sore, maybe a little light-headed. They nearly fall once they're on their feet.

"Did you eat dinner?" I ask, steadying them.

Wren bites their lip, thinking. "I can't remember."

"Are you hungry?"

Wren pauses, as if it takes great effort to tell whether they are hungry or not. They even touch their stomach. "A little," they finally say.

"Come on, I'll make you something," I say, gesturing toward the kitchen.

Wren glances longingly at the piano, but when I frown at them, they follow gingerly behind me, still sipping their tea.

"Do you have any food in here?" I ask.

Wren shakes their head.

"Neither do I," I admit. "We'll have to purloin something."

Wren laughs, the sound breaking up the heavy atmosphere of the sleeping house. "Purloin?"

I grin back. "It's a good word."

"All right, Agatha Christie," Wren says. "Make us some eggs. Neil always keeps some in there for his keto nonsense."

I frown. "I don't know. Neil already hates me."

"He'll never know it was us," they say. "Besides, he deserves it after he was so rude to you."

Wren goes to one of the fridges and pulls out three eggs. They toss one to me without warning, and I barely manage to catch it before it hits the floor. Before I've recovered, they've tossed another one. I catch this one too, but it hits the other egg in my hand and cracks.

"Wren, stop!" I laugh. "We want to eat the eggs, not wear them."

Wren snickers and walks the last egg over to me and places

it gently in my hands. "Scrambled?" they ask. "I bet we can rustle up some cheese too."

Wren sits on the counter while I make the cheddar-covered eggs. They chatter about Magni Viri gossip for a while—who's sleeping with who, who's fighting for a top spot—but then they go quiet and their fingers start to move against the mug like they're feeling out musical notes. Even away from the piano, it drags them back. Their compulsion is almost unnerving, going far beyond ordinary artistic obsession.

"Eggs are done. Grab me some plates?" I ask, nudging their leg.

Wren startles. "What?"

"Plates and forks?" I ask.

Wren eases themself slowly off the counter and searches in the cabinets. But they don't seem to know where to look. They have to try three different ones before they produce a plate. It's as if they've never been inside this kitchen. I guess exhaustion can do that to a person.

We sit at the table and eat our stolen breakfast, exchanging a few tired words now and then. When we're done, Wren goes groggily up to bed. By the time I've finished washing away all evidence of our crime, the sky is a deep, dark blue through the window, the first signs of dawn beginning to stir.

I decide there's no point in going back to bed now, and besides, I don't want to return to those horrible dreams I was having. So I put on a pot of coffee and tiptoe up the stairs and into my room to get my computer and books. Wren is passed out on their bed, still in the clothes they were wearing, mouth open and snoring.

Once downstairs and in possession of my coffee, I set up in the library, turning on every lamp to banish the shadows. I open a new Word doc and stare at the blinking cursor. I have to figure out what to write for Dr. O'Connor. I have only one week. I need to have something to show him. I sit for ten minutes, racking my brains for a place to begin—a setting, a character, even just an interesting sentence. But nothing comes. My mind is as blank as the page. There's no way I'm returning to my awful flash fiction piece. I need something much, much better than that. Something like Meredith would write.

Against my will, my mind wanders up the stairs and into Meredith's room. I think about the notebooks sitting on her desk, the laptop that probably contains dozens of stories and novels. What are they about? What worlds did she weave with only her words?

For a moment, no matter how weird and creepy I know it is, I close my eyes and pretend that I am Meredith Brown— gifted, prolific, effortlessly cool. I sit at my desk, bright red hair pulled up into a voluminous, gloriously messy bun, green cardigan draping my thin frame. I take a deep breath, the air scented with the lily of the valley perfume on my skin, raise my fingers above the keys, and—

Nothing. Nothing comes. The fantasy dissolves into mist. I am Tara again—average looks, average style, average brain. There is no story inside me waiting to get out. There's no work of genius brewing. Pretty soon, O'Connor is going to realize what a mistake he made in choosing me for Magni Viri.

I stare at the blank screen, watching the cursor blink, willing words to appear. I have to write something. I have to prove to O'Connor and to myself that I belong here. Because what happens if I can't do it? Will he kick me out of the program?

If I can't write, I don't deserve to be here.

A wave of despair and self-loathing washes over me. All this time, I've been saying I couldn't write because I didn't have time, because I had to focus on work and school. All this time, I thought my mediocrity was because of other people, because of circumstances outside my control. But what if it's just me? What if it's always been me?

With a moan, I slam my laptop shut. I can't look at that blank screen any longer, can't face the emptiness for one more second. I need something else to do, something to distract me. Something that won't make me feel lost and ashamed. I remember I have problems to do for quant reasoning and a reading response for Freshman Seminar. Those, I know I can handle.

I'm reaching into my bag for a textbook when suddenly I freeze. The fine hairs at the back of my neck stand up and goose bumps sweep across my body. Cold spreads through me, as if my blood has turned to ice in my veins. Slowly, slowly, I lean back up, the book clutched in my hand. My body begins to tremble, and my shoulders go rigid.

My mouth goes dry, and my chest tightens. I'm afraid, but I don't know why.

A feeling grows around me, greater than my fear. It's like . . . loathing. Contempt. Like the very walls of Denfeld are watching me and finding me wanting, finding me weak and unworthy. I feel judged, scorned, despised.

I would get up and flee the room, but my legs have stopped working. I am rooted to the couch, my feet frozen on the floor. Terror fills me.

Is it . . . Meredith? Is this her hatred I feel? Does she see my mediocrity and despise me for it?

My ears fill with the sound of screaming cicadas, an insect tinnitus so loud it makes me dizzy. For a moment, I'm not sure where I am, cast back into the horrible dreams I woke from this morning, confused images flashing across my vision.

Softly, beneath their screams comes the sound of footsteps in the hallway, heading toward the library door. I turn painstakingly slowly to see who's there, my heart pounding.

Jordan stands at the door, wearing a striped blue-and-gray sweater, a mug in one hand and his messenger bag slung over his shoulder. He smiles at me. "Morning."

Relief floods through me at the sight of him, and the cold in my bones seems to abate. The horrible feeling of being hated subsides. The cicada screams fade to a distant pulse.

"Hey," I say, all my panic releasing in a shaky breath. I don't know what that was, but it's over now. It's almost like I gave myself a panic attack—thinking about Meredith, thinking about all the ways I can't measure up to her. All the ways I wish I could be her.

"Did you make this coffee?" Jordan asks, holding up the mug.

"Why, is it bad?" I ask, struggling to sound normal.

He smiles. "No, it's the best I've had this semester."

"Well, at least I'm good at something," I say, my voice still tremulous.

He comes and sits next to me on the couch, dropping his leather satchel on the floor. "Quantitative Reasoning, huh? The bane of every English major." He says it so seriously I can't tell whether he's teasing me or not. "Half the students I tutor need help with this class."

"Really?" I ask, clinging desperately to the normalcy of the topic, relieved he didn't notice my earlier panic. "So it's not just me who finds it impossible?"

He shakes his head. "Can I help?"

"Are you sure?" I ask. "I don't have any money to pay you. I haven't gotten my stipend yet."

"I think my help is a fair exchange for this coffee," he says, then takes another sip.

"Wait," I say as his earlier comment finally filters through to my tired, shocked brain. "You tutor? But I thought we weren't allowed to have jobs?"

Jordan puts a finger to his lips. "What O'Connor doesn't know won't hurt him. Besides, it's only a few hours a week. I like teaching."

It's a pretty tame rebellion, but I'm still surprised by it. Jordan seems so upright and rule-following. Maybe he has to behave that way to survive in this rarefied space.

I smile and mime zipping my lips. The last of my fear subsides, only a shaky unease left behind in its wake. It's hard to feel afraid with Jordan next to me, solid and reassuring, making the dim library feel warmer and brighter than it was.

I show him some of the problems I've been struggling with, and he explains what I'm missing in such a calm, patient way that for once I don't feel like a complete failure at math. He nods approvingly as I apply his advice to the next problem. Then he pulls out his laptop and starts doing his own work.

We go on this way for an hour, him pausing every ten or fifteen minutes to help me get unstuck. Jordan is revising an essay and asks for my help a few times—whether to use a semicolon or a colon, how to reword an awkward, clunky phrase. I'm not sure whether he genuinely needs the help or wants to make me feel better about myself. Either way, I do feel like less of a charity case.

Around seven, the rest of the house finally starts to wake. Voices drift from other rooms, footsteps sound overhead, a blender runs in the kitchen. The force of what I felt earlier fades, the ordinariness of the day smoothing it away.

I move on to my reading for Gothic lit. Jordan disappears, but Azar shows up before long to take his place, as well as several older students I don't know. The library and the house itself hum with activity and life. I can practically feel the thinking happening all around me as the others work at their laptops, scribble in notebooks, flip rapidly through pages. That sensation I felt during the initiation ceremony, of an immense electrical current running through us all, joining us together—I feel it now, here. We are part of something; we *are* something.

But doubtful questions keep breaking through my feeling of belonging. What if I don't have the same genius as the rest of Denfeld's students? What if there is no story inside me waiting to get out?

What if that cold hatred I felt earlier was more than my own nerves? What if it was a warning? A reminder that I don't truly belong in Magni Viri?

ELEVEN

These questions don't stop once I leave Denfeld Hall. They dog me all the way across the sunlit campus, up the stairs to the English building, and into Dr. Hendrix's classroom. For the first few minutes of class, I have to work hard to pay attention, but soon I get wrapped up in the day's discussion of the reading.

Dr. Hendrix sits patiently at the front of the classroom, hands clasped in her lap, waiting for someone to attempt to answer the question she just asked. It's our first class back since she found Meredith's body in the library. She canceled the last two class meetings, assigning us discussion board posts instead. Judging by how she looks now, she needed a rest. Her face seems thinner and paler, and her hands tremble sometimes when she lifts them, which is probably why she's keeping them clasped in her lap. Meredith's death has clearly taken a toll, and I'm not sure a discussion of vampires is the best thing for her right now. But I suppose she must soldier on through the syllabus she set.

After a long and painful silence, she clears her throat. "Let me ask the question a different way, then. What makes vampires so emblematic of the Gothic?"

"The juxtaposition of desire and fear," someone says from the back of the class.

"Can you elaborate?"

I turn and recognize an upperclassman from Magni Viri, a Latino boy with gold-rimmed glasses and shoulder-length curls. I think his name is Gabriel. He tends to sleep through half of our classes and crack dark-humored jokes in the other half.

"Well," he says, "vampires are simultaneously beautiful and terrifying. They are monsters with angels' faces."

"Well put," Dr. Hendrix says. "What else? Tara?" she asks, turning her eyes to me.

I hate when professors put me on the spot like this. A hot blush spreads up my neck. But I make myself answer. "Vampires are aristocratic—wealthy, refined . . . cultured. And yet at heart they are beasts and murderers, who prey on human blood. Plus—"

"Sounds like the one percent to me," Gabriel quips, and everyone laughs. But Dr. Hendrix's eyes are still on me, waiting for me to finish my thought.

I continue. "Well, when you consider the political heart of Gothic literature . . . I mean, it's about more than aesthetics and the supernatural, right? So maybe what he said about the one percent is right. The wealthy and privileged have always preyed on the poor, sucking their life away."

Dr. Hendrix leans forward, her eyes brightening. "How do we see this playing out in the literature, in *Carmilla*, for example? After all, Carmilla's victim, the naive teenaged Laura, is an aristocrat herself."

"Well," I say, self-conscious at having the entire class's attention on me for such a long stretch, "well, Laura wasn't Carmilla's only victim during the novel, was she? Carmilla also preyed on young women and girls in the area. Farmers' daughters, maids, all working class. Laura is our narrator because she was the only one with the privilege to be able to tell her story."

"Very, very good," Dr. Hendrix says, and I try to suppress my pleased smile at her praise. I might not be able to write, but at least I'm still good at this.

Dr. Hendrix turns to the rest of the class. "Now, of course, we can't talk about nineteenth-century vampires without talking about anti-Semitism."

She launches into a mini lecture on the historical context of the novel and how its depiction of vampires compares to that of *Dracula*. I take notes, waiting for the blood to leave my cheeks. Right before class ends, Dr. Hendrix asks us to consider contemporary vampires, especially the ones we see in YA novels and teen TV shows.

"How much of the Gothic have they retained? More specifically, how well do they reflect the image of the aristocratic vampire preying on good and ordinary people?"

"Well, they're always rich, aren't they?" a girl says. "Because who would want to go out with a broke-ass vampire?"

Dr. Hendrix laughs along with the rest of us and tells us to consider this question for our two-page reflection essay, due next class. She answers a few questions and then dismisses us, standing behind her table and shuffling through some papers. I can tell she's hoping we'll all leave quietly and not disturb her. The effort of teaching seems to have exhausted her. Yet when I pass her, she looks up and touches my arm.

"Tara. Are you all right?"

"I'm fine," I assure her. "Are you?"

She blows out a shaky breath. "It was such a shock to find Meredith that way. I think it will take me a long time to get over it. I hope it will be easier for you."

I shake my head, thinking of how I dream of Meredith every night, how I feel her in the rooms of Denfeld Hall. Everything reminding me she's still here, still watching. But of course I can't admit to any of that.

"I . . . I was offered her place in Magni Viri," I say instead.

Dr. Hendrix's eyes widen. "What?"

"Dr. O'Connor . . . he said I was originally in the running for her spot, that it was between her and me. So they gave it to me."

"Oh. Well, congratulations," she says coldly.

I wince at the condemnation in her voice. "I know it seems kind of callous, taking her spot like that so fast, but the offer was too good to pass up. I'm on scholarship, and I had to take out so many loans," I explain. I'm desperate for her to understand, the one other person who found Meredith in that library with me. I can't stand for her to think badly of me.

Dr. Hendrix's face softens. "I don't blame you, Tara. Not at all. It isn't you who . . ." She presses her lips together.

"You don't like Magni Viri?" I ask. I vaguely remember some look or word from the night we found Meredith, some hint that she disapproved of Magni Viri.

Dr. Hendrix makes sure the room is empty before she answers me. "Dr. O'Connor is my ex-husband. I know what

he's like. How he drives those students. Half of them walk
out of Corbin looking like shades of themselves. Many have
had breakdowns. I'm not saying they don't produce brilliant
work. But it's clearly an unhealthy atmosphere for many of the
students, and I don't know why the administration allows it
to go on." By now she's breathing heavily, clearly worked up.
She shakes her head. "Forgive me for raining on your parade,
Tara. Theodore's running of Magni Viri was one of the many
things we disagreed about."

"Oh," I say, surprised and embarrassed. "That's okay,
but . . . um, well, I'm really liking the program so far though.
I've made good friends already."

"I have no doubt," Dr. Hendrix says kindly. "You're a
smart girl with a good head on your shoulders. But if you ever
find you need to talk to someone outside of Magni Viri, I'm
here, all right?"

"Sure," I say, anxiety starting to make my insides writhe
like snakes. "Thanks—thank you, Dr. Hendrix." I start toward
the door, ready to be done with this awkward conversation.
Not that Dr. Hendrix is totally off base. I have noticed that
some of the upperclassmen look run-down and that students
push themselves really hard in Denfeld, but it can't be as bad
as she's making it out to be.

"Oh, and Tara," Dr. Hendrix calls before I pass into the
hall, "your thoughts on *Carmilla* today were very astute. You
seem to have an instinctive grasp of the Gothic. I'm looking forward to reading your next reflection. By the way, you
should think about taking my Southern Gothicism course
next semester. I think you'll love it."

"Thank you," I say again, more sincerely this time, happiness at her praise breaking through my anxiety. It has been so long since I truly felt like I stood out in any way. "I'll definitely think about it. See you next time." I hurry out the door, flustered and confused.

But as I walk out of the humanities building and into a moody, gray afternoon worthy of a Gothic novel, I realize Dr. Hendrix has helped me solve my schedule dilemma. I'll drop American History I and take American History II next semester, along with Dr. Hendrix's Southern Gothic class. Those fit together and will be a good follow up to Gothic lit. I don't think Dr. O'Connor can argue with that logic.

With that decision made, I realize I can skip American history and squeeze in a nap, something I've never once had time to do at Corbin. As I walk back to Denfeld, I push away the doubt that Dr. Hendrix's tirade against Magni Viri stirred up in me. Things are going to be all right. I'm going to pass my classes. I'm going to make solid friends. And maybe if I can get out of my own way, I'll even be able to write these pages for Dr. O'Connor.

But my nap is the same as last night's dreams, only more detailed. Cicadas buzz in the treetops of the cemetery below Denfeld Hall, then raise their song to a long, drawn-out scream. The trees sway overhead, branches rubbing against each other, creaking and groaning. I'm alone in the cemetery but not alone—another walks beside me, invisible. She takes my hand, and though I can't see her, I can feel her. Her fingers are soft and cool against mine, but they cling tighter than I would like. My heart pounds hard and fast, and the one who walks beside me seems to cling all the harder, as if she could steal away the pulse at my wrist. She wants to, I realize with a bolt of fear. She wants my life.

From the dark, in the distance, comes a scream. My head snaps toward it and then I'm awake in my bed, trembling. My alarm sounds from across the room. I let it go for a moment, waiting for the dream to loose me from its eerie hold, but it lingers. *She* lingers. The ghost who held my hand was Meredith, I feel sure of it. I can almost feel her now, lying beside me in the narrow bed.

Wren comes into the room and turns off the alarm. "Get up, Tara. Your alarm was going off," they say as they tip an armful of books onto their bed.

I sit up and rub my forehead, ignoring the way my skin feels all shivery and cold. "What time is it?"

"I don't know," Wren says with complete disinterest. They find my phone and toss it at me. I look at the cracked screen and am thrown back to the night I dropped it, when I found my way to the gate of Denfeld's cemetery like a sleepwalker. The night I heard voices calling out something that sounded like "Isabella." Now I'm sure it was Latin—just like the song we sang on initiation night.

I've let myself get spooked by it all. By Meredith's death; by taking her place; the initiation in the cemetery; the strange, isolated way we live up here on our hill at Denfeld. Magni Viri is a dream waiting to wrap you up in cobwebs if you let it.

Perhaps, I realize, I *should* let it. Maybe that's the way to succeed here. You have to give all, everything, let it take you over like the ghost in my dream. Maybe that's how I'll finally start writing. It's certainly working for Wren.

I watch them as they lean against the edge of their bed, dashing music notes onto staff paper in a composition book nearly as big as they are. They're nowhere near a piano, and yet they are composing, writing, creating art from nothing.

I want that. I want to be absorbed like that. Look how Wren's eyes smolder, how fast their pencil moves across the page, as if it can barely keep up with the movement of their mind. Wren is like flames dancing through a forest, catching every tree in their wake. I'm watching genius at work.

And what have I been doing? Agonizing over class choices, dreaming about dead girls. I see now what Dr. O'Connor meant about focus. Wren is like an object lesson before my eyes. Does Wren go too far sometimes, exhaust themself? Yes. But isn't it worth it, for this? For the art they're making, which will outlast them? Isn't that what I want too? To leave something of myself, of my mind, behind in the world?

Dr. Hendrix said Dr. O'Connor pushes Magni Viri students too hard, but maybe she's wrong. Maybe Dr. O'Connor is doing what it takes to pull greatness out of us. Maybe accomplishing something of value in this world takes sacrifice, maybe even a little suffering. A little bit of madness, even.

Wren freezes, their pencil poised above the page, their mouth slightly open, as if music itself has disappeared from the world. Their expression is shocked, terrified, bereft. I almost ask what's wrong, but then Wren nods once and their pencil starts dancing across the page once more.

I climb out of bed and go to class.

❦

For the rest of the week, I try to write. I sit on the couch in the library with a notebook and pen. I sit at my laptop in my room. But nothing comes. The cursor blinks, the blank page screams. The world is as empty of words as if language never existed, as if humanity were still prehistoric, apelike, swinging in the treetops. That moment of Wren's I witnessed, when the music disappeared from their mind, is my every waking moment.

I go to class and do my assignments. I eat lunch with my new friends. I try not to let my panic grow, try not to obsess over the fact that I will never get out from under Meredith Brown's shadow in this house.

But Neil reminds me daily how different from her I am. Never overt, like the first time. Always little offhand comments that sound harmless.

On Friday morning when I come downstairs, Neil is making eggs at the stove, and Azar is steeping a pot of fragrant tea that fills the room with the smell of cardamom.

"Nice jacket," Azar says, nodding at the gray herringbone blazer I wear over a black sweater.

"Oh, thanks," I say self-consciously. "Quigg gave it to me. He said my wardrobe wasn't scholarly enough." I laugh, but I'm pleased at Azar's compliment. My outfit is simple, structured. I felt very chic when I left my room, which I'm not sure I've ever felt before.

Neil turns and glances at me, uninterested. "Remember that dark gray blazer Meredith used to wear all the time?" he asks Azar. "How she'd pop the collar up?"

"Oh my God, she looked like a sexy spy or something," Azar says. She laughs and launches into a reminiscence about Meredith and one of the first Magni Viri parties.

Neil joins in, adding details where Azar forgets them.

I stand for a moment listening, trying to smile. But I realize they're not talking to me. I've disappeared for them. The very memory of Meredith is stronger than my physical presence in the room. I move around them, making my coffee, listening to their stories like the bystander I am. When I finally walk out of the kitchen, they don't even notice.

Back at my desk, my anxious mind returns again and again to Meredith, to her brilliance. What was her novel about? What words had she written that Dr. O'Connor believed would define a generation, leave a mark on the world that could never be rubbed out? I wish I could see them.

No, more than that—I wish her words were *mine*, the way her place in Magni Viri is mine, her friends are mine. I wish I could wear her clothes, her hair, her skin. Wish I could have her heart beating in my chest. This girl taken too soon from the world who had something to say, something to offer. I wish I could become her.

After another hour in front of the blank page, something in me snaps. I pull Meredith's stolen pen from my desk drawer. I need to know more about what she was working on. I need to know what caliber of writing O'Connor is going to be expecting from me. The kind of person everyone in Magni Viri wants me to be. If I'm going to fill Meredith Brown's shoes, I need to see exactly who she was.

I get up from my chair, gripping the pen. I know Azar just

left for the robotics lab and won't be back for hours. This is my chance. If someone catches me, I'll say I was returning the pen I took by accident.

I nod to myself, satisfied with the excuse. On socked feet I sneak down the hall and try the doorknob to Azar and Meredith's room. It's unlocked. Apparently the residents of Denfeld Hall are more trusting than those in my old dorm. I make sure no one is watching from the hallway before I slip inside the room, leaving the overhead light off in case someone looks up here from the grounds. I cross the room quickly and pull the heavy maroon curtains closed. Darkness fills the space, and an icy fear inches up my spine, making me hesitate.

I take several deep breaths, searching the air for Meredith's telltale perfume. But the room smells only of coffee and Azar's almond-scented lotion. I cross over to Meredith's desk and flick on her lamp. I sit in her chair.

I know it's wrong to go through someone's belongings, to violate their privacy, but a feverish voice inside me presses me along, tells me that this could be the key to finally unlocking the words stuck inside my head, that Meredith is dead, so it doesn't count—right?

With a racing heart, I open her shiny new MacBook and power it on. I groan when I see it's password protected. I try a few obvious passwords like *password*, *MagniViri*, even *NeilByrd*—just in case Neil's love wasn't as unrequited as I suspect. But none of them work. I'm way too technologically ignorant to try to get around even this basic security. With a sigh of frustration and maybe relief too, I power the laptop off again.

When the screen goes black, I startle at the pale face reflected at me. It takes me a beat longer than it should to realize that the face is my own—frightened, with dark, hollowed-out eyes like a corpse. I shut the laptop with more force than I ought, my breaths coming ragged.

But a second later I wish I hadn't—a cool wind blows against my bare neck, making my entire body go rigid, and I wish I could look in the screen's reflection and see what's behind me. I don't want to turn around.

I take a deep, purposeful lungful of air, determined to get my nerves under control. Denfeld is an old building and probably full of drafts. Quietly now, I open the shallow drawer in the center of the desk, hoping to find printed copies of her work. That's when I smell it—when I smell *her*. Lily of the valley surrounds me, as potent as if I were wearing it myself. My hands start to shake, cold spreading up my fingertips.

But then I spy a perfume bottle in the corner of the drawer, delicate and expensive-looking, half wrapped in a headscarf. I let out a small whimper of relief and get back to the task at hand. There are no papers in the desk. What happened to the story she brought to the lit reading? I glance quickly through Meredith's possessions, looking for clues to unlock her, to understand what made her the magnetic, brilliant, irresistible person she was. But what can a desk drawer really tell you?

She was tidy, based on how neatly everything is laid out—several identical pens, blank index cards, a mini stapler. She had a sharp, well-organized mind. I already knew that.

Where did she keep her secrets?

I close the drawer and turn to the pile of plain black

Moleskines on top of the desk, each of their spines num-
bered with a metallic marker. I open the notebook on top,
my hopes rising—only to be immediately dashed. It's full of
lecture notes, all of them written in dark ink in an elegant,
italicized print. I go methodically through the pile, and each
is the same. There's nothing of Meredith's own writing here.
Nothing of her thoughts, apart from a few questions she jot-
ted down about syllabi and exams. Nothing to tell me how to
become someone like Meredith Brown.

Aren't brilliant writers supposed to be messy scribblers,
leaving napkins with half-baked ideas all over the place? Aren't
they supposed to doodle in the margins of their notebooks?
Meredith may as well be an engineer like Azar for all the artistic touches I see here, in the place where she supposedly created Pulitzer-worthy fiction.

It must all be on her laptop, I realize. Everything she truly
was—all of her hidden behind a password I can't guess.

But there must be something here in this room, one single
clue to who Meredith Brown was beneath her cool, unruffled
surface. There must be something to hint at what she was writing. Or what it was like inside her mind. Or even . . . something to explain why she was crying on the night she died.

I open the closet on Meredith's side of the room. As I
expected, Meredith's wardrobe is as ruthlessly simple as that
stack of Moleskines on her desk. I run my fingers over the
clothes—crisp, monochromatic button-downs, a few dark-
toned blazers, sweaters in gray, black, and the darker earth
tones. Everything she owned was cool and sharp-edged, classic
and modern at once. It seems too put-together for a college

freshman, even one as accomplished as Meredith. I fish in the pockets of each blazer and oversize cardigan, searching for anything she might have accidentally left behind. There's nothing, not even a forgotten receipt or a balled-up tissue.

Almost ready to give up entirely, I walk to Meredith's dresser. I can't quite bring myself to open her underwear drawer, so I scour the top of the dresser instead, squinting to make out the objects arranged there in the dim light from her desk lamp. There's a tube of the dark brown lipstick she always wore, the inky eyeliner she drew on so sharp and perfect, mascara and blush. I pick up the lipstick and open it, raising it to my lips. I pause, my hand trembling.

Just as I'm about to touch it to my top lip, a door slams somewhere down the hall, startling me so badly that my hand spasms, drawing a brown line right above my lip.

"Oh my God," I whisper, panic thrumming through me. I recap the lipstick and drop it fast. I wipe feverishly at my face. If someone were to come in here and see me like this . . .

Deeply creeped out by my own behavior, I hurry out of Meredith's room and back to my own. I lean against my closed door, trembling, my breaths coming fast, the smell of Meredith's perfume choking me.

I have to get over this obsession with her. Knowing what she was writing wouldn't have helped me anyway, even if I had found it out. I need to get past this block, this paralysis, and find words of my own. Fixating on Meredith will only make it harder, will only make me more afraid.

With new resolve, I sit at my desk and open my notebook, cheap ballpoint pen poised above the first line, willing words to appear. The blank page stares at me the same way it has all week. It seems to look through me, as if I'm made of mist. I do the only thing I can think of and write the very first words that enter my head, even if they're not fiction.

I think Meredith Brown is haunting me, I write. And beneath that: *Or maybe I'm haunting her.*

TWELVE

Sunday arrives, and suddenly everyone in Denfeld is simmering with a strange, jittery, overwrought kind of energy I can't quite put into words. Quigg wheels a keg into the house, and some upperclassmen come back from a trip to the nearest town with armfuls of liquor. After hearing whispers all week about the Sunday night MV parties, I'm about to find out exactly what goes on at them.

Neil starts drinking before noon. I smell it on his breath when I take a seat next to him at lunch. His clothes and skin are smeared with paint, and he says he's been in the art studio all morning. When Azar comments on the smell of whiskey at the table, he says it's paint thinner. No one believes him.

"Neil, I know it's going to be hard without Meredith at the party," Jordan says. "It's going to be hard for all of us."

Neil shrugs, not meeting his eyes.

"Maybe it's time for you to go talk to someone," Jordan says quietly. "It's not healthy, the way you're dealing with her death."

Neil sighs and lowers his forehead into his hands.

"Leave him alone," Azar says gently. "I know you mean

well, but . . . just leave it, Jordan."

"Sorry," Jordan says. "I'm trying to help."

"You don't have to fix everything. It's not your job," she says. "And some things can't be fixed." Her words sound tired, resigned.

"All right," Jordan says, the barest edge of hurt in his voice. "I won't say anything else." As if to prove his point, he pulls out his phone and starts scrolling through Twitter.

"I didn't mean . . ." Azar hesitates, then shakes her head, as if she can't find the right thing to say. Instead, she touches Jordan's wrist, and he gives her a small smile, some wordless understanding passing between them. The tension at the table fades but doesn't disappear entirely.

But as Azar starts talking to Neil about the girl she likes, a sophomore named Zoe, her voice grows more cheerful. "I think tonight's the night," she says with a sly grin. "A little moonlight, a little liquor."

Neil snorts.

"Is it going to be weird if I don't drink tonight?" I whisper to Penny. I've seen my mom drunk one too many times to have any interest in drinking.

She shakes her head. "Alcohol doesn't pair well with my meds, so I don't drink. But if you feel weird about it, just hold a red cup and no one will know the difference."

"Magni Viri stoops to the level of the SOLO cup?" I whisper back.

She laughs. "What? You think we only use crystal goblets?"

"I was expecting brandy snifters and tasteful charcuterie boards," I say around a smile.

"What the hell is a brandy snifter?" Penny asks, dissolving into more laughter that attracts the attention of the rest of the table.

"It's a very fancy glass for very fancy people," Jordan says without looking up from his phone.

"Is it called that because you sniff the drink before you drink it?" Wren asks.

No one answers. But Neil rolls his eyes and says he's going back to the studio.

"Penny, what are you two talking about? You're not spoiling Tara's first Denfeld party, are you?" Azar asks suspiciously. "None of us got a heads-up, and neither should she."

I think Azar is kidding, but there's a strange note in her voice that almost sounds like a warning.

"I said nothing," Penny says, still wiping tears from her eyes. "Brandy snifter." She shakes her head.

"Y'all aren't gonna haze me tonight, are you?" I ask anxiously.

For some reason, the entire table bursts into hysterical laughter.

"What?" I ask defensively.

Penny grins. "Tara, you know I love your accent, but the way you just said that." She shakes her head.

"It wasn't just the accent. It was like you'd wandered in off the set of *The Andy Griffith Show*," Wren says. "Pure, wide-eyed Southern innocence."

I'm a little offended, but I remember what Azar said before about the chip on my shoulder, so I shrug and laugh. They didn't mean any harm by it. I did sound a little like a hayseed visiting the Big Apple or something, afraid of being corrupted by city slickers.

Next to me, Penny shifts closer until her knee touches mine. "I won't let anybody haze you," she whispers in my ear. "I promise." Her eyes are merry, her cheeks pink from laughter.

When I look around the table, I realize that everyone else is looking at me in almost the same way: friendly, open, accepting. I remember the other thing Azar told me: I belong to them now, and they belong to me. I can let down my guard.

By seven, the restless energy of the house has infiltrated my body too. I change my clothes twice, try to work on three different assignments without any success, and can't even make it through a single episode of *What We Do in the Shadows*, which I've been watching in hopes of comparing it to *Carmilla* for my final Gothic lit paper. Finally, around eight, Wren bursts into the room and starts looking frantically through their closet.

"Party's starting. We gotta go!" they say. They throw a corduroy jacket on over their jeans and embroidered white button-down. "You'd better dress warmer than that. Come on, come on!"

I grab my coat and yank on my boots as I follow Wren down the hallway, nearly tripping in the process. "Isn't the party here?" I ask.

"You'll see!" Wren says, practically skipping down the stairs. My stomach lurches. I think I know exactly where we're going.

A few minutes later, we pass through the gates of the cemetery. It is utterly changed from the night of my initiation.

There are lanterns hanging from tree limbs, groups of people laughing and joking. A makeshift bar is set up on the steps of a huge mausoleum that bears a half-effaced name: *Walter W—th —orge.*

I puzzle over the missing letters for a moment before it hits me. It must have once said Walter Weymouth George. This is where one of Magni Viri's founders is buried. This is the mausoleum his bereft friend built for him. I wonder how they'd feel about it being used as a bar.

"Tara! Wren!" Quigg yells when he sees us. He is already well into his cups, his cheeks flushed ruddy, his eyes bright. He grins and puts an arm around each of us.

"Tara, your first night of revelry!" he exclaims.

"So the Sunday night parties are always in the graveyard?" I ask. "Why?"

"'Tis tradition!" Quigg says. "It's the heart of Magni Viri! We are communing with our forebears."

"It's not very festive." I don't say the rest of what I'm thinking: that it seems disrespectful to party on the graves of the dead.

"What could be more festive? They're dead, and we're not," Quigg says with a wild laugh before leaving Wren and me to our own devices. Wren starts helping themself to the liquor.

"I'm gonna go find Penny," I say before setting off into the dimness of the cemetery. I sense I'm going to need a sober buddy tonight. These Magni Viri kids clearly party as hard as they study.

I pass Azar and Zoe, who are making out against a tree.

Azar gives me a wink when she comes up for air. After a few minutes I find Jordan sitting with Trey and Jessica, the only other Black students from Magni Viri, laughing like I've never seen him laugh before.

"Hey, have you seen Penny?" I ask him.

He beams at me, and I can't tell whether he's buzzed or just really enjoying himself. But the smile is transformative, opening him up. "Yeah, she's lying on the ground under those cedar trees over there," he says. "She's in a mood. Maybe you can cheer her up."

Based on the way he's looking at me, knowing and a little teasing, I can't help but wonder if Penny has talked about me to him, if she's told him that she likes me.

"I'll try," I say, trying not to smile too widely at the thought of Penny Dabrovsky having a crush on me.

I leave Jordan with his friends and weave my way through tombstones and undergraduates to the place he pointed. Soon, I make out Penny's long-legged form stretched out on a blanket in the grass. Her eyes are open as if she's gazing at the stars. I feel a little chill at my heart, thinking of Meredith in the library. But then Penny turns her head.

"Hey, you," she says, her voice full of affection. "I'm star-gazing. Wanna join?"

My heart beats a little faster as I lie down next to her. The ground is cold, even through the blanket. I shiver, and she moves closer to me so that her side is pressed against mine.

"Do you know the names of the constellations?" I ask, wondering if she can hear my racing heart.

"Nah, not really," she says with a sigh. "Azar is kind of a

space geek and could tell you most of them. But I just think they're pretty."

I roll over and lean up on my elbow to look down on her. "Jordan said something's bothering you."

"Did he now?"

"You do look kind of gloomy. Bat research not going so well?"

One side of her mouth quirks up. "Something like that."

"You can talk to me, you know. You've listened to all my problems with O'Connor and classes and stuff," I say.

Penny blinks at me. "I've only known you, like, a week and you want me to spill my guts?"

"Oh," I say, wincing. "Right."

Has it only been a week? I feel like I've been in Denfeld Hall for half a semester already, my life has changed so much. Maybe I'm assuming intimacy where there is none.

But she's smiling now. "Don't you worry your pretty head about me. Except to keep me warm. It's freezing out here," she says, pulling me back down. She tugs the blanket on her side up to cover us. I do the same with mine, realizing with a rush of happiness that she called me pretty. We lie under the stars, surrounded by the smell of damp cedar and earth, wrapped up together like a little burrito. It's cozy and close.

Around us, the party grows, everyone's voices getting louder and wilder as the night progresses. We're a little world of our own, made of silence and starlight. For a moment, I think about kissing her, but instead I press closer into her warmth and wait, giving her a chance to open up to me, if she wants to.

"I'm tired," Penny admits after a while. "I'm in a flare."

"A flare? What does that mean?"

"It's when my autoimmune disease is worse than usual. It makes me really tired and achy. It feels like gravity is pressing harder on me than on everyone else."

"Where does it hurt?" I ask.

Penny lets out a bleak laugh. "You'd be better off asking where it doesn't hurt."

"I'm sorry," I say. "That sounds rough."

"Yeah, it is," Penny says.

"I don't think anyone would mind if you left the party and went to bed."

She sighs again. "I want to be here."

"Well, I'm glad you're here," I say, laying my head on her shoulder. I breathe in the woodsy smell of her.

"Sometimes I'm afraid . . ." She pauses to grope for words. "I'm afraid that my illness is going to get so bad that I won't be able to do the work I want to do. I'm afraid that I don't have enough time to accomplish anything. My disease is mostly managed right now, but that doesn't mean it will stay that way."

I'm quiet for a long time, unsure how to respond. She's trusting me with something, and I don't want to fuck it up. "That sounds scary," I finally say.

"Yeah." She leans her head against mine.

"You hide it really well," I say. "Being afraid. You seem so solid and balanced compared to everyone else."

Penny snorts.

"What?"

"I actually have terrible balance. Haven't you noticed my cane?"

I laugh into her shoulder. "I had no idea you were a pun-as-humor type. I don't know if we can still be friends."

"Puns are the height of humor," Penny says in a dignified tone.

"Sure," I say.

"Okay, I told you my fear. Now you have to tell me yours," Penny says. "Even trade."

"I have a deep-seated fear of puns and the people who make them," I say seriously.

Penny elbows me in the side.

"Fine, fine," I say through a laugh. I stare up at the bright pinpricks of stars. "I'm afraid . . . that I'm actually just a big giant nobody who is never going to accomplish anything of value." The admission makes my cheeks burn. "I'm afraid of being mediocre." I'm afraid of never measuring up to Meredith Brown, I add silently to myself.

"Do you want commiseration or advice?" Penny asks after a moment.

"Why not both?"

"Okay. So your fear is the same as pretty much everyone's in Magni Viri. We're all terrified of being average. Terrified that we're not as brilliant as we've been led to believe or as talented as we think we are."

"So you're saying I *am* mediocre?" I laugh.

"You're human," Penny says. "But here's the thing I think about all the time: So what if I am ordinary? My dad is ordinary, and I think he's the best person alive. So what if I don't accomplish anything that changes the world? He didn't, and I still love and admire him. Why is my value all tied up in accomplishing things? What's so terribly wrong with being ordinary? It's not like greatness ever made anyone happy."

The love she feels for her dad is so pure it makes my chest ache. I wish I had a simple, uncomplicated feeling like that for either of my parents. I wish I had nice, dependable, ordinary parents I could be proud of, whose lives were something to emulate rather than something to escape from. But to me, ordinary has always looked like giving up. The struggle for greatness might not be the answer, but the inertia of ordinariness didn't do much for my mom either. Or for me, caught in her orbit for so long.

Of course, I can't say any of that. I search my brain for a lighter remark. "Well, have you convinced yourself with that speech yet?" I ask.

Penny laughs. "Not even a little bit."

"It was so heartfelt though," I say. "Very earnest."

Penny snorts. "I can't believe we're lying in a graveyard talking about mortality and the meaning of life while a bacchanal practically rages around us."

"We are the very definition of square."

"You want to go join the party?" Penny asks.

"All right," I say. I get up and help her to her feet. Her hands are cold.

"Thanks," she says.

We start toward the glow of the party.

"Hey, Tara?" she asks a little shyly. "Can I hold your hand?"

I glance at her. "Yeah, of course. Do you feel unsteady?" I hold my hand out to her.

"No," she says with a smile. "I just want to hold your hand." She pauses to gauge my reaction and then slips her fingers into mine. A warmth rushes up from my belly, making my skin tingle. Our hands fit together like they were always meant to be touching. My heart is racing again, and now I know she can feel it. But I can feel hers too, beating a fast tempo against my wrist.

My cheeks burn, and I'm glad it's too dark for her to see. I bite my lip to keep from smiling too hard. Penny Dabrovsky is holding my hand.

We find Wren and Quigg first, who are singing "Bohemian Rhapsody" together. Even drunk, their voices are beautiful. They both hold out their arms when they see Penny and me like they want to pull us into a group hug. Quigg is too drunk to notice Penny and me holding hands, but Wren grins at us. We join in their song, all swaying together to the music in our heads. Penny never lets go of me.

Pretty soon it doesn't matter that I haven't had a drop to drink. The energy of the party is contagious, and I feel tipsy on it alone. I laugh more than I ever have in my life. I wouldn't have guessed that Penny was popular since she's kind of reserved, but she clearly is. Loads of older Magni Viri students drift over to say hello, and soon I've met a half dozen people I've never spoken to before.

It makes me wonder why Penny has picked me of all people, when there are so many others here—boys and girls—who she could have if she wanted them. An even more unwelcome question drifts through my mind: if she ever thought of Meredith in that way; if she ever asked to hold Meredith's hand.

The thought of Meredith recalls me to where we are. We're in a cemetery, surrounded by moldering bodies, graves that have been here for centuries, as well as newer ones, whose owners have hardly had a chance to rest. We are like a mockery to the dead—so young and so alive, our blood beating hot and excited in our veins. If the roles were reversed and it were me who lay beneath the earth, beneath this thoughtless revelry, I would want to grab hold of the revelers; pull them by the ankles; suck the breath from their mouths, the blood from their veins; steal their young bodies, young hearts, young dreams for myself.

The thought makes me feel so strange and dizzy that when Penny turns to say something to me, her face inches from my own, I can't help but reach out and touch her cheek, run my thumb across her skin. The words disappear from her surprised lips, and her gaze goes to my mouth. Without another thought, I kiss her, feeling the chapped ridges of her lips beneath my own, tasting the root beer that lingers on her tongue. When I pull away, her eyes glimmer, as if catching starlight. She smiles and draws me back in for another kiss, her fingers caught up in my hair. I kiss her and kiss her as the party rages on around us, aware of nothing but her warm lips and the cold tip of her nose when it touches mine.

It feels like getting lost in the woods at night. It feels like being found.

I only pull away from her when a flame goes up from the

ground a few yards away, a white-hot, burning pillar that lights up the entire cemetery. The upperclassmen who surround it scream and stagger away from the flames. I recognize Bernard in his dressing gown, his usually gaunt, exhausted face transformed by a wild, giddy laugh as he falls backward onto his ass, just a few feet away from the fire. Everyone roars with laughter, the noise of it fearful and exhilarating both. I laugh too, the sound wrenched from my chest the same way the Latin song spilled forth on the night of my initiation.

Neil stands nearby, silent and alone, leaning against a ten-foot obelisk, smoking a cigarette. He watches the fire with a strange, trancelike expression, as lost in the flames as I had been in Penny's kiss.

"What's up with him?" I ask Penny, nodding at Neil.

She laughs. "He probably ate one of Dennis's gummies and is stoned on ancient herbs or something."

Before I can respond, she pulls me down to the cold grass and kisses me with her warm lips until I forget my fears, my anxieties, until I forget my own name. When I lean back against a tombstone, Penny's limbs and hair tangled with mine, I no longer feel like we're disrespecting the dead by partying on their graves. I feel like our lives are all weaved together, the living and the dead, the past and the present, bound together in a moment that has no beginning and no end.

So when I smell Meredith's lily of the valley perfume on the air, so far from that drawer in her room, I do not feel afraid. We are all one creature tonight. We are all Magni Viri.

THIRTEEN

I wake at my desk, my face smashed against the pages of a notebook. Sunlight trickles in from a slit in the curtains. I sit up slowly, my neck and shoulders aching. I blink my crusty, tired eyes at Wren's side of the room. It's empty. Their bed is still covered in the same litter of books and clothes as it was last night. They must have never made it back to our room after the party.

I try to recall everything that happened last night, but it's a blur. I remember lying under the stars with Penny; I remember kissing her. I remember the wild, reckless energy that swept me up. But that's all. The rest is a hazy memory of faces and laughter and the cold, damp smells of the cemetery, mingled with smoke and liquor and beer.

I feel hungover even though I didn't drink. My lips are puffy and bruised from kissing. I touch them and can't help but smile. Then my eyes land on my notebook. The pages are covered top to bottom in my handwriting, or at least a version of it. My usually neat print is a dashed-off scrawl, pressed hard into the page, as if the words were coming too fast and too intensely for my hand to keep up.

I flip backward in the notebook a few pages, and then a

few more. There are at least twenty-five pages filled. Did I write all of this last night? I couldn't have.

But the handwriting is mine, and the phrasing is familiar. It feels like something I would write. There are sentences here and there that feel like déjà vu.

And yet . . . I rub my eyes and try again, starting from the first page of messy, scrawling words. It's a story about a place that reminds me eerily of Corbin College, but Corbin College if it were made up entirely of buildings like Denfeld Hall. All dark stone and creeping ivy, closed in by green hills. It's set sometime in the past, though how far back I can't tell. There is a family that lives on the grounds as caretakers, which they've done for generations, as long as the college has stood on this land. Always caretakers and never students. Always sneered at, imposed upon. There's a growing hatred in their hearts, a cankering ill will toward the school and its buildings, the faculty, but most of all toward the students—"soft, pampered creatures with hard souls" my pen declares them.

I want to say that's not how I feel about the people at Corbin, but I know it is. All this anger and resentment has been inside me for months. And now I've put it onto the page.

But there's no Jane Eyre stand-in here, no put-upon teacher fighting thwarted dreams. In fact, the story doesn't have a single main character like I would usually write. Instead, it centers on three siblings: Coy, Hazel, and Eugenia Dossey. Coy is good-natured, hardworking, and handsome enough that the college girls make eyes at him when they pass him on the grounds. He has flings with some of them but never gets attached. His sisters are just as beautiful as Coy but less even-tempered. Hazel pines over the boys on campus until she is sick. But Eugenia nurses a hatred for them, passed from her father the way a knocked-over candle sets the curtains—and then the whole house—ablaze.

I read over the pages twice before I'm entirely convinced I wrote them, despite how true they feel. The thing is that they are simply too good. I've never written anything so good.

I shake my head. It must have been the effect of the party—kissing Penny, singing and laughing with Wren and Quigg, running like children through the tombstones, playing hide-and-seek in the trees. It must have loosened something in me. There's been a hard, stonelike thing lodged in my chest since I got to Corbin. Last night must have shaken it free. And words came with it.

I bite my lip, smiling at the pages, the most intense rush of relief breaking through me. I *am* a writer. It wasn't a pipe dream. It wasn't foolish. I am exactly who I want to be. And now I have the words to prove it.

I spend an hour typing up the pages, correcting minor errors of punctuation, filling in a few words where I omitted them in my rush to get the narrative on the page. In a Word document, double-spaced, in Times New Roman, the story feels even more like mine than it did in my own handwriting. When I finish transcribing the last of the previous night's scrawl, I scroll back up to the top of the document and type *By Tara Boone* with a little disbelieving laugh. I click the line above, where a title should go. The cursor blinks while I think.

CICADA, I type, though I'm not sure why. There is no mention of cicadas in the pages I wrote last night. But the word feels right somehow, the sound and shape of it. I think of the exoskeleton Penny showed me, how it clung to the side of the tree even without its host. I think of the hum and scream from the treetops in the cemetery, from my dreams. *Cicada*. That's what this book is called. And it *is* a book, I realize. Not a novel but a novella.

I know I'm putting the cart so far before the horse that the two may never meet again, but I can't help but picture the book, how it would look as a finished thing you can hold in your hands. A small, slim volume you could sit and read in a day, your legs thrown over the side of a chair, mouth slightly open, totally absorbed in the words on the creamy pages. I can see the title on the cover, my own name at the bottom, beneath a moody illustration.

I am deep into a daydream about walking down a city street and spying *Cicada* in a bookstore window, face out on a New Releases table, when my phone's alarm goes off from inside the pocket of the jacket I wore to the party last night. It's only seven in the morning. I've been awake for hours already, and I know I couldn't have slept for more than a few hours last night. But it's worth it, for this. A novella.

I look back at the typed pages. Only a beginning, I remind myself. The start of something. Beginnings are so much easier than middles and ends.

But it's something I can send to Dr. O'Connor. Proof that I belong in Denfeld Hall, in Magni Viri. Proof that I am not a second-rate Meredith Brown, forever living in her shadow.

Before I can start to doubt myself, before I can lose my nerve, I email him the pages.

I go downstairs in a flurry of high spirits, eager for a cup of coffee. I can't stop smiling, and if I weren't so tired, I think I would skip down the stairs. Last night I wrote the beginning of my novella, and last night I kissed Penny. I remember how she looked after we kissed, surprised and bright-eyed and eager. She wanted me every bit as much as I wanted her.

What did it mean? I wonder. I feel so hopelessly inexperienced. Was it just one night—a single moment in time? Or will we be a couple now? It was my first kiss. My first anything. I can't believe I had the courage to do it. I can't believe she kissed me back.

I bite my lip at the memory as I swing off the banister at the bottom of the stairs and launch myself right into Neil. He steps back from me and squints at me blearily. He is haggard and paint-spattered and still smells of liquor and smoke. I expect a nasty comment, but he maneuvers around me and goes upstairs without a word. Maybe all the vitriol has finally left him, though I suspect he's only too hungover and exhausted to be spiteful.

After I eat a Pop-Tart, I carry my coffee and books to the house library to finish my reading before I head to Gothic lit. But I don't make it through the door. Because over the mantel an unframed canvas is propped, the ink still wet.

It's a portrait of a girl with long curly red hair. Her eyes are like the flames that Bernard let loose last night. She is beautiful and terrible, all-consuming. She looks out over the library as if daring us to say she's dead.

All the buoyancy goes out of me. My blood freezes in my veins. Once more, I am small and gauche and frightened, out of my league, an interloper in a house of geniuses.

It feels like a message from Meredith, like she's watched me these last few days, walking the halls that were hers, hanging out with the friends that were hers, trying to become the writer that she was meant to be.

Whether Neil knew what he was doing or not, the meaning of this painting is clear: whatever success I might have, whatever inroads I might make, Meredith Brown still reigns in Magni Viri.

I back out of the library doorway, and then, like a coward, I flee.

I avoid Denfeld's library and the rest of the house for the remainder of the day, Meredith's blazing gaze burned into my memory. Even the campus library is too full of her, and I am forced to abandon my old refuge for the noisy campus café. Every time I let my mind drift from my studies, it returns to Meredith, to her face, to the memory of her voice, the smell of her perfume. A cold thrill goes through me each time I picture the painting, leaving me shaky and sick. How can a dead girl hold so much power over me? Last night I thought I was done being frightened of her, that I could bear the way her ghost lingers in our midst. But I was wrong. I was horribly, horribly wrong.

I am still thinking of her as I walk down the hall to O'Connor's office the next morning. I'm afraid that my confidence in the pages I sent him was misplaced, that he's going to raise his eyebrows at me, asking silently if this is really the best I can do. That all the while he'll be remembering Meredith's writing and comparing me to her.

But when I enter his office after a quick knock, he positively beams at me. "Tara! Tara, those pages you sent me." He shakes his head in wonder. "I knew you had it in you."

"You really liked them?" I ask as I take a seat.

He laughs. "They are brilliant. *You* are brilliant."

A small smile escapes my lips, the heavy dread lifting from my heart. "Really?"

"My God! The writing is so controlled, so measured, not a word wasted. There is this perfect tension. I held my breath through most of it. Do you know whose writing it reminds me of? Shirley Jackson's."

My heart explodes inside my chest. "Shirley Jackson?"

"Mmm, yes, there's the same tension, the same foreboding." He shakes his head. "Of course, it's entirely your own though. It doesn't feel at all derivative."

"So you approve of this as my project for the year?" I ask, feeling my pride stir for the first time since I saw Neil's painting of Meredith.

"Absolutely. Entirely. I cannot wait to read more."

"Didn't you say we need to bring in another faculty member? Someone from the English department?"

"Ah, yes," he says. "I was thinking of Jimmy Coraline. He teaches creative writing."

"Oh," I say, remembering how awed Dr. Coraline was by Meredith at the lit club reading and how rudely I behaved. Facing him again so soon would be excruciating.

"Did you have someone else in mind?" Dr. O'Connor asks, cocking his head.

"Well . . . I was hoping we could ask Dr. Hendrix," I say, pouncing on the idea with relief. I know Dr. Hendrix admired Meredith too, but she wasn't Meredith's creative writing teacher. "I'm in her Gothic lit class, and I'm going to take Southern Gothicism with her next semester."

A muscle near his mouth twitches, almost imperceptibly. "Ah, well. That might be a bit awkward," he admits. "She and I used to be married."

"I know," I say. "But you wouldn't have to see much of each other, would you?"

He rubs his chin, considering. "To be honest, she and I do not see eye to eye as scholars or teachers."

"Aren't differences of opinion and pedagogy good?" I press, though I know their differences are way beyond ideological. She thinks he's a monster. But I'd rather have them at each other's throats than bring in Professor Coraline.

Dr. O'Connor laughs. "All right, then. But you ask her. And I'd still like to show your work to Dr. Coraline, if that's all right. He's a Magni Viri alum, you know."

"Sure, of course," I say, accepting my partial win.

He pushes a class change form toward me. "Now, let's talk about your schedule."

When I say I want to drop American history, he nods and fills in the form without comment. I feel strangely validated, as if I made exactly the decision he'd hoped I would. Or perhaps it was never about the class to drop at all, more about my being thoughtful about my own education.

The form completed, he leans across the desk. "Now, tell me how things are going for you at Denfeld."

I falter, my thoughts full of the uneasiness of the last week—the strange phone calls, the lingering sense of being watched, my worries about the well-being of some of the upperclassmen. Meredith everywhere I turn. And now the painting.

"Have you made friends?" Dr. O'Connor prompts, recalling me to the good parts of joining Magni Viri.

I smile. "I have, actually. My roommate, Wren, and Penny, and I guess Jordan and even Azar. Only . . ."

"Neil?" he guesses.

"He's not a fan," I admit.

"Neil's not a fan of much of anyone except himself, in my opinion," Dr. O'Connor says.

I blink at him, surprised that he would so openly criticize another student.

"Don't get me wrong, he's a very talented artist."

"Oh, I know," I say. Meredith's fiery portrait hovers behind my eyes. "It's like something you'd see in a museum."

Dr. O'Connor nods. "It's almost ghoulish to say, but I think Meredith's loss will benefit his art greatly. Up until now, he has been a spoiled child who has hardly experienced anything. Now he knows loss and grief. Those are powerful emotions that create powerful art."

He's right—it *is* a ghoulish, unfeeling thing to say, but I'm quickly learning that O'Connor doesn't mince his words or pull his punches. Besides, I think he's telling the truth about Neil. I don't know what Neil's art was like before Meredith died, but now it's brilliant.

"He painted her," I say quietly. "A new one, just this morning."

Dr. O'Connor's eyes gleam. "I believe he will be able to hold a show of his work next semester if he keeps up at his current rate. I have a connection in New York."

"An art gallery?" I ask. I wonder if he has connections that would help me too—literary agents, editors.

"Yes, precisely." He must read something of these thoughts in my expression because he adds, "And when the time comes, I'll help you place your work too."

"Really?" I nearly laugh at the thought of it, how far-fetched it seems, yet how easy it might be.

"Really," he says. "But first you have to go write me some more pages." With that, his attention shifts away from me, back to something on his computer monitor. I've been dismissed.

"Next week," I promise.

He waves me away, already immersed in someone else's needs.

This time when I break into the cool air outside of the social sciences building, I don't feel overwhelmed or inadequate. I feel . . . elated. The air is crisp and smells of fall, the trees are dotted red and orange and yellow. The sky is a brilliant blue, as if it has never known rain.

Talking to O'Connor actually made me feel better about everything, made me realize how silly I've been. Neil's painting of Meredith had nothing to do with me. It wasn't a message or a portent. It was merely a painting expressing his own feelings, just like the novella I'm writing expresses mine. Everything is going to be all right.

As if the universe wants to confirm this feeling, Penny

gets up from a bench and comes walking toward me, a small, secret smile on her face. She's limping slightly, her cane in one hand and book in the other. She comes right up to me, where I stand on the bottom stair, which raises me to her height.

"Hello," she says, and she leans forward and gives me a peck on the cheek that makes goose bumps spread over my skin. "I was waiting for you."

"Hey," I say, touching her arm. My insides glow. "What have you got there?"

"Just a bit of light reading." She shows me the book's cover, which features a bat in flight. It has Dr. Coppola's name beneath it.

"Bat girl," I say teasingly.

"Oh, I've never been called that before, not even once," she says with a smirk.

"What's your favorite kind of bat?"

"Little brown bats," she says without hesitation. "That's the kind we have in our cave here. Did you know that just one of them can eat a thousand insects in an hour?"

"I love how nerdy you are. If I were a bat, what sort of bat would I be?"

"Vampire," she says with a grin.

"Come on," I say, "seriously? A bloodsucker?"

"No, you'd be . . ." She steps toward me and twirls a strand of my hair around her fingers. "You'd be an epauletted fruit bat. They're very cute."

"Are you calling me cute?"

Penny smiles, biting her lip in a way that makes my stomach swoop. My eyes follow the movement, and I'm thinking about kissing her again when the door behind us opens and Dr. O'Connor comes out.

"Penny," he says. "I hope you've made some progress before our meeting tomorrow."

"I'll do my best," she says, her voice suddenly strained, the ease from a moment before lost.

"Do better than your best," he says as he passes us down the stairs and hurries off.

"What's that about?" I ask.

She rolls her eyes. "Nothing. Just O'Connor being O'Connor. Want to go study somewhere with me? I need a break from Denfeld," she says, clearly eager for a subject change.

I hesitate. I am itching to get back to *Cicada*. To see where the story goes next. But I won't be able to write with Penny there.

"Come on, please," she says. "Surely you wouldn't deny yourself the pleasure of my company."

"Well, when you put it like that," I say. I hop off the final step. Penny starts toward the campus café, her book under her arm. I watch her for a moment, a tall, athletic-looking girl in corduroy pants, green suspenders, a cream-colored button-down. She turns and raises her eyebrows at me, leaning on her beautiful cane. Bat girl.

I smile and follow her through the dreamily autumnal campus. For perhaps the first time, I feel like it belongs to me. I feel as if the world is opening up before me—many worlds, all stacked against each other, their doors flung wide.

FOURTEEN

I wake at my desk again. Morning light streams in through the open curtains, which I never closed. Wren isn't in their bed.

My notebook is filled with more inky scrawls. Pages and pages of it. I close my eyes again, as exhausted as if I'd never slept at all. I want nothing more than to climb into my bed and go to sleep. Instead, I stand and stretch, working the aching tightness out of my muscles. I notice that my fingers are smeared with ink, the middle finger on my right hand red and sore where I held the pen. I must have written for hours last night.

I pick up the notebook and pace slowly through the room, turning pages as I go. The middle Dossey sibling, Hazel, is dead, having drowned herself in the lake. Coy is steeped in grief. Eugenia, though, has gotten a college boy named Frederick in her snares. She's working him as surely and darkly as Circe worked the shipwrecked men on her shores. It will not end well for him, I know.

When I reach the end of the pages, I look up, surprised to find myself in this sunlit room, in this body of mine. The pages are good, perhaps even better than what I'd written before. Darkly atmospheric, taut, simmering with suppressed violence. I shake my head in wonder.

But I am a wreck, exhausted to my core. It takes all I have to drag myself down the hall and into the shower. I tip my head back and let the hot water pummel my skull, sluice down my face. I could fall asleep standing. When I finally open my eyes to lather myself with soap, I'm shocked to find an enormous purple bruise on my hip. I touch it gingerly, wincing. When did I get this? *How* did I get this?

I must have crashed into something last night, maybe my desk or the chair. But I don't remember doing it. I blink at the bruise, trying to recall the sharp, surprising pain I must have felt. But it's not there.

Did I get out of bed last night in the dark and feel my way to the desk to write? I must have. That must be what happened. But the sight of the bruise fills me with a vague unease. Something niggles at me, just out of reach of my thoughts.

I finish washing myself, rinse the conditioner out of my hair, and climb out of the shower, shivering in the cold air. I swipe the foggy mirror so I can see my reflection. There are dark circles under my reddened eyes. I blink at myself. Nothing a little concealer can't fix. Besides, dark circles are a badge of honor around here, practically a fashion accessory. Almost everyone has them.

I lean forward, studying myself. My face looks a little thinner. I haven't been eating enough perhaps. It's such a long way to the cafeteria from Denfeld, and I always seem to have other things to do. But I'd better stop skipping meals.

There's something else in my face that feels unfamiliar though, more than tiredness and a few missed dinners. It's the way my eyes look. Despite the red squiggles on my sclera, the puffiness of my tired eyelids, my gaze is direct and assured in a way it's never been. I hold my head higher, surer.

That girl who ducked her head through the halls, who moved like a ghost through the crowded cafeteria, she's gone now. Someone else has taken her place: a new Tara. A writer, someone with friends and an almost girlfriend, someone who doesn't have to scuttle through this campus like an unwelcome parasite.

The rattle of the bathroom doorknob and a disappointed sigh break me out of the trance of my own gaze. I throw on my bathrobe and hang my towel, then go over and open the door. "I'm done," I call to the figure slowly shuffling down the hall.

Wren turns. They walk slowly toward me, exhaustion evident in every limb.

"You all right?" I ask, moving out of the way of the door.

Wren nods, not speaking.

"Come have breakfast in the cafeteria with me, all right?" I say, studying their wan face. They look even worse than I do. We both could clearly use a square meal.

Wren nods again, then closes the bathroom door.

Fifteen minutes later, we're trudging down the hill toward the main campus. Wren is uncharacteristically silent, wrapped in their own haze of exhaustion—and I in mine. It's only after we've started on our breakfasts and drank half a cup of coffee each that conversation feels possible.

"Wren, where have you been sleeping?" I finally ask.

They blink at me over the rim of their cup. "In my bed?"

I shake my head. "You haven't touched your bed in days. Are you hooking up with someone?" I really hope they say yes.

But Wren laughs. "Who would I be hooking up with?"

I shrug, picking up a piece of bacon. "I don't know, anyone. You're a catch."

Wren's mouth turns up in a wry smile. "Neil complained that my piano playing was keeping him awake at night, so I've been in the twenty-four-hour practice rooms a lot."

"Neil is full of shit," I say. "He's been up every night painting anyway." I squint at Wren. "Have you been sleeping in the practice rooms?"

"A little," Wren admits. "It's such a long way back to Denfeld, so sometimes I nap on the couch in the big practice room."

"So you *are* sleeping?" I press.

Wren shoves a big spoonful of oatmeal into their mouth. "Of course," they say thickly. They swallow a bite and cock their head at me. "Are *you*?"

"Touché," I say with a laugh. I feel a little better now, with breakfast in my belly. Not so totally wiped out. I glance at my phone. "I gotta go to class. Can we hang out later? I feel like I've barely seen you lately."

Wren smiles. "How about dinner? Six o'clock?"

"It's a date." I grab my stuff and hurry to the humanities building. Dr. Hendrix is at the front of the room, setting up for class, when I come in.

"Hi," I say with a smile.

"Tara, how are you?" Dr. Hendrix asks, appraising me. I'm glad I showered and ate breakfast before coming here. If she'd seen me in my earlier state, she would probably assume Dr. O'Connor was driving the newest Magni Viri recruit to exhaustion, and be too mad to agree to join my project committee.

"I'm great actually," I say brightly. "I'm working on a kind of Gothic novella, and I wondered if you might be willing to be one of my readers."

The words fill me with a fierce, happy pride that makes me hold my head a little bit higher. I'm writing a book, just like I've always dreamed of. Those words in my journal have proved I have what it takes. And that makes all the exhaustion worth it, though maybe I won't tell Dr. Hendrix so.

"A Gothic novella! How thrilling!" she says. "I would love to read it."

"It would be for my independent study with Dr. O'Connor," I add, and her smile falters.

"He wanted to ask Dr. Coraline, but I'd much rather have you," I say, hoping she's susceptible to flattery. "You're such a good teacher, and I think you could really help me."

She hesitates, a visible wince on her face.

"Please," I say. "I would really love for you to be involved. I'm going to take your Southern Gothicism class next semester like you suggested. It all fits so perfectly."

"Well, all right," she says.

"Great! I will send you what I have so far, once I finish transcribing my new pages."

"Are you writing by hand? How old-fashioned," Dr. Hendrix says with a smile. "I wasn't entirely sure students knew how to write by hand anymore." She laughs and then shakes her head. "Sorry, that was very boomer-y of me, wasn't it? Though I'm actually a member of Gen X," she adds, patting her hair self-consciously.

I laugh. "I don't usually write this way, but it's how the book seems to be coming out. Maybe because it's set in the past it wants to be written with old ways too."

"Set when?"

"I don't know," I admit. "Sometime in the past, somewhere in the Appalachians."

"Ah, well, that's very Cormac McCarthy of you. Have you read *Outer Dark* yet?"

"No," I admit. "I've always been afraid to read anything by him after seeing the movie version of *The Road*."

"We'll read him next semester, so gird your loins," she says. "Gosh, that's an awful expression, isn't it?"

"It is," I agree with a laugh, trying—and failing—to imagine how this funny, self-conscious, fragile woman was ever married to a man like Dr. O'Connor. I'm curious to see what they're like together when we have a meeting.

By this time, half the class has trickled in, so I let her get back to preparing her notes. A movie still from the 1940s film adaptation of *Jane Eyre* is on the screen. A rather sinister Orson Welles looks down on a much too pretty Joan Fontaine.

We've moved on from vampires to the Brontë sisters, with their wild moors and troubling men. It's a lecture day, and I sink gratefully into my seat to take notes, glad I don't have to try to wow anyone with my intellect for the next hour. Writing *Cicada* has taken every last drop of it.

Wren doesn't show up for dinner. I text them twice and even call them, but it goes straight to voice mail. As the minutes tick by, my stomach tightens with worry. Penny and Jordan turn up together, and then Azar and Neil.

"Y'all, I'm really worried about Wren," I say once everyone's seated. "They were supposed to meet me for dinner, and now they're not answering their phone."

"They're probably at the piano, completely oblivious to the time," Azar says around a mouthful of salad.

"That's what I'm worried about," I say. "I get being wrapped up in your work, but it's way more than that. Wren hasn't been sleeping in our room. I've barely seen them. And when I do, they look totally exhausted, like to the point of it being kind of dangerous. I think something's wrong."

Neil rolls his eyes, and I turn on him, surprising even myself with my ferocity. "And why the hell did you send Wren to the practice rooms? You couldn't put on noise-canceling headphones or something?"

"They've been playing the same damn song for weeks! I can't stand it anymore," Neil says.

"You know how far away the practice rooms are. Wren isn't sleeping. They're barely eating. At least if they're in the house, we can keep an eye on them."

"Wren's not a child, and I don't think they'd appreciate you treating them like one," Neil shoots back. "In fact, you've all got a nasty habit of infantilizing them."

I sit back, wounded, my words curdling on my tongue. Wren said almost the same thing the first day I met them, about hating how the others babied them. But this isn't the same. I genuinely think Wren is in trouble.

"Wren isn't a child, but they are young," Penny says, coming to my defense. "Barely even seventeen, which is younger than all the rest of us. And you know how obsessive they are, how hard it is for them to pull away from their work."

"Look around this table," Neil says. "Show me one person at this table who isn't bone-tired right now. Show me one person who got more than five hours of sleep last night."

Met with silence, he waves his hand. "There you go."

"This is what Magni Viri is," Azar says hesitantly, as if she's not entirely sure whether she believes it. "This is what it takes." She rubs her face, and I notice for the first time how exhausted and stressed she looks. Azar is so good at projecting confidence and competence, but now I see the cracks in her armor.

Jordan shifts uncomfortably. "That doesn't mean we shouldn't look out for each other," he says quietly. "And Tara's right. Wren has gotten way worse lately. We've all noticed it."

"I've been worried about them for weeks now," Penny says. "Even Quigg said something to me yesterday about how bad Wren looked. I think it might be time for an intervention."

"So let's go find them," I say. "We'll sneak some food out for them and go find them in the practice rooms. We can all go do something fun together, maybe just casually bring up how we're worried about them."

"What are we going to go do?" Neil spits. "We're in the middle of Hillbillyville, in case you haven't noticed. We can't exactly run up the road to see a movie."

"Tara's right though," Penny says, a protective edge to her voice. She touches my knee under the table. "We don't want Wren to feel like we're ambushing them. Besides, we all need a break. Something normal and nice. What should we do?"

The whole table falls into silence. No one can remember how to have fun, I realize. Except for the wild Sunday night cemetery romps, no one at this table does anything except study and work on their independent projects. We've all become a bunch of work-obsessed robots. And we're wearing ourselves out. I can see the exhaustion and strain written plainly on each of their faces, just like I know it's written on mine.

"How about a game night?" I suggest tentatively.

"What kind of games?" Jordan asks, brightening. "Like Monopoly?"

"No," everyone else says in unison.

"Oh, let's do charades!" Azar says excitedly. "I always played that with my astronomy club friends in high school. Or Pictionary. Something like that."

Neil rolls his eyes again and mutters something about being surrounded by nerds, but he doesn't argue. Everyone else seems to think it's a good idea. So we finish dinner quickly, wrap a tuna sandwich in a napkin for Wren, and set off toward the practice rooms. My panic fades now that we're in action. Maybe I was overreacting. Wren's probably fine, but a night of fun and rest won't hurt anyone.

We hear the practice rooms before they loom up out of the gloaming. A single saxophone croons into the night, lovesick and warbling.

"Jesus, at least Wren only plays the piano," Neil says with a shudder.

We wander down the hallway of practice rooms, peering into the window of each door. Most of them are empty. But in one a girl leans over a cello that's between her bare knees, playing feverishly, her eyes closed.

"What are you looking at, Tara?" Azar asks, putting her face next to mine to peer in at the glass. She laughs, throaty and dirty-sounding.

"Pervert," she whispers in my ear, but she stares too.

We have to jog to catch up with the others.

"Wren is usually in the big piano room at the end of this hall," Penny says.

Azar elbows me in the side. "So are you and Penny exclusive yet," she asks with a grin, "or are you going to go back and ask out that cellist?"

"Oh, don't worry, I won't stand in your way," I whisper back.

She laughs and puts her arm in mine, and I feel like we're finally, really friends.

"How's your independent project going?" I ask. "I've never really asked you much about it. It's something environmental related, right?"

Azar's smile falters. "Yeah, I'm exploring how robots might be used to remove particulate pollution from the air, the way they're starting to be used to clean up the ocean."

"Wow, are you serious? Didn't know I was arm in arm with—"

"Oh shit!" I hear, and I nearly give myself whiplash turning toward the yell.

It's Penny, panic in her voice. She hurries into the last practice room on the right. We all run to see what's the matter.

Wren is passed out on the floor, their face pale, a bit of blood at their temple.

"No no no no no no no," Azar says, her voice a disbelieving moan. "Not again. Please not again."

The room swims before me, and where Wren lies, I see Meredith. Eyes open and staring. Tear tracks on her cheeks.

But no, it's Wren, with Penny on one side and Jordan on the other.

Jordan feels at Wren's throat for a pulse.

"They're breathing," he says, loud, relieved. He pushes back Wren's hair. "The cut isn't too bad either." He puts his hand ever-so-gently on Wren's shoulder.

"Hey, Wren. Hey, buddy, can you hear me?" he asks, his voice shaking.

Wren's eyes flutter open. "Ehhmmm," they say.

Azar lets out a relieved, inarticulate cry. The tight pressure in my chest eases slightly. Neil says something I don't catch and slams out of the room.

"What happened? Did you fall?" Jordan asks, voice tight with worry.

Wren blinks at us, struggling to focus. "Got dizzy. Must have hit my head on the piano. Did I hurt the piano?" they ask worriedly.

Jordan laughs gently. "The piano's fine. You don't look so good though. I think we'd better get you to the hospital."

"Should I call an ambulance?" Penny asks, phone at the ready.

"Or health services?" I add.

Jordan glances up at us, his eyes wide despite his apparent calm, chest heaving a little. "No, they'd just call an ambulance anyway, and those are slow as hell out here, not to mention expensive. It'll be faster to drive Wren ourselves. Who has a car?"

"Oh, I do," I say. I'd nearly forgotten about my car, still sitting in the student parking lot, where I left it when I first arrived on campus.

"Can you go get it, pull it as close to here as possible?" Jordan asks, though really it's a command. He's taken charge of the situation.

"Hurry, Tara," Azar says, tears in her voice.

"I will," I say, and sprint out of the room. Luckily, the parking lot isn't far from the practice rooms, but every step I take feels miles longer than it should until I'm there. My breaths come short as I scan the parking lot for my car. My hands shake as I fish my keys out of the cluttered recesses of my backpack, and I drop them twice before I manage to get the door open.

I text Penny once I'm parked outside the music building. They all hurry out together, Wren held up between Azar and Jordan. Penny opens the back door, and they ease Wren down onto the seat. Jordan gets in beside Wren and buckles their seat belt.

"I'd better go check on Neil," Azar says, clearly torn between us and him. "After Meredith—"

"That's fine, we've got Wren," Penny reassures her before climbing into the front seat. Azar strides away, her phone already to her ear.

We're silent as I pull the car out of the parking lot—fast, fishtailing a little. It's very dark, and there aren't nearly enough lights to show me where to go, but I barely slow down. I peer into the blackness, searching for the way to the highway. Penny opens Google Maps and locates the nearest hospital. It's twenty-five minutes away.

"God damn it," Penny whispers, shooting a panicked look at the back seat.

"It'll be okay," I say. "I'll drive fast."

I finally find my way off Corbin's campus and onto the long gravel drive through the forest. I've always liked the idea of Corbin's remoteness, set in its own little world in the hills. But now it feels like we're a million miles away from the help Wren needs.

Jordan has to work hard to keep Wren conscious and talking. "I'm so tired. Let me sleep," Wren says, their voice wretched.

"You could have a concussion," Jordan reminds them. "You're not supposed to fall asleep with a concussion."

"Why'd Magni Viri have to let in a premed major, any-way?" Wren says. "I hate you."

"I know," Jordan says. "That's all right. Tell me how much you hate me." He's trying so hard to keep his voice even, to keep the panic inside, where it can't touch Wren.

But it hardly matters. Wren is sinking again.

"Turn on some loud music or something," Jordan says. "Blast it."

"There are CDs under your seat," I tell Penny. She fumbles around and pulls out a black CD case.

"Under different circumstances, I would ask you what decade you're from," she says as she thumbs through the choices with the aid of her phone's flashlight. "My great-uncle has a CD collection like this in his car."

"They were in the car when I bought it," I say, glad of the distraction. "The stereo doesn't have any way to connect to a phone. There's a Queen CD in there," I add, thinking of how we sang "Bohemian Rhapsody" at the Sunday night party.

Penny laughs, delighted, as she pulls out *News of the World*.

"'We Will Rock You' is number one. That ought to be loud enough to keep Wren awake."

Penny hands me the CD, and I eject the last one I was listening to and throw it into her lap. I slam Queen in and turn the volume dial way up. The sounds of clapping and stomping fill the car.

We finally make it off the gravel drive and onto the main road. I drive as fast around the tight curves of the hills as I dare. We rocket through the night, Freddie Mercury's voice the only thing between us and our panic.

When we're a few minutes away from the hospital, I turn off the stereo. "How's Wren?" I ask.

"Asleep," Jordan says. "I tried everything short of slapping them in the face."

"You did your best," I say.

We spend the rest of the drive in tense silence. When we pull up to the dinky little hospital, Jordan runs inside for a wheelchair and help. Penny starts getting Wren ready to move.

After they get Wren out of the car, I go park. I sit alone in the darkness for a few minutes, listening to the car cooling down. I realize that my heart is racing, my whole body trembling. I've been gripping the steering wheel so hard my fingers ache. I unclench them and rest my head against the steering wheel, taking in deep breaths.

Once I feel more stable, I walk into the hospital, looking for the others as I go. Penny and Jordan sit in a nearly empty waiting room. The only other occupant, an old white man who clutches his stomach, eyes them with evident distrust. Are rural townies truly suspicious of college kids like they are in the books and movies? With their dapper clothes, Jordan and Penny are very clearly not locals. Then again, maybe the old man is just racist.

When I sit down next to them, the man's gaze softens. In my thrifted jeans and sweater, I must look more ordinary, more familiar, like the girls who live in whatever town this is.

"They took Wren straight back," Penny says, reaching across Jordan to squeeze my arm. "Wouldn't let us go with them."

Jordan rubs the side of his face tiredly. He had the worst of it during the drive. "That nurse asked me if I hit Wren," he says. He sighs.

"I'm sorry," I say. "That's fucked up."

"I butted in straightaway and let them know they had it

wrong," Penny said. "I don't think we'll have any more problems with it."

"I hope not," Jordan says, putting his face in his hands, which I realize are trembling. "They keep calling Wren 'she' and 'her' though. It didn't seem like the time to correct them, not that I think it would help."

"We're not at Corbin anymore, Toto," Penny says.

The three of us laugh weakly, though the statement makes me a bit self-conscious. I feel, uncomfortably, as though I've switched sides—now I'm one of the college kids who laugh at the hillbilly locals. I push the thought away.

"God, what a night," Jordan mutters.

"Well, I wanted us to get out tonight. I guess I got my wish," I say quietly. I lean my head against Jordan's shoulder. Penny leans against his other one. We sit in silence for a long while.

"The worst thing," Jordan says suddenly, "is that right now instead of thinking about Wren, I'm actually thinking about my project."

"Tell us about it," I say around a yawn. "It will pass the time."

"Well," Jordan says, "I'm interested to see if—" The rest of what he says is made up of so many unrecognizable scientific terms that the words are more like poetry in another language. Something about cancer cells is all I can grasp. I listen to the soft lilt of Jordan's voice, follow it through unrecognizable lands, caring only for the sound of his voice and the evident pleasure he takes in his subject. Eventually, it lulls me to sleep.

When I wake again, Jordan and Penny are still talking. But they've moved on from Jordan's project. I keep my eyes closed, listening.

"How much do you think she knows?" Jordan asks Penny, his voice hardly more than a whisper.

"I don't know," she says. "Not much, I don't think."

"It's getting harder to keep from her, isn't it?"

"God yes. But O'Connor . . . ," Penny says, hesitating. "You know what he said."

"We've got enough to worry about as it is, I guess."

"Never a shortage of that," Penny agrees tiredly.

Then they lapse into silence. They might have been talking about anyone, anything. But I can't help but think that "she" might be me. It would have to be either me or Azar, wouldn't it? I don't think they could keep anything from Azar.

But what could they possibly be keeping from me? More Magni Viri secrets? Even after the initiation, the Sunday parties, everything? I thought I was supposed to be one of them now, fully. Would Penny do that to me now that we're together? Hurt and worry start to gnaw at my insides. I consider pretending to stay asleep for longer in case they start talking again, but I don't think I want to hear any more. I don't want to risk hearing something that will ruin things between me and Penny. Besides, maybe I've got it all wrong. Maybe it's nothing to do with me.

With a fake startle, as if I've been woken suddenly from deep sleep, I lift my head from Jordan's shoulder. I make a production of rubbing my eyes and yawning. "Any news yet?" I ask.

Penny has a guilty look on her face as she starts to answer, but then a doctor in a white coat comes bustling toward us.

Anxiety clenches my heart—for Wren most of all, but for myself too, and for the secrets the others are keeping from me. Because as much as I want to believe they weren't talking about me just now, I know better. I might be a part of Magni Viri, but I guess I'm still not one of them.

FIFTEEN

Dr. O'Connor asks Neil, Azar, Jordan, Penny, and me to meet in his office late in the afternoon the next day. Laini, the resident director, comes too. I've barely seen her since my initiation. She rarely leaves her study.

"Thank you all for coming," Dr. O'Connor says. "As I said in my email, I wanted to give you an update on Wren and talk about what happened. I'm happy to share that Wren will be coming back to school tomorrow. I spoke to the doctor myself. He said it was nothing worse than a bad case of exhaustion and dehydration, perhaps a lack of regular meals. No concussion, only a few stitches from hitting their head when they fainted."

Of course, we know all this already. We were the ones who found Wren bleeding on the floor, who took that horrible, strained drive to the hospital, who sat anxiously in that waiting room for hours. I bristle at the casual way he brushes off Wren's injury and how little concern he seems to feel about the state they were reduced to.

Perhaps O'Connor realizes he's been too blasé because he clears his throat and adds, "I'm sure it was very unsettling for all of you to find your classmate in that way. Frightening even.

But Wren is fine. They will come home tomorrow, hardly any worse for wear. I want to commend you for the maturity you all have shown, as well as the care and concern you've demonstrated for your friend. Things might have been much worse if you hadn't gone looking for Wren when you did. We take care of one another in Magni Viri. You are all a shining example of that."

No one says anything, but Laini nods and gives us all an approving smile. I cross my arms over my chest. I'm not sure what they think I'm supposed to feel. Proud of myself? Sickness still curdles in my gut at the memory of how Wren looked lying on the floor, small and pale and bleeding. All alone.

"Did you all know that Wren was in that bad of shape?" Laini asks us, her voice tentative. "If you did, why didn't you come to me?"

"Isn't that your job, to make sure things like this don't happen?" Neil interjects, an edge to his words. I wonder if it's guilt for sending Wren out to the practice rooms to begin with.

Laini's cheeks redden. She opens her mouth to say something, but Dr. O'Connor waves her off.

"Let's not point fingers. Let's not blame one another. Wren is an adult, and they—"

"They're not, actually. Wren is seventeen," Neil points out.

We all look at him in surprise. Only last night, he accused us of infantilizing Wren. "And so am I, for that matter."

"Me too," I say.

Dr. O'Connor looks annoyed at the interruption. "Your age isn't important. You are independent people with autonomy, directing your own lives. That's what I meant," he says.

"That is part of the promise of Magni Viri."

Neil snorts. "Our own lives? That's rich," he says.

The others shift uncomfortably.

I have no idea what he's talking about. But everyone else seems to know. Maybe he means he's tired of being controlled by O'Connor.

"You'd think after what happened to Meredith that you'd take a little more care with your students," Neil continues, his voice full of venom.

Dr. O'Connor shoots an equally venomous look at Neil. "This is nothing like what happened to Meredith, and you know that."

"But it's understandable that you would feel that way," Laini says, butting in. She shoots an unreadable look at me. "Meredith hasn't been . . . gone . . . for very long. Of course you can't help but think of her. You can't help but worry that something bad might happen to another of your friends. But Wren is going to be fine," Laini says. "Right, Dr. O'Connor?"

"Correct," he says tightly.

"But how do you know that? What are you going to do to make sure Wren is okay?" I press. A part of me needs to know that this won't happen again, that it won't just be me and the others looking out for Wren, when we failed so miserably this time around.

Dr. O'Connor lets out a frustrated breath. "Look, I know it's cute in our current culture to talk about self-care and boundaries and all that, but to get anything done in this world, you can't think in those terms. You have to give every-thing; you have to give all. Your time, your body, your energy, your youth. You cannot hold back. I am not glad that Wren is in the hospital, but nonetheless, I applaud them. No one in Denfeld Hall works harder or is more devoted than Wren Norwood. No one will make more of a mark upon the music world than Wren will.

"Do they go too far in failing to eat and sleep and care for themself? Perhaps. But Wren is not the first genius to live only for their art, and they will not be the last." O'Connor's eyes light up with an almost religious fervor. "This academic society is utterly devoted to the human capacity for greatness, brilliance, genius. And Wren is the prime example of that. In fact, I would much rather you follow Wren's example than not."

The words hang heavy in the silent room. I look at the others, expecting to see the same shock on their faces that I am feeling. But they don't even look surprised. Maybe they've heard speeches like this before. Jordan's face is serious and composed as always. Neil leans forward with his face in his hands. Azar bites her bottom lip, gazing at the floor. But Penny stares straight at O'Connor, a look of deep dislike on her face, an open contempt that shocks me almost as much as O'Connor's words did.

"However," Dr. O'Connor says, pausing, "we don't want any more accidents this semester. Please make sure that you are eating, sleeping, and caring for yourselves. Keep tabs on one another, look out for one another, just as you have been doing. If the pressure starts to get to you, talk to Laini or to me. But do not let up. Do not become complacent. Do not let this setback keep you from your goals. You all have work to do."

With that, he dismisses us. Neil bolts from the room

without another glance at anyone, his hands clenched into fists. The rest of us file out of the social sciences building, not speaking. But when we break into the open air, Penny swears, which I've never heard her do.

"That son of a bitch," she says quietly, vehemently. "That absolute bastard."

Azar puts a quiet hand on Penny's arm. "He's an asshole, but he's not wrong," Azar says. "This is what we signed up for."

Penny shakes her head. "There has to be another way."

"There isn't," Azar says, her voice tired and resigned. She shrugs. "I gotta go study for my physics exam. See you all later." She turns and walks away without another word. The rest of the group disperses with her, leaving only Penny and me behind.

"Do you really think that's true?" I ask her. "Do you think it has to be like this? Everyone working themselves half to death?"

Penny lets out a frustrated breath. "I think Magni Viri is a fucking cult. You want to go for a walk with me?" She looks at her watch. "Might be able to catch the bats' emergence."

"Thanks, but I think I'd rather be alone," I say. I'm too unsettled to talk to anyone right now, even Penny. I keep replaying what I heard her and Jordan whispering last night, trying to figure out what they meant. They mentioned O'Connor, and their anger at him today seems like it's about more than Wren. Neil brought up Meredith's death, almost as if it was related.

But what does O'Connor have to do with any of that? What does Wren overworking themself have to do with Meredith's aneurysm? Can a brain aneurysm be caused by stress? Maybe they blame O'Connor for Meredith overworking? I can't help but feel that I'm missing something here, something important that everyone else seems to know and understand. But I don't know how to ask what it is. And they're clearly not going to tell me.

I could ask Penny if she and Jordan were talking about me last night and what they meant, but then I'd have to admit I was listening in on their conversation. And I don't want to give Penny a reason to lie to me.

She studies me for a moment before she brushes a fall of hair out of my eyes. "Another time, then."

She gives me a sad, tired smile. I almost lean forward to kiss her, my body drawn to her despite my conflicted thoughts. But I pull myself back.

"See you later," I say, then head back to Denfeld.

Once there, I sit on my bed and stare at Wren's side of the room. Even though they're hardly ever here anyway, I feel their absence keenly. I guess because I know where they are now, what they've been through. They are probably lying in their hospital bed composing in their head, their fingers itching for the piano. But I hope not. I hope they're sleeping, eating, resting. I lie down and pull the blankets up to my chin, my own exhaustion hitting me. It makes me feel guilty, but if I can wish rest for Wren, why not for myself?

Dr. O'Connor said not to let up, not to grow complacent. Maybe how badly I want to close my eyes and sleep shows how unlike the other Magni Viri students I really am. I'm not a genius. I'm not a true artist. I'm a wannabe scribbler.

But at least I'm not in a hospital bed right now.

I try to resist it, but I fall asleep.

When I wake, I am lying on my back in the pitch-black dark. My eyes feel so heavy it's almost as if they are glued closed. I don't try to open them. I lie still and wait for my body to rouse itself. The house is completely silent, except for the distant hum of cicadas. Shouldn't they all be dead by now, or back in the ground?

My thoughts are muddled, confused. The room smells strangely musty, of dirt and rotting things. Close and airless. I shift on my bed, trying to make myself open my eyes and get up. But my sheets feel different, like satin instead of cheap cotton. I run my fingers over them. I touch cool, soft material and then the edge of the bed, a smooth, hard wood, which makes me startle. This isn't my bed. My bed has a metal frame. I try to open my eyes again, but they are unwilling.

Where am I? Did I sleep in someone else's bed? My head swims, fuzzy. I reach a tired hand up to touch my face and meet wood overhead too. My heart explodes in my chest. Frantically, I reach all around me, touching, groping. But I'm completely enclosed—in a closet? A box?

No, I realize, panic surging through me—it's a coffin.

I scream. I scream and I scream and I scream.

I come to at my desk, sitting straight up, pen poised above my notebook. I blink down at my handwriting. The paragraph is barely legible, hardly more than scratches on the page. The pen's ink is all gone. The sentence I was writing hovers in midair, half-finished. *Eugenia knew that she—*

What did Eugenia know? I have no idea. I shiver again and again and again, my teeth clattering together. I'm out of the coffin, but I still feel frozen, the pen clutched in my fingers. My heart pounds like I was running, and sweat beads on my clammy skin.

I was buried alive. I was buried under the ground in the cemetery, my eyelids glued closed. I was buried in a box with satin pillows. Cicadas hummed, their song audible even beneath six feet of dirt.

With enormous effort, I make my fingers drop the pen. Horror spreads through me, metallic and sour on my tongue, cold as damp earth between my toes. I wrap my arms around myself.

It was a nightmare, only . . . I wasn't asleep. I didn't come to, slumped over my desk, drooling on the page. I was sitting upright. I was writing. Was I sleepwriting, the way others sleepwalk? Is that even possible?

Frantic, I flip through the new pages. I don't remember writing a word. It's like I sat here, my brain elsewhere, while someone else's words poured from my pen. The worst part is, they're good. Much better than anything I've ever written.

Because I didn't write this, I realize with sudden, certain shock. It's in my handwriting, and I was sitting here moving my hand across the page, but I didn't write this. Not a single word is mine.

I stagger up out of my chair and back away from my notebook as if it's a repulsive, disgusting thing. If I didn't write these pages, then who did?

The answer comes all too easily: Meredith. It was Meredith

Brown. I took her spot in Magni Viri, I took her friends. Now I'm writing her book. The idea is so bizarre I almost laugh. But I know, deep down, that it's true. I'm being haunted—no, not just haunted. *Possessed.*

I thought I was taking over her life, but what if it's the other way around? What if she is taking over mine?

Pacing, frantic, I think back over the past couple of weeks. I remember walking behind Meredith's body as the EMTs wheeled her out of the library, how I felt like someone walked beside me. That must be the moment it all started. The moment her soul latched on to my body.

And all those creepy phone calls? They were her, just as I suspected. She was trying to make contact. So why have the calls stopped now?

Because she succeeded, I realize, my heart skipping a painful beat. She did more than make contact; she took over. She possessed me.

This time I do laugh, a high, giddy sound that makes me clap my hands over my mouth. I look around, as if someone might have heard.

Only someone did hear. Meredith. She's been with me constantly, watching me move into her house, sit in the library where she sat, eat in the kitchen, hurry down the stairs. She has watched me go to class and answer questions she could have answered better. She has watched me argue with Neil and kiss Penny. And she has waited, ever so patiently, for me to fall asleep.

And then she would creep into my dreams, into my body. She would write her words with my pen, with my hand, with my mind. Like the automatic writing that spiritualists used to do. I remember reading about how the poet W. B. Yeats's wife used to do it. She would let the spirits guide her pen, conveying messages from beyond the veil.

But I didn't agree to this. I didn't invite Meredith in. She stole in, when I lay asleep, vulnerable, unable to fight her. She stole in, and she took over.

Suddenly I am desperate to get out of this room, out of this house, as far away from Magni Viri and Denfeld as I can. I throw on clothes and boots and grab my backpack, then sprint down the hall and down the stairs, through the imposing foyer, and out into the night. I walk fast, as if I can leave Meredith behind, as if she is rooted here in Denfeld Hall. She's not, I know that. But I have to try. I have to get away.

I don't look down at the cemetery. I pretend it isn't there. Meredith isn't buried there, but it doesn't matter. Her spirit is here. Her spirit is here and sending me to sleep in her coffin while she uses my body.

I don't think about where I'm going. After all, I have nowhere to go. I don't have friends on campus, except the ones back in Denfeld. And I can't tell them their beloved Meredith is possessing my body at night. It's impossible. They would look at me with disgust in their eyes. They would hate me.

There's no safe place for me. There is nowhere that Meredith cannot find me, nowhere she cannot reach. I walk all over campus, from north to south, east to west. I watch the other students living their normal lives, laughing and talking. I walk past a guy leaning against a tree, strumming a guitar. When I come across a couple making out in one of the gardens, pressed up against a low wall, I walk as softly and quietly as I can, so I don't disturb them.

I walk until I am nearly insensible, until there is nothing but darkness and sidewalk and cold. I'm halfway down the hallway toward Mr. Hanks's office before I realize where I am. I don't know what's led me here. Maybe my feet are just walking a familiar path. Maybe a part of me wants to go back to an easier time. I start to turn around, but Mr. Hanks hears my footsteps and comes to the door.

"Tara," he says in surprise. "Are you all right?"

"Hi," I say, forcing a bright, cheerful tone, even though the familiar sound of his voice has brought tears to my eyes. "It's been a while, so I thought I'd come see you."

Mr. Hanks laughs. "Miss cleaning floors already?"

I laugh too, though mine is shakier. "Sometimes. It was always quiet, gave me time to think, I guess. Not so much of that these days, what with classes and writing and everything." I babble on, hardly aware of what I'm saying.

"Come in," Mr. Hanks finally says, when I pause to catch my breath. "You want a cup of hot tea to warm you up?"

"You drink tea?" I ask with some surprise.

He smiles a little bashfully. "I seem like a black-coffee man, don't I? But my sister is a tea fanatic. We've lived together ever since her partner died, and she always had a pot around. I developed a taste for it. Now she says I make a better cuppa than she does."

He busies himself with an electric kettle and an old chipped teapot. Before long, he puts a mug of very black tea into my hands. "Milk?" he asks.

When I nod, he pulls a little container of milk out of a minifridge and pours it in. "No sugar, I'm afraid."

I take a sip and smile. The tea is strong and malty, its bitterness cut by the milk.

"You do make a good cup of tea," I say.

He nods but doesn't reply.

We sit in silence for a few minutes, sipping our tea. It warms me from the inside, dispelling some of the sick horror of the last few hours. My mind finally stops whirring.

"Do you believe in ghosts?" I ask him, relieved to hear that my voice is no longer the bright, forced thing of earlier. It's my own, anxious but normal. As if he's noticed it too, Mr. Hanks's shoulders relax, despite my strange question.

"I do," he says simply. His answer doesn't surprise me. The working-class people I grew up around believed in the supernatural too. My mom always swore our old trailer was haunted.

"I think . . . I think one has gotten hold of me," I say. "A ghost."

I expect him to startle, but he stares steadfastly into his mug of tea. It's got the Corbin College logo printed on it. A black swan, beak pointed at the sky.

"The dead girl?" he asks. "From your academic society?"

"Yes," I say, surprised. "I think—I think she's haunting me."

He nods. "They do that, sometimes."

"What should I do?"

He looks up. "Well, it's your life, ain't it? She's got no claim to it. You fight for it. You fight 'er off."

"I could leave Denfeld," I say, "drop out of Magni Viri."

"No," he says sharply. "That's running, not fighting. Don't let her drive you out of your life."

"I'm scared," I say.

"Well, life is scary, girl." He doesn't say it cruelly, only matter-of-factly, the same way you'd say that water is wet, that the sky is blue. "But either it's worth fighting for or it ain't."

Is my life worth fighting for? How many times have I thought that Meredith would live it better, that she deserved breath in her lungs more than I do, that she would make more use of my flesh and blood than I ever will?

And she already has. She's the one who has been writing *Cicada*, not me. Those are her brilliant words, ideas, characters, everything. I am nothing more than a vessel to pour from. A chipped, tea-stained mug with a faded logo.

"Thank you for the tea," I say, setting my empty mug down on Mr. Hanks's desk. I stand to go.

"Tara," he says, and I turn. "Come back anytime. And if you . . . if you ever need help, I'm here. You can always come to me." His voice is gruff, but there's so much gentleness in it that tears spring to my eyes once more.

"I will," I promise him.

He nods. "You're a good, smart girl. You deserve more than the whole lot of these kids put together." He waves his hand, indicating all of Corbin College. "And I believe you'll do more than the lot of them too. I really do."

"Thank you," I say quietly. As I walk alone back to Denfeld Hall, I wish I could believe him.

SIXTEEN

I've been in my room for an hour, but I'm afraid to go back to sleep. I keep thinking about how Mr. Hanks said to fight, but I don't know how. I can't imagine where to even begin. Finally, I head down to the house library to read, hoping it will distract me from my thoughts—and keep me awake.

I stop short in the doorway. Meredith stares back at me from the mantel, brilliant and burning, more alive even in paint than I'll ever be in life. This is the ghost I'm supposed to fight? Her? This girl who latched on to me moments after her death, determined to claw her way back? I was such an easy mark, lonely and drifting, hardly alive myself. Perhaps she knew what was coming even before she died; maybe that night she stared at me in the auditorium with that searching glance that tore right through me, maybe even then she knew. She was waiting for me. Waiting to claim me so she could pick up where she left off.

Anger burns in my chest, momentarily overpowering the fear. Mr. Hanks is right. Why should she have my life? She already had everything—wealth, beauty, genius. Why should she get my life too?

Before I can stop to think, I've reached up and plucked the

painting from the mantel. This close, the smell of the paint is strong, almost dizzying. I squeeze the sides of the canvas, my heart racing and my breaths coming shallow and fast. I could destroy it. I could paint over her face. I could burn her burning eyes. I could rip the canvas into bits and throw it in the swan fountain on the lawn, extinguishing her.

I take a few steps backward, my eyes still on the painting in my hands. But before I reach the door of the library, I thud into a hard, broad chest. I yelp, turning to see who it is.

Jordan.

"You okay?" he asks, steadying me with his hands on my shoulders. Then his eyes narrow as he takes in the way I am gripping Neil's painting. "What's going on?"

I stumble forward and put the painting back on the mantel, nausea boiling in my gut. My face goes hot.

"Are you all right? What's wrong?" Jordan asks.

But I push past him, not answering. I rush out of the library, half-blind. All I can see are Meredith's burning eyes—daring me, mocking me, despising me.

"Tara," Jordan calls after me. He follows me to the foyer. "Tara, what's the matter?"

I shake my head once before I slip out the front door and back into the night. He doesn't come after me, but I walk fast anyway, as if I can outrun him and Meredith both, as if I can turn a corner and she'll lose sight of me, like in a cheesy detective novel.

As if she's not already *inside* me.

I don't know where to go. My feet are still tired from pacing campus earlier. It's the middle of the night. I wish I could go back to my old room with Helena, with her horrid haughty silences. I wish I could climb into that bed and go to sleep and forget that Magni Viri exists, that I had ever set foot in Denfeld Hall. Maybe my ID will still get me into the dorm building. I can go the common room and sit on the couch and watch TV.

Buoyed by the idea, I head straight for my old dorm. It feels like walking back in time. Back before I had friends, when I was drowning in student debt, when I was only a wisp of myself.

Now that my anger has burned off, despair takes its place. I can practically hear Meredith's honeyed voice in my mind, asking me questions I'm not sure I want to answer. *Was she better off, that Tara? Was she truly? Who was she anyway? No one. A girl who had done nothing, been nothing, who hadn't been loved by anyone. Not even her own parents.*

Pursued by these hateful thoughts, I hurry toward my old building. When I hold my ID to the scanner, it clicks and lights up green. My heart leaps. I hurry inside, my head down. The building is nearly silent, the common room deserted.

I collapse onto the couch, relishing the pure animal relief of getting off my feet. But that lasts only a moment before shame and terror and despair creep back in. I'm such a coward, such a waste of space. For the first time since this all started, I hang my head and let myself cry. I clutch the textbook I was carrying to my chest like it's a favorite childhood doll and not a hard-edged, overpriced anthology.

It's a relief to cry, to stop trying so hard to hold myself together. The tears come and come and come. I cry as quietly as I can, my shoulders shaking with sobs no one will hear. Once my tears have finally stopped, I lie on the couch, my back to the room. I feel numb and spent, the sharp blade of fear dulled. My eyes blink closed. And then again.

I'm going to have to sleep, I realize. If I try to stay awake, I'll only make myself sick. I'll only be exhausted and vulnerable. But I know as soon as I surrender to oblivion, Meredith will come. She will come inside and take over.

I set an alarm on my phone for half an hour. How much damage can she do in half an hour? That's what I tell myself, knowing it's a lie, a pitiful deluded hope. But there's no choice. Exhausted, I drop off into darkness, the low buzz of cicadas already filling my head.

Bright sunlight falls across my face, waking me. I blink groggily at the ceiling, the events of last night rushing back.

I sit up fast. It's morning. But that's not possible. It can't be tomorrow already. Eyes barely open, I scrabble in my pocket for my phone, where I placed it after setting the alarm. It's 8:06, four hours past when I was supposed to wake.

I look around, frantic. I'm not in the common room on the nubby old couch. I'm back in my own bed in Denfeld Hall.

Fuck. *Fuck.*

I don't have any memory of leaving the dorm, walking across campus, coming home to Denfeld. There's only the vague atmosphere of a nightmare lingering around the edges of my mind. I push my aching body out of bed, despite wanting to lie there forever. I'm so tired. I don't feel like I've slept at all. What did Meredith do while she was inside my skin last night?

I cross the room to the desk. My notebook is there, closed, a pen on top of it. I open it and flip fast until I hit the last filled page. New words. Of course. Meredith walked my sleeping body all the way back here so she could write. She doesn't care about anything else. She just wants to write her novella. She wants to finish it.

I rub my face, so sick with exhaustion I sway a little. Maybe . . . maybe if I let her finish it, she'll leave me alone. She'll give up this body. Her unfinished business will be done, and she'll go sleep in the earth, where she belongs. Isn't that how ghosts are supposed to work? There's a kind of relief in the idea, an easier path in just letting her take what she wants and moving on after.

I turn away from the desk, not even wanting to read the words Meredith wrote. The excitement of *Cicada* is gone for me. I walk to the full-length mirror attached to the back of the door. I stare at myself.

My eyes are bloodshot, circled with purple. My skin is pale and wan. My hair hangs limp and slightly greasy. I look as used up as an old dishrag. This is after only a few weeks of Meredith's nighttime writing. What will I look like by the end of the semester? Will I even be alive? Or will I follow Meredith to her grave?

I shake my head, pushing away my defeat with the last energy I have. I can't let her do this to me. This isn't why I came to Corbin. If I wanted to look like this, I'd have stayed home, worked a shitty job, got old and exhausted and bitter before I'd even turned thirty. I wanted a different life for myself. I wanted to be more, to do more. I wanted to be happy.

Someone knocks on the other side of the door, startling me. My heart beats so hard I feel it in my throat.

I open the door a crack. Penny is there, looking fresh and clean and sharp as a J.Crew ad. "Good morning. I brought you some coffee," she says, cradling an oversize mug in two hands.

I let her in and take the mug. "Thanks," I say. My voice is hoarse, creaky. I take a sip of coffee. It's bitter and too sweet.

"Are you sick?" Penny asks, putting a hand to my forehead.

I move away, not quite wanting her to touch me. I feel contaminated, made dirty by Meredith's ghost inside me. "I don't know," I say. "Just tired, I think." I set the coffee on my dresser.

Penny sits in my desk chair and crosses her legs, one oxford shoe jiggling. "Jordan said you seemed upset last night. He said you left Denfeld really late and didn't come back before he went to sleep."

I rub my face. "Yeah, I went to my old dorm."

Penny scrunches up her face. "What? Why?"

I study her. She's so logical, her brain so scientific. I don't think she'll believe me if I tell her I'm being haunted by Meredith Brown. Besides, the secrets she's been keeping from me feel like an invisible barrier between us, a warning not to let her in.

"I needed a break from this place," I say, which isn't entirely a lie. "You told me yourself that you find it claustrophobic sometimes, didn't you? So you go to the woods."

"I guess so," Penny says uncertainly. Then she stands and comes toward me, a hesitant concern on her face. "What's wrong, Tara? You can talk to me. I don't want you to get sick and hurt like Wren did. I want to help you if I can." She reaches for my hands, and this time, I steel myself to her touch. I let her take my fingers in hers and warm them. She looks into my eyes. I can see that I'm hurting her feelings by being so cold.

"I'm sorry," I say, looking away. "It's not you. I am just . . . kind of overwhelmed. It's embarrassing."

Penny laughs, relieved. "You don't have to be embarrassed by that. We're all overwhelmed."

"Sure," I say, wanting to end the conversation there. "Look, I had better take a shower and get ready for class. I've got Gothic lit soon. I'm going to be late as it is."

"Of course," Penny says, backing away from me. "We'll talk later, okay?" She smiles, reassuring, but her eyes study mine, as if looking for some sign that we're okay. That I still like her, despite my coldness. That must be what she's worried about.

I'm going to have to do what Mr. Hanks said and fight this ghost, I realize with a pang. Because I won't only lose my nights to Meredith. I'll lose my whole life, including Penny. Maybe I don't totally trust her right now, but I don't want to lose her, not when we've only just begun.

"Penny," I say as she turns away.

She looks back at me. I go to her and give her a quick kiss on the lips.

"Thanks for checking on me. I really appreciate it."

Relief fills her eyes. "Anytime."

I meant to send her away, but her nearness somehow makes me feel more present in my own skin, so I wrap my arms around her in a hug, bury my face in her neck. She squeezes me back, and I hear her breathe in the scent of me.

"You smell good," she says, pulling away with a smile. "Green and sweet like spring."

Her words make me go cold because I smell it too. It's lily of the valley.

Penny kisses me once, softly, not noticing my distress. "I'll let you get ready for class," she says, and then she's gone.

I stand in the doorway for a long moment, feeling sick. Meredith's scent is all over me because she's inside me, because she has me utterly in her grasp.

But I won't let her do this anymore. I won't lie still in her coffin while she finishes her book, while she uses my body like a helpless, lifeless instrument. I refuse. There's too much at stake, too much I have to lose. I don't know how, but I will find a way to make her leave me alone. I *will* find a way to get my life back.

My eyes dart to the notebook on my desk, filled with the pages of Meredith's novella. "I'm not writing your book anymore," I say, my voice fierce. I snatch up the notebook and rip out a big handful of pages, tearing them in half before shoving the whole mess deep into the wastebasket.

As if to mock me, the smell of lily of the valley grows even stronger, a sickly haze that fills the room. Throwing out Meredith's notebook won't be enough.

I need to get her off me, I think, seized with a desperate need to scrub my skin clean. I hurry to find my towel and bathrobe and get in the shower. Luckily, it's free. I soap up and scrub my skin hard, letting the scalding water turn my skin red. I do the same to my hair. The cloying raspberry scent of my drugstore shampoo takes over, and gradually the horror I felt leaves me, replaced once more by exhaustion.

I let the hot water pound my skull, wishing it would wake me up. But it doesn't. If anything, it makes me want to go back to bed even worse than before. I should have drunk more of that awful coffee Penny brought me.

I put conditioner in my hair and then zone out while the water strikes my back. I don't think about anything, my mind nearly perfectly blank with exhaustion.

When I zone back in, I'm standing in front of the foggy bathroom mirror, my finger on the glass. It's like when you go for a drive and suddenly you're at your destination, not remembering any of the turns or red lights in between. I blink at the mirror. There are words scrawled across the glass, words I just wrote with my fingertip.

You promised, they say.

A whimper escapes my lips.

I wasn't asleep. How did Meredith grab hold of me? I was awake. I was moving, showering. I wasn't thinking of anything; my mind was blank. But I wasn't sleeping. This shouldn't be possible.

You promised stares back at me, the letters beginning to drip and fade. I grab my towel from the rack and wrap myself up. I feel faint, sick. Everything seems unreal, impossible. Meredith is growing in strength, I realize, even as I get weaker.

She can control me in any vulnerable, inattentive moment. I'm at her mercy.

Can she read my mind too? Are my thoughts even my own anymore?

I shiver hard, nausea crawling through my stomach and up my throat. What does she mean by *You promised*? What did I promise? I never agreed to anything. I never spoke to her at all.

I stare at the now distorted, disappearing words, paralyzed by dread. But I can't stay here. I can't wait around for her. I have a life to live.

I dry myself off roughly and throw on my bathrobe. I hurry down the hall and get dressed quickly, hardly noticing what I put on, consumed by the need to move. I walk as fast as I can to the English building, shivering as the cold wind whips through my wet hair.

When I open the door to the classroom, everyone turns to look at me. Dr. Hendrix scrunches her brow, glances at her watch. I'm seriously late. I put my head down and find a seat near the back of the room. Once there, I sit up straight, keeping my eyes trained on Dr. Hendrix. I don't let my mind wander, not even for a moment. I take notes and listen carefully to even the most inane of my classmates' comments, determined to not lose an instant of awareness. But I don't raise my hand, and Dr. Hendrix doesn't call on me. She keeps shooting worried little glances at me. I must look completely awful.

After class, before I can rush out, she calls me to her desk. "Tara," she says, trying and failing to smile. "Are you quite all right?"

I rub a hand over my eyes and laugh. "I look that bad, huh?"

"Well, and you were very late today. You're never late," she says.

"I haven't been sleeping well."

"Ah. I see," she says. She pauses. "You're not pushing yourself too hard, are you?"

I shrug. "Maybe."

Dr. Hendrix touches my elbow. "Magni Viri has already had one student in the hospital this semester, Tara. Don't be the next one, all right?"

I nod. Then I realize that Dr. Hendrix might be able to give me information about Meredith. "Have you had a chance to read any of the novella I sent you yet?" I ask.

She smiles. "I actually started it last night. Oh, they are beautiful pages, Tara. Really sharp writing."

A few days ago this would have made me blush with pleasure, but now the compliment suffocates me. I know she's praising Meredith's writing, Meredith's words.

"Did they remind you of anything?" I ask. "Of anyone else's writing?"

"Like whose?" she asks. "A literary inspiration?"

I hesitate. "Like . . . like another student's? Maybe Meredith Brown's?" I bite my lip so hard I taste blood.

She shakes her head, looking surprised at the question. "I never read Meredith's fiction, only her essays for class. But no, no, I wouldn't say that your writing is anything like hers actually."

"Oh," I say, my thoughts grinding to a halt at her words. I thought for sure she would see the similarities. She would have to, right?

"Why did you ask that?" Dr. Hendrix asks, cocking her head. "Is it because of what Dr. O'Connor said at her memorial? You're not comparing yourself to Meredith, are you? You two are very different people, after all."

"I don't know," I mumble. "I don't know what I was thinking."

"I'll read the rest in time for your next tutorial," Dr. Hendrix says. "I look forward to discussing it with you."

"Thank you. Thank you so much," I say, giving my best impersonation of a smile. "I'd better get to my next class. Goodbye."

I leave the room with my head spinning. Why isn't my writing like Meredith's? Maybe it's because her fiction and her essays were written in different styles. Maybe Dr. Hendrix couldn't see the similarities across such different mediums. That must be it. I rack my brain, trying to remember everything about the short story she read at the lit club reading. Was it similar to *Cicada*? Was the cadence of the words the same? The building tension?

My phone dings, startling me. It's a text from Penny saying Wren is back at Denfeld.

SEVENTEEN

When I get to my bedroom, the others are already there. They all go quiet when I come in, an uncomfortable silence that reminds me vividly of the discussion I overheard at the hospital. Were they talking about me? Maybe Jordan told them what he saw in the library, the way I was holding the painting of Meredith. Or maybe they were talking about the thing they've all clearly been hiding from me.

Penny and Azar sit on my bed, which one of them must have made for me because the blanket is spread neatly over the mattress and pillow, unlike the mess I left this morning when I fled this room. Jordan sits at my desk, and Neil leans against the wall. Wren is cocooned in a fluffy throw blanket amid the clutter on their bed, clutching a mug of tea. All my suspicions soften at the sight of them, here and alive and hopefully well.

"Hey," I say, going to Wren's side, steadfastly ignoring Jordan's eyes. I push some books out of the way and climb onto the bed, putting my arm around them in a quick embrace. "How are you?"

"Fine," Wren says. "Still a little tired." They smile. There are dark circles under their eyes, and they are paler than they should be. I can just make out some stitches at their hairline.

"I'm really glad you're back," I say. "I missed you. It was lonely here without you."

"Me too, and I'm glad to get out of that hospital. So many horrible noises everywhere, and the whole place smelled like bleach."

"Sorry," I say. "That sounds rough. Were the doctors any good?"

Wren shrugs. "They were all right. A little clueless. But some of the nurses were really nice." Wren fidgets, uncomfortable. I can't tell if it's from being the center of our collective attention or from something else—like a hankering to find a piano.

"You're going to take it easy for a little while, aren't you?" I ask.

"Of course they are," Penny says, coming from across the room to sit on Wren's other side. "We're going to make sure of it."

Wren looks at me, a hint of concern in the little space between their dark eyebrows. "You look like you've been burning the candle at both ends yourself."

"Oh, come on, enough small talk," Neil says, pushing off from the wall. "Wren, don't go back to the practice rooms. You can play downstairs as much as you want. Just don't be an idiot and get yourself killed, all right?"

Azar laughs. "That was the closest thing to an apology I've ever heard Neil utter. You'd better enjoy it, Wren."

Wren grins.

Everyone stays a while longer, laughing and talking, glad to have Wren back with us. I stay mostly quiet, content to see Wren enjoying themself, even though I can't do the same, not with Meredith's ghost and the others' secrets dogging me, not with my torn-up notebook still in the trash can across the room. But after they all go and it's just Wren and me, Wren slumps down onto their pillows, clearly exhausted by the effort of socializing.

"What really happened?" I ask them. "What made you hit your head?"

"It's like the doctor told you. I hadn't eaten anything. I was dehydrated and going on hardly any sleep. I was run-down," Wren says, but there's a shadow across their expression that makes me think they're hiding something.

"But why did you do that?" I ask. "Why did you push yourself so hard?"

Wren stares at me. "You really don't know?"

"Know what?"

Wren shakes their head. They open their mouth like they want to say something, but then they close it again. "It's the Magni Viri way," they say, with a wry twist of their lips, either unable or unwilling to tell me the truth. I wonder if the others know the real reason, if it's what they were talking about before I came into the room and they all fell silent.

I think it's time to try to get some answers. Because maybe the secret they're all keeping from me has to do with Meredith. Maybe they know something that will help me. Penny, at least, will hear me out, I think desperately. I really didn't want to tell Penny about Meredith haunting me, but I have to tell someone. And Penny's the most likely to open up.

Wren can barely keep their eyes open now, so I leave them

to their nap and go in search of Penny. I know she doesn't have class, so she can't be too far away. But she's not in her room, the library, or the conservatory. I'm about to text her when I glance out a window and see her sitting outside in the back garden, staring off into the trees.

I go to her. She must have earbuds in because she doesn't notice my approach. She's sitting on the strange circular bench that wraps around a tree. It's old and made of black iron, and the tree has grown too big for it, bulging out over the bench in places. Penny leans against the trunk, her long legs spread out in front of her. I can only see half her face, but the expression there is anxious, moody, like she's puzzling over a problem she can't solve.

I touch her shoulder, and it's the sort of thing that would startle most people, but Penny takes a long time to look up at me, and when she does, her expression doesn't change. It's like she's looking at me from within a deep well, not entirely sure whether or not I'm real. The sight makes my skin creep, but then I realize what the expression reminds me of—someone on heavy pain medication. Penny has the same look in her eyes, lost inside herself, like my mom did when she was taking opioids for her back. She must be having a bad pain day and just taken some meds.

I brush some yellow leaves off the bench and sit. I put my head on Penny's shoulder, taking her hand in mine. After a moment, she pulls out one of her earbuds, wipes it on her corduroy pants, and hands it to me. When I put it in, classical music pours into my ear. It sounds familiar, though I don't think it's one of the really famous composers. There's something mesmerizing about it, something that catches you up in its flow and carries you . . .

It sounds like Wren's music, I realize. Maybe this is one of Wren's influences, music that helped shape their style.

"Who is this?" I ask.

Penny pulls her phone from her jacket pocket and shows me the screen. I don't recognize the artist's name, but the composer's leaps out at me: Walter Weymouth George.

"The founder of Magni Viri?" I ask, surprised. It's hard to reconcile his faded image in the painting with this very real music, a song you can listen to on Spotify.

She nods.

"Look, can we talk?" I ask, taking out the earbud and cleaning it on my shirt. There are more important things to discuss than classical music. Penny pockets her earbud, along with its mate when I pass it to her. "Are you up for that on your pain meds?"

"I don't take that kind of medicine," she says, still in that distant, abstracted way from before. It's like she's coming out of a trance. "I'm on anti-inflammatory and immune-suppressing drugs. But yeah, what's up?"

"Oh, sorry," I say, "you just seem . . ." I trail off, afraid of offending her. "Never mind. It's just that—well . . . some weird stuff has been happening to me."

Penny stiffens beside me. "Oh?"

"I'm afraid I'll sound . . ." I taper off, biting my lip.

"What is it?" Penny asks, sitting up straighter, suddenly alert. She puts her hand on my knee. She looks like she's steeling herself.

I take a deep breath, then let it all out at once. I may as well put all my cards on the table. Maybe if I'm totally honest with her, she'll tell me what they've all been hiding too.

"I don't think I'm the one who's been writing *Cicada*," I say in a rush. "I think . . . I think it's Meredith. I always write at night when I should be sleeping, and I wake up and there are all these pages I barely remember writing. And I'm having these dreams, Penny. They feel so real. Like I'm in a coffin."

Penny doesn't say anything, her face grave. I press on. "And this morning when I got out of the shower, I wrote these words on the mirror. Only . . . I didn't know I was writing them. It was a message for me, from Meredith."

"What did it say?" Penny asks quietly, her voice strained.

"It said 'You promised.'"

Penny nods. "You tried to stop writing the novel, didn't you?"

"Yes," I say, shocked. "How did you know?"

She looks away, back toward the trees. Several emotions pass over her features, and I can tell she's wrestling with herself. She opens her mouth and closes it. She takes a deep breath. Finally, she shakes her head and turns to me. "Look, why don't you just finish it? Just write the book and then see how you feel after?"

"What?" I say through an incredulous laugh, my insides turning to ice. She can't possibly be serious. This can't be her response. I shake my head.

"Don't you understand?" I press. "It's not my book to write. It's *Meredith's*."

Penny stares at me, her eyes pleading. She swallows hard,

as if to push down words she can't say. When she finally speaks again, her voice is low and soft. "What is your biggest dream? The thing you want more than anything?"

"I want to be a writer," I say. "But—"

"And you got your wish. You're writing, and Magni Viri is footing the bill." Penny smiles, but it's a desperate, terrified thing.

I stand up fast, my face hot with anger and disbelief. "Magni Viri is paying my way, so I should just shut up and be grateful? Are you serious right now? Have you heard a word I said? I'm being haunted by Meredith!" I nearly scream the last words, all of my fear and frustration coming to a head.

Penny leans away from me, shocked, before she regroups. "No, you're not," she says evenly. "You're not, Tara. I promise. Meredith is way down in Savannah, Georgia, in one of those fancy family plots in Bonaventure Cemetery you always see in the movies. She's hundreds of miles away from here."

I shake my head hard, infuriated by the calm, soothing way Penny is speaking to me, as if I'm delusional. "Remember this morning, when you told me I smelled sweet and green like spring? Wasn't that scent familiar to you?"

Penny's brow scrunches. "What are you talking about?"

"That wasn't my perfume. It was Meredith's!" I say, desperate for her to believe me. "I smelled it on her when she died, and then later in her room. And now I smell like it too."

Penny blinks, confused or maybe just pretending to be. "Mer didn't even wear perfume. She had a fragrance allergy or something. Neil had to stop wearing cologne because it made her throat close up."

"Why are you lying to me? I saw the bottle of it in her desk," I say, my face flaming as I realize I've admitted to snooping through Meredith's things.

Penny raises an eyebrow as she realizes it too. "Her asshole of a mom sent her perfume for her birthday, perfume she knew Meredith couldn't wear. That's it."

I stare at Penny, uncomprehending. She's lying to me. She has to be. And it's not like when I overheard her talking with Jordan either, keeping secrets from me. This time she's looking me straight in the face and lying. She didn't even react to the outlandish idea that I'm being haunted, which means whatever secret the rest of Magni Viri is keeping, it's definitely about Meredith, and not even Penny is willing to tell me what it is.

"I thought I was one of you now," I spit, anger briefly eclipsing the hurt. "What happened to Magni Viri taking care of its own?"

Penny smiles, sad and resigned. "We are taking care of you. This is me taking care of you. Go write your book, Tara. That's all I can say."

I stare at her, realizing what a mistake I have made. Life has taught me again and again that I'm on my own, that no one is going to take care of me. Of course Penny isn't any different.

"I knew I shouldn't have trusted any of you," I say, shaking my head, backing away from her. "And I shouldn't have tried to talk to you about this."

"Yeah, maybe you shouldn't have," Penny says, wiping her eyes, which are suddenly red-rimmed and shiny, as if she's holding off tears. But instead of explaining or apologizing, she gets up and walks away from me without another word. She heads straight into the woods, not even bothering to find a trail. I stand gaping at her retreating back, as she is swallowed up by brush and leaves.

"Penny!" I yell, fury filling my chest. "Penny, come back here!"

She doesn't reappear, and I don't expect her to.

"Fuck," I say. "Fuck."

I sit down hard on the bench and lean forward, clutching my hair at the roots. I'm so tired. God, I'm so tired. And I don't understand what in the hell just happened between us. How she could act like that and then just walk away from me.

Before I can stop myself, I start to cry. Hot tears pour down my face, and my nose starts to run. Before long, it builds to a shuddering sob. I don't know what else to do, so I let myself cry, a cold breeze doing its best to dry my cheeks.

Once all the tears are gone, I wipe my face on my sleeve and stare blearily at the ferns in the flower bed, still vibrant green, even as the rest of the world has begun to fade.

I don't understand why everyone is lying to me, hiding things from me. I keep trying to think of an explanation, but it's like grasping at straws. Did they *kill* Meredith? Is that why she's here and haunting me, clinging desperately and obsessively to Magni Viri through me? But that doesn't explain everyone's behavior, like why Wren is so fixated on their music they could have died from it. Why Penny was just zoned out like she was high. Why Neil paints half the night and drinks for the rest of it.

Azar and Jordan are a little better, though Azar seems tired and almost despondent in her acceptance of Magni Viri's demands. Jordan is always up studying earlier than anyone, and whenever I ask where Azar is, the answer is invariably the robotics lab. Still, they're both even-keeled and never seem to go too far. At least not that I've seen yet. I don't think they could have been involved in Meredith's death.

With a shuddering sigh, I realize none of them could have. They're not killers. I'm sure of it. It's the only thing I'm sure of.

So maybe every member of Magni Viri is exactly what I thought they were when I first arrived: Exceptional. Obsessive. Brilliant. Doing work that matters.

And me . . . I am too, at least with Meredith inhabiting my skin. She's the only thing that makes me fit into Denfeld Hall. Without her, I don't make sense. Without her, I'm no one special, an ordinary girl among prodigies.

Maybe Penny's right. Maybe I should write my little book and keep my mouth shut. That's what I've told myself half a dozen times already. Don't look a gift horse in the mouth. Don't rock the boat. Don't go digging for things better left buried. Just keep going. Keep writing.

I'm not sure I have any other choice.

Because as horrifying as the thought of sharing my body with a ghost is, Meredith might be the only chance I have of achieving my dreams. Even if it's not *my* mark I'd be leaving on the world.

This morning I was prepared to fight for my life, but that's over now. I was worried about losing Penny and the others, but I can see I've already lost them. They were never mine to begin with. My life in Magni Viri was always a lie. I close my eyes and let the resolution grow inside me: I won't fight her. I won't try to run. I will let her write her novella. I will let her fulfill her unfulfilled business.

And once she's done, I can only hope she'll move on and let me live inside the existence she has built for me. That's my only way ahead.

At least for now, my life belongs to Meredith Brown.

EIGHTEEN

The weekend and the following week pass in a sleepless haze. I skip the Sunday night party, texting Quigg to say I have food poisoning, the only excuse I can think of that will let me stay in my room all weekend.

At some point, my notebook finds its way out of the trash, its torn pages taped back inside, jagged as a living wound. I write, go to class, do my homework. I keep mostly to myself, and Penny doesn't seek me out. She's avoiding me. She lied to me, walked away from me when I needed her, and now she's doing everything in her power to avoid being in the same room with me. Once, I catch her watching me from across the quad, her hair fluttering in the cold wind, but when our eyes meet, her mouth goes hard and she turns away, as if I'm nothing to her.

Maybe this is who she is—a liar, a fake, someone who pretends to care right before she breaks your heart. I thought we had a connection, something special. But I see now that she never felt about me the way I feel about her. It was stupid to throw myself into a relationship with her so fast; stupid to trust her so completely. I won't make the same mistake twice. I won't make the same mistake with anyone.

I eat lunch with the others sometimes and see Wren often enough. But Penny must have told them about our conversation because there's a charged kind of silence between me and the others now. We all know that something fundamental has broken between us. I'm not sure it can ever be repaired. They aren't avoiding me, but they might as well be.

Cicada inches forward, page by dreadful page, its eerie, tense world as real to me as my own. More real perhaps. I spend more time with Eugenia and Coy than with anyone else. I live inside the world that Meredith is creating.

Each morning, when I wake stiff-necked at my desk, my fingers ink-stained and sore, I dutifully type the pages that Meredith wrote with my hand. I correct the typos and supply the missing words. I email them to Dr. O'Connor and Dr. Hendrix.

I go through the motions of being a college student, but there's nothing of me left for anything more. Meredith uses nearly every drop. I feel heavy in my body, my mind dull. I walk slowly, speak slowly. My joints hurt, and my limbs feel like they're filled with lead. I wonder if this is what Penny feels like during one of her flares.

I begin to think that Meredith is doing more than inhabiting my body. I think she's changing it, reshaping it.

Because every time I catch sight of myself in a mirror, just out of the corner of my eye, I have to do a double take. I never look quite like myself. Sometimes my straight eyebrows are too angled, or my mouth is wider than it ought to be, or my hair is a shade darker than its usual dirty blond. Even my freckles seem to fade sometimes, as if the pigment is leaching from my skin. In those moments, I blink at myself until the wrongness disappears, until it's my own face again.

But as the week crawls on, I grow afraid of mirrors and stop looking at all, ignoring my reflection everywhere I go.

I'm afraid that one day I'll look into a mirror and Meredith's face will be staring back at me.

By the time Sunday comes around again, I've realized the enormity of my mistake. The truce I've made with Meredith isn't temporary. I've surrendered to her, body and soul. And it's too late for take-backs. I'm completely in her grip—why would she ever let go?

As the daylight wanes, the house grows restless and tense, everyone keyed up in preparation for the cemetery party. But I lie in bed all day, too exhausted to do anything. I don't even sleep. I lie still while the sun's rays move across the hardwood floor of my bedroom.

Wren brings me tea and water, a few snacks. I drink and eat without tasting anything. They try to talk to me, but the words don't make the transition from sounds into meaning. I feel suspended, as if in a twilight state, the world not entirely real.

I've made my body and my mind a perfect dwelling place for Meredith Brown, so soft and easy for her. Helpless to her control.

When the sun goes down, my body gets up. I don't mean for it to. But it does. It puts on its clothes and brushes its hair and its teeth. Like a plucked string, it hums with the collective energy of Denfeld Hall, all those excited voices, those hurrying feet.

My own feet carry me down the stairs and across the lawn. I pass the black swan statue. The water has been turned off, so the creature's beak points meaninglessly at the dark sky, heavy with gray clouds.

It makes me think of how Meredith looked when she died, her body in the library so cold and so still, the light gone from her eyes. An empty shell.

But she found another shell, didn't she?

I recognize the silhouettes ahead of me—all of the other Magni Viri freshmen, Penny at their center. They walk in a tight group, their heads together, talking. My body quickens its pace a little, as if it wants to hear what they say.

"Look, we knew what this was, when Tara came here. We all knew what we were agreeing to," Neil says.

"But—" Penny starts to say.

"It's not like she has other options," Azar says, cutting across her. "With *her* background."

"But I just feel—" Penny tries again.

"Hey, no one told you to date her," Neil says brutally.

Penny rubs her face tiredly. "I know. Maybe that was a mistake."

"Well, what about me? I'm the one who has to share a room with her. Do you know how hard that is?" Wren says.

"I'm sorry, Wren—" Jordan says, breaking off, as if he senses my presence. He turns and sees me. "Oh, hey. You feeling better? Wren said you were in bed all day."

I stare at them, some distant part of me curdling at the casual way they're looking at me, as if they weren't just complaining about me, talking dismissively of my *background*, as if they weren't regretting my existence. As if all along they haven't been pretending. And why? What are they getting out of it?

"Yes," I say. "Yes, I'm better." My voice doesn't sound like my own, too low and somehow old-fashioned, almost monied-sounding. Is that what Meredith sounded like? I can't remember.

Perhaps the others hear it too because they exchange glances I can't read. We keep walking, now in silence, almost at the cemetery. Suddenly, Penny stops and turns to me. "Listen, Tara, there's something I need to say."

"Penny," Azar says. "Not now, not here."

"No, it's time. It has to be time," Penny says. "This has gone on too long." She takes a deep breath, as if she's steeling herself. Is she about to break up with me? In front of all our friends? *Her* friends, I accept dully.

"Someone's coming," Jordan says, a warning in his voice. He looks over my head and waves. I turn. It's Quigg, dressed to the nines and carrying a bottle of bourbon in either hand. He's smiling hugely, clearly already well on his way to drunk. He lifts up one of the bottles, as if to make a toast, and I half expect him to yell something about partying, as if we're in a nineties teen rom-com. But instead, he starts reciting a soliloquy, his voice deep and resonant. It's mesmerizing, even in my hazy state of mind. I can imagine what he's like onstage, utterly transformed by the magic of theatre. Dimly, I recognize the words from *Macbeth*.

"Tomorrow, and tomorrow, and tomorrow,
Creeps in this petty pace from day to day
To the last syllable of recorded time,
And all our yesterdays have lighted fools
The way to dusty death. Out, out, brief candle!
Life's but a walking shadow, a poor player
That struts and frets his hour upon the stage
And then is heard no more. It is a tale
Told by an idiot, full of sound and fury,
Signifying nothing."

At the end of his speech, Quigg lowers the bottle. "Ha!" he says. "Shakespeare was wrong, wasn't he? At least about some of us!" Then he laughs and laughs and laughs. He wraps an arm around me, still clutching the bourbon. Neil snatches it from his grasp and unscrews the bottle, then takes a big swig.

I'm not even sure why, but I grab the bottle from Neil and take a sip. It burns like fire going down my throat, making me grimace, but it's the first thing I've been able to feel in days. I take another sip. The liquor matches my mood: sharp and bitter. It tastes like disappointment and grief and simmering anger. I lift the bottle to my lips once more.

"That's my girl!" Quigg says, leading me into the cemetery. I look back once at Penny, who shakes her head. I don't even want to know what she was going to tell me. I don't want to hear any more lies.

The fairy lights glitter in the trees, and my head swims pleasantly. I wish suddenly that I could leave this body to

Meredith and float free in the treetops, free as dandelion seeds on the breeze.

I take another sip of bourbon, and then another.

And after that, I get my wish.

I wake up sometime in the early morning, when the birds are starting to stir but the sky is still blue-black. For the first time in my life, I am hungover. My mouth tastes terrible, and my stomach feels like its lining has been burned away. Everything hurts. I feel a little ashamed of myself.

But at least I *can* feel.

At least I'm in my bed, and not at my desk. At least I slept. I guess my drunk body wasn't any use to Meredith. Or maybe I washed her away with all that bourbon. My head throbs and my stomach lurches. But I feel less vague than I have in days, more like myself, more like the body I inhabit is my own.

But now that I can feel again, the memory of how my friends were talking about me last night comes rushing back, and this time the pain isn't dim and distant. I feel the betrayal like a huge fist squeezing my heart. Wren said they hated rooming with me. Penny said it was a mistake to date me. All along, they've been pretending. All along, they've been using me for some obscure reason of their own.

My stomach churns with nausea, and I can't tell if it's from the betrayal or the alcohol. But when the nausea reaches its crest, I shoot out of bed, still in last night's clothes, and stagger down the hall to the bathroom, a hand over my mouth.

I throw up three times. When I'm finally able to peel myself off the cold tile, I stick my head under the faucet to rinse my mouth. I wash my face with soap and cold water. But as I pull the towel away from my face, I forget to avoid looking in the mirror.

A strangled scream dies in my throat.

Someone else's face stares back at me.

I blink, thinking it will go away like all the times before, that it's a trick of my tired eyes and the weak morning light. But the same wrong face stares at me from the mirror, a pleased little smirk on its lips. My worst fears have come true, and they are mocking me.

The face's eyebrows are angled up, the eyes are brown, the nose is blunt and small. The mouth is wide, with frown lines on either side of it. There's a funny little divot on the right side of the forehead, as if this girl lifts her eyebrow a hundred times a day.

Except that she's not a girl at all. She's a woman. She must be at least thirty years old, maybe even forty.

I lean toward the mirror, barely breathing, feeling like I might pass out. She leans in too, her eyes studying mine. She smirks again and lifts her eyebrow.

I touch the little divot in her skin with trembling fingers and see the motion reflected in the mirror.

Her face is my face.

My skin goes hot and then cold. Panic courses through me.

Because the woman in the mirror is not Meredith Brown.

NINETEEN

I stare at myself—not myself—

I stare at *her*. My hands shake. Or are they her hands?

This woman in the mirror . . . Is she my ghost, my captor, the author of my book? Did she dream up Coy, Hazel, Eugenia, and all the rest? Is this the one who drags me each night from my bed to tell their story? To tell *her* story?

"Who are you?" I whisper, half expecting the reflection in the mirror to answer, as if it has a body separate from mine. But my lips don't move, and neither do hers. She stares at me, waiting.

With a cry, I turn away from the mirror, shoving my fingers deep into the roots of my hair. I pull hard, and the sensation returns me to myself a little, makes the bathroom stop feeling like one of those funhouse-mirror attractions they have at the fair.

"I am Tara Boone," I say to myself, my voice a strained, wild thing. "I am Tara Marie Boone. I'm seventeen years old. I was born in Gaiman, Florida. My mother's name is Bethany Charles. My father's name is Thomas Boone. I have no brothers and no sisters—well, I do, but they don't really count. I . . . I broke my arm when I was seven, falling out of a tree. I scored a twenty-nine on the ACT because I bombed the math. My favorite book is *Jane Eyre*. My favorite color is . . . is maroon."

The basic facts of myself make me feel a little more tethered to earth. I'm still *me*, despite the ghost taking up residence inside me. After a few deep breaths, I turn back around and look in the mirror. I instinctively flinch away, but it's my own face that I now see there. My own tired, haggard, exhausted face. Little red dots have risen to the surface of the skin around my eyes, thanks to all that puking. My eyes are bloodshot and my own usual blue. There's a pimple on the side of my nose. My skin looks oily and pale, my freckles brighter than usual.

I've never been so glad to see my own face, terrible as it looks. But I know it's not the entire truth. *She's* still under there. I can feel her beneath my skin. I can see her features like smudged-out pencil beneath my own. She has taken root in my body, in my mind. This stranger. This woman.

It was bad enough when I thought that beautiful, mysterious, brilliant Meredith Brown was possessing me. But this is abhorrent, unbearable. I don't want a strange woman sharing my brain, my blood. It's a violation. It's disgusting. I feel like cockroaches are crawling under my skin.

"Get out," I growl at the mirror. "Get out! Leave me alone. Get out!"

My own face stares back at me, its features twisted with despair, revulsion. The woman who has stolen my body doesn't answer. She doesn't acknowledge me.

Someone knocks on the bathroom door, making me jump. I stare at the door. The knock comes again.

"Hey, let me in! I really need to go!" someone shouts, banging on the door again.

I cross the room and open the door, and Azar nearly tumbles into the bathroom. She barely looks at me before she pushes me out and slams the door behind her. A moment later I hear her throw up.

Like a sleepwalker, I pad through the hall and into Azar's room. I walk straight to Meredith's desk and open the drawer. The little bottle of perfume sits there in its silk scarf. I pull it out and spray it on my wrist.

Roses. It smells like dried roses, crushed and spiced.

Not lily of the valley.

I drop the perfume bottle back into the drawer and leave the room, drifting down the stairs, as if I'm searching for something I've lost but I can't remember what. My mind can't take all of this in. Am I having a psychotic break? Is this what schizophrenia feels like? I never even considered the possibility before, when I thought it was Meredith haunting me.

But this is something completely different. This is . . .

I stand in the doorway to the library, staring at the painting of Meredith. All this time, I've been obsessed with her. Half in love with her at times, half enraged by her at others. Always jealous, always insecure. Sometimes giving myself over to her power, sometimes fighting her with all I'm worth. But she was never here. She was only a memory.

The painting is as alive and vibrant as ever, but it has lost its terror now. Meredith is only a girl, a dead girl. She's nothing to do with me. Someone completely different has me in her clutches. Someone older and smarter and far more powerful.

I wish it had been Meredith now. I could bear it if it were Meredith.

I turn away from the painting and pad into the kitchen for a glass of water. Just as I bring the water to my lips, Penny walks into the room. She flinches and takes a step back. We stare at each other for a long moment. I remember how I told her that I was being haunted. She wasn't surprised. She wasn't concerned. She told me that I should just finish the book and see how I felt.

She knew. She wasn't surprised because she knew. She knew it wasn't Meredith but someone else. And she didn't say anything. She walked away from me.

And last night, she said our relationship was a mistake.

Anger flares up in my chest, hot and bright, blotting out even my fear. I want to yell at her. I want to scream. I want to throw my glass against the wall. Instead, tears prick my eyes and clog my throat, the way they always do.

"Morning," Penny says awkwardly, going to the teakettle.

I watch as she fills the kettle and places it back on its heating element. She pulls down a mug from the cabinet and a little metal strainer. She measures a teaspoon of black tea into it. Then she has nothing else to do with her hands; she has to wait for the water to boil.

She risks a glance at me. I can't read her expression. I have no idea who she is, I realize. She's a stranger, same as the ghost inside me. I might have kissed her. I might have lain under the green canopy of the conservatory with her, swapping quotations from *The Secret History*. I might have held her hand in the cemetery. I might have memorized every detail of her face.

But I do not know her.

She's a stranger, and she lied to me. Whatever we had together is over now.

"Tara," she says. "I want to—"

Without a word, I leave the room, tears rolling down my cheeks.

As if on autopilot, I take a shower and get dressed, instinctively avoiding every mirror. Wren is still sleeping, their face smooshed into a pillow. I gather my books and papers and leave the room, and then the house.

It's a cold, clear morning. The leaves on every tree are stark red and bright yellow, ochre and bloody pink—each of them printed against a cloudless, cerulean sky. It's almost too perfect, like a picture for the college website, captioned "Corbin College in the fall." Laughter rings out across the courtyard, red-nosed coeds hurrying to their classes. Everyone looks sharp, definite, unbearably vital and alive.

But I pass through it all as if in a dream. Maybe I'm in shock.

I even cross paths with Helena, who sneers at me and then does a double take. I wonder if she can see the woman too, or if she's just surprised by how run-down I look. It doesn't matter. She can't help me.

I go to my classes. I barely listen, my entire attention focused on the woman inside my skin. What did she do with me in all those lost hours? Did she only write her book? She could have taken me anywhere, done anything with me, and I wouldn't know.

The thought sends a cold, leaden feeling through me.

Vaguely, I recognize it as dread.

What if she's dangerous? What if she makes me hurt someone?

What if she makes me hurt myself—more than she already has?

I shiver, hard. So hard my teeth clack together. The girl sitting next to me looks over and then leans away from me, as if afraid I'm contagious.

I squeeze my eyes closed. I have to get control of myself. I have to do something.

The second class is over, I gather my things and rush out of the classroom. I decide to skip lunch. I didn't eat breakfast, but I'm not hungry at all. The thought of the woman hiding beneath my skin, inside my mind, has obliterated even the thought of food. I go straight to my bedroom. Wren is gone, their cheerful clutter everywhere.

I sit at my desk and pull out the notebook that I've—that *she's*—been writing *Cicada* in. I open it with shaking hands. I study the shapes of the letters on the page, the places the ink blots and scratches, as if the markings can tell me something about her. My hand formed each word, but her mind wrote it, not mine. There must be something of her here. Something that will tell me who she is.

I start at the beginning of the novella and I read, looking for clues of her. The first thing I realize is the tenderness with which she writes about Eugenia. Eugenia ought to be the villain of the book. She is clearly evil, seducing unsuspecting college boys and leading them one by one to their deaths. But she . . . isn't.

The woman paints Eugenia as beautiful and intelligent, as someone who feels deeply, someone with a righteous cause. How did I not see this before? The readers aren't meant to condemn Eugenia; they're meant to root for her.

I would never write a character like that . . . would I?

I read on, letting myself get caught up in the story in a way I couldn't when I thought I was the one writing it. I read it like I would a book from the library, turning the pages with breathless urgency.

And I start to understand it—her fondness for Eugenia. Eugenia's family has always been downtrodden, looked down on. She is smarter than all the boys at the college, smarter even than many of the professors who cross her path. But she's seen as nothing more than a cheap body to be used and discarded. Isn't her anger reasonable? Isn't it righteous?

The writing stops at what must be the midpoint of the novella, a tense and almost visceral scene where Eugenia realizes she's pregnant. She wraps her hands around her stomach, and a flow of terrible, possessive love washes over her. I shiver, knowing that this love won't make her milder, more tender, won't stop her ruthless quest for revenge and dominance. It will only lead her to ever bloodier lengths. Because now she won't act only from a place of frustration and nihilism. She has something to fight for, something to kill for. Eugenia is more dangerous than she has ever been.

With a little gasp, I sit back in my chair. The woman I saw in the mirror this morning has a mind far darker and far bleaker than my own. And I want it out—I want her mind out of my brain. I want *her* out.

Without thinking, I scrape my nails viciously down the front of my arm, as if I could scratch the woman out of my skin. I cry out at the pain. My nails are trimmed short, but they still leave deep red lines across my skin, blood welling up in a few spots.

Just then, the door opens and Wren hurries in. "Are you okay?" they ask. "I thought I heard you— Oh. Oh, Tara." They drop their stuff at the door and walk slowly toward me. "You hurt yourself." Their voice goes soft, as if speaking to a wounded animal. "I've got a first aid kit. Let me help you."

I gape at them, unsure how to explain myself. Or if I should even try. Talking to Penny didn't go so well, after all. Besides, I heard what they said about me last night, about the burden of rooming with me. I pull my sleeve down to cover my arm.

"I'm fine," I say. "I— My arm was itching and I guess I scratched a little too hard." My voice sounds strained and rusty around the edges.

"Pull your sleeve up. You'll get blood on your shirt," Wren says matter-of-factly.

I stand up. "No, I should—"

"Please," Wren says. They hold out the first aid kit. "Let me help you."

I'm too overwhelmed to argue. I sit back down and pull up my sleeve, smearing blood across my skin.

Wren pulls their desk chair over and sits beside me. Without a word, they start to clean my arm.

"I really wasn't trying to hurt myself," I say. "It was an accident."

"Okay," Wren says. "But even if you were, I'm not judging you. And I'm not going to fuss over you, because I hate when people do that to me."

"Thanks," I say, struggling to reconcile this kind, thoughtful person in front of me with the one who complained about rooming with me last night, the one who has been lying to me. It doesn't make sense.

They put antiseptic on the worst of the cuts, along with a few Band-Aids for the bleeding spots. "There you go, that should heal up nicely." They push back their chair.

"Thank you," I say, pulling my sleeve down again.

Wren looks at me like they want to say or ask something. "Are you . . ." Their words trail off, and then their eyes fall to the notebook on my desk. "How's your novel coming along?" they ask instead.

"Novella," I say automatically. "It's . . . fine. Maybe halfway done." My face burns with shame, as if I'm taking credit for someone else's work.

"You'll feel better when it's done," Wren says. "I always do, when I finish a composition. It's like a release."

My head snaps up. That's the same thing Penny said to me out on the bench under the tree the other day. To just finish the novel.

Another thing from that conversation comes back to me. "Walter Weymouth George," I say, and Wren flinches.

"What?" they ask, already on guard.

"Penny was listening to some classical music the other day. By one of Magni Viri's founders, Walter Weymouth George. It reminded me of your music. Is he an influence of yours? Is he why you wanted to join Magni Viri?" I keep my voice as level as I can.

Wren stares at me for a long time, their expression stricken. "Yes, yes, I suppose so," they finally say. Then, "Tara, are you— Do you . . . ?

I wait, my eyebrows raised, my heart starting to race.

But Wren shakes their head, fear in their eyes. "I—I'd better go. I told Quigg I'd help him with something." Before I can open my mouth to call them back, Wren is out of the room.

And now I'm sure. Penny knows what's going on with me, and so does Wren. All of the first-years know. All this time they've known and they kept me in the dark. None of them tried to help me. Not even Wren. Not even Penny. Instead, they pretended to care about me, to be my friends. They're still pretending, even now.

Because they're wrapped up in this too, in ways I don't understand. There have been so many signs. I've been a fool to miss them. The way Wren plays the piano, the way Neil paints. The way Penny was zoned out that day we fought. How they're all working on projects that are more advanced than they have any right to be. How they've all resigned themselves to the brutal demands of Magni Viri, as if there's no other choice.

Could they . . . ? I hesitate. Could they be going through what I am? Could they have ghosts of their own, ghosts like mine? But if they did, why would they hide it from me? What would be the point?

Penny could have told me when I tried to talk to her about being haunted. But she didn't. She walked away from me, left me to deal with it alone. They all did, in their own ways. Is that what she and Jordan were whispering about that night at the hospital, wondering if I'd figured things out yet? Was that the unspoken thing in Wren's eyes every time we talked about Magni Viri? The secret behind Neil's opaque comments and Azar's careful answers? They all clearly decided not to help me. But more than that, they made a conscious choice to leave me in the dark, for some reason I can't begin to fathom.

They have secrets of their own, secrets they've been determined to hide since the day I set foot in Denfeld Hall.

TWENTY

It's late. Again. I know I need to go to bed. I know my body needs rest, especially after I poisoned it with alcohol at the cemetery party. But I can't stand to fall asleep and lose control, not any longer. Not now that I know a total stranger is waiting in the wings to possess me. A stranger with a dark mind and questionable morals.

So I go walking. It's very cold—a sharp, insistent bite of air against my skin. The sky is clear and scattered with stars. The campus is quiet. The cicadas have finally finished for the season, the newly hatched nymphs crawling back underground for another thirteen years.

As I walk toward the cemetery, I wonder if the ghosts can hear the cicadas moving in the earth, or if the cicadas sleep quietly the way the dead are supposed to. The thought makes me shiver worse than the cold night air.

Because some of the dead don't sleep. They don't rest. They rise up from their graves to steal hours from the living.

A graveyard at night is the last place I ought to want to be, but I'm already haunted, so what harm can it do? I stand at the cemetery gate, my hands clenched around the cold iron bars. I hold still for a moment, thinking of my initiation night, when

I was so hopeful, so excited to join Magni Viri, to give up my solitude in exchange for their strange belonging.

The latch gives, and the gate creaks open.

As I walk down the path, that night rushes back to me. My friends giddy on the stairs, running across the lawn with Azar. The circle of candles, the eerie music. The feeling of leaving my own body and joining up with something greater than myself.

I abandon the path and wander among the gravestones. It's dark beneath the trees. Near the middle of the cemetery, Walter Weymouth George's mausoleum glows a little in the moonlight. The cold air breathes against the back of my neck, stirring my hair. I shiver and keep walking.

Here's where I lay on a blanket with Penny, gazing up at the stars. I walk on. Here's where I leaned against a tombstone, kissing her. Isn't this close to where I stood when I made my vows too? I run my fingers over the damp, mossy stone.

Tears burn my eyes. I turn too quickly and trip, landing hard on my knees, scraping my palm against rough stone. The smell of the earth surrounds me, damp and cold, just like in my dream of being in my ghost's coffin. But then, rising above it, sharp and sweet, is lily of the valley.

I let out a horrified moan and scramble for my phone. I don't want to be alone in the dark with her. I flick on the flashlight, and its cold white beam illuminates the grass and the fallen leaves, the gravestone shaped like an open book that I must have scraped my hand on.

I kneel in front of it and brush the damp, clotted leaves off the tombstone. A cicada exoskeleton rolls off with them.

I shiver, and then I freeze.

The name on the tombstone is Isabella Rebecca Snow. Born 1931, died 1967.

Isabella. Why is that name familiar?

I squeeze my eyes tight, suddenly dizzy. I remember voices calling in Latin, desperate cries echoing through the woods.

That's right. The night that Meredith died, I went walking in a haze and ended up here at the cemetery . . . and I heard the Magni Viri students yelling for someone named Isabella. I'd thought I was wrong, that they were yelling something in Latin. But what if they really were calling for Isabella?

This Isabella? Not a lost dog or a person . . . but a ghost.

I scramble back from her gravestone, my mind racing.

This is where I stood when I made my vows and gave a drop of my blood. This is where it all started. My new life. My initiation into Magni Viri. What did the words on that paper Laini gave me say? What words did I speak into the darkness?

I promise to be a vessel for genius, for the profundity of the human mind, for the sacred act of creation. That's the only part I remember.

I open my eyes and blink into the bright light from my phone. *A vessel.*

I promised to be a vessel.

I thought it was some silly metaphorical crap, a testament to Magni Viri's collectively massive ego. But what if it was more than that? What if it was a literal vow? What if when I spilled my blood on this grave, I actually promised my body to . . . to what? To a ghost? To Isabella Snow?

I remember the words I—*she*—wrote on the bathroom

mirror the other day. *You promised.* That's what it said.

I promised.

I did this to myself, I realize, a hollow desolate darkness opening up inside me. She didn't snatch my body; I let her in freely. I gave myself over to her power.

All for Magni Viri.

"I didn't know," I say to Isabella's grave, my voice nearly breaking. "No one told me. I thought it was a silly ritual. I didn't know it was serious. How could I have?"

Isabella doesn't answer. The tallest treetops sigh in the wind. It's the only sound for a hundred miles. There's nothing else. The world is wrapped in cold and silence.

"I didn't know," I say again. "This isn't fair."

But I'm old enough to know it doesn't matter.

And so does Isabella. She was only thirty-six when she died—that's hardly even half a lifetime. I wonder how it happened, whether accident or sickness or violence. A part of me hopes that she suffered, the way I'm suffering now.

This is where I woke up in her grave, the sound of cicadas in my ears. This is where I scratched at the lid of her coffin. This is where I screamed.

All while she sat at my desk, writing *Cicada.*

Tears roll down my cheeks. I wipe them off with my sleeve before they can fall onto her grave. I don't want to give her even one more drop of myself.

In a shaky voice, I read aloud the inscription beside her name and the dates of her birth and death. "*Magni animi numquam moriuntur.*" More fucking Latin. I reach for my phone and type the phrase into Google Translate.

Great minds never die.

My jaw tightens. Anger surges through me, enough to drown out my ever-present fear. I didn't do this *for* Magni Viri; I did it *because of* Magni Viri.

I thought I was pledging myself to the other students and the program. I thought I was promising to work hard and do my best. Instead, I was binding myself to a ghost, making myself into a vessel. Not for Magni Viri. But for *her*. For *her* genius, not mine. For what *she* could create, not what I could.

I stalk back up to the house, which rises like a sinister beast on the hillside, black and austere. The moon shines across the lawn, casting shadows everywhere. I remember how I felt looking up at Denfeld for the first time, like Jane Eyre at the gate of Thornfield. I couldn't have known how right I was then, what lies and deceit I would find here, what dangers.

And love too, a stubborn part of me whispers. Friendship, belonging. Penny. Jordan and Wren. All the rest of them.

I shake my head and continue on. It wasn't friendship. It wasn't love. It was a charade. It was a game that Magni Viri was playing with me. They lured me in and trapped me. I thought I was Jane Eyre, but maybe I'm truly Bertha Rochester, the mad wife in the attic. Locked up and hidden away—inside my own body. I was never anything more to these people than an empty shell, waiting to be inhabited.

TWENTY-ONE

The final hours of the night are the bleakest I've ever known, steeped in grief and anger. But Tuesday morning feels like yet more darkness. I would rather do almost anything than go to my tutorial with O'Connor. I would rather do anything than sit across from him in his plush office while he pontificates about human genius and pretends to advise me on my book. But I need information, and he's the head of Magni Viri. That also means that I can't let him know that I know about Isabella. I need to act like my usual naive self. Considering how exhausted I am, it shouldn't be hard to pretend to be stupid.

I'm a few minutes late getting to the social sciences building. As I near O'Connor's door, I hear raised voices. I pause at the threshold, listening.

"My God, you haven't changed at all!" a woman snarls, fury lacing her words.

I'm shocked to recognize the voice as Dr. Hendrix's. "This is—this is practically criminal!" she yells.

"Andrea, you're being—" Dr. O'Connor starts.

"No, no, I'm done. I listened to you for twenty-three years, and I won't listen for a single moment more. This was a terrible mistake. I ought to have known better. I *did* know better!" The door slams open, and Dr. Hendrix barrels out, her nostrils flaring, her cheeks bright red. Her ever-present shawl is in disarray, falling off one shoulder.

"Oh!" she says when she nearly runs into me. "Tara, I'm so, so sorry. But I simply cannot." She shakes her head. "I cannot—" Too angry and flustered to finish the sentence, she brushes by me with a muttered apology, heading for the exit.

I watch her disappear down the hallway before I poke my head into Dr. O'Connor's office. Considering Dr. Hendrix's state, I expect to find him pacing and upset, but he sits calmly at his desk, rifling through some papers.

"Ah, Tara, come in," he says with an easy smile, as if his ex-wife didn't just barge out of his office in a rage. "I'm sorry if you heard any of that. I did warn you about my history with Dr. Hendrix."

"You did," I say, taking a seat across from his desk.

"I suppose we'll need Jimmy Coraline after all," he says with a laugh.

"Is she going to be okay?" I ask, glancing back at the doorway.

He waves a hand lazily. "Oh, she'll be fine. Divorce. It does interesting things to people, I suppose. But let's talk about your pages."

"Were they all right?" I ask, making my voice shy, hesitant. "They feel . . ." I let myself seem to grope for words. "They seem . . . like something someone else would write. They don't feel quite like me."

Dr. O'Connor freezes, his eyebrows raised. When he smiles, it doesn't reach his eyes. "Sometimes we do better work than we expect," he says carefully. "We're not aware of the depths of talent inside us."

I bite my lip and look down, since I can't force a blush. "Thank you, but I only mean that the story is darker than I expected. I didn't think I had a dark side like that."

"Ah," Dr. O'Connor says, his shoulders relaxing a fraction. "I see." He pauses as if thinking carefully of what to say next. "I was not surprised to see pages like this from someone like you."

"Someone like me?"

"You have been through a great deal. I believe you feel a great deal too, though you try to hide it. Resentment, class rage, ambition. I see so much of you in these pages, even in Eugenia."

I'm taken aback by his directness. I think he might be right, at least a little, but I don't like the casual way he presumes to know my feelings, smugly summing me up like a character in a story. I shake my head. "I'm nothing like her. I would never kill someone."

"Wouldn't you?" O'Connor volleys back. "If it came down to it, and someone was in the way of what you wanted, what you loved?"

"I . . . I'm not sure." I look away from him, my eyes wandering across the walls of his office. They land on a row of fussily framed black-and-white photographs, all portraits of tweedy, academic-looking men, seemingly from different eras judging by their haircuts and clothes. But one photo is of a dark-haired woman in mid-century fashion posing outside Denfeld Hall. I noticed it last time I was in here.

"I know I would," O'Connor says, drawing my gaze back to himself. He smiles. "I would fight tooth and nail for what matters to me. I would pay any price. Then again, my ex-wife never tires of telling me that I'm a ruthless man." His eyes flicker, and I wonder if he's warning me. "Perhaps that is why I like your writing so much. It is absolutely ruthless."

I stare at him a long moment, taking in what he has said. When I turn my head again, I only mean to avoid his eyes, but mine are drawn inevitably back to the photograph of the woman, and this time I see why. The breath leaves my body. Because I recognize her.

The woman in the photograph is the ghost I saw in the bathroom mirror. It's Isabella Snow.

At first all I can grasp is her face, that mocking face that stared back at me from the mirror—clever, haughty, implacable. She smirks at the camera the same way she smirked in my reflection. She's a little younger here, the lines around her mouth less pronounced. But it's her. My ghost.

Her dark hair is short and curled in a conservative style. She stands with lifted chin, her hands clasped in front of her. She wears a white blouse with a Peter Pan collar. There are cat-eye reading glasses on a chain around her neck. She is thinner than me, small-boned, almost petite. But a ferocious intelligence radiates from her.

There's something familiar about the way she looks at the camera, as if she can look right through time and space and into your soul. As if she can see you, down to the cells that make up your body.

Her picture frame has a brass placard at the bottom, same

as the others. I squint to read it. *Isabella Snow, Director, 1961.* She was here the whole time, waiting for me to recognize her.

"Tara?" O'Connor says.

But I can't respond. All I can do is blink at her, my tired brain struggling to take her in. This is the author of *Cicada.* This is the woman who has taken over my life. Who stuffs me in her coffin while she uses my body to write her novella. She wasn't some scholarship student, some hapless creative grasping at a better life. She was a professor. A director of a prestigious academic society. She had a good life, and now she's stealing mine.

Hatred rises in me like a wave, more powerful than anything I ever felt for Meredith. It takes all my self-possession not to leap from my seat, snatch her photograph from the wall, smash the glass, rip the picture into a thousand little pieces. I squeeze my fists at my sides and stare into her eyes.

"Tara? Are you all right?" O'Connor asks.

I turn to face him, my breaths coming short. It takes all my effort to swallow down my rage. But I can see that he has seen it and knows what caused it. My little naive schoolgirl act is over.

"Ah, Isabella Snow. She was before my time, but I am absolutely fascinated by her," he says casually. "Our first female director. A brilliant writer like yourself." He smiles at me, showing nearly every tooth in his mouth. It's a smile that tells me clearly that he knows how I am connected to her. A smile that tells me he knows how trapped I am. "Imagine what works of genius she might have produced if she had lived a little longer."

Bile rises in my throat. There's no more point in pretending. I can't even find the words to try. I gather my things and start to leave, my hands shaking all the while. The only thing I can think about is getting out of this room, away from both of them.

I've reached the door when O'Connor calls my name. I turn.

"You're doing brilliant work, Ms. Boone. You're living your dream. I'm so glad that Magni Viri has given you everything you hoped for."

His words are like an ice shard in my heart, sending their brutal cold all the way to my fingertips and toes. I don't think his ex-wife was even a little bit wrong about him. I think he is an absolutely ruthless man.

By the time I break into the cold morning, I am gasping. All this time, my ghost's photograph was hanging on Dr. O'Connor's wall. While he talked to me of my own brilliance, she was staring down at me. And he knew. Of course he knew. He set it all up.

As I walk across campus back to Denfeld, my shock begins to recede. But the anger stays, burning beneath my skin. They stole my life. Dr. O'Connor, Magni Viri, and Isabella Snow, they lured me in with the promise of a better future, and they stole my life.

But they aren't going to keep it. O'Connor says I'm like Eugenia Dossey? Well, maybe that's true. Because I will not lie down and let a bunch of rich assholes treat me like trash. Not anymore. I don't know how, but I'm going to get rid of Isabella Snow.

I know who she is, when she lived and died, where she's buried. She's not just a ghost in a mirror now. She belongs to the physical realm, and that means I can find a way to deal with her.

I refuse to let her win. She had her chance at life, and this is mine.

And I will fight with everything inside me to keep it.

Back at Denfeld, I launch into action. No more sitting around feeling sorry for myself. I have work to do.

First, I make a fresh pot of coffee and steal a Pop-Tart from someone's shelf in the kitchen, hoping the caffeine and sugar will help me survive the rest of this day. I check my email on my phone while I wait for the coffee to brew. There's already a sheepish message from Dr. Hendrix apologizing for storming out of the meeting. She offers to meet with me one-on-one to discuss my writing. I close out of it without responding. I have too much else to worry about.

Coffee in hand, I lock my bedroom door and get ready for research. I pull up Corbin's library page so I can check the databases and open a new Google search tab. I take a deep breath and type Isabella's name. It's time to learn everything I can about the woman who is trying to steal my life.

Thankfully, the library digitized every single edition of Corbin's student newspaper, *The Corbin Review*, so it doesn't take long for me to find Isabella's obituary. My breath catches when I see it. The obituary takes up half of the front page, which is considerable page space in a year that must have been dominated by news of the Vietnam War and civil rights protests. There's a black-and-white photograph of Isabella, looking much as she did in the photo from O'Connor's office. This one is more recent, the lines around her mouth deeper, the little divot in her forehead more pronounced. It must have been taken very near her death because she looks exactly as she did in my mirror. Her face is too thin and her eyes are shadowed, but she still has that indomitable eyebrow lifted, that haughty smirk.

I start to read.

Ms. Isabella Snow passed away on August 4 from a long illness. She was a member of the English department faculty for nine years, teaching English composition and creative writing. Among students, she was known as a teacher whose passion for her subject was rivaled only by her nearly unobtainable high standards. Perhaps this is why she became an adviser to, and then director of, the secretive academic society Magni Viri, from 1961 until her death. Hers was an unusual position for a woman and a professor lacking a doctoral degree, as the position of director was previously held only by tenured male faculty members. Her appointment caused a considerable stir among both faculty and students.

Little is known of Ms. Snow's history, except that she was born in this very county in 1931. She attended Corbin College as an undergraduate and returned to teach here immediately after completing a master's degree at Emory University in Atlanta, Georgia. Her family could not be located for comment.

As well as a teacher, Ms. Snow was an author in her own right, with stories published in several literary journals and a recently signed contract with Harcourt Publishers for a novel. Ms. Snow has been called the next Flannery O'Connor—

I immediately click off the tab and start searching for Isabella's published stories. After several minutes, I find her name mentioned in connection with an obscure literary magazine, but there's no full text in any database. Her stories haven't survived into the twenty-first century. I let out a disappointed sigh.

There's also no mention of her novel anywhere, which means she died before she could finish it. Was it *Cicada*? Or something else?

I sit back in my chair. It seems strange that she was born in this area—I've never met a single student who's also a local. Is that what drew Isabella back to Corbin College, to Magni Viri? Did she live with her family when she came back to teach? If they were blue collar like most people around here, it's hard to imagine that a woman as successful as Isabella would live comfortably among them.

I try to find records of Isabella's birth, but there's nothing. I can't find a death certificate either.

Eventually, I shrug and give up the search. It doesn't matter who her family was, does it? It's more important to know her personality, her goals and ambitions. And I think I've learned those.

Now I know that her life was bound up with this college

and with Magni Viri. I think of the photo on O'Connor's wall, of her haughty, self-satisfied smirk, standing in front of Denfeld Hall like she had conquered it. I bet Magni Viri was the most important thing in the world to her, apart from her own writing. I wonder if she lived on campus. Maybe she even lived in Denfeld Hall. Chill bumps break out all over my skin at the thought. Maybe she slept in a room like this one, hurried up and down the stairs, sat in the library writing.

Then I realize—maybe she left more of herself behind than her ghost. Maybe there are clues of her life scattered all through this house, if I can only figure out where to look for them.

After all, if she didn't have any family, where else would her belongings have ended up? Who would have taken possession of her writing? It must be Magni Viri. She wouldn't have wanted it to go to anyone else.

There's a chance it's all still here, under this roof. And maybe there will be something that can help me get rid of her. Where would it all be stored? Denfeld Hall has only a small basement, and it's filled with washing machines.

But there's also an attic.

I bolt from the room and up the stairs, all the way to the top floor. There must be a way up to the attic. I walk through one wing, but there's nothing that looks like an attic door. I cross over to the other wing.

And there it is, a plain, unadorned wooden door squeezed into the wall at the end of the hallway. I jiggle the handle, but it's locked. Of course. I look around, trying to think through my haze of exhaustion. Maybe Laini has the key? Or

O'Connor? Should I just break in?

On an impulse, I reach up and run my fingers over the top of the doorframe. A key falls down, along with a cloud of dust. I wipe the key off on my pants and shove it into the lock, my hands trembling with adrenaline. The door opens. The smell of mold and dust and animal droppings wafts out. My heart beats hard and fast. I pull a string dangling from the ceiling, spreading light up a set of cramped and spindly stairs. And then I start to climb.

At the top of the stairs is a light switch. I flick it on. The attic is huge, much bigger than I expected. It's filled with old furniture, dusty boxes, and endless piles of paper. There must be at least a hundred years' worth of stuff up here. But the care taken with these possessions is evident. All of it is neatly stacked, the boxes are labeled, and little aisles run all over the attic. This is a storage space that gets used. You're meant to be able to find the things you come looking for. Somehow that's creepier to me than a messy, abandoned attic would have been.

I follow the dates on the boxes, winding around and around until I'm near the middle of the attic. It reminds me of looking for Isabella's grave this morning—so much searching, only to find her at the center of everything. And her boxes are there, labeled with her name and the date she died.

I let out a breath. This feels too easy. It's almost as if I was supposed to be able to find Isabella's things. I shake my head and kneel in front of the boxes. One is a cedar chest. In it, I find Isabella's personal effects: clothing, shoes, jewelry. It's all surprisingly well preserved and tidy, as if someone expected her to come back for it.

The thought sends a shiver down my spine. Because that's what's unnerving about this attic. I'm not the one who's supposed to be able to find Isabella's things here—*she* is.

When I unearth an empty bottle of Dior perfume, I have to resist the urge to throw it at the wall. The crystal bottle might be empty, but I know exactly what its contents would smell like. Lily of the valley. Isabella Snow.

I slam the chest closed, then move on to a cardboard box. It's filled to the brim with notebooks. I pull the one on top out and open it, sucking in a breath. Every page is filled with tight, slanting cursive handwriting that is illegible to me. I can only guess at a word here and there—*summer, laugh, poor*. A diary? I put it to the side and pull out a big armful of identical notebooks. I leaf through them quickly, but there are no dates, no capital *I*'s like you'd see in a journal. There are quotation marks sometimes, enclosing what looks like dialogue.

I realize it must all be fiction. Stories and novels. Isabella's literary legacy. My head buzzes.

At the bottom of the box is a manila file that contains official-looking papers. A signed teaching contract. A yellowing immunization card. And a birth certificate. I pull it out with careful fingers, wincing at the way it crinkles with age. The space under *Father* is blank. But the name listed under *Mother* is impossible. I read it three times, and I still don't believe it.

Eugenia Rebecca Dossey

Eugenia?

Why would Isabella use her mother's name for such an awful character?

I pause. No, it's more than that. I know the pages of *Cicada* as well as I know myself. Eugenia's character is imbued with all of Isabella's pain and rage and ambition. She is as real as Isabella was.

Eugenia isn't just named after Isabella's mother. She *is* Isabella's mother. I can feel it, as surely as I feel Isabella's presence inside me.

Before she was Isabella Snow, she was Isabella Dossey.

Before she belonged to Corbin College's student body or faculty, she belonged to its family of caretakers.

Isabella is the child Eugenia is pregnant with in the story. Isabella is the daughter of a murderess. Isabella's *mother* is the character at the bloody, vengeful heart of *Cicada*.

It all makes so much sense now, the obsession Isabella has with this book. *Cicada* isn't just a novella. It's a family history.

TWENTY-TWO

I bring the entire box of Isabella's notebooks and papers back to my dorm room. I pull out the notebooks and typed pages, stacking them around me in untidy piles. I ought to be systematically searching for information here, but my head is already too full of what I learned from her birth certificate. I leaf idly through the notebooks, Isabella's tight, dramatically slanted cursive appearing like words in another language. The writing looks angry and deliberate, the pen gouging deep into the paper. Beyond that, I can't make much sense of her notebooks, only a few words here and there. It would practically take a historian to decipher them, I think. I abandon the notebooks and turn to the typed pages instead.

These were typed on a typewriter on yellowing paper, the ink faded with time. I read mostly without comprehension, too distracted and too tired to make meaning of Isabella's words, though these are printed clearly. I vaguely recognize some of what I read, as if I've read it before—a kind of déjà vu. From Isabella's mind? A published novel I read a long time ago?

Finally, I decide it doesn't matter. There's nothing here that can help me. The only thing this trove of her writing can do is sink me more deeply into her mind, which I'm realizing now is the very last thing I need. What I'm truly looking for is a way to get rid of her, and I won't find that here. I throw everything back into the box and kick the entire thing underneath my bed, too weary to take it back to the attic, where it belongs.

I go to the window and look out over the grounds, thinking hard. Isabella clearly loved this college and Magni Viri. So much that she wanted to be buried in the graveyard outside Denfeld Hall. So much that she clung to this place, bound her spirit to it.

But she didn't do it alone. No, Magni Viri made it possible. With those vows, that ceremony. Has she been lying in wait, all these years? Or am I just another of her victims? So many students have passed through this program. She could have possessed dozens by this point, made them write and publish her words. She could have possessed—

Meredith.

Of course. She must have possessed Meredith Brown. But Meredith's brain aneurysm ruptured before Isabella could finish her novella. Then Isabella needed a new vessel, so she attached herself to me. She followed me around, waiting for me to let her in too. Because so what if she lost Meredith, when there were so many others eager to take her place? There will always be more bodies. We are utterly replaceable.

But Isabella isn't. *Magni animi numquam moriuntur.*

Great minds never die.

She thinks she deserves an eternity more than I deserve my own life. More than all of us do. Look at her writing— O'Connor was right when he called it ruthless. *She's* ruthless.

The fierce and bloodthirsty joy she takes in Eugenia's darkness, the vicious way she stuffs me into her coffin at night, the merciless way she robs me of health and sleep. She can't be reasoned with. There's no compromise to be had. She'll never stop unless someone makes her. Unless *I* make her.

I have two choices now. I can give up and go home to Gaiman with my tail between my legs, forfeiting my chance at a college degree and a better future. Or I can do what Mr. Hanks told me I should: fight for my life.

Isabella might be an angry, spiteful ghost hell-bent on immortality, but I am angry too. I want more than I've been given too. And I'm willing to fight for it. Haven't I clawed my way here to Corbin College? Haven't I had to blaze and rage too?

Isn't that why she picked me, at least in part? When she looked at me through Meredith's eyes at the reading, didn't she see something of herself in me? Didn't she see a little spark of herself in my eyes, hear it in my voice?

She thought I was someone whose resentment she could harness, whose weakness she could exploit. But I will turn that spark against her.

I will burn her out of my life. Tonight.

The cemetery is dark and dim, filled with the rustle of small animals. The only light comes from the moon, which is half-hidden behind a bank of clouds. But I'm glad it's not a bright night. I don't want anyone to see what I'm doing out here.

I find Isabella's grave quickly. And then I don't waste any time. I start to dig. The soil is much harder than I expected, tightly packed and cold. And I'm not exactly in the best shape of my life, having missed a few meals and a night of sleep, plus whatever sleep I ought to be getting right now.

But I can't think about that. I push the shovel in with the heel of my boot, scoop up a big tangle of dirt and roots, and toss it to one side. I do this over and over and over again. Soon, it becomes a rhythm, one I barely need to be conscious of. My body takes over, going on autopilot. I dig and dig and dig, and the moon moves across the sky, and the skittering in the bushes quiets down. My mind goes as blank as the darkness.

I'm halfway across the cemetery before I realize what I'm doing. What *she* is doing. My hands are empty. The shovel is gone.

"Fuck!" I whisper.

"What are you doing?" says a voice just to my right.

I swivel fast, my heart exploding, but I can't see who spoke. They're in the shadow of an oak, leaning against something. Cigarette smoke wafts toward me.

"Who's there?" I ask, my voice shaking.

They laugh. I recognize it.

"Neil," I say, releasing a breath. "Why are you out here?"

He peels away from the darkness and comes into the moonlight. I can just make out his silhouette—the peculiar slump of his narrow shoulders. He raises his cigarette to take a drag, and the tip burns bright red in the darkness.

"Why are *you* out here?" he echoes, releasing a cloud of smoke.

I cough. I'm so tired, I can't think straight. I can't think of a lie. "Are you following me, or what?"

He laughs again. "Not everything is about you, Tara. So conceited."

I'm covered in grave dirt, but it's too dark for him to see that. Maybe he hasn't noticed what I'm doing. Maybe he just came out for a smoke right as I left off digging. Maybe.

"You've been avoiding everyone," he says.

"So what?" I shoot back. "Miss me?"

"You're in the wrong program for going it alone," he says.

"Fuck off, Neil. Like you care."

"I never said I cared." He tosses his cigarette on the ground and stamps it out. "Sweet dreams, Tara." With that, he ambles away into the darkness, back toward Denfeld.

I let out a long breath. I don't know what the hell that was. What he was trying to say to me. And I don't care. I just need to get this done.

I stride back to the grave and search for the shovel. I don't see it anywhere. She must have made me throw it in the bushes. I shine my phone along the ground until I find it. Then I start digging again. I clearly hadn't been at it very long before she made me stop. I've barely made it a foot down and only in one small area. My arms already hurt. Even through my thick winter gloves, blisters are forming. Exhaustion looms, waiting for me to give up.

I grit my teeth and keep going. To avoid letting my mind drift, I recite every poem I can remember. Emily Dickinson and Edgar Allan Poe. Robert Frost and Edna St. Vincent Millay. It helps. I have to keep reaching for words I've forgotten. It keeps my mind occupied so she can't get a handhold. It keeps her in the dark where she belongs.

But after an hour of digging, I realize I won't be able to reach her casket tonight. What little strength I had is giving out, and I'm nowhere close to deep enough. I need help. But who could I possibly ask? There's no one. Only me.

A wave of despair engulfs me, washing away the earlier resolve that came with my anger. I sit down, hard, right in the hole I've been digging. Tears rise to my eyes. I glance at my phone's screen. It's two in the morning.

I don't know why I do it, but I pull up my contacts and scroll to Neil's name. Maybe it's because he's the only one who has never pretended to be my friend, who never hid his disdain. *Come back to the graveyard*, I text. *Please.*

The text status changes to "Read." But he doesn't respond. I groan and put my head back on my knees. I let my eyes close.

A few minutes later there are footsteps in the leaf litter. I look up to see a dark shape standing above me, a shovel thrown over its shoulder. "Get out of the fucking grave, Tara," Neil says.

I scurry up, nearly twisting my ankle in the process. "Why are you—"

"Don't say a word. Don't ask me anything. I am nothing but a shovel tonight. Deal?"

"Deal," I say, even though a hundred questions spring to my lips.

We dig for hours, the only sound the rasp and thud of our shovels, the spray of dirt as we toss each shovelful from the grave.

When my shovel strikes wood, splintering it, I nearly

scream. We're only about four feet down. "Why's she so close to the surface?" I hiss at Neil.

He laughs. "What? You think she is willing herself out of the ground?"

"Shut up," I say tiredly, though that's not far off from what I was thinking.

"Probably water tables rising or storms disturbing the ground. I'm sure Jordan or Penny could explain it," Neil says.

"Not that we're going to ask them," I remind him. "This is between you and me."

"I'll keep your dirty secrets," Neil says with a lecherous purr in his voice.

"Keep digging," I respond, too exhausted for banter.

We widen the hole and scrape out the last of the dirt. It takes forever.

Neil climbs out of the grave. He turns on his phone's flashlight and shines it onto the casket. "Open it, then," he says.

I look up at him, his face lit from below. He looks sinister in this light, his eyebrows dark, his mouth a hard line.

I can't find the casket's clasp, but I don't need it. The wood is water warped, nearly rotted away. I pull the pieces off and toss them behind me.

A vague smell of damp and rot wafts up from the casket. Isabella is unrecognizable, little more than bone. There are nasty strands of what might be mummified skin or might be synthetic fibers that even a half century underground couldn't break down.

I stare at her, completely numb. I can't even summon disgust.

I glance back up at Neil. His face is twisted with hate. "We'd better hurry. It's going to be morning soon," he says.

I reach down to try to pick her up. She comes apart in my hands, sending up dust and mold. I turn my head away, coughing.

"Be right back," Neil says. He disappears, leaving me alone in the dark with Isabella. I try not to think of my dreams of being buried in this grave, how I battered the top of the casket with my fists and screamed until my voice gave out. How the cicadas sang around me, an underground symphony of horror.

When Neil returns, he tosses down brown paper leaf litter bags. "Put her in these. You can pass each one up to me."

I nod and start opening one of the bags. I realize how impossible this task would have been without Neil. Even if I'd managed to somehow dig the whole grave by myself, I would have had a hell of a time getting the body out once I'd finished.

I wrap my scarf around my nose and mouth and start stuffing bits of Isabella into the first bag. Her arms, her torso, her pelvis. I pass the bag up to Neil, who takes it without comment.

I put her legs into the next bag. One of the feet falls off, and I have to search around for it.

"Come on, Tara, hurry up," Neil says, his voice tight. I scramble around, exhausted, making sure I haven't missed any other pieces. I don't want any of Isabella left here.

I bag the last few pieces, which could be her clothes or her tendons, I don't even know. I take one last look at her empty, skeletal face before I drop her head into the bag. Then I pass it up to Neil. "That's everything," I say.

Without a word, he reaches down and helps pull me out of the grave. I collapse onto the dirt beside him.

"Look, go do what you have to do. I'll take care of refilling the grave," he says.

"Are you sure?"

"You've got about two hours before the sun comes up," he says. "Just go."

"Thanks," I say. "Seriously, Neil, I—"

"Fuck off," he says. He turns his back to me and starts shoveling dirt into the hole as fast as he can.

"Right." I grab the leaf litter bags, one in each hand, and take off at a trot. The body weighs barely anything now, all of its substance rotted away. I might as well be carrying actual leaves in these bags.

I keep to the shadows as much as I can. The last thing I need is for campus security to stop me. After what feels like an hour but is probably only fifteen minutes, I make it to the parking lot, the one everyone complains about because it's so poorly lit and they're afraid they'll be murdered getting out of their cars.

I toss the bags of Isabella into the trunk and start my engine. I sit for a moment while the car idles, my mind gauzy with exhaustion. Where should I take her?

God, I just want to sleep. I just want to be done with this.

I turn on the stereo, and Queen blares out. I haven't driven the car since taking Wren to the hospital. For the second time in a month, I leave campus with Freddie Mercury singing along to my frayed nerves.

I drive for a long time, barely paying attention to where

I'm going. There are no cars on the road. The sky is dark, but there's the barest lightening on the horizon. The green-brown hills loom all around me, offering no easy place to stop the car. But finally, I come down a long, steep stretch of highway, and the forest opens up. I pull onto the shoulder of the road and grab the bags from the trunk. I march several yards into the trees, not even bothering to turn on a light.

I trip over a raised tree root and crash down hard onto my belly, dropping the bags.

I lie still, and for a moment I think about staying where I am. Just falling asleep here on the cold ground. But I grit my teeth and get back to my feet.

In the shadowy dawn, I find a dip in the ground between two trees that's full of leaves and woody debris. I open each of the bags and let Isabella's remains fall into the leaves. Then I scatter it all so that her body is covered again. Reburied. I rip the leaf litter bags into several pieces and throw the pieces into the wind, to be carried off.

That's the best that I can do. That's the best burial I can manage.

I sway on my feet as I stare down at the leaves. It looks the same as before, as if I'd never been here.

"Rest in peace, you heinous bitch," I say.

And then I stagger back to my car. I start the engine and do a U-turn. I drive back to campus, so exhausted I can hardly keep my car from swerving off the road. Thankfully, the police are scarce out here. I pull into the parking lot just as the sun comes over the hills, casting its golden light across the campus.

I am completely filthy, grime on my clothes and in my

hair, smeared on my face, crusted beneath my nails. If I walk across campus like this, it's going to attract attention. I look in the back seat. There's a jacket that Jordan must have left behind. I shimmy out of my filthy coat and drop it onto the floor of the car. I grab a wet wipe from the glove compartment and scrub my face and hands with it. Then I put on Jordan's jacket.

I walk fast back to Denfeld, my hands in my pockets and my head down. I don't cross paths with anyone except for a professor who's too busy staring at his phone to notice me.

Denfeld is starting to stir, but there's no one on the stairs. I hurry up them and let myself into my room, my strange and sleepless night already feeling distant and unreal. Wren is asleep in bed. I should take a shower, but all my strength is gone. I pull off all my clothes and collapse into bed, pulling the covers over my head.

I shiver for a few minutes. My body wants to sleep, but I don't let it. I need to be sure that Isabella is gone.

I wait, trying to feel her presence. Trying to feel her slipping around the edges of my tired mind. But there's nothing. No one.

I am myself again. Isabella Snow is gone.

Relief spreads through me, the tight spiral of anxiety in my belly finally unwinding and letting my exhausted body relax for the first time in two days. I drop into a level of sleep so deep that even dreams cannot break into the darkness.

TWENTY-THREE

I wake slowly, at first aware only of the way my body aches. Against the soft sheets, cushioned in the blankets, I am warm and tired, and I never want to crawl out of bed again. But gradually the rest of the world demands my notice. Twilight seeps in at the windows, and from downstairs comes the usual noise of a house full of college students—laughter, arguments, music.

I slept, I realize with relief. For a whole day, probably. Hours and hours. I missed my classes, but I slept. That means Isabella is truly gone. That means I'm myself again. I'm free of her.

The events of the last few days pour in on me. I couldn't fully feel it all while it was happening, but now, with my mind rested, the numbness has faded. And I realize how monstrous it all has been. How horribly monstrous. I dug up a woman's grave. I removed her corpse and scattered it in the woods.

And Neil helped me do it. Why? Why would he risk himself for me? He hates me. But he seems to hate Isabella more. I wonder if he hates his own ghost too.

I sit up in bed and stretch, wincing at the aches all over me. There is no part of me that does not hurt. But it was worth it. Every aching, screaming muscle and ruptured blister was worth it. I got rid of her. My life is my own again.

I blink at the window, its curtains thrown open to the indigo sky. My stomach growls, and I realize how long it's been since I've eaten. There's plenty of time to make it to the cafeteria for dinner, if I can just get myself out of this bed.

With enormous effort, I throw my legs over the side of the bed and stand, scratchy fabric riding uncomfortably up my thighs. A new wave of pain washes over me as my feet and knees take the burden of my weight. I limp around my room, gathering stuff for the shower. I am about to put on my bath-robe when I catch sight of myself in the full-length mirror that hangs on the back of the door.

I scream, stumbling backward, away from my reflection. Away from *her*.

She stares at me in the dim light, her short hair in disarray, her cream-colored blouse wrinkled from sleeping in it. She wears a knee-length wool skirt and nylon stockings as if she's about to go teach a class.

Except, I realize after a long moment of shock, that this isn't like before. This isn't some disturbing mirror trick. It's not Isabella's face in the mirror where mine should be, only her hair and her clothing. My own frightened face stares back at me. But I've been dressed and styled like her as if in a cos-tume. The musty smell coming off the clothes tells me they're the same ones I found in her attic storage.

My hands go automatically to my head. What I feel there matches what the mirror shows. It's not a wig. Someone has cut and dyed my hair. It's shorter and dark brown, curled in an old-fashioned style. There are bangs.

Without my blond hair, I look nothing like myself. I'm pale and washed-out; a stranger. I may as well be wearing Isabella's face instead of my own.

My hand goes to my mouth. *No. No, no, no, no, no.*

There's only one person who would have done this.

I didn't get rid of her at all. After everything I went through, she's still here. She's still haunting me. She's still in control.

And this haircut isn't some joke, a ghostly lark. It's punishment for what I did. For what I tried to do. It's a message, clearer than the words she wrote with my finger in the steam of a bathroom mirror.

You are mine, it says.

She's never going to give me up. No matter what I do.

With a convulsive cry, I rip her clothes from my body, sending buttons flying with the force of my desperation to be rid of her. I push the ruined clothes deep into the trash can beside my desk before I run down the hall to the bathroom and jump in the shower. I scrub my skin and my scalp, pulling the shampoo roughly through my now-short hair, watching brown water swirl down the drain. I scrub and scrub, but it won't change anything. She'll still be haunting me.

I avoid looking in the mirror as I dress in my room. I brush my hair and throw a beanie on over it, shoving the strands up inside the hat. I don't want to see it anymore. I don't want anyone else to see it either.

I'm trying to decide what to do next when someone knocks on my door. I pause, considering who it might be.

Neil? Penny? Maybe just Wren.

I open the door. Quigg smiles at me. "Hey, Tara."

"Now's not a great time, Quigg," I say. "Sorry."

"Dr. O'Connor is downstairs and wants to talk to you," he says quickly, before I can close the door in his face.

My stomach clenches. "He's here?"

"In the library." Quigg gives me a sympathetic smile. "I wouldn't keep him waiting if I were you. He seems pretty mad."

I close my eyes. "Fine, I'll be right down."

"He wanted me to . . . escort you."

"Are you serious?"

Quigg looks mortified but only gives me a dignified nod.

I clench my jaw. Just when I thought this couldn't get any worse. "Okay, let's go," I say. I close the door behind me. We walk slowly down the stairs, and Quigg doesn't say anything. He just shoots surreptitious little looks at me, both curious and pitying.

When I walk into the library, Quigg leaves me with a gentle squeeze of my shoulder. Dr. O'Connor is standing at the window, his back to me. I'm reminded again of what a small, slight man he is. It's astonishing how much power he manages to exude.

He turns, and I suck in a breath. His eyebrows are drawn together, his mouth hard. "Tara, what were you thinking?" he asks, his voice quiet but sharp at the edges, rage held barely in check. "How could you do this?"

"How could I do what?" I ask, looking down at my shoes. I had to wear an old scuffed-up pair of Chucks because my boots are caked in mud.

"Don't play games with me," he says, his voice dropping half an octave. He steps toward me, and I try not to flinch away. "What you did is a crime. A felony, actually. You could go to prison."

My mouth drops open. I'd never even considered the legal ramifications of digging up Isabella's grave, only the spiritual ones. "How did you find out?" I ask, my heart racing.

"Does it matter?"

"Yes, it does," I grit out.

I wonder if Neil told him. But that would implicate him too. I remember how Penny said the walls of Denfeld have ears. Anyone could have seen me digging up Isabella's grave and told O'Connor.

Dr. O'Connor shakes his head. "That's all you have to say for yourself? No apologies? No explanations?"

"You know why I did it," I say quietly. "You tricked me. You made me—"

Dr. O'Connor takes another step toward me. "I made you do nothing, young lady. I thought we had an understanding. I thought you *understood*."

He thought he'd cowed me yesterday. He thought I'd keep my mouth shut and write my book. He didn't expect me to fight back.

"I understand *nothing*," I spit. "I didn't agree to this. I want out of this."

O'Connor raises a finger to point at my face, all pretense of politeness gone. "Now you listen here. I have taken your trailer trash ass out of a place of obscurity and lifted you into a position that others would kill for. You will be quiet, and you will be grateful. You will do what's expected of you. No more foolish games."

I meet his eyes, fire kindling in my chest. "And if I don't?"

"You will be out of this college so fast, with a mark on your record so black that you won't be able to get into community college, let alone another school of this stature," O'Connor snarls.

That takes me aback. I wasn't expecting outright threats from him.

"Fall in line, Tara. Now. Fall in line or you're done. You can stay here and write your book and start a career for yourself, or you can go back to Yeehaw, Florida, and work in a convenience store for the rest of your life. That's your choice."

My face burns. I clench my fists at my sides. No words will come to me.

O'Connor stalks past me, letting his shoulder knock into mine as if to emphasize his point. Once he reaches the door, he turns. "Oh, and by the way, Isabella Snow's remains will be reinterred tonight."

"What? How? How did you find them?" I ask, but he's already walking away.

I stand alone in the library swallowing down my anger, my shame, my despair. My shoulders rise and fall with my breaths, but no tears come to my eyes.

"What the fuck?" I whisper, sinking into the nearest chair.

O'Connor said no more games, but what is everyone else doing except playing games? Him? Neil? Even Penny, Wren, and Jordan? They've all been toying with me. No one ever comes right out and says anything. It's always sideways looks and allusions. But everyone knew what was happening to me.

Everyone except me.

Neil steps into the room. "So it didn't work," he says, leaning against the wall by the door.

I leap to my feet. "Did you tell O'Connor?"

Neil laughs cruelly. "Just when I was starting to think you weren't stupid after all."

I shake my head in disgust and turn away. "God, why did you bother to help me? You don't even like me."

"No, I don't, but I hate her."

"Isabella?" I ask. So I was right about that.

"Of course, Isabella. I *hate* her," he says so viciously that his top lip peels back in a snarl. "I mean, I knew your plan probably wouldn't work, but it was worth it just to fuck with her. Just to get back at her a little."

"Get back at her for what? You're not the one she's haunting. You're not the one she did *this* to," I say, pulling off my hat.

Neil blinks at me. "So she gave you a bad haircut. So fucking what?"

"So what? Are you—"

"She killed Meredith!" Neil screams, pushing off from the wall. "She killed the girl I loved. Ended her life. Like that." He snaps his fingers.

"Meredith died of a ruptured brain aneurysm," I say quietly. "That's why Isabella moved on to me."

Neil stares at me, eyebrows raised, like he's waiting for me to catch up.

My stomach turns to ice. All along, I never questioned what O'Connor told me about Meredith's death. People have brain aneurysms all the time, don't they? At worst, I thought the stress of Magni Viri caused it. But not that Isabella did it on purpose. Maybe I just didn't want to let that idea into my head. Maybe it was too scary to even consider.

I remember Meredith lying on the library floor, tear tracks on her cheeks. She didn't die. She was murdered.

Fear leaps into my chest, followed by a rush of rage. "Isabella *killed* her? And you didn't think you should tell me that? You didn't think I deserved to know what I was walking into here?"

Jordan comes to the door, the others behind him. "Hey, the whole house can hear you two arguing."

I look at him, at Penny, at Wren. At Azar, standing slightly off to one side like she's not sure she wants to be here.

The rage in my chest explodes. And for once, it's not tears that come out. "Who fucking cares if they hear me?" I yell. "Everyone already knows! Everyone in this house knew what was happening to me, and no one said anything. No one cared. All of you pretended to be my friends, and all this time, you were—you were—" I shake my head, unable to find adequate language for their betrayal.

Jordan ushers everyone into the library and shuts the door, sealing the six of us inside. "We *are* your friends, Tara. We were never pretending about that."

I laugh. "If that were true, you would have warned me. You would have told me what I was walking into. . . . She killed Meredith," I add weakly.

Penny steps forward, her hands reaching out. "We wanted to tell you. We wanted to tell you so badly. But O'Connor . . ."

She looks helplessly at the others.

I shake my head, backing away from her. "Why? Why would you keep this from me?"

They all look afraid, like even now that I know, they aren't allowed to say it out loud. Penny shocks me by bursting into tears, her usual calm, detached manner giving way. "O'Connor said that if we told you what was happening to you, you would fight it. And Isabella would kill you too. We thought you might die . . . like Meredith did. We thought you would die, Tara! Do you know what that has felt like?" She knocks a closed fist against her chest, overcome. "To be with you and care about you and not be able to tell you anything?"

For a moment, I'm moved by her emotion, the anguish in her voice. But I shake my head. I signed on to Magni Viri before Penny ever knew me. Before any of them did. "Why did you let me walk into this at all? Didn't you know what was going to happen when I joined Magni Viri? Don't you all have ghosts of your own?"

She opens her mouth only to close it again.

I glance away from Penny to the others, watching emotions pass over their faces. Guilt, fear, and something harder-edged I can't name. Everyone is afraid to speak.

Finally, Penny seems to gather her courage. "O'Connor said that Isabella had already picked you, that she'd made her choice and there was nothing we could do about it. All we could do was try to keep you as safe as possible," she says. "And—" She glances over at Jordan. There's something else she doesn't want to say.

"Well, you see," Jordan says, "it's— Well, we . . ."

Azar swears. "If we didn't let Isabella have what she wanted, it would have cost all of us something, not just you."

"What do you mean?"

"When we joined Magni Viri, we were told what we were walking into. We all agreed to it: that we'd allow our bodies to be used as vessels by brilliant minds for four years. Whatever the partnership created during that time, we got to claim credit for. We would already have careers started for us before we even graduated. We would be successful. We would be taken care of."

"And you didn't want me to jeopardize that? God, you're all so selfish! I would never do something like this to someone."

"Shut up and listen," Azar says, her eyes flashing. "The way this all works . . . it's complicated and it's delicate. The ghosts are all bound together. If one of them isn't getting what they want, it can be dangerous for everyone. And Isabella is powerful. I don't know why. But she has the ability to disrupt the entire system. To throw the whole thing out of whack." Azar looks almost frightened. "The night she killed Meredith and was disembodied . . ." She shakes her head.

"I heard you all yelling for her that night. Somehow I ended up by the cemetery, and I heard you."

Azar's eyes widen slightly. "We didn't know where she'd gone. We didn't know yet that she'd already chosen you. That she'd chosen you even before she killed Meredith."

I remember the way Meredith stared at me when I saw her at the reading, the way her gaze cut right through me, to my very heart. It was Isabella's stare, not hers. She'd picked me out. But why, when she had brilliant, beautiful Meredith Brown already?

"Why did Isabella kill Meredith?" I ask.

"That's what we've been trying to tell you," Wren says, a hitch in their voice like they're trying not to cry. "She killed Meredith because Mer was resisting her. Mer wanted to do her own work, write her own books. And she was doing everything in her power to stifle Isabella."

Neil cuts in. "That night at the reading, the night she died—the story she read—do you remember it? 'Incubus'?"

I nod.

"That was Meredith's writing, not Isabella's. It was *about* Isabella."

"Oh," I whisper. The story I didn't really understand at the reading now makes perfect sense. The relentless dread, the nightmarish, surreal atmosphere of it.

"That was the last straw for Isabella, I guess," Neil says. "Mer wasn't being a good, obedient vessel and so she killed her. And then she chose you to take Mer's place."

"That's why we didn't tell you," Penny says, wringing her hands. "We were afraid she would kill you too."

"Oh my God. And last night I dug up her grave!" I shake my head, realizing how lucky I am that all Isabella did was dye my hair and dress me in her clothes. I could be dead now, just like Meredith.

I stare into Penny's eyes, which are wide and worried, still leaking tears. I almost believe her, that it was about me. Almost. But then I remember the way they talked about me the other night, how Penny said dating me was a mistake.

How Wren whined about having to room with me. They were only pretending to be my friends because they needed me.

That's what people are like, I hear inside my head. For a lurching, sickening moment I'm not sure if it's my own thought or Isabella's. *That's why you're on your own.*

"You weren't afraid for me. You were afraid of what she would do to the rest of you," I snarl.

"Of course we were afraid," Neil says. "We're not fucking saints. We have our own lives and our own futures to protect. Between the ghosts and O'Connor . . . well, rock and hard place, you know?"

I shake my head, backing away from them.

Wren reaches for me. "Tara, please. We do care about you. We really, really do."

I snatch my arm away from them. "Don't touch me."

"Tara," Penny says, "let us help you now. Now that you know, we can teach you how to manage it. How to make it more bearable. It doesn't have to be so hard. There are ways—"

"And you," I growl, interrupting her. I feel my lips twist with suppressed tears. My chin quivers dangerously. "I heard you say it was a mistake to go out with me. Why did you do it, then? Why did you get close to me, make me think you wanted me? For O'Connor, for Magni Viri? Was it all a lie—what was between us?"

Penny's gaze softens with something like pity. "Of course not. It was never about that. I swear. I liked you. I wanted to be with you."

I look around at all of them. I still can't believe what they've done to me. The web of lies they've built around me, trapping me inside. Neil? Sure. Azar? Maybe. But Jordan? But Wren, who seemed so completely guileless, so open and real? And Penny? Penny who asked my permission to even hold my hand? How could she do this to me?

It hurts. It hurts so much. I've never felt more betrayed.

A breath shudders out of me. "I can't believe—I just—I thought I'd finally found a place to . . ." I shake my head, unable to make the words come. "I couldn't have been more wrong. God, you're . . . you're all just a bunch of selfish ass-holes! You're heartless. I can't believe I thought you were my friends."

"Tara, we're sorry. We're all so sorry," Jordan says.

I shake my head. "I'm done with all of you. I'm not your plaything anymore."

The five of them stand together in a group, bound together as they've always been.

And I stand apart, on my own. Like I've always been.

There's nothing left to do but walk away.

TWENTY-FOUR

I sit on my bed, feet on the floor. I stare at the wall. I feel empty, spent. Worse than I did after two nights of not sleeping.

I finally had friends, or at least I thought I did. And every last one of them betrayed me. This program, which promised to lift me up and make my life better, has instead stolen what little life I had. If I keep trying to fight Isabella, either she will kill me or O'Connor will burn my life to the ground.

There is only one other option, the thing I swore I would never do.

I have to go home.

Back to Mom and our little apartment. Back to the sad, strained life we led together. Back to my little town, where nothing ever happens and no one hopes for anything to. Where there is no life and no future.

Either I can give my body over to a vengeful, dangerous ghost or I can become a ghost again myself.

I lie back in bed and close my eyes. I can feel Isabella inside me, stirring at the edges of my conscious mind, waiting and watching for her moment to get out. I run my fingers through my shorn hair. Neil's right—all she did was give me a bad haircut. But there are so many worse things she could do. She could hurt me. She could make me hurt someone else. She could kill me like she killed Meredith.

I lie still for a long time, and it feels like I'm already mourning my lost life. My four years here at Corbin, the career I would have had, the books I would have written, the classes I would have taught. Silent tears run down my cheeks.

But finally, there's nothing else to do but the inevitable. Maybe it was always going to come to this, even without Isabella, without Magni Viri. Mom told me that Corbin College wasn't for people like us. She was right.

I scroll to her name in my contacts and hit the Call button. The phone doesn't ring, but a woman's voice comes on immediately. "We're sorry, but the number you have dialed is no longer in service."

I sit up fast, holding out my phone to see if I called the wrong person. But I didn't. It's Mom's number, the one she has had since I was a kid. And it's disconnected.

I dial it again to be sure. But the same thing happens.

My heart rate explodes. Why is my mom's phone disconnected? Did she go off the deep end without me there to keep an eye on her? Or did she change it on purpose? She said she never wanted to speak to me again. Maybe she meant it.

I squeeze my eyes tight, pushing the horrible possibility away. I dial the McDonald's where she was working last. But when I ask for her, the girl on the phone says that my mom doesn't work there, hasn't worked there for weeks now. She can't tell me anything else. I hang up, my lungs constricting in my chest.

My hands shaking, I text Robin: *Hey, my mom is MIA.*

Have you seen her around town at all?

A notification that she's typing appears immediately, then vanishes. Appears and then vanishes.

Shit, that's not good.

Finally, she responds: *Oh no, sorry to hear that! I saw her two weeks ago at Walmart with some guy I didn't know but she turned and went the other way.*

I wonder what else Robin chose not to say, what got deleted while I was watching those three dots start and stop. I could ask her to go by the apartment and see if my mom is home, but there's one other thing I can try first. I dial our landlady, a cranky old woman who lives next door to us. She has an ancient beige-colored landline phone, and it always takes her an eternity to get out of her chair in front of the TV and walk across the room to where it's mounted on the wall. I know because I listened to it ring all day every day when I lived there.

This time, the phone rings sixteen times before she answers.

"What?" she yells into the receiver.

"Hi, Mrs. Norris? This is Tara from next door."

"Who?"

"Tara Boone, Beth's daughter? Your neighbor? Remember, I'm at college in Tennessee now?"

She pauses, thinking it over. "What do you want? If your mama is trying to take back that doll she gave me, she can forget about it. The mess she left behind in that—"

"Doll? What doll?"

"The Cabbage Patch one. She doesn't know this, but it's

worth a pretty penny. Vintage and all that. Might just about pay for—"

"She gave you my doll?" I ask, shocked. That was the last thing my dad gave me before he and my mom split up for good. I nearly brought it to college with me but had left it on my bed at the last second, afraid it was too babyish.

"I told you, I'm not giving it back," Mrs. Norris warns. "Now, if you'll excuse me—"

"Mrs. Norris, wait. I'm not calling you about the doll. I'm trying to find my mom. Her phone is disconnected and she's not working at McDonald's anymore. Can you tell her to call me?"

"No, I can't. She moved out two weeks ago. If you'd stopped interrupting me, you'd already know that."

All the air leaves my chest. "Wha-What? She moved out? Why?"

"I don't know and I don't care. I was glad to see the back of her. Constant loud noise. Always arguing with that new boyfriend of hers. She almost set the place on fire once. Good riddance."

Panic crawls up my throat. "Mrs. Norris, did she tell you where she was going? Or did she leave you any way to contact her? A forwarding address?"

"No, she didn't."

"But . . . how am I supposed to find her? She doesn't even have Facebook anymore."

"Well, bless your heart, I thought you were supposed to be smart, all up in college and everything. You don't know much, do you?"

"I really don't," I say, too overwhelmed to be offended. "You can't think of any way to get in touch with her?"

Mrs. Norris pauses. When she speaks again, her voice is surprisingly gentle. "Listen here, little girl. Your mama took off, and if she wanted you to find her, she'd ha' told you where she was going. But she didn't. And if I were you, I'd count myself lucky to be rid of her. You've taken care of that woman for long enough. She's a bad seed, but that doesn't mean you have to be one too. And it doesn't mean you have to clean up her messes. You be a good girl and stay in college. Everything'll turn out all right for you in the end, you hear? Forget about your mama and live your life. You'll be better for it."

"Yes, ma'am," I say mechanically. "Thank you. Goodbye." I end the call before she can reply.

My mom is gone. She changed her number, quit her job, and moved—all without telling me. She left her life behind like it was nothing. She left *me* behind like it was nothing.

Because I left her first.

To come here and follow my dream, to become someone she wouldn't want to know.

Mom was childish and needy, irresponsible, undependable. But she was my family. My only family.

And now what am I left with? I have nowhere to go. I have no way to support myself. If I leave Corbin College, I'll be homeless. If I stay here, I'll be sharing my body with Isabella for the next four years, completely at her mercy.

Dr. O'Connor has me exactly where he wants me. I have no choice but to stay. I can't quit Magni Viri. I can't leave this house. I can't fight Isabella. I belong to her now.

The reality of my situation crashes down on me with enormous, irrefutable force. All my fighting was for nothing. Isabella has won, completely and irrevocably. There's absolutely nothing I can do about it.

With a sob, I pull the covers over me and lie down on my bed, tucking my knees against my chest. I have never felt more alone or more helpless. I have never felt less loved.

Because there's no point in fighting it any longer, I go to sleep.

TWENTY-FIVE

After a few days the world starts to blur. Sleeping and waking, nightmare and reality, it all runs together. I go to my classes, mostly. I do some of my assignments. Sometimes I shower, sometimes I don't. It doesn't seem to matter much, and Isabella doesn't care. I don't really taste my food—whenever I remember to bother to eat any, which isn't often.

Dr. Hendrix keeps emailing me and trying to talk to me in class. I manage to fend her off at first, but she grows more insistent, so I finally stop going to Gothic lit. I know that deep down I love that class, but I can't seem to remember why.

All that matters is *Cicada*. Isabella writes all night long, leaving me to catch true sleep here and there as I'm able, mostly in between classes, though sometimes I sleep right through them. Even when I'm awake, I'm in a haze, hardly aware of my surroundings. People talk to me and I don't really hear them. Penny keeps coming to my door, and I open it and stare at her while her lips move. I close it again without saying anything. I don't see Wren at all, so they must be bunking with Penny or sleeping in the practice rooms again. I can't bring myself to care.

The truth is that I'm not really here. And I don't want to be. It's a relief to sink down into Isabella's coffin while she sits at my desk and writes. It's a relief to lie in the darkness and listen to the world creak and groan and creep around me. It's a relief not to exist.

I wonder if it's possible for me to crouch in some dark little corner of my own brain and for Isabella to have this body all to herself, twenty-four hours a day. I'm not sure I would mind. It might be better that way.

There are times when I think Isabella and I are merging into one. My hands are her hands. My neurons, my synapses are hers. But I'm not just a vessel for her to inhabit. We're intertwined, our thoughts and feelings mixing. I feel her impulses as if they are my own. And more and more, they are the ones that rule me. The story she's writing is twined around my brain, my heart. I can't stop thinking about it. It feels more real to me than my own life.

Eugenia, her swelling belly. The bloody climax she's hurtling toward.

Every morning I type Isabella's words. They frighten me because I know that at least some part of what she writes is real. That it truly happened. But Isabella frightens me more, the dark edge of her mind sharp and slick as a bloodied blade. I can feel her craving, her bloodthirst. She loves the damage Eugenia is doing. She relishes every dark turn. She can't stop writing because she needs, desperately, to reach the apex of horror and watch humanity unravel. She is, in every possible way, her mother's daughter.

And I—at least in some sense—am her. I *am* Isabella Snow.

Right now, at this moment, I am glad to be her. I am glad to have my brain and my body put to a greater use than I could ever give them. Isabella might be bloody, but she's also brilliant. She came from dark and humble beginnings just like me. But she made something of herself. She built herself up into a person even death could not conquer.

She deserves the use of my hands. She deserves it more than I ever will.

Isabella is the writer I could never be.

But in a way, because of her, I get to be that writer. Because of her, I get to make something great, just like I've always dreamed of.

Tonight, I watch her as she writes. I follow the lines of her story across the page, as rapt as she is. She is nearly there, to the point of crisis. She writes feverishly, her pen scrambling. If it weren't my handwriting, I wouldn't be able to read it.

Eugenia, hugely pregnant, meets the boy who impregnated her late at night, deep in the woods, next to a stream. He wants to marry her. He begs her, on his knees. But Eugenia knows she would never be accepted in his world, not even by him, no matter how much he professes to love her. Her place is too well established. To Frederick she would always be a girl he saved. He would come to despise her.

He would raise her daughter as a hated thing, an object of shame. And that Eugenia could never allow.

So she refuses. The boy becomes angry at first, yelling at her that the child is his and he'll claim it. That she won't raise his blood among lowly people. But when he catches sight of the rage in her eyes, he changes tack, going back to confessing his love for her and the child.

The boy grovels before her; he presses his face to her belly. He gazes up at her, moonlight reflecting in his eyes. And Eugenia loves him, as well as she's able to love a pampered, privileged boy. But she loves herself more. She loves the child growing inside her more.

With her left hand, Eugenia smooths the boy's hair off his forehead, her touch gentle. She makes his head fall back, exposing the white expanse of his throat.

And I want to stop Isabella's hand. I want to scream at her not to do it. Not to let her father be killed. But I am as powerless against her as the boy is against Eugenia.

Eugenia brings her right hand up fast, sinking a knife into the side of Frederick's throat. His eyes open wide with shock and disbelief. She yanks the knife back out and lets the blood splatter the ground, the water, her dress. When his eyes go empty, she pushes him backward until he falls onto his back in the stream.

Eugenia wipes the knife on her bloody dress and goes home to have her baby.

Elation and triumph pour from Isabella's mind and into my heart, a feeling so intense and all-consuming that I lose track of myself, that I can no longer tell where Isabella ends and I begin.

TWENTY-SIX

"Tara," someone is saying. "Tara, can you hear me?"

Blurred shapes pass to and fro in front of me, but I can't make my eyes focus. I'm so cold. My teeth knock together in my skull.

"Oh my God, I think she has hypothermia or something," the voice says.

A warm jacket is draped around my shoulders. Someone takes me by the arm, and I let them, my body shuffling forward automatically. We must be in the woods because the world smells like damp earth and rotting leaves.

We walk for what feels like a long, long time. The two people whisper back and forth as they half carry me between them. Vaguely, I recognize them as Wren and Penny.

After a while their voices become more than empty sounds, and I start to piece together what's happening. They found me wandering in the woods without a jacket. I was missing for hours. My feet are bare, except for a pair of dirty, torn socks with blood on them. I'm so cold. I feel like I'll never be warm again.

"I can't believe I fell asleep and lost track of her," Wren says, their voice wretched.

"It's not your fault," Penny says. "You couldn't help it. You did your best."

I blink up at the leafy sky. It must be midmorning, judging by the sun. I don't remember coming to the woods. I don't know how I got here. I don't know how they found me. But I must have wandered a long way because I still don't recognize where we are.

"I should give her my shoes," Penny says. "Look at the state of her feet."

"No, you can't risk cutting up your feet when you're immune suppressed. You might get an infection. I'll give her mine."

"Wren, you wear, like, a size six. Her feet are at least a nine, maybe a ten."

"All you giant feet people," Wren grumbles. "Well, it's not too much farther. Do you think we should drive her to the hospital?"

"Of course we should," Penny says.

"No hospital," I say, my raspy voice interrupting their bickering. "I'll be fine."

They stop in the path, apparently shocked that I'm coherent.

"Tara, are you all right? What happened?" Wren asks, chafing my fingers.

Penny stares at me with enormous, worried eyes.

I shake my head. "I don't know." I don't know whether I'm fine and I don't know what happened. All I know is that I'm exhausted and my soul feels wrung out. My brain feels like someone padded it with gauze.

I try to think through the last few days, the last few hours. I remember watching Isabella write, watching *Cicada* hurtle toward its ending. Eugenia meeting her lover in the woods, stabbing him in the throat. Going home and laboring for hours and then screaming in triumph as Isabella slithered into a world scented with both her mother's and her father's blood. In the final scene, Eugenia held the baby in her arms, and she was as mighty and vengeful as any god, a dark queen who brought life into the world on her own terms, who would destroy anyone, anything to see her child thrive. The baby girl drank her mother's milk, and Eugenia whispered the child's name like an oath, like a threat, like a spell.

For one moment, Isabella and I were both that child, safe in its mother's arms, cherished, beloved. And then there was a wave of grief, a tsunami of despair. I was obliterated, torn apart. I disappeared into the darkness.

I don't remember anything after that.

"I guess what happened is that Isabella finished her book," I say.

"Tara, I—" Penny starts to say, but then someone yells.

We all turn, and there's Jordan, jogging up the path toward us.

"Hey," he calls. "Is she okay?"

"Thank God, you got my text. Can you give Tara your shoes?" Wren asks. "Oh, and does she have hypothermia, do you think?"

Jordan approaches me warily, as if I'm a wounded woodland creature. He feels the pulse in my wrist and studies me for a moment. "No, I don't think she has hypothermia." He bends to inspect my feet and grimaces. "Come on, then," he says to me. "Put your arm around my neck."

I do as he asks, and he lifts me into his arms. "This will be faster. Let's get you into the warm."

I know I'm supposed to be mad at him—at all of them—but the only thing I can feel is relief. I'm not alone in the dark with Isabella anymore. I lay my head against Jordan's chest and feel the tears start to come. I'm too tired to fight them, and soon they grow into sobs.

"Shh, it's all right," Jordan says. "Everything will be fine." He's so gentle and so good, and I can't quite remember why I thought he wasn't my friend.

I wipe my eyes with a shaking hand and take a shuddering breath, hiccupping around a final sob. "I'm okay," I say, more to myself than to the others.

"How are you this buff?" Wren asks Jordan after a few minutes of silence. "When do you even have time to work out? The rest of us have the muscle tone of jellyfish."

Jordan laughs, and I feel the rumble in his chest. "I do push-ups every morning when I wake up."

"Oh, for God's sake," Penny says. "Have you considered taking up a vice? Allowing yourself an imperfection?"

When Jordan speaks, I can hear the smile in his voice. "Well, I'm friends with you lot, aren't I?"

Wren boos him and Penny laughs. I shiver into Jordan's warmth and listen to the music of their voices as we make our slow and steady way through the woods. I'm cold and achy and miserable, but it's better than it was before, while I was lost inside Isabella's mind. Here, in the warmth of Jordan's arms, surrounded by my friends, I feel almost like myself again. I feel almost safe.

But while Isabella has released me from her hold for the moment, I know she isn't gone. She's still inside me, waiting. *Cicada* might be finished, but Isabella isn't finished with me. I'm bound to her for the next four years, if not forever.

Still, for a few minutes, I allow myself to feel safe, even if I know the safety isn't real. For a few minutes, I let myself pretend that my life doesn't belong to Isabella Snow.

By the time I'm showered, dressed in warm clothes, and tucked under the blankets in my bed, I realize that I don't want to be at Denfeld Hall. I want to be almost anywhere else but here. Jordan bandages the cuts on my feet, which thankfully aren't deep. Wren brings me a bowl of chicken noodle soup and watches while I eat it. Penny sits next to me on the bed and explains how they looked for me for hours after a senior Magni Viri student saw me walk into the woods at dawn. She keeps reaching out to touch me but then drawing back her hands as if she's afraid.

"What can I do for you?" Penny finally asks. "What do you need?" She looks guilty and helpless.

I can feel the tears near the surface, wanting to break free again. "I don't want to be here," I say miserably. "I can't go back to sleep and let her . . ." I shake my head. "It was—she was . . ." The tears roll down my cheeks, irrepressible. "It's like I was gone. And I wanted to be gone. She's too strong for me."

"Is there somewhere I can drive you?" Penny asks.

I cry harder. There's nowhere for me to go. Mom has disappeared. I don't even know how to get in contact with my dad, not that I'd want to. And Robin's parents would never let me stay with them.

Penny scrunches up her face. "Is there someone from campus you know? Someone you trust? Like, a professor maybe?"

I think of Dr. Hendrix's frequent offers of help, but I can't call her, not after how I've been skipping her class and ignoring her emails. Besides, if I tell her what's going on, she'll go straight to O'Connor, and I can't have that. Knowing him, he'd make good on his promises to kick me out and destroy my academic prospects.

Who else is there?

"Mr. Hanks," I say, alighting on the idea with relief. I remember his gruff affection, the quiet sureness of his presence. He did say that if I ever needed help to ask him for it. It's Saturday, so he won't be on campus. But I have his cell number.

I look around for my phone. Penny puts it into my hand.

"Can you give me a minute?" I ask her.

She nods and leaves the room. I know she wants things to be normal between us again, but now that I'm thinking clearly, I'm remembering all the reasons I have not to trust her. Not to trust any of them. They all lied to me. They all betrayed me.

I dial Mr. Hanks. He answers on the third ring.

"Tara?" he asks, surprised and worried-sounding. "Are you all right?"

I gulp down a sob. "No," I say. "No, I'm not all right."

"Where are you?" he asks, alarmed.

"Denfeld. Can you—can you come get me? I know it's a lot to ask, but . . . but do you think I could stay with you for a little while? With you and your sister?"

He pauses for a long time, and if I were in better shape, I'd be embarrassed for asking. I wouldn't blame him for saying no. It would look strange to people—a female student staying at a school employee's house, and a male one at that.

"Of course you can," he finally says. "But my truck's in the shop today. And my sister's out running errands. Is there someone who could drive you?"

"Yes," I say. "What's your address?"

At first, Penny is quiet as she drives, lost in thought, her eyes on the road. I'm too tired to make an effort, still exhausted from Isabella's ravages. I lean my head against the window and struggle against the urge to fall asleep, watching the endless woods rush by my window. But finally, after I don't know how long, Penny clears her throat.

"Tara? Are you awake?" she asks.

"Yeah," I say, not moving.

"Look, I don't know where to begin. How to say I'm sorry. It's all so complicated."

I pull myself away from the window and look at her. Even in profile, she looks tired and guilty, her shoulders hunched as if the steering wheel is holding her up.

"Did you ever even really like me?" I ask, my voice hard. "Or were you pretending?"

Penny glances at me, her brow furrowed. "Of course I liked you. God, from like the first time I met you, I liked you."

"Why?" I ask, a feeling of emptiness washing over me again. *I am nothing, I am no one. I am a vessel for Isabella Snow.*

"Why did I like you?" Penny asks.

I nod.

She purses her lips, thinking. "Because you're so earnest."

"What?" I say, almost laughing. It's not what I expected to hear.

"I'm serious," Penny says, smiling. "You bring this incredible focus and attention to everything you do. Like, when you're listening to someone tell a story, you listen with your whole body, taking it all in. When you work on an assignment, you give your whole self to it. And when you kissed me that first time in the cemetery . . ." She shakes her head, smiling. "It felt like I was the only thing in the world."

"You were," I say.

Penny's eyes go shiny. "Tara, I like everything about you. I like the freckles on your nose. I like the way you walk in those boots you're always wearing. I like how kind you are, how much you care about everyone. I like how you cry when you get mad. I like how real you are, how you're never pretending to be someone you're not. Tara, you are, like, basically, my dream girl."

Her words cover me in warmth, like a weighted blanket. I could curl up in them and rest. But it's not enough. It doesn't excuse what she's done. I rub my face, frustrated. "But you lied to me. You kept things from me," I finally say. "You let Magni Viri ruin my life."

She sighs. "I never planned on . . . falling for you. For a while, I wished I hadn't. When things got so bad and I wasn't able to tell you anything, I wished that you had been someone else, someone I didn't like so much. That's all I meant."

"What you meant when?"

"When I said that maybe it was a mistake to date you. Because falling for you . . ." She shakes her head. "God, it made everything so much harder. That's why I've been avoiding you. I guess I was afraid of causing you even more harm."

"Avoiding me caused me harm," I say.

Penny blows out a hard breath. "I know. I fucked everything up."

I stare at her, wanting so badly to forgive her. But there are still so many unanswered questions, so many things I can't let go of. What if I forgive, and nothing changes? Will I just be repeating my relationship with my mom all over again? Allowing her to hurt me over and over, only to keep letting her back in, always wanting to believe that this time she'll be different?

But I never really found the words to tell my mom how I felt. I was never sure she'd listen. Now, after everything that's happened in the last few weeks, after being silenced by Isabella again and again, I don't want to bury those words anymore. I can find them now, after all I've been through. I have to, if I want to be more than a casualty in my own life. I have to learn to stand up for myself, to tell people what I feel, what I want.

I'm quiet for a long moment, thinking over what I want to say. Finally, haltingly, I begin to speak. "I want to move on. I want to forgive you," I say. "But you hurt me, Penny. You hurt me so badly." I take a deep, shuddering breath. "All of you did, but you especially. I—I mean, I opened up to you, I trusted you. That's not easy for me to do." Tears are running down my cheeks again, and I wipe them angrily away.

Penny nods, swallows hard. My chin starts to quiver, and when I'm able to speak again, the words come out strained, half a sob. "And then you—you ripped my heart out of my chest." I gasp in a breath, trying to get my voice under control. "I haven't ever felt so alone. These last weeks have been awful."

"I know," Penny says, her voice anguished. "And if I could find a way to undo it all, I would. I understand if you can't ever forgive me. I'm not sure I would be able to forgive me if I were you. But . . . well, I really hope you can."

"Me too," I say, almost in a whisper.

Before I can say more, the GPS notifies us of the next turn. It's the road Mr. Hanks's house is on. We're out of time. I wipe the last of my tears away, wait for my breathing to steady.

"We're here," Penny says a minute or so later as she pulls my car up Mr. Hanks's long, rugged, tree-lined drive. His house is about an hour from school, but it feels farther. It feels a million miles away from Denfeld, maybe because instead of sitting down in a valley, it's perched up high on a ridge.

It's an old wooden house that's clearly been lovingly maintained. The white paint is fresh and bright and the flower beds are tidy, even now in late autumn. It's surrounded by a bit of forest in the back. The whole place looks homely and peaceful—the absolute opposite of Denfeld Hall. Just the sight of it makes me feel better.

Penny turns to me, her eyes traveling over my face, unsure of herself, unsure of what to say. "Is this really where you want to be?" she finally asks.

"Definitely," I say as Mr. Hanks comes out the front door

and stands on the porch. Instead of his usual work uniform, he's wearing a pair of blue jeans and a flannel shirt. A woman in a Corbin College sweater follows him out to the porch, and I realize she must be his twin. They're the same height and build, and they look almost exactly alike, except that on her Mr. Hanks's features don't look so forbidding. She smiles at us and waves.

When we open the car doors, she calls out to us. "Welcome. Come on in when you're ready!" Then she turns and goes back into the house. I adjust my beanie as I climb out of the car, making sure it covers my hair.

Mr. Hanks walks down from the porch. He nods at me and goes around to the trunk to get my bag. "And who might you be?" he asks Penny.

"She's my friend from Magni Viri," I say. "Penny Dabrovsky."

"Pleased to meet you," Mr. Hanks says, hefting my bag onto his shoulder.

"Can I—can I come in for a little while?" Penny asks.

Mr. Hanks nods.

At first I think she wants to check up on the place, make sure I'll be safe, but then I realize she's limping. Sitting in the car for so long must have made her stiff and achy, not to mention half carrying me through the woods to keep me from dying of exposure. My anger at her softens, and without thinking, I touch her hand as we go up the porch.

She glances at me, relief washing over her features. But then we're inside, and our attention is taken up with looking around.

The inside of Mr. Hanks's house is floor-to-ceiling book-shelves.

"Wow," I say. A quick scan tells me there's a ton of history, astronomy, and geology.

"More than one way to get an education. Remember that," Mr. Hanks says. He motions to the right of the front door with his head. "There's a guest room back here you can stay in. Right next to Marla in case you need anything. I'm gonna put your bag in there."

"Thanks," I say, my eyes still on the books.

"We're so glad you're here, sweetheart," Marla says, coming out of the kitchen. She wraps me in a big, welcoming hug. I stiffen at first but then relax into it. Marla holds my shoulders and studies me. "You look like you could do with a bit of feeding up." She puts the back of her hand to my fore-head. "You feel a bit feverish too." She smiles sadly. "Never you mind. We'll get you sorted."

"This is Penny," I say, extricating myself from Marla's grip.

Marla hugs Penny too. "I saw you were walking gingerly, honey. What have you girls been up to?"

Penny and I exchange a dubious look.

Marla laughs lightly. "We'll worry about it later. Penny, are you going to stay for dinner?"

"Oh. Oh, I don't know," Penny says, sticking her hands in her pockets.

"You're welcome to. Y'all aren't vegetarians, are you?"

"No, ma'am," I say. "Penny, you should stay," I add. Even if I'm mad at her, I don't want her driving back to campus in pain. Besides, I want to finish the conversation we started in the car.

Penny nods and smiles, and her shoulders come up around her ears in the most awkward, charming kind of way. I feel more of my anger chip away.

Marla looks around us. "Hey, Coy, get your butt out here and give these girls a tour while I fix dinner."

I flinch. "Did you call him 'Coy'?" That's Eugenia's brother's name in *Cicada*, a strange name I'd never heard before and had written off as one of the odder, old-timey names. But maybe it's common in these parts.

"You can call me Coy too if you want," Mr. Hanks says. "Now that you're not my employee."

"Oooh, he was sad as an old cow when you went and quit on him, Tara," Marla says, bustling off to the kitchen.

"I wasn't either," Mr. Hanks says. "My sister exaggerates. I do miss your help though. This new boy I hired can't even work a broom. Come on, I'll show you 'round."

He leads us around the house, showing us the kitchen and dining room, living room, bathroom, all the usual stuff. He leads us out of a sunroom attached to the back, which is full of houseplants, and into the backyard. There's a strange sort of little shed in the middle of the yard.

"Look here," he says, a note of pride creeping into his voice. He leads us over to the shed and opens the door, flicks on a light. There's a big piece of machinery right in the middle of the floor. It's a long cylinder painted white, mounted on a complicated-looking metal stand. Parts of it are covered in silver duct tape.

"Oh, a telescope," Penny says. But it doesn't look like any telescope I've ever seen. She approaches it, circling, studying all the pieces. "You made this, didn't you?" she asks, looking up at him in surprise.

He gives a sharp, short nod. "Ground the lenses myself."

"Oh wow, that's impressive," Penny says. She glances at me. "Azar would flip over this."

"Our friend Azar Davani," I explain. "She's an engineering major—and a space geek." I try and fail to suppress a yawn.

"I'll give you a demonstration sometime when you're not about to keel over," Mr. Hanks says, leading us out of the shed and back toward the house. He opens the door to the sunroom for us. "Why don't you girls go relax for a little while? Tara, you can get settled in."

After a few words with Marla, Penny and I head back to the guest room. We collapse onto the bed without speaking, and then we both laugh. We roll over to face each other.

"I've missed you," Penny says, so much longing in her voice I almost reach for her. Almost.

"I've missed you too," I admit, but I know I'm not ready to let her back in. Not yet.

She must read something of my thoughts because her face falls. "I'll keep saying I'm sorry as long as I have to, until I've earned your forgiveness. I'm sorry for letting O'Connor do this to you. I'm so sorry for not telling you from the beginning, for letting it go on so long. I'm sorry for hurting you. For all of it."

I nod. "Can you just . . . go over it all again? Why you lied to me. Help me understand."

Penny's expression opens, a bit of hope creeping into her eyes. "It's like we told you before, we were scared. Isabella killed Meredith, and we were afraid that if you knew the whole truth, you'd resist her and she'd kill you too."

"But if you'd just warned me before I joined Magni Viri—" I start, unable to let that idea go. If they had stopped me from joining, if they had told me what I was truly signing up for, none of this would have happened, would it?

Penny lets out a long, regretful sigh and pauses as if gathering her thoughts. "When O'Connor told us that Isabella had already picked you and there was nothing we could do about it, we did try to argue with him . . . at first."

"You did?" I ask, grudgingly surprised. That can't have been easy. My own confrontations with O'Connor have been awful.

Penny nods. "Yeah, but the more we pushed back, the madder he got. He said that if we tried to keep you from joining, it would mess up the whole system, that Magni Viri would fall apart without everything in place as it should be. That if we thought dealing with our ghosts was hard now, it was going to get nearly unbearable as Isabella disrupted the other ghosts' equilibrium.

"And when that didn't work, he started in on the personal threats. He asked if we wanted to lose our scholarships, our futures. He laid it on so heavy that finally we accepted what he was saying. We thought we didn't really have a choice. I think it felt too hard not to believe him, you know? Like, it was in our best interest to believe him and go along with his plan."

That part stings. That they chose to believe O'Connor for their own sakes. But I get it too. Would I have behaved any differently with my own future at risk? Besides, I'm not entirely sure O'Connor was lying. It does feel like Isabella marked me for her own.

"I swear, we did everything we could to keep you safe. We watched over you. We did it in shifts, someone always keeping an eye out for you."

"So you spied on me?" I ask tiredly.

"No, not all!" Penny says. "It's not something O'Connor told us to do or anything. We just wanted to make sure you were safe. And we wanted Isabella to know we were watching too, that you weren't alone."

"I felt alone."

"I know," Penny says, something in her voice twisting. Tears brighten her eyes. "But you're not alone now, not if you don't want to be. I'm here, and I'm not going anywhere." She meets my eyes, her gaze fierce and protective, almost possessive.

I know I could hold on to my anger, that I could withhold forgiveness. I'd be well within my rights. But I also know that it's what Isabella would want me to do. She'd want me to stay alone, isolated, resentful, angry. Just like her.

I don't want to be like Isabella. I don't want to keep a wall between me and the person who cares about me more than anyone else does. I'm tired of being alone, and Penny is right—I don't have to be. With a shuddering breath, I reach out for her hand.

Penny's tears finally overflow and trace their way down her cheeks as she laces her fingers in mine. "Thank you," she says. She brings our clasped hands to her mouth and brushes her lips over my knuckles, featherlight. We hold each other's gaze for a long moment.

I cross the distance between us until our bodies lie pressed together, my lips inches from hers. "I forgive you," I say. And then I kiss her, long and deep, for the moment forgetting everything except the relief of being held in her arms. At home, at peace.

But when we pull away from each other, all my worries come rushing back. "Will she be able to get to me here?" I ask, taking off my beanie. My hair is a constant reminder of Isabella's power over me.

Penny considers. "No. No, I don't think she will. Or at least, not like before. The ghosts need the proximity to Denfeld and all the Magni Viri students. It's why most of us don't go home for the holidays, why we do summer school. Or at least that's what Quigg told me. The nearness to Denfeld is super important. That's partly why we do the Sunday night parties in the cemetery, to sort of tighten the bonds between us and the ghosts. To keep the connection strong."

She bites her lip. "You're not going to leave for good, are you? You're not going to go home?"

"I don't have a home to go to," I admit.

"What? What do you mean?"

I hide my face in the pillow. "After I realized about Isabella . . . I tried to call my mom and ask to go home. But she—she's gone. Moved, quit her job, changed her number. She doesn't want me to find her."

"Jesus, Tara," Penny says. She scoots closer to me and wraps her arms around me again. "I'm so sorry."

I let Penny hold me. The tears rise to my eyes, but I'm about cried out at this point. I just lie close to Penny's warmth and breathe in her woodsy smell. I let myself be comforted.

"You can sleep if you want to," she says into my hair. "I won't let anything happen to you."

"Thank you," I whisper. I close my eyes. I lie still, listening to Penny breathe, and before long, I'm asleep.

Someone knocks on the half-open door. Marla sticks her head into the twilight-hued room, her features lit by the hallway light. "Girls, dinner's ready if you're hungry."

I lift my face out of Penny's hair. "Thanks, Marla. Be right there."

Marla smiles gently at the way Penny and I are twined together. "I'm sorry to wake you. You two looked so peaceful." There's a wistful quality to her voice.

"It's all right," Penny says, slowly and painstakingly sitting up. "Thank you for letting me stay for dinner."

Marla winks at us and disappears.

The table is piled high with Southern food: cornbread, pork chops, collard greens with ham. There's even a pecan pie. I haven't eaten food like this since coming to Corbin.

The four of us eat in silence for a while, too occupied with the meal in front of us to bother speaking. The food tastes so much like home that tears sting my eyes.

"Good?" Marla asks us.

"Marla, you're a wizard," Penny says. "I didn't even know I liked Southern food."

"Where are you from, honey?" Marla asks.

The two of them carry the conversation, talking about Pennsylvania and food traditions. I am content to listen, to soak in this atmosphere of safety and warmth and wholeness. Penny puts her hand on my knee, and I twine my fingers through hers. Mr. Hanks shoots me little concerned looks, probably worrying over what might have happened to bring me to his door. I wonder how long he'll let me stay before he asks why I'm here.

By the time dinner is over, I'm swaying in my chair from exhaustion.

Penny says she had better get started on the drive back to campus. I walk her to the door, a little awkward on my bandaged feet. "You sure you'll be all right driving back alone?" I ask. "I'm sure they wouldn't care if you want to stay the night."

She shakes her head. "I'll be fine. I have to take my meds, and there are some things I need to do."

"You need to get back to your ghost, don't you?" I ask, seeing what she's carefully avoiding saying. "It's the bat researcher who had a heart attack over the summer, right?"

Penny nods. "Yeah, Dr. Coppola." She hesitates. "I'm sorry. I wish I could stay, but—"

"No, don't worry about it. We'll talk tomorrow." There's so much Penny and I still need to say. So much she needs to tell me. But tonight I'm glad to leave it be, to leave everything be.

"You'll be all right here, yeah?" Penny asks.

I nod. She kisses me, and before I can say anything else, she's headed down the porch steps, moths flying around her head. "Call you in the morning," she says. And then she's gone, the taillights of my car disappearing into the dark. I watch until I can't see the faintest glimmer of them.

I sit in a rocking chair on the porch and listen to the

nighttime sounds, not quite ready to go inside yet. I expect to feel lonely, but I don't. I just feel tired. Tired and in need of rest.

After a while, Mr. Hanks comes out and sits in the rocker next to mine. "It'll be nice to have you stay here, Tara. Gets awful quiet with only Marla and me."

I smile at him. "How'd you get such a nice sister anyway?"

He laughs. "Well, we had to share a womb, you know. Maybe the niceness got poorly distributed."

"Nah. You're a lot nicer than you let on. Thank you for helping me. I really needed it," I say.

"You can stay as long as you want. I mean that. And you don't have to tell me anything unless you want to."

"I do, it's just . . . maybe tomorrow. Is that okay?"

"Absolutely," he says. He stands up. "You get some rest. You'll feel better in the morning."

Once he's gone, the night descends again. I think about Penny driving through the dark on her way back to campus. I think about the others, all of them moving around Denfeld Hall, doing their work—or doing someone else's. I think about Isabella's ghost—untethered, searching for me, itching to get back into my skin. I shiver and pull my sweater closer around me.

I still don't know how I ended up in the woods this morning. Why Isabella sent me wandering there without a coat or shoes. I remember writing the last line of *Cicada*. But after that, it's all gone. Maybe she wanted a walk and couldn't be bothered to protect me from the cold. Maybe she wanted to remind me of her power over me. Or maybe she felt as lost as

I did after *Cicada*'s bloody ending.

I take a deep breath of the night-scented air. I'm so glad I'm not at Denfeld tonight. And I'm not sure I'll ever go back again.

Mr. Hanks is right: there's more than one way to get an education. Having a college degree isn't the only way. And Magni Viri sure as hell isn't.

Maybe I need to find my own path.

But for now, I mostly need a place to recover from Isabella Snow.

TWENTY-SEVEN

I get a good night's sleep for the first time in weeks. No nighttime writing. No nightmares. No waking with an aching neck, hunched over my desk. Instead, I wake to the sound of birdsong, warm in my borrowed bed. I feel like I've truly escaped from Isabella, as well as from Magni Viri's clutches. I feel like my life is my own again, even if it's a giant mess and I don't know what I'm going to do next.

I luxuriate in the feeling, lying in bed until I hear Marla and Mr. Hanks clattering dishes in the kitchen. I dress slowly, watching myself in the mirror, looking for signs of Isabella. But my face is my own. No smile lines, no divot in my forehead. Just my own freckled nose and too-small lips, my own blue eyes. I smile at my reflection, and there's nothing sardonic or mocking in it. I'm myself. Ordinary. And for the first time, I'm glad to be ordinary.

Mr. Hanks and his sister are lovingly bickering their way through a pot of tea when I come into the kitchen. Mr. Hanks jumps up to get a cup for me and pushes the milk jug in my direction. Marla makes me a plate of eggs, grits, and biscuits without breaking her conversational stride.

I eat my breakfast and sip my tea, listening to them argue about whether the roses need to be cut back. I wonder what it would be like to wake up every day like this, in a small, homely life; to have a normal job and hobbies and never think about college again. To forget about greatness. To forget about achievement. To choose smaller dreams.

It doesn't look so bad.

But my peace only lasts an hour. I'm helping Mr. Hanks clear away the plates from breakfast when I notice a framed picture in the corner of the glass-fronted china cabinet. My hands go numb and cold. I walk slowly toward the frame and pick it up. The photograph shows a woman holding two fat laughing babies in her lap. The woman is Isabella Snow. Her hair is dark, her eyes are bright, her lips are painted burgundy. It's the first time I've seen her in color—except, of course, in the mirror.

"What have you got there?" Mr. Hanks asks. I turn mechanically toward him and hold out the photo. A sad smile passes over his face. "My cousin Isabella," he says. "And me and Marla, if you can believe it."

"You're related to Isabella Snow?" I ask, trying to keep my voice even, trying not to panic.

Mr. Hanks's eyebrows come together in surprise. "How did you . . . ?"

I shake my head, close my eyes. Mr. Hanks's first name is Coy. He said he's lived here all his life. He's a caretaker of Corbin College, just like Isabella's family was. It seems impossible, but . . .

"Tara?"

I swallow. "Do you remember when I asked if you believe in ghosts?"

Mr. Hanks nods, though he looks bewildered.

"The ghost . . . it wasn't the girl who died. I was wrong. It wasn't Meredith."

His eyes widen with understanding, and then with dismay.

I stagger to a chair, still clutching the picture frame. "I asked you about Magni Viri before I ever joined. You could have told me your cousin was a director in it."

Mr. Hanks sits too. "We don't . . . we don't tend to talk about her in my family. Is she really . . . ?" His words trail off helplessly.

"She's why I'm here. She's why I'm in this state," I say, gesturing vaguely at myself. I laugh. "And even here, all these miles away, here she is."

Mr. Hanks rubs his face. "She died when I was a child. Some kind of cancer; I never heard what."

"Is that why y'all don't talk about her?"

He shakes his head. "No, it's . . . complicated. My grand-daddy, Coy Dossey, who I was named after, he was her mama's brother. Eugenia was her name. But she's—well, she's not the one who raised Isabella. You see—"

"What? Who raised her?" I ask, interrupting him. Isabella's father couldn't have done it; Eugenia had killed him. But I don't believe Eugenia would have given Isabella up to *anyone*, not willingly. Not with the fierce way she loved her baby at the end of *Cicada*. I remember the way that love felt.

Mr. Hanks rubs his cheek, which needs a shave. "Isabella

was born out of wedlock. That was a much bigger deal back then than it is now, especially in these parts. Her daddy was a boy up at the college."

I steel myself for what comes next. The murder. The inevitable scandal that must have followed.

"Eugenia, she didn't want a baby. She tried to get rid of it, of Isabella, but it didn't work. Abortions weren't legal in the US at all then, and the ones you could get . . ." He shakes his head. "So when Isabella came, Eugenia hated her. She was a danger to that baby, and everyone knew it. After a few weeks, my grandaddy took Isabella to the boy's family—to Isabella's father's family, I mean. They raised her. They were wealthy folk. The one condition was that no one from our family could have contact with Isabella. And so no one did until Isabella came back here to the college as a teacher. Then she sought us out, and we all—"

I hold up a hand. "Wait, so Eugenia never got in trouble for killing the boy?"

Mr. Hanks's head snaps up. "What? What boy?"

"Isabella's dad, Frederick."

Mr. Hanks scrunches up his face. "She didn't kill him. Where did you hear that? That boy left her. My grandaddy had to track him down to make him take responsibility. And even then he didn't. He left it to his parents to handle. Went off to law school someplace."

My head spins. The story Isabella wrote wasn't true. It didn't happen. It seems impossible that the events of *Cicada* are merely fiction when I practically lived through them myself, tangled up in Isabella's mind, Isabella's words. But here's the truth in front of me. Eugenia didn't kill Frederick. She didn't love her baby.

"So Isabella was raised by these rich people, and no one in your family ever saw her?" I ask, incredulous. The events of *Cicada* still feel absolutely real to me.

Mr. Hanks shakes his head. "It was a shock when she came 'round all those years later, so well educated and all those fancy manners and everything. My parents couldn't figure out what on earth she wanted to do with all of us. Eugenia had run off years ago, nobody knew where. So Isabella didn't get a chance to meet her mother. Only to hear about her secondhand, and I don't think she much liked anything she heard. Maybe she thought her mama would be waiting for her with open arms, glad to have her daughter back. It must have been a disappointment."

His words feel like a punch to my stomach. A *disappointment*? That word can't begin to describe it. I know what it must have felt like. Like living through her mother's rejection all over again, the scar that never healed tearing wide open. The same thing I feel every time I try to call my mom and she doesn't answer, knowing deep down that she's never going to answer.

Maybe that's another reason Isabella picked me. Neither of us got the mother a kid deserves. Maybe she sensed that in me—that place where a mother's love is supposed to be. I bet that's why she chose Meredith too, judging by what Penny told me about Meredith's hateful mother. We were like mirrors for her, reflecting her greatest wound.

"What was Isabella like?" I ask, trying hard to picture the events he's describing.

"I didn't really get to know her. I was too young. I only know what my parents and other relatives said about her."

"What did they say?"

Mr. Hanks sighs. "That she was a very complicated woman. Brilliant, a mind like nothing they'd ever seen. But hard-hearted, angry. I don't think she was treated well by the people who raised her. I think she felt she had quite a lot to prove. She was very ambitious. She had enormous aims for herself. I have no doubt she would have achieved them if she'd lived."

I sit quietly for a few moments, absorbing this information. So much of what I assumed was fact in *Cicada* is false. But why? Why did she rewrite her own history, especially in such a bloody, violent way?

"That's pretty much everything I know," Mr. Hanks says. "Is she really— What exactly has been happening to you?"

I don't even know where to begin. But I try to tell him. He's opened his home to me; the least I can do is be honest with him. I tell him everything, right up until the point I landed on his doorstep.

Mr. Hanks looks astonished. "How is this all possible?" He shakes his head. "I'm a scientific man, but I'm not so proud as to reject what my parents and grandparents taught me about this world. I've heard of hauntings and I've seen a ghost or two myself. But this . . . this shouldn't be able to happen."

"It's Magni Viri," I say. "They've done some kind of ritual that binds the dead to new students. The others, they all walked into it knowing what was happening. But Isabella picked me for herself and no one told me. No one told me what I was agreeing to when I joined."

"Is she—is she here now?" he asks, looking around as if to catch sight of her.

I shake my head. "I'm far enough away from campus to be rid of her, I guess. She lost her hold on me. But if I go back . . ." I look up at him. "I'm scared. I'm scared of what she might do to me."

"I hate to think that my own flesh and blood could do this to a girl. Could steal a life that's not hers. Makes me ashamed," he says. "I'll do anything I can do to help you. You just say the word."

I touch his arm. "Thank you. And don't be ashamed. You're the best person I know. You've helped me more than anyone."

He gives me a brief nod. It's the same one he's given me a dozen times before, but now I can see the warmth in it. "I'm proud to know you," he says.

Talking to Mr. Hanks has lifted my spirits a little, made me feel less alone in my own mind. But nothing has changed. Isabella is still waiting for me at Denfeld Hall, and probably growing angrier by the minute. And now I know she didn't just record history; she re-invented it in some bloody vision of her own.

What future does she have planned for me if I go back?

I sit on the bed in the guest room for an hour, mulling over everything Mr. Hanks told me. Isabella's life seems suddenly sadder and smaller—she was abandoned and unloved, unwanted, lonely. She must have created *Cicada* in a desperate attempt to rewrite her mother's feelings for her, to rewrite the trajectory of her own life. But this knowledge doesn't make her less frightening. After all, she's still rewriting reality—now, in my body, with my life.

But it wasn't only my body she borrowed. She was drawing on my feelings and experiences too. She tapped into my own longing for a mother who would do anything for me, who would protect me. She tapped into my own resentment at the mom I got instead. Only she twisted it all. She twisted it to make Eugenia Dossey.

And Isabella wasn't satisfied in the end, no matter how brilliant and powerful her new story was. Because rewriting history doesn't erase what truly happened. A novella is a poor substitute for parents who love you and give you a stable home.

But I think Isabella will keep trying to rewrite history anyway. She's stuck in a lifetime's worth of pain and resentment and anger. She'll write the same story over and over again for the rest of her immortal existence, trying to convince herself it's true.

Or at least she will if I ever go back to Denfeld. But I can't stand to think about it anymore, so I turn my attention to the work I missed while Isabella was wrecking my life. It's probably a waste of time since I can't go back, but I don't have anything else to do. I need something to keep my mind occupied.

When I pull out my Gothic lit folder, guilt floods me. I remember the half dozen emails from Dr. Hendrix. I think she even left me a voicemail once, when things got so bad I stopped going to class. I open my laptop and read through her emails, starting with the oldest. At first, they are apologetic, embarrassed. She was ashamed of losing her temper at my tutorial. But then the tone turns worried. "I am very concerned for you, Tara. Please let me know you are all right," the newest email says. She includes the number for the campus counseling center and closes with the promise that she will contact student services for a wellness check if she doesn't hear from me soon.

"Shit," I breathe. I feel awful that she's been so worried. And I definitely don't want student services in my business. How long ago was this e-mail sent?

I relax when I see it was only a day or so ago and reply quickly, assuring her that I am okay. I apologize profusely for missing class and not responding to her emails. My fingers hover above the keys as I consider how to account for my behavior. "The truth is that I have been a little lost," I write. "I've been having some personal problems that have affected my mental health." It's not exactly the truth, but it's as close as I can get to it without mentioning ghosts. I include another apology and then send the email, holding my breath.

I email my other professors too—all except for O'Connor—to give them a similar excuse for my poor attendance and missing assignments. A few of them email me back over the next few hours to offer extensions. When Dr. Hendrix's response arrives, I let out an enormous sigh of relief. She's not even mad at me. She says she's glad I'm okay and hopes to see me in class. She says to take all the time I need to complete my next essay because "mental health is more important than classwork."

I almost laugh at the difference between her and O'Connor's views on academic achievement. Then I get back to my homework. It feels good to work on essays and math problems, as if I'm just a normal college student. It's good to use my own mind again, separate from Isabella.

But I haven't quite recovered from the beating she gave my body, and I'm drowsing in bed with an anthology of Sumerian poetry draped over my chest when someone knocks on the guest room door. I expect to see Marla or maybe even Penny, but it's Wren standing there. "Hey," they say. "You're looking a lot better. How are you feeling?"

I sit up. "Okay. Still tired, but I don't seem to have any lasting damage."

Wren comes in and sits on the edge of the bed. "I brought you this." They slide a plastic grocery store bag across to me. Inside is a box of hair coloring. A beautiful blonde smiles from the front of the box, her hair cascading over her shoulder. "It's the closest I could find to your natural color."

"Thanks," I say. "And thanks for coming to find me in the woods."

Wren looks at me with enormous, shining eyes. "Tara, when I said that about having to room with you . . . I didn't mean it the way you thought. I only meant that it was so much harder for me to keep things from you because we lived together, not that I didn't like having you for a roommate. I love living with you."

I swallow down another round of tears. "Really?"

Wren nods. "Really. I'm so sorry about everything. God, what a mess."

I study them. Wren is too thin, their eyes too big in their face. They look as tired and frightened as I feel.

"Are we okay now? I really want to hug you," they say.

"Come here," I say, opening my arms. Wren's face breaks into a smile and they practically leap into my lap.

"Everyone else is here," they say once they let go.

My stomach drops. "Everyone who?"

"Jordan, Azar, and Neil. And Penny and me, of course."

"Why?"

"We all need to talk. We need to figure some things out," Wren says. "But it can wait. Right now, they're outside with Mr. Hanks; he's showing them the telescope and his space photography. He and Azar are best friends now. So if you want, I can dye your hair for you."

I nod, glad for a reprieve from what is sure to be another exhausting confrontation, and we head into the bathroom. There's a stack of old towels on the counter. "Marla said we could use these," Wren says. "It might not be perfect, especially on top of that brown, but we'll do our best. Are you okay with bleaching it first?"

"You know how to do this?" I ask nervously.

Wren snorts. "I used to dye my hair twice a month."

"What color?"

"All of them," Wren says with a laugh. They motion to a chair in front of the sink. "Sit here and lean back. I'll work my magic."

When I emerge from the bathroom, I feel a little more like myself. My hair is blond again—the wrong shade, but still— and Wren has trimmed it into a more modern cut. It actually looks pretty good. I know it's just hair, but it feels like having a little piece of myself back.

We make our way through the house. Jordan is sitting on the floor in the living room, poring over a giant geology book from Mr. Hanks's collection. He jumps to his feet when he sees us. "Hey, you're looking better," he says with a smile. When I remember the gentle way he carried me out of the woods yesterday, I decide to skip all the stuff we need to say and go straight for a hug. I squeeze him so hard he lets out a soft little *oof*.

"Everyone else is in the sunroom," he says when I let him go. When we walk into the brightly lit sunroom, Marla and Mr. Hanks excuse themselves, leaving the six of us alone.

My eyes find Penny first. She's sprawled out on the floor, her back against the wall, sun cascading over her upturned face. Her smile widens into a grin. "You look *hot*."

I touch my bangs self-consciously as I take a seat next to her.

"Seriously, Tara, wow," Azar says. "That shag loves you." She's sitting primly on a garden bench, a stack of glossy astronomy photographs in her lap. Neil is next to her, tapping his feet nervously on the ground.

"Thanks," I say. "Why are you all here? If it's to take me back to Denfeld, you can forget it. I'm not going back."

Azar grimaces. "Look, we've behaved like shits. And we're all sorry for it. But you need to understand. See, O'Connor . . . you know what he's like. He didn't give us a lot of choice."

"There's always a choice," I say.

"Oh, fuck you, Tara!" Neil snaps. "Ever since you got

here, you act like you're the only one with problems. We've all got our whole lives riding on Magni Viri. We all stand to lose everything if we step out of line."

The others try to shout him down, but he keeps talking. "Every single person in this room has a reason for what they did. We all have a reason that we need Magni Viri. No one would agree to join the program without one."

"That's true," Azar says.

"Well, what are they?" I ask, crossing my arms over my chest. "What's so important that you would do this to yourselves—and to me too?"

Jordan leans forward on the wooden swing where he sits next to Wren. "My grandparents raised me. They are both disabled and on a fixed income. They could never afford a school like Corbin, or any school at all. They've got so much medical debt. I need to be as successful as possible so I can take care of them. I owe them everything I am." He lifts his chin slightly, and I see the steel beneath his gentle surface.

Penny nudges me. "I couldn't afford this school either. And you already know how I feel about . . . how I'm afraid I'll run out of time."

I meet her eyes. "I remember."

Wren bites their lip. "My family has money, but they're really conservative. My parents cut me off when I came out."

That surprises me. Wren never mentioned any family issues to me. Maybe Neil is right that I act like I'm the only one with problems. "I'm sorry," I say. "I had no idea."

Wren shrugs. "I don't like to talk about it."

After a beat of silence, Azar huffs. "Everyone in my family

is so successful. My older siblings are all at Ivies. It's ridiculous. And I work so hard, but . . ." She shakes her head. "It's never enough. I'm good at understanding concepts and ideas, and I'm good with my hands, good at building things, but nothing else comes easy to me. The essays, the tests . . . it's all a struggle. I just wanted a chance to prove what I'm capable of."

"But, Azar, you're, like, a genius," Wren says.

Azar shrugs. "I'm not. I just work my ass off."

Everyone turns to stare at Neil, the only one who hasn't offered up a secret.

He grits his teeth. "Not that it's any of your fucking business, but I guess we're kumbayaing, so I'll tell you. My parents wouldn't pay for college unless I major in business and work for my dad's firm when I graduate. I'd rather die than do that soul-killing shit, so I am renting out my body to a dearly departed Magni Viri alum in exchange for a successful art career. Fucking sue me."

Azar snorts.

"Who . . ." I try to find words for the question I want to ask. "I've got Isabella. What about the rest of you?"

Wren gives me a lopsided smile. "Don't you already know mine?"

"Walter Weymouth George?" I guess.

Wren nods. "WWG, yeah. I was worried you had guessed when you asked me about him."

"It was a pretty big clue actually, when I was trying to work everything out."

"How *did* you figure things out?" Azar asks.

I sigh. "I mean, once Isabella showed me her face, I was

bound to find her. Her picture was hanging in O'Connor's office, for God's sake. But when I found her grave, I remembered the vow I made in the cemetery. In the end, it wasn't that hard to put the pieces together."

"A little harder to dig up a corpse," Neil quips.

"That wasn't supposed to happen," Azar says sternly. "We were taking turns keeping an eye on you when things got so bad. That night was Neil's turn and he went way off script."

"I can't believe you were all keeping an eye on me that whole time."

"You thought we'd all abandoned you, huh?" Wren asks guilty.

I nod. "And then when Penny told me about it yesterday, I kind of thought you had been spying on me for O'Connor."

Wren wrinkles their nose. "We deserve that. But we were really just trying to find ways around him. We couldn't tell you anything, but we thought at least we could make sure you didn't get hurt. Or at least we tried."

"Well, I know now. So there's no reason to hide things from me. I need y'all to tell me everything. Everything you know."

The others look at each other. "Honestly, we don't know that much," Jordan says. "O'Connor explained only the bare minimum to us. Some other stuff we've heard from older students. We don't exactly know what's true and what's rumor."

"But we'll try to answer your questions," Wren adds hurriedly. "It's the least we can do. What do you want to know?"

One question after another presents itself to me. It's hard to know what to ask first, what to focus on. "So how much of the work students are doing is theirs, and how much is the ghosts'?" I finally settle on.

"In theory, it's supposed to be 50–50. And for some of us it is," Azar says. "Though there are definitely days we have to fight for that 50 percent. Seems like a lot of days lately," she adds in a murmur.

"For me it's almost like a mentorship," Penny says. "Dr. Coppola is really easy to work with. Our minds are compatible, I guess. It's not just her work. It's mine too. We're working together."

"It's mostly the same for me," Jordan says. "Welty can get out of hand sometimes, and lately, he's been getting worse, but we're basically a team. We're able to combine a lot of his natural instinct with my modern knowledge."

"But not all the ghosts are like that," I say. "Isabella isn't."

"No, Mer always said that Isabella was like a steamroller, trying to completely take over," Neil agrees. "She picked the wrong vessel because Mer wasn't willing to take a backseat."

"I think Isabella picked me because she thought we were the same, that I'd be a better vessel for her story. Because I was so angry and empty and alone." I look away from them, embarrassed. I didn't want to believe O'Connor when he said he saw me in Eugenia, but he was right all along.

Cicada might have been a product of Isabella's skill and ideas, but she filtered everything through me. My perspective, my feelings, my way of seeing the world. Twisted and nearly unrecognizable, but there.

"Hey, you're nothing like her," Wren says. They put a hand on my arm. "And you're not alone anymore. You have us."

I try to smile. I want Wren to be right. I want to be better than Isabella was. I think I can try to be. I know I want a different life than she did, that I want to let go of old hurts, that I want to let new people love me instead of pining for those who never will.

"What about the rest of you?" I ask. "What are your ghosts like?"

Wren smiles wistfully. "You know how something can be absolutely terrible for you and absolutely wonderful at the same time? That's WWG."

We talk on and on, and I learn about the other ghosts who are tethered to mine. A musician, an artist, a scientist, an engineer, an ecologist. I have to admit that some of the work they were doing when they died is hugely important, that it ought to be carried on. If Jordan is able to finish his ghost's research, he could cure nearly every type of cancer there is.

But is that truly worth everything Jordan has to give up? There are other ways to carry on a person's work without loaning them your body, your mind, your well-being. And shouldn't every person only get one shot at life, no matter how brilliant they are?

"So when O'Connor dies, does he get to be buried in the cemetery by Denfeld and have his work carried on?" I ask.

Neil snorts. "What work? O'Connor hasn't done anything worthwhile. He's just a suit."

"A fanatical suit," Azar says, raising an eyebrow. "Nobody believes in Magni Viri the way he does."

"He was in Magni Viri when he was a student," Penny says. "And he stayed on as a resident director like Laini. But he never did anything really remarkable after that time. He's still riding his ghost's coattails. He knows he won't get a grave, but he wants to be near the program. He wants to protect it."

"That's why he was willing to sacrifice you to Isabella, even after she killed Meredith," Wren says. "The Magni Viri bylaws say that a ghost that causes serious physical harm to a student will be cut off. Isabella should have been released after that. But O'Connor wasn't willing to let her go. He thought her work was too important."

"More important than Meredith's life," Neil snarls. "And yours."

"He's kind of a monster," Wren says sadly.

"When he brought us in, he lied about what it would all be like too," Azar says. "He said it would be an equal partnership, that we would still be in charge of our own work and futures. But most of us don't have any true autonomy, any choice. We're stuck, even those of us who like the work we're doing."

"We're all giving up a lot more than we planned. He manipulated all of us," Jordan says. "And we're only a few months in. A lot of the older students . . . well, you can see what they look like. The ghosts seem to take a stronger hold the longer they are embodied. It affects everyone differently. Like, Bernard Cottingham? He's going to get someone killed, if not himself. And O'Connor won't lift a finger to stop it."

"Can't we do anything about him?" I ask. "Isn't there, like, a board or something? And, wait, did you say there are bylaws?"

"We only know about that because of Quigg," Penny says.

"O'Connor tells him more stuff than the rest of us since he's his assistant. But O'Connor keeps most of us in the dark as much as possible. He tells us only the bare minimum, and if we ask questions, he threatens us. Hell, maybe the board wants it that way so we can't make too much trouble. I don't know."

"I mean, there's a reason they picked us all, isn't there?" Jordan says, an edge of anger in his voice. "It's not because they love diversity. Not because they believe in educational equity. They picked us because we all have a vulnerability to exploit. We can all be manipulated for one reason or another." He pauses. "There are a lot of reasons playing host to a white dude didn't feel good, but knowing where this is going . . ." He shakes his head.

"Yeah, exactly," Azar says. "The word *colonization* comes to mind."

I look between the two of them, taken aback. Sharing my mind with Isabella has been horrible. I hadn't even considered what it might be like for Azar and Jordan to have white men inhabiting their psyches.

"Even if we could get through to the board members, it wouldn't matter. They don't care about us," Azar says. "O'Connor has all the power here."

"Who's on the board?" I ask. "Do you know?"

"Major donors, MV alums, former directors. Some businesspeople who must know enough to want to keep an eye on young people to invest in," Jordan says. "No one who's going to give a shit about our well-being."

We fall into silence. Finally, Neil asks the question

everyone else is thinking. "Tara, are you really not coming back to Denfeld?"

"How can I? Isabella is going to kill me." Before, I thought I could let her take the reins and try to make it through in one piece. I know better now.

The others exchange a pained glance.

"What?"

"For all his bullshit, I don't think O'Connor was lying about the damage Isabella could do," Neil finally says. "She's stirring the other ghosts up. They're getting harder to control, intruding more, working us harder. Things were always precarious. But we . . . we think it's about to get dangerous for everyone."

"So don't go back," I say. "Let's none of us go back."

Penny shakes her head angrily. "It's not fair. None of this is fair."

"What can we do?" I say desperately. "There has to be something we can do."

"Well," Wren says quietly, "I do have one idea." Their mouth turns up at the corner. "How do you all feel about breaking and entering?"

TWENTY-EIGHT

Once we all quiet down, Wren explains. "One night when Quigg and I were hanging out, he told me that O'Connor keeps a locked cabinet under his desk that contains decades' worth of information about Magni Viri. Occult books, records and paperwork, the bylaws, everything. It's all there. Everything he doesn't want the students to get their hands on. If we had that information, I bet we'd actually have some power."

"So you want to steal that stuff?" Azar asks skeptically.

"Well, if we can see it, maybe there's something in there that will help us. Maybe there's a way to protect Tara from Isabella. To protect all of us."

Everyone is quiet a long moment, thinking. "How do we get into O'Connor's office?" Penny asks.

"Maybe Mr. Hanks can get us the key," Neil says.

I shake my head. "I don't want to risk getting him in trouble. Not when he's done so much for me already. Besides, even if we get into the office, we'll still have to unlock the cabinet."

Azar closes her eyes and groans like she's about to say something she knows she'll regret. "I'm an expert lock picker."

"What?" everyone yells at the same time. Neil laughs with obvious delight.

"I used to practice lock picking as a . . . hobby," Azar says. "And, fine, I was a horrible bratty little snoop when I was a kid and liked to break into my siblings' rooms to read their diaries and shit like that. I'm not proud of it."

"You're kidding," I say.

Azar's stony face says she's not. "I can do it. But the question is, is this really what we want to do? If O'Connor finds out, he'll rain down fire on our heads."

I remember what he was like after I dug up Isabella, how angry and vengeful. He really would end my academic career without a drop of remorse. Everyone else's too.

"Let's just you and me do it," I say to Azar. "He's already against me. If we get caught, the rest of them can say they don't know anything about it. And you can say I made you do it. I'll take the blame. What do I have to lose?"

"That would mean you have to go back to campus," Penny says. "Where Isabella is. Are you willing to do that?"

I take a deep breath. I feel braver now, surrounded by my friends, knowing they've got my back. Knowing I'm not alone. I don't want to leave Corbin and give them up. I want to stay with them. I want four years with them. And while I know college isn't the only path, it's the path I want, the path I chose. I want my life back.

"I can do it," I say. "I *will* do it."

To my surprise, Azar grins. "Let's do it then."

Neil snorts. "I know you two want to feel all heroic right now, but you're going to need a lookout. So I'm coming too."

"Me too," Wren says. "You'll need two of us for that."

I smile. "All right. But Jordan and Penny, you guys stay out of it, okay?"

"Deal," Jordan says. "We'll just be lying to everyone about where the rest of you are."

"Why?" I ask. "Why would anyone care?"

"Because you're going to do it tonight, aren't you?" he asks. "It's Sunday. You'll all be missing the cemetery party."

I say goodbye to Mr. Hanks and Marla while the others wait outside. I grip my backpack straps, trying to ignore the queasy feeling in my stomach. "Thank you both for everything," I say. "For opening your home to me and—"

"Don't mention it, sweetheart," Marla says, giving me a big hug. "You're welcome here any time. Come right back if you need to." She kisses my cheek and bustles off to the kitchen with a sniffle.

Mr. Hanks rubs the side of his face. "Tara, are you sure about this? About going back—to her?"

"No," I admit. "But you told me before you gotta fight for your life, right?"

He gives a short, sharp laugh. "I did. But that was before I knew the whole of it. I'm worried for you."

"I'm worried for me too."

"But you're right, you can't let her win. Not if there's any way to stop it. You deserve to live your life. If anyone can do it, I believe you can."

"You might have too much faith in me."

"Never," he says. "But you'll come back, won't you? If you

need to? You can consider this your second home now." He lifts his chin, and something in his eyes tells me he knows what my family situation is like. That he's offering me a better one.

"I will," I promise. "And even if I don't need to, I'll still come back to see you and Marla."

"Good girl," he says with a small smile and a nod.

I step forward and hug him tight. I'm so, so glad that I have a place to escape to if our plan fails. I only hope I don't need it.

I open the front door and hurry down the front steps, my jaw clenched tight. "Let's go," I say to the others, tossing my bag into the trunk. I slide into the front seat and start the engine.

Part of me wants to stay here and be at peace. But I know I'd only be hiding, and that wouldn't make me happy. So as we drive away from Mr. Hanks's house on the ridge, I force myself not to look back. I have a life to fight for in Denfeld Hall.

We drive back in the dark—me, Azar, Neil, and Wren in my car. Jordan and Penny left in Neil's SUV hours ago. They're going to tell anyone who asks that the rest of us broke down in my shitty car on the way back from seeing a movie in a nearby town.

It's about 9:00 when we make it to campus and park the car. We sit in the washed-out light of the parking lot for a moment, listening to the engine cool down.

"Are we really going to do this?" Wren asks, disbelief in their voice.

"Yes," Azar says tightly from beside me. "Yes, I believe we are." She digs in her bag for a while before producing a slender leather pouch. When she opens it, metal lock picks gleam in the low light.

"Wow," I breathe. "Oh wow." My heart rate accelerates.

Neil leans forward from the backseat. "Oh, come on, Tara, we've already dug up a grave together, and that's a felony. We're practically partners in crime at this point."

I laugh, though it sounds more like a sob.

"No time like the present, I guess," Wren says, pushing open their door.

Wren and Neil climb out, leaving Azar and me in the car. They're going to scope out the building and make sure we can get in without being seen.

Azar and I sit in silence until the others disappear into the darkness. "I can't believe you're helping me," I finally say. "This is the last thing in the world I expected."

"I'm helping myself too," Azar says. "I'm helping all of us. Stop being so self-centered." But there's a smile playing around her lips.

I laugh. "All right."

Her face turns serious. "I'm doing it for Meredith too. She was our friend, and O'Connor let Isabella kill her and toss her out like a jacket that didn't fit anymore. There should be consequences. Even in a fucked up situation like this, there are supposed to be rules, ethics, lines that don't get crossed. But O'Connor isn't honoring that."

She shakes her head. "All this time, I thought—or maybe I wanted to think—that he picked all of us because we were so smart and so deserving, because he believed in us. I thought I finally had something to make my parents truly proud. But that's not even why I got picked." She sighs. "All of us are disposable in his eyes. It's only the ghosts he cares about."

"Maybe at some point you just have to be proud of yourself and let that be enough," I say.

Azar lets her head fall back against the seat. "Yeah, maybe so. But it's not just about competing with my siblings or pleasing my parents. I really wanted this. I would never have signed on otherwise. I mean, my family isn't really religious, but I still knew better than to fuck around with ghosts. You hear enough stories about jinn . . ." She rubs her eyes. "Anyway, that's why I tried so hard to keep believing in Magni Viri. The work I'm doing—it matters. It could change the world. But I wanted to change the world as *myself*, not as a vessel for someone else."

"I know exactly what—" I start to say, but then my phone dings. I read the text. "Wren says the building is deserted. No one seems to be around. But the outside doors are locked."

Azar shrugs. "One more door won't kill me."

We walk silently through campus to the social sciences building, which thankfully isn't near any popular hangouts. No one is around, except for Wren, who lounges on the steps looking at their phone. We go around the building to the back, which is half-hidden in the gloom of tall trees. Neil's nowhere to be seen, so he must be lurking in the shadows.

Azar gets us inside in under a minute. I shiver in the unheated air of the building as we walk up the stairs and then down the dark hallway. There's not a sound in the building except for a low electrical humming.

Azar stops outside O'Connor's office and puts her ear to the door for a few moments before she gets to work with her lock picks. This time I get to watch her do it, and it's basically the coolest thing I've ever seen. The lock clicks and Azar pushes the door open, revealing a dimly lit office, curtains wide open. "Child's play," she whispers. "Two down, one to go."

"Good luck. Make sure to stay low; someone could probably see inside the window from outside," I whisper back, then turn to keep an eye on the hallways around us.

Azar drops to her knees and crawls inside. I can see through the crack that the room is partly illuminated by a lamppost from outside. Azar ought to be able to make her way without too much trouble. I check my phone to make sure Wren or Neil hasn't texted.

"Found it," Azar calls from inside. Quiet metallic sounds follow. After a few moments, she grunts. "This one's tricky. Really well made."

"Can you get it?" I whisper.

"Oh, I'll get it all right."

I alternate between watching the dim hallways and my blank phone. My pulse ratchets up as the minutes tick by.

"Got it!" Azar says, a little too loudly. I hear her fumbling around. "There's a lot of stuff in here, Tara. What should we take?"

"Let's take everything we can carry," I whisper back.

"Okay, but you're gonna have to help."

I glance at my silent phone once more before shoving it into my back pocket. Then I crawl into O'Connor's office, pulling the door closed behind me. I scurry under the desk where Azar sits, shining a tiny keychain flashlight into the small cabinet there.

"Whoa," I say. My fingertips tingle. There are about twenty leather-bound, crumbling books as well as a smaller volume that turns out to be a journal. "We won't be able to carry out all of this. Unless Wren or Neil comes inside to help."

"I know, I didn't think there'd be so much," Azar breathes. "Plus, whatever we take out, we're gonna have to sneak back in."

"Okay, let's look through everything and only take the stuff that seems most promising," I whisper. Azar nods and pulls out a book. I pull out one too. The spine cracks when I open it, releasing a whiff of incense and blown out candles. It's a heady scent, and despite the precariousness of the situation, I can't help but take a moment to breathe it in. I run my fingers lovingly across the faded pages.

"Stop lusting after the books and get busy," Azar hisses.

I pull out my phone so I can shine a light on the pages. That's when I see Neil's text—from a minute ago.

"Shit!" I whisper. "Quigg's coming. We've got to—"

The stairway door slams. Uneven footsteps come down the hall.

Azar's eyes widen. We start shoving books back into the cabinet. Quigg is singing tipsily to himself, so we know when he reaches the door. He rattles his key in the lock, apparently not realizing it's already open.

We push ourselves deep beneath the desk and hold our breath. I want to believe that Quigg wouldn't rat us out, but he's O'Connor's right-hand man. He has his own skin to save.

The door bangs open, and the light flips on, flooding the room with artificial light. Quigg keeps singing to himself, some showtune I don't quite recognize. He pushes stuff around on the desk for a while before sighing. With a muttered curse, he drops his phone onto the carpet next to his feet. The screen has O'Connor's number pulled up.

"Ughhhh," Quigg says, lurching forward to pick it up. He grabs it and dials O'Connor. "I can't find it," he says into the phone.

I can hear O'Connor's annoyed voice clear as day. "What do you mean you can't find it? It's right on my desk. Quigg, are you drunk?"

"Of course I'm drunk," Quigg says with a dark laugh. "It's Sunday night and I'm slowly losing my bodily autonomy to a fossil from the 1950s, who is frankly much less talented than I am."

O'Connor huffs loudly. "Look on the left hand side of the desk. There's a manila folder. The one on top. You see it?"

Quigg shuffles over, and Azar and I have to pull ourselves in even tighter. "Yes," Quigg says.

"Open it, take a picture of the document on top, and email it to me."

"I see it. The donation summary? Can I text it?" Quigg asks.

"No, email it," O'Connor says curtly. He hangs up.

"Well, fuck you very much," Quigg says to the silent phone.

He stomps out of the office, flicking the light off as he goes. He locks the door and we hear him go off down the hallway, singing.

Azar and I let out a collective breath. "Jesus, that was close," I say. "Think he would have turned us in?"

"I don't know," Azar says. "Quigg's hard to read. He plays the party animal angle pretty hard, but he has a lot riding on Magni Viri. Corbin's the only school that would take him because he has a juvenile record. And some people think he's basically O'Connor's mole, carrying everything he learns back to this office. I mean, O'Connor knows way more than he should about what goes on in Denfeld, and it's sure not Laini telling him. She hardly ever even comes out of her study."

"Unless it's the ghosts who tell him," I say. "Is that possible?"

Azar shrugs. "I hadn't really thought about it before, but yeah . . . absolutely. If they're in control, I mean. They could call him or go to his office."

"So that's how O'Connor knew I dug up Isabella's body," I say, finally putting all the pieces together.

Azar pauses, and when she speaks again, her tone shifts, turns worried. "I feel like Edgar—that's my ghost—I feel like he's getting more and more obsessive, you know? Like, he won't leave the robotics lab. He made me miss a date with Zoe. He's a resentful little shit too."

"So is Isabella," I say, thinking of how she dressed me up and cut my hair after my grave robber stunt. I wonder if the others' ghosts have done things like that too to punish them. "I know she'd go straight to O'Connor if she could. So that means we can't fall asleep and give them control until we finish all of this. We can't risk it."

"It's gonna be a long night," Azar says with a sigh.

There's no sign of any bylaws or other modern documents, but there's plenty else that looks useful. We decide to take the journal and ten of the occult books. I'd rather call Wren in to help us so we could carry it all, but we've already had one near discovery tonight, so I don't want to get greedy.

I text Wren and Neil telling them we're coming out. Then we gather everything up and get out of the building as fast as we can. If we're lucky, we can put all this back before O'Connor even knows that it's gone.

We go out the back door, and Neil steps out of the shadows beneath a tree, startling me so badly I nearly drop my load of books.

"Did Quigg see you?" he demands.

"Obviously not, dumbass," Azar says. "Here, take some of these." She puts half her stack of books in Neil's arms.

"Thanks for the warning," I say. "I saw it just in time."

Neil nods.

Wren comes jogging around the side of the building. "Good work, you two!" they say, grinning. They pull the top few books off my stack. "Wow, these feel ancient."

"Any word from Penny and Jordan?" I ask.

Wren grimaces. "Yeah, Penny texted and said Quigg asked where we were, so our absence was definitely noted."

"Well, what if we go now?" I ask. "Say a kind stranger stopped and fixed the car?" It's the last thing I want to do. I don't want to be anywhere near that graveyard.

"No, let's not waste time," Azar says. "We need to get through these as quickly as we can, right?"

Everyone agrees, so we head to Denfeld. We keep to the shadows as we near the house, not wanting to be spotted by any of the revelers. It's cold enough to make me shiver even though we're walking fast, so the rest of Magni Viri must be miserable down there. It doesn't sound like anyone is having a particularly good time at the party tonight. I can hear low-key indie music and occasional laughter, but it's nothing like the first few raucous Sunday night parties I attended.

We make it up the stairs without being spotted and ensconce ourselves in my and Wren's room. Jordan and Penny promise to join us and bring coffee as soon as the party starts winding down.

We lay the books out in two rows, and as scary and stressful as all of this is, there's a little fizzle in my stomach at the thought of handling arcane research materials like these. The books are weathered and well-used and have mysterious titles like *Binding the Spirits* and *Beyond the Veil*. Their copyright dates are all mid-to-late-1800s.

"Well, here we go," I say, choosing a book at random. "Let's hope we find something before Isabella throws me off a cliff."

"Huzzah!" Azar says. "To Tara not getting thrown off a cliff!" She holds out a book and I gently tap it with mine as if they were wine glasses. Neil mutters something under his breath.

"This is the weirdest study group I've ever been to," Wren says, stretching out on their bed with a particularly fragile-looking book.

After that, the only sounds in the room are pages turning.

TWENTY-NINE

I quickly realize the book I chose is useless. It's a primary text on spiritualism, but it's all theory, and we don't have time for theory. I put it back in the pile and pick up the journal. Maybe we need something more personal to find answers.

The handwriting is archaic, written in a strange, spiky cursive that is nonetheless more readable than Isabella's journals were. The flyleaf tells me it belonged to John Bauer, the bearded, determined-looking cofounder of Magni Viri, who I remember was a professor of metaphysics and theology, as well as an ordained minister.

But this journal was written before he ever came to Corbin, during his student days in Boston. He was part of a student-led occultist club, attempting séances and automatic writing. He mentions someone named Walt over and over again, a dear friend judging by the way he describes him. Was that Walter Weymouth George? Is this when their plans for Magni Viri began?

The journal charts Bauer's increasing obsession with the idea of communing with the dead. For him, it wasn't just a fashionable hobby. He believed that ghosts could be like Virgil in Dante's *Inferno*, guiding a person through the truths of the universe.

So that's how this all started—an undergraduate's spiritual longing. If only he knew how it would all turn out.

As I flip through the pages, Bauer's ideas become more ambitious, his prose more feverish. He felt he was on the verge of finding a way to merge the mind of a spirit and a man, as he put it.

At some point Jordan and Penny come into the room, but I hardly notice them. I'm immersed in Bauer's writing. His mind is nimble and imaginative. He sees possibilities everywhere. Even though I know the horrible outcome of his ideas, I'm still drawn in by his passion for them.

Penny puts a cup of coffee into my hand. I drink it automatically, wincing at the bitter taste. The girl really should not be allowed anywhere near a coffeepot. I see now why Jordan thought the coffee I made was adequate payment for his help with my math homework.

I dive back into the journal. Three-quarters of the way through it, Bauer decides that he needs a way to open the veil between worlds, to either let the ghosts in or to let himself out. If he can do that, then he feels he can offer them fair trade.

"Has anyone found anything yet?" Neil asks around a yawn, interrupting my reading. He stretches like a cat before collapsing onto my bed next to Azar.

There's a half-hearted collective murmur that amounts to "not much."

"Well," I say, "listen to this." I fill them in on what I've

learned from Bauer's journal, right up to the point where he
decides he needs a way to open the veil.

"Don't we open the veil every time we have an initiation?"
Penny asks.

I think of the charged atmosphere of my initiation, the
feeling of immense connectedness. Looking back, it's clear
when the ghosts all arrived. I felt it, a shift in the air. But what
caused it? The ring of candles? The song we sang?

"Didn't the candles blow out all at once, at the same
moment the song ended?" I muse aloud, my eyes squeezed
tight, trying to recall every detail of that strange night.

"Oh my God," Wren says, sitting up fast. I'm so startled
I nearly spill my coffee. "The music. WWG." They look
between the rest of us, as if we're supposed to understand.

"What?" Neil asks around another yawn.

"Walter Weymouth George," Azar says. "The founder of
Magni Viri?"

"AKA Bauer's dear friend Walt," I add.

"Yes!" Wren yells. "My guy. The composer."

"What about him?" Penny asks, rubbing her eyes. Fatigue
is clearly slowing down everyone's thinking.

"He— It's the music. His music. That we sing at the initiation."

"Oh," I say, finally understanding. "The music opens the
veil." This is what Bauer needed. He couldn't figure out how
to get the ghosts to come. So he teamed up with a musician. I
bet Weymouth George is the reason Bauer ended up at Corbin
College. Or vice versa. They wanted to continue their occult
club in another form.

"Yes!" Wren says, practically bouncing on the bed. "It's not just tradition or ceremony. It's part of the spell."

"An invocation," I say, borrowing Bauer's word for it.

"WWG wrote it for Magni Viri. It's one of his only compositions he never allowed to be performed or recorded," Wren says. "It's only ours."

"The lyrics are all about coming in out of the darkness and dwelling in the light," Jordan says, nodding. "So, yeah, that makes sense. It's the music."

"You know Latin?" Azar asks, scrunching up her nose.

"Yeah, don't you all?" Jordan asks, surprised, looking around at each of us. We all shake our heads.

Azar rolls her eyes. "So we sing this song and wake the ghosts or whatever," she says, "and then what?"

My initiation is fresh in my mind. "We offer them our blood."

"We pledge ourselves to be their vessels," Penny adds.

"Is it really that simple?" I ask. "A song and some blood and a promise?"

"Well," Jordan says, "the blood part is." He holds up the theory book that I'd discarded before. "According to this, blood is a common offering to the dead. It's our life force. That's powerful."

I think of how thin many of us have gotten, how pale. The condition I was in when Isabella finished writing *Cicada*. It wasn't only fatigue. It was more than that. And I've only been at Isabella's mercy for a few weeks. The older students have been living with theirs for years. No wonder they look far worse, gaunt and exhausted and ill.

"They feed on our blood. They feed on *us*," I realize with a shudder.

Jordan's mouth twists. "Even the ones who are like partners . . . they're not truly. They're slowly draining us dry."

Azar shakes her head. "Another thing that fucker O'Connor never mentioned. So what do we do about it?"

"We break with them," Penny says quietly. "We take back our vows."

"Can we do that?" Azar asks.

Penny shrugs. "All agreements can be broken. There might be a cost or a punishment, but they can be broken. People get divorced all the time, don't they? People break contracts at work. They run away from the military."

"Yeah, but that's humans. Ghosts are different, aren't they?" Azar asks.

"Besides, if you go AWOL you go to jail," Jordan adds.

I put my head on my knees and groan. I'm so tired. Even after the coffee, I'm tired. My body still hasn't recovered from the beating Isabella gave me. She knows it too. Since I returned to campus, I can feel her lapping around my edges, waiting for me to let go. And when I do? What will happen then?

Penny puts a hand on my back. "We'll figure this out, Tara. I promise."

I nod tiredly. "But we need to do this tonight. We need to get those books back in O'Connor's office before he notices them missing."

"Okay, everyone read. Find something useful," Penny says. "Anything about breaking the connection with the ghosts. Like, I don't know, maybe banishment? Or an exorcism?"

"How about a séance?" Neil suggests, holding out his book so we can see it.

I'm so shocked Neil is actually offering a suggestion instead of a caustic comment that I just blink at him.

"A séance?" Jordan asks skeptically. "Like with a Ouija board?"

"No," Neil says, "not exactly. We wouldn't need a physical means of communication because we're pretty much already walking Ouija boards, aren't we?"

"Uh, aren't we trying to take the ghosts' power over us away, not give them more?" Azar interjects. "You really think opening ourselves up to them more is a good idea?"

"It does sound dangerous," I say. "Isabella can grab hold of me even when I'm not asleep, if my mind wanders a little. I can't imagine what she could do if we tried to summon her up."

"I mean, yeah, it's dangerous. Obviously. But if we summoned one of them and let them speak freely, maybe we would learn something," Neil says. "And of course there's a chance we give them a stronger hold, but they've already got all the power anyway. We're always at their mercy. My little freeloader doesn't give a shit about my life or what I want. Isn't it worth the risk if we can get the upper hand?"

"He's right," Penny says. "If we don't take whatever chance we have now, we might as well just lie down and give up, let them take over completely."

Everyone is quiet for a long moment, weighing the risks against the potential rewards.

Jordan is the first to speak. "Who did you have in mind,

Neil?" he asks, his voice cautious. "I can't imagine most of the Magni Viri ghosts would be particularly helpful."

"WWG," Wren says before Neil can answer. "He's our guy. I'm sure of it."

"The asshole who started all of this?" Azar snaps, sweeping her hand in the direction of the cemetery.

Wren nods vehemently. "Look, I understand why he wanted this. It was for his music. It was because he knew he was going to die too young, and he couldn't stand it. He had so much more to offer the world, and he knew he wouldn't get the chance."

"I get that," Penny says quietly.

"See?" Wren says. "Maybe he was an egomaniac, maybe he was shortsighted, but he really only cared about the music. About his art. He never envisioned Magni Viri becoming this tool of control, I know it. And I don't think he would appreciate where it's all gone. I'm sure he'll help us." Wren waits impatiently for us to think through it, eyebrows raised.

"Even if he doesn't want to help, he'd probably be our best bet to tell us something useful," I finally say, hedging. "I mean, all of this started with him. Maybe he's the secret to ending it."

"It's worth a try," Jordan says, leaning forward, his brow scrunched up in concentration. "But what we're talking about is thinning the barrier between us and them, aren't we? I want to make sure we all understand the risk we're taking. We don't know what the consequences might be. Are you all up for that?"

"Yes!" Wren says.

"I'm game," Penny adds.

Neil and I nod.

"And look, Azar," Neil says, showing her the book. "There are instructions for protecting yourself from the spirits. It says we need to form a circle and maintain our connection to each other physically. It's like putting a protective wall between us and them. If we do this, we should be safe."

We all stare at Azar, waiting. She rubs her temples like she's getting a migraine. "Every cell in my body is screaming at me not to do this, but . . . fine. If this is our only option, we'll do it," she says. "But when this goes to shit, I want you all to remember that I said it was a bad idea."

Inside me, Isabella begins to churn and fume, agitated by our plans. But I can read what's underneath her anger. She's afraid of what we're about to do. And that means it has a chance of working.

"What does the book say we need?" I ask Neil, the tiniest ember of hope beginning to flicker to life inside me now that we have a plan. Maybe, just maybe, we can find a way to get free.

We wait until the cemetery party has finished and the house has gone quiet before we sneak out of Denfeld into the pre-dawn darkness. I shiver as we walk, both from the cold and my own anxiety. We're going to call forth a ghost—and not just any ghost, but the man who helped start all of this. We're going to get the answers we need. I'm sure of it. This is the right thing to do. It's the only thing to do. Even if it's dangerous.

The cemetery is quiet with the hush that precedes morning, before the birds have awoken, before squirrels have started to skitter in the trees and bushes. It's just past 4:00 a.m., and the cemetery feels as dead as the cicada exoskeletons that litter the ground, crunching beneath our shoes as we walk.

"Here," Wren says when we reach the mausoleum. Their voice sounds so small and quiet in the dark.

The mausoleum looms up, hardly more than a shadow. Inside, WWG's body molders, but, of course, he is already here with us—living inside Wren, undead and undying.

I shine my flashlight on the stone that marks the details of his life, half-effaced though they are. Beneath his name, there's a smaller message I hadn't noticed before: *Brilliant and beloved, his soul endures in us*, it reads. It's a gentler inscription than Isabella's grave had, written not only with respect for the man's mind but also his heart. I wonder if Bauer chose it. Of course, while an outsider might read these words and see only affection, Magni Viri students can see another truth: that WWG literally endures in us, carried forward by each new generation.

The six of us kneel in a circle in the center of the cemetery, at the door to WWG's resting place. For a moment I feel as if I've gone back to the night of my initiation, the enormous circle of Magni Viri students lighting up the night. But this time, instead of candle flame and blood, we offer only darkness and the mist of our breaths when we speak. Weymouth George is already here; we only need to help Wren channel him fully. But the lack of lights is unnerving. It feels like we don't have anything to defend ourselves against the dark, against the ghosts. We're putting ourselves more at their mercy than we ever have before.

"Bottom's up," Wren says, popping one of Dennis's herbal gummies into their mouth. The others explained to me that the gummies are used by most of the MV students when they need to make it easier for the ghosts to do their work. It certainly can't hurt to include them here.

We hold hands, making a fortress of our bodies as the book instructed. "Ready?" I ask, my voice shaky.

"Ready," everyone says. Except Azar, who only sighs.

"Wren, are you sure you're okay with this?" Penny asks for the third time.

Wren is the one who will have to bear the greatest burden here.

"I'm sure," Wren says, lifting their chin bravely.

"Okay, each of us should scoop up a handful of dirt in our right hands, and then rejoin the circle," I say. Everyone does as I ask. As we grip each other's hands again, cold moist earth mingles with our skin. This is the earth that Magni Viri students have shed their blood on for a century. If blood is life force, like Jordan said, we have offered these ghosts a whole lot of life force.

"Wren, you're going to have to take the lead here," Penny says. "You know better than the rest of us how to talk to him. We'll just support you."

"Okay," Wren says. They are quiet for a long moment. We wait in the silence of the cemetery, bound together by hands and blood and something more. We wait so long that my knees start to ache. The sound of my own breathing starts to get under my skin, too loud in the darkness. It sounds magnified, doubled, as if Isabella is breathing inside me too, poised for her chance to break free.

The book said to name the ghost you hope to speak to, but instead, Wren begins to hum. To my surprise it's not the initiation song; it's soft and sad and lilting, like an old ballad a mother might sing to a child. After a few minutes, all the hairs on my arms stand on end, and my skin feels electric, lit up. All of my instincts are telling me that Walter Weymouth George is here.

"Walter?" I ask, a lump in my throat. I call him that because he doesn't feel like Weymouth George or WWG in this moment. He feels real, present, himself. *Walter.*

Wren stops humming. "Yes?" they ask softly. It's Wren's voice, but not. It's too dark for me to see anyone's expression, but I can feel the others' tension, their held breaths. Inside me, Isabella pulses and beats, her fury an onslaught of waves wearing down rock.

I push back against her, anchoring myself to Penny and the others.

"Walter, we need your help," I say, my voice strained, desperate. I don't know how long I can hold Isabella off.

Wren starts humming again. Penny squeezes my hand hard, as if to remind me we're only supposed to ask clear, direct questions of the spirit.

"How do we break the bonds of Magni Viri?" I ask.

Wren stops humming. "Magni Viri?" Walter asks, sounding a little confused.

"How did you join your spirit to students, so that you could live on?" I try again.

"Oh, that was John," Walter says.

"John Bauer?" I ask, my breath quickening. "He knew how? Did he tell you how to put an end to it?"

Walter starts to hum again, apparently reluctant to speak. Or perhaps he finds it difficult. "He wrote it all down, of course. He was always writing it down," he says fretfully. "He left half a dozen journals behind, here 'at the heart of Magni Viri.'" He chuckles and shakes his head.

"Where?" I press, but Walter is still speaking.

"Oh, how he regretted it all. He tried to stop it. He never meant for it to . . ." Walter's attention wanders, and he starts humming again.

We don't have time for this. I can feel Isabella raging within me, a force of nature. We can't hold our ghosts off forever. "How do we end Magni Viri?" I ask again.

The air around us grows even colder, and it feels like frost creeps across my skin. I shiver and shiver. On either side of me, Penny and Neil do too. I can hear Penny's teeth chattering. I squeeze her hand harder, feeling the gritty dirt between our palms. The ghosts are closing in. Across the circle, Azar is doubled over and moaning as if in pain. I'm not sure she can last much longer. We're going to have to end the séance without getting what we came for.

But then the darkness is replaced with hazy light. I'm in the cemetery, but in a different part. I'm standing instead of kneeling, my hands bound with rope. I can hardly see anything, but someone stands near me, his face very close to mine. He whispers to me, his voice afraid and trembling. I can hardly make out the words over the sound of chanting all around us. But I understand their meaning.

He touches my cheek and kisses me, and I feel the scratch of his beard on my skin, taste the salt of his tears. I know I ought to be terrified, but all I feel is love, radiating out from my chest, reaching for him.

When the knife enters my heart, his lips are still on mine.

The world goes dark. I gasp back into my body, still linked to Penny and Neil.

"What the fuck was that?" Azar asks, her voice quavering.

Apparently, the others all experienced the same thing I did—being murdered.

"Who did that happen to?" Jordan asks, his breaths coming hard and fast.

"I think it was WWG. He didn't die of sickness," Penny says. "John Bauer killed him."

I realize she's right. Walter took us inside his memories, perhaps the one memory he relives over and over again—the memory he lives inside. John Bauer killed Walter Weymouth George. But how could he have founded Magni Viri if he was murdered?

Before I can open my mouth to ask another question, I feel something on my skin. Something slimy and wriggling. I look down and see a worm trying to escape between my and Penny's hands. It works itself free and falls to the earth. That's when I notice the mold creeping up my wrist. Green, thick, fuzzy, it spreads up my coat sleeve, and judging by the way my skin crawls, beneath my sweater too, working its way up my arm. The same thing is happening to Penny. She looks at me, her eyes wide and frightened.

Worms begin to heave and crawl all around us, and insects too. Their sharp legs skitter over my knees and start to climb, their antennae wheeling.

Across the circle Azar screams. She leaps up, breaking our connection, desperately trying to shake off the creatures. And that is what the ghosts were waiting for.

My breath freezes in my chest. My brain seems to shiver in my skull, fracturing my vision. I feel the moment Isabella seizes me, and it isn't like before. I don't watch her from a quiet place in the corner. She claims me. Her rage is cold and endless, a wind whipping through snow-blasted plains. It scours me.

She knows I'm looking for a way out of my vow, and so now she will break me. The way she broke Meredith.

I fall forward to the earth, where worms and insects still throng. I gasp and claw at the soil, trying to raise myself. But it's too late. Cicadas scream inside my brain.

Someone pulls at my arm, trying to yank me up, but I can't get my feet under me. Another person joins them, and together they carry me.

That contact of my body with theirs, it's all that keeps me tethered. It's the only thing that makes it possible for me to breathe. I feel like I'm in two places at once—here, being dragged out of the cemetery by my friends; and in a cold, dark place with Isabella where my body turns to rot, where I am endlessly devoured.

They drop me on the ground outside the cemetery gate, and we all fall together in a pile. I hear the others gasping, whispering, moaning.

"Tara?" Penny asks, kneeling in front of me with a wince. She takes my face in her hands. "Tara, come back to us."

At first, I can't see anything except the darkness, can't feel anything except Isabella's rage. But I follow the sound of Penny's voice, search for her in the endless night. Slowly, slowly, she comes into focus, and I feel the way her hands grip my cheeks. Finally, I look into her eyes, and they fill with relief. Then I notice the others behind her, all of them staring at me with worried eyes.

"I'm . . . okay," I rasp.

Penny laughs, the sound more like a sob, and kisses me hard. Her kiss is the only warm thing in the world. It spreads through me, bringing me back.

But Isabella is still here. I feel her closer than ever before; I hear her thoughts murmuring in the back of my mind.

"What happened?" I ask. I look down at my hands. There's no rot there, no mold. Only dirt. Were the worms real, the insects?

"We saw that stuff too," Penny says. "We really pissed them off, huh?"

I nod numbly.

"Ugh," Neil groans, drawing out the sound. He pulls at his hair. "Anyone else feel like you've got a parasite in your brain?"

"Yes," we all say. Wren is crying. Jordan has his arm around them.

"Wren, are you all right? Did he hurt you?" I ask.

They shake their head.

"We strengthened their hold," I say. "We gave them more power over us." Which is exactly what we were afraid of, exactly the risk we decided to take anyway.

"Come on, let's get back inside before we freeze to death," Azar says. Her voice is strangely toneless, as if she's shell-shocked. She turns away robotically and starts toward Denfeld.

I push to my feet and help Penny up. She's limping a little, so I put my arm around her waist. She's shivering hard too, and her skin feels feverish. I wonder what her ghost is doing to her.

I feel Isabella settling more firmly than ever into my skin. I might be in control for the moment, but she's growing, her mind filling mine. I can almost hear her thoughts. They are like echoes, muddied and distorted. And there are emotions inside me too, ones I'm sure don't belong to me. It's not only the anger. It's . . . all of her. The full human being that she was.

Somehow, feeling Isabella's sadness is more disturbing than feeling her rage. There's a loneliness inside her like an ocean, and I'm afraid I might just drown in it.

I can feel the ways that we're alike now. I can sense how much she needed to prove herself, how much she needed to claim her own life, same as me. I can feel the resentment festering in her heart for all the people who have the things she's been denied. But it's the loneliness—that vast and endless solitude—that almost takes my breath.

It's less dark now that we're out from under the trees, and I can see the others more clearly. Each of their faces look strained, as if they're holding back their ghosts from sheer force of will. Maybe they are.

"Well, we're fucked!" Neil yells, his voice thick with tears. His body curves over his knees, and he rocks back and forth.

"Shhh, shut up!" Penny hisses at him. "You don't want to wake the whole house up."

"Who even cares? Things can't get worse than this," Neil says. "God, I was so stupid. It was manageable before. Now it's . . ." He gasps. "It's unbearable."

"Calm down," Azar says, still in that toneless voice. "It's going to be okay."

Jordan rubs his hand over his heart as if it hurts. "I guess that's what we get for blindly following instructions in a book that was probably written by a charlatan."

"I'm so sorry, y'all. I'm so, so sorry," I say. I know we all agreed to this, but it still feels like it's my fault. Like I'm the one who set this all in motion.

"Do you all feel it too? The boundaries are breaking down—between us and them. The walls are growing thinner," Penny says as if in a daze. "I can hear Dr. Coppola's thoughts, feel her feelings."

"We rushed in," Azar says, picking absentmindedly at her cuticles.

"We had to," I reassure her. "We had to try."

"We didn't know what we were doing. We should have waited," she says, raising a now-bleeding hangnail to her mouth.

"Yeah, we all know you thought it was a bad idea!" Neil snarls.

Azar only stares at him, but Wren shakes their head. "No, let's not blame each other. We didn't have any other choice. Besides, it's not like it was a total failure. We learned a lot."

"Did we?" Neil asks, his voice loaded with scorn.

"Of course we did," I say. "We saw how WWG died. He was ritualistically killed. The chanting, the candles, the knife in his heart . . ."

"I didn't understand it though," Jordan says. "He wasn't scared. He wanted it."

"And he was gay," Penny says. "Did you know he was gay, Wren?"

They nod. "He always felt that way to me. But I didn't know he was in love. I think John Bauer loved WWG too. The way he killed him was . . . so gentle."

I close my eyes, trying to remember everything. The memory feels lodged inside me, as if it belongs to me.

Penny lifts her hand to her cheek as if remembering the way Bauer's beard scratched against Walter's face when they kissed.

"So John Bauer killed Walter Weymouth George to create Magni Viri," Jordan says slowly. "But he loved him?"

"He definitely did," I say, remembering the way that Bauer's lips felt on mine in the memory. Even with my limited romantic knowledge, I know that most kisses don't feel like that. "He loved him desperately."

"Then why did he kill him?" Penny asks.

Wren squeezes their eyes shut, as if searching inside for the answers. "WWG was sick and running out of time. Tuberculosis, I think."

"So he was willing to sacrifice his life to create Magni Viri?" I ask.

Wren nods. "Yeah, I think so. He was dying, and he wanted more time."

"And I bet Bauer didn't want to let him go," Penny says. "If they were in love. And so young."

"You don't kill someone you love," Jordan says.

"I would," Neil says, his eyes feverish. "If they were dying anyway, and I could find a way to hold on to them. I would have done it to Meredith."

I stare at him, and I know he means it. He would have driven a knife into her heart if it allowed him to be with her forever. Is that beautiful or evil? I don't know, but mostly it's heartbreaking, devastating.

"All right, so Bauer kills WWG and takes his spirit into himself? He makes himself the first vessel?" I say. "And from there, he created Magni Viri."

"But he regretted it," Wren says, their eyes bright. "WWG said Bauer regretted creating Magni Viri."

With a lurch, I remember the rest of what Walter said about Bauer. That he was always scribbling; that he had written everything down.

"The journals that WWG mentioned . . . he said they were in the heart of Magni Viri," I say. "What does that mean? Denfeld Hall?"

Jordan looks back toward the graveyard. "No, the cemetery. That's what people have always called it. The heart of Magni Viri."

"Oh, that's right. It was in my vows. And I think I heard

Quigg call it that," I say, excitement surging through me. "But where in the cemetery?"

Wren laughs. "Where else? The journals are buried with WWG. They must be in his crypt."

"Because who would disturb a grave?" I say.

"You mean besides you?" Jordan asks. When I wince, he laughs and adds, "Sorry, too soon?"

"Well, let's hope the second time's the charm," I say.

My heart races with expectation, despite my exhaustion. The séance wasn't a failure, even if it cost us more than we meant to give. We know where to look now.

We're going to find the secrets to ending Magni Viri, and then we will rid ourselves of the ghosts that are devouring us whole.

THIRTY

"We don't need six people for this," Jordan says. "I think only two or three of us should search the mausoleum. The rest of you can go back to Denfeld to keep an eye on things, watch to see if O'Connor turns up."

"I'm staying," Wren says. "WWG is my ghost."

"Wren, I think what we need this time is muscle, not spiritual connection," Jordan says gently.

"I'm stronger than I look," Wren says. "It takes a lot of upper body strength to play as much piano as I do."

"Wren's right; they should stay," I say. "And I'm staying too."

"You know, I've already dug up one corpse this semester, so I'll sit this one out," Neil says.

"Me too," Azar says, gazing to the east, where a band of light has appeared on the horizon.

"We'd better hurry," I say. "The sun is coming up."

"How about I find a vantage point from the woods where I can keep an eye on the cemetery gate?" Penny suggests. "I can text you if I see anyone coming."

"That's a good idea," Jordan says. "But guys, whatever you

do, don't fall asleep. The ghosts will go straight to O'Connor with our plan."

After a little more discussion, we disperse.

When Wren, Jordan, and I step back through the gates of the cemetery, I want to laugh. Of course this is where the answers are buried. The only thing Magni Viri cares about are the ghosts whose original bodies decay under the ground. The heart of Magni Viri is death and rot, like so many institutions.

But as we approach Weymouth George's tomb, I wonder if that's entirely true. The beautiful Gothic building where WWG's body rests speaks of something higher, something truer. I hate that we are about to desecrate it.

As we walk up the steps of the mausoleum, all my hair stands on end. Even though I know Penny is watching over us, I feel exposed, vulnerable. I want to get inside as quickly as possible. To my relief, the doors to the mausoleum aren't locked like they always are in public cemeteries. I pull one side open, fumbling in my pocket for my flashlight to make sure there aren't wild animals or anything dangerous inside.

But I quickly realize I don't need it. Early-morning light pours down through a stained glass window very high up, illuminating a white marble angel, its face lifted in a rapturous expression, a goblet clutched to its chest.

"Tara, let us in," Jordan says from behind me, and I realize that I've been frozen in the doorway for I don't know how long. I step inside to let the others pass. Jordan closes the door behind us.

"It's beautiful, isn't it?" Wren whispers with a soft smile.

"You've been in here before?" I ask, looking around the space. Apart from the angel, there's nothing here but bare stone and echoes.

"Yeah, but I haven't come in a while. I used to visit twice a week at the start of the semester. It's peaceful in here," Wren says, sitting on the floor with their arms around their knees. "I really hate that we have to mess it up."

"You kind of love WWG, huh?" I ask.

"Yeah, I guess I do," Wren says.

"Why couldn't I get WWG?" I say. "Mine's such an asshole."

Jordan and Wren laugh.

"Yeah, but don't forget he's the reason we found Wren passed out on the floor of the practice room with a head injury," Jordan points out.

"At least he didn't dye anybody's hair," I grumble.

"You're more upset about that than Isabella almost causing you to die of exposure in the woods, aren't you?" Wren asks disbelievingly.

"It was mean-spirited and rude," I say with a shrug. "You shouldn't mess with someone's hair. It's, like, psychological torture or something. Like those parents who shave their daughters' heads for missing curfew and put it on social media for everyone to see."

"The worst YouTube trend of all time," Jordan agrees.

"What made her so awful, do you think?" Wren asks. "Isabella, I mean."

I pause, my eyes settling on the angel statue. "From the

pieces I've put together, she was born to caretakers of this college, but her dad was a wealthy student. Her mom gave her up to his family, and I don't think they loved her. I don't think anyone loved her. So she had all this genius and resentment and pain, and this is what she decided to do with it."

Jordan scratches his chin. "If she's been in pain like that for all these years, maybe it will be a relief for her to be free of Magni Viri. She could finally let go."

"Maybe," I say, though it's hard to imagine Isabella willingly letting me and her chance at life go. "I'm not sure if a person like her is even capable of finding peace and rest."

"Well, I hope WWG will be at peace once this is all done. I hope we can give him that," Wren says.

Jordan glances at his phone. "Anything from Penny or the others?"

Wren and I both check ours. "Nope," we say in unison.

"Then let's find those journals."

We gaze around at the walls, trying to figure out how to begin. "This place is awfully big for one body," I say. "Do you think someone else could be buried in here too?"

Jordan brandishes the pickax we found in the garden shed, the closest thing to a sledgehammer we could manage. "Only one way to find out."

"Here," I say, pointing at a place near the floor where the stone looks different, the surface uneven, as if it was broken and resealed. "He must have put them here."

Jordan kneels and inspects the place. "Yeah, it was definitely disturbed at some point," he says, running his hand over the stone. He clenches the handle of the pickax, then draws back his arm.

I close my eyes, not wanting to see the old stone crack and crumble.

"Wait!" Wren yells just before Jordan can bring the pickax down on the stone. He nearly drops it as he tries to avoid the wall.

He cocks an eyebrow at Wren. "Are you kidding me right now?"

"Sorry," Wren says, a little breathlessly, "but look." They try to dig their fingernail into a small crack at the base of the angel statue. It's not solid as I suspected. There's clearly a front panel that is wiggling. "I can't quite get it though," Wren says with a frustrated grunt. "Tara, are your nails any longer than mine?" They hold up their hands to show me how their fingernails are bitten down to the quick.

I laugh and show mine, which aren't much better.

"Here," Jordan says, handing Wren his student ID. "Try to wedge that in."

Wren fiddles with the card, angling the corner of it into the loose corner of the statue's base. There's a small grinding of stone on stone, and then the panel falls open, landing on the hard floor of the mausoleum with a satisfying crack.

I shine my flashlight into the space. There's a silver box inside.

"Oh my God," Wren whispers, a hand over their mouth. They seem frozen, unable to touch the box.

I crawl forward and hand Wren my flashlight. Then I

reach into the dark space and pull out the box. It's made completely of silver, engraved all around with ivy leaves, a bit tarnished from the damp. It's heavy.

"Open it," Wren says, angling the flashlight to search for clasps.

On the front, two hands grasp each other, forming the clasp. I lift them separately, and the mechanism clicks, opening the box. A faded, water-stained envelope lies on top of the contents, the name *Walt* inscribed there in Bauer's now-familiar, spiky handwriting.

My hand shakes as I reach for it. The envelope is unsealed, and I pull out a single-page letter. *Walt, my love, my life*, it begins. My eyes speed down the page, landing on the signature at the bottom.

"It's from Bauer," I say.

"Oh my God," Wren says again.

"Read it, Tara," Jordan says.

"Okay," I say, my voice shaking, tears already pricking my eyes. I clear my throat and read.

Walt, my love, my life,

I had to keep you, my love, I had to keep you. I could not let you pass beyond the veil, beyond my reach. I could not let you go where I was unable to follow. I thought it was love, perfect love. I thought I could hold your beautiful soul within mine, let you nest there, little bird. I thought I could keep you with me.

But like all men, I erred. You are closer than breath,

yet as far from me as heaven is from earth. I cannot reach you, cannot commune with you. It is maddening, as if my every arrival coincides with your departure. I go to sleep and you are not here. I wake and you are gone, only your music left behind.

Pure music, your soul's essence, the only thing that has kept me tethered to my own body all these years, the only thing to make my fading life worth living.

But now I grow old and weak. Soon, I will leave this earthly existence and join my Maker. And because I have no genius worth passing on to a new generation, and no desire to continue this shadowed life where I cannot truly be with you, I will share the fate of regular men and die. I will leave you behind. You will have a new body, young and bright and, I hope, worthy of you.

Yet I fear that I have done you a wrong, my love. I fear what might grow from our blood twined together in the earth. I wish I could believe my legacy will remain pure, but already I sense how darkness will bloom. Men care only for money and ego and power. I might have acted once and put an end to all of this, but I was afraid and selfish, and now it is far too late. I do not have the power, and the others would never allow it. I am sorry, my love. I am sorry for all the ways I have failed you.

Forgive me for asking too much of you, for clinging too tightly to that which belongs rightly to God. Forgive me for failing to set things right, though I had the means. When you are released, if ever that day should dawn, find

me. Come and find me. I wait for you through decades and centuries, through all the ages of mankind, with unending devotion, with constant hope. But for now, I leave all my knowledge, all my workings, to rest here with you. Because whatever Magni Viri becomes, it was all . . . all of it, every act and every word, for you alone.
Always,
Your adoring servant,
   John Bauer

When I finish, silence falls and settles in the mausoleum. Tears run down my cheeks, and when I look at Wren, I see theirs are wet too.

"They really were in love," Jordan says wonderingly. "All of this was because they loved each other, because they couldn't let go."

"So if we end Magni Viri, if we set WWG free, maybe they'll be together again," Wren says.

"Do they deserve it?" Jordan asks quietly. "After all the harm they've caused?"

"Of course they do," Wren says simply.

"Let's see what else is in here," I say, wiping the tears off my face. I pull the box toward me, half expecting to find a shriveled, blackened human heart inside. Keeping your lover's heart in a box, Mary Shelley style? I would not put it past Bauer. Not for one second.

There is no heart, but there is a knife, wrapped in a piece of leather. It is silver like the box, engraved with ivy leaves.

The initials J.B. are on the hilt. I hold it up, letting the golden light fall across it.

"This is the knife that Bauer drove into his lover's heart," I say, caught up in the drama of the moment.

"Jesus," Jordan breathes.

"Are the journals in there?" Wren asks, recalling me to the reason for our quest.

I put the knife back and pull out a stack of six leather journals. I open the one on top and breathe a sigh of relief when I recognize Bauer's handwriting. "They're here. This is what we need. This is everything we need."

Just then, my phone starts to ring. I yank it out, my heart racing. It's Neil. I quickly put him on speaker so the others can hear.

"He's here," Neil says without preamble. "O'Connor's here at Denfeld, and he is pissed. He got here like twenty minutes ago, and he came in screaming for Quigg. Like, roaring through the fucking house, waking everyone up. That was who he suspected first since Quigg had a key to his office. But then Quigg denied everything, and so O'Connor started banging through the house, yelling and knocking on everybody's doors. Laini tried to get him to calm down, to leave the house, but he gathered us all in the sitting room. He said he would expel us all if we didn't say who broke into his office. I've never, ever seen him lose his cool like this."

"Is he still there?" I ask, my heart rate exploding.

"No, but he's looking for you."

"For me?"

"Yeah, you are the obvious next suspect, Tara. You dug up

Isabella's grave, for God's sake."

"*We* dug up Isabella's grave," I remind him.

"Whatever, but it's you he's gunning for. You can't let him find you. Actually, you can't let anybody find you. He set all of Magni Viri on you."

"Well, we got the journals," I say. "They were here. So we just need to read them and find the answers to ending Magni Viri. We can do it tonight if we're able to figure it out."

"That's a big *if*. And there are a lot of hours until dark. What if O'Connor finds you first?"

"If I didn't know any better, I'd say you're worried about me," I say.

"Oh, go fuck yourself," Neil says, but this time, there's something like fondness in his voice.

It's damp and cold in the mausoleum, but we can't go back to Denfeld. We can't even go to the campus library because if a single member of Magni Viri spots me, we're screwed. So instead, we hunker down in Walter Weymouth George's tomb and make ourselves as comfortable as we can—at least, as comfortable as we can without the danger of falling asleep. We can't risk even one of us giving control to their ghost, which means another sleepless day. After a few hours, Penny joins us, and not long after, Neil slips in too, carrying a backpack full of food and bottled water and Penny's meds.

But there's someone missing.

"Where's Azar?" I ask.

"She's out," Neil says, handing me the last bottle of water. "I kept texting her and she wouldn't answer, so I finally called her. She said she didn't want to be a part of this anymore, that it was too much."

"We shouldn't have pushed her to do the séance," Wren says.

Neil shrugs. "This is textbook Azar. She gets overwhelmed and she disappears."

"She did seem really freaked after the séance," I admit.

Neil scowls and doesn't say anything. There's a ball of anxiety in my chest, but I ignore it. Whatever is going on with Azar right now, we can't fix it.

"It's okay. We can do it without her," Penny says. "At least we know she's safe, right?"

I wish Azar were here, but even with just the five of us together, I feel more secure. Penny stretches out on the floor, her head in my lap, to try to rest a little. Sitting watch in the woods for hours took its toll.

If it weren't for Isabella roaring inside my head and my worry for Azar, I'd almost feel peaceful here in WWG's tomb, surrounded by my friends, poring over Bauer's journals. But Isabella is still loud and angry in my mind, surging against my defenses like an invading army. I rub my temple and grimace at the pain she's causing. I'll be lucky if we figure this all out before Isabella kills me like she did Meredith.

Penny blinks up at me. "You okay?"

"Yeah, it's just Isabella," I say. "But don't worry. I'm still in control." I run my fingers over Penny's long soft hair, grounding myself with the touch. "Rest."

Penny smiles and nuzzles her face against my leg. I gaze down at her, and I realize that this is what Isabella was missing. This is what makes me different from her. Isabella had so much talent and genius and drive. But she didn't have the things that make a person feel whole: love and friendship and belonging. Maybe that's why she clings so hard to her writing.

I hope that if we figure out how to break the spell that binds Magni Viri, I won't lose the best thing I've gained from that bond: Penny, Wren, Jordan, Azar, and even Neil. I hope I don't lose my friends. I hope I don't end up on my own again.

Slowly, over the course of the day, we pool together information from Bauer's notes and descriptions of Magni Viri's rituals. The way the candles ought to be arranged, the kind of language to use. Precautions to take for safety.

I have to skim a lot of Bauer's self-recriminating thoughts, trying to weed out his personal angst from the useful information. Despite his growing distaste for everything concerned with Magni Viri, he cannot bring himself to put an end to it because that would mean letting go of WWG. He can't stand the thought of Walter's spirit ceasing to be, yet he is filled with so much self-loathing that he looks forward to his own death. Even the thought of inhabiting a new body as a ghost of Magni Viri repulses him. He considers the possibility of his spirit joining with WWG in new bodies, and it makes him physically ill. Yet he never stops longing for Walter.

Once, on a particularly bleak night, Bauer considers using the knife that ended his beloved's life to end his own. I cover my mouth as I sink into his dark thoughts.

"So we need to use the song from initiation night, right?"

ERICA WATERS

Penny asks, interrupting my reading. "If we want to get the ghosts all in one place?"

"Yeah, we guessed correctly about that. In this journal I've got, Bauer talks about how music is the only thing that can truly pierce the veil," Jordan says, tapping the pages. "It can draw the spirits to the living."

"So you were right to hum that song at the séance, Wren," I say. "How did you know to do that?"

Wren shrugs. "I don't know. It just came to me. I think it's one that Walter's mom used to sing to him when he was little. It has the feel of something deeply buried and comforting, you know? You can hear strains of it in several of his compositions."

"So we arrange the candles, we sing the initiation night song. And then what?" Jordan asks. "How do we break the connection? Do we need to use a different song for that?"

Everyone shakes their heads, unsure.

"WWG said that the answers to ending Magni Viri were in these journals. Bauer must have written down how to do it, even if he never intended to follow through," Penny says.

"Let's just keep reading," I say. I skim through my journal faster, and then pick up the final one that no one has looked at yet.

It's the last journal that Bauer wrote. We saved it for last because we didn't want to rush into anything like we did with the séance. But if the answer exists, this is probably where we'll find it. I take a deep breath and start to read.

Halfway through, Bauer stops complaining about his loneliness and disappointment, his disgust at the money-minded benefactors of Magni Viri. Instead, he starts thinking, speculating, weaving new ideas together. I realize he's making a plan, building a new ritual.

He suspects that spirits who have become used to being embodied will fight with every tool at their disposal to avoid losing their hosts. Judging by the way that Isabella still rages inside me, I know he's right. And we'll be up against more than her: two dozen ghosts, many of whom are probably as ruthless as Isabella. We can't afford to get anything wrong if this is going to work—and if we're all going to make it out alive.

I could assault the walls of Magni Viri all day long and the structure would not fall, Bauer writes. *But with my silver knife, I could pry up the foundation stone, and with a single breath, crumble the house into ash. If I were a braver, better man, I would.*

"Hey, y'all, what do you think this means?" I ask. I read the puzzling sentences aloud. "What is the foundation stone?"

"He means Walter," Jordan says. "He's the heart of Magni Viri, the thing that started it all."

"So that means he's the way to end it too," Penny says. "But how do we 'pry up the foundation stone'?"

We are quiet again, thinking. "With his silver knife, he could pry up the foundation stone," I murmur to myself. Bauer doesn't say he would smash it. He would pry it up and remove it, letting the house crumble around it.

And he'd use his silver knife, the same one that killed Walter. So maybe it's not about saying the right words or performing things a certain way. Maybe it's about the emotional connection between the two of them. There's a reason he held on to that knife, a reason he left it behind with his letter and journals.

"I think I've got it," I say, the truth landing in my belly with the weight of lead. "I know how to put an end to Magni Viri."

THIRTY-ONE

We talk for a long, long time. We read every word in every journal. Finally, near the end of the last journal, we find a heavily crossed-out ritual titled "Words of Breaking." It's in Latin—because of course it is. Jordan reads it aloud, and even without knowing the words, I can catch the ritual's rhythm. It feels like a poem or a song.

Jordan quickly translates it for us: it's all about letting go of the past, old wounds, and vain ambition and seeking rest from long labor.

Neil groans. "Oh, God, does this one need to be sung too, like the initiation song?"

"It certainly seems like it was meant to be," Wren says, peering at the words. "If music opens the veil, maybe it helps keep it open too?"

"Well, it certainly can't hurt," Penny says.

Wren pulls a pencil stub from their breast pocket with a tired smile. "Let's get composing, then."

Jordan helps Wren pair the Latin words with a simplified version of the composition that Wren has been writing with WWG, the same one Wren played for me on my first day in Denfeld Hall. Even without the piano, the song is eerie and emotional, making me feel like I've been stripped to the bone. I can't help but wonder if WWG has been thinking of ending Magni Viri for a while now, if his longing to reunite with Bauer has grown greater than his desire to make music.

We practice chanting the song together until we're all sure we know the words—or at least the sound and shape of them. After that, the only thing left to do is wait for night to fall, which doesn't take long after all our preparation. I pull Wren a little aside to talk through the more personal aspects of the ritual, to get their consent and input since they'll once more be playing host to WWG. Once it's dark, Neil sneaks back up to Denfeld to pilfer the few supplies we need. By the time he makes it back to the graveyard, the sky is black, with dense dark clouds scudding across it.

We're quiet as we leave the mausoleum, tired and achy from hours of being crammed inside, each of us lost in our own thoughts and fears. What we're about to do is incredibly dangerous, and the slightest error could unravel the whole plan. The consequences if we fail loom over us; with the threats we face from O'Connor and our ghosts, our futures depend on this working. That's not reassuring considering our plan is made up partly from rituals crafted by a lovesick priest, partly from guesswork, and partly from our own desperation. We have to summon the embodied ghosts—*all* of them, which means summoning every member of Magni Viri. We have to protect ourselves from them completely, not allowing them into our circle. And given the horrifying tricks they pulled during the séance, that likely won't be easy, though at least now we know we need to use candles. We have to loosen the ghosts' hold on their hosts, to whom they cling like parasites. And most important, we have to release Walter Weymouth George. If that step fails, nothing else we do matters.

But now it's time. There's no light from the moon or stars, so we have to go carefully, using our flashlights when we lose our way. Mine falls across a stone angel's face, half-covered in ivy, a snail crawling up its cheek. It reminds me once more of what happened at the end of the séance, with the worms and insects and mold creeping up our skin.

"Are you all absolutely sure you want to do this?" I ask the others.

"Too late for take-backs, isn't it?" Neil asks. "O'Connor's onto us, and I don't think he's going to take a full-scale mutiny as well as he did your little rebellion."

"He didn't take that well either!"

"Exactly," Neil says darkly.

"Shut up, Neil. It's going to be okay," Jordan says. "It's going to work. And, yes, this is what we want to do, Tara. After everything we've learned in the last two days . . . I seriously don't want to turn into the next Bernard Cottingham."

Penny puts her hand in mine and squeezes, and a little fire kindles in my chest. "We're all together in this," she says. "Don't worry. This is the right thing to do. For all of us."

"Okay, let's start here," Wren says once we reach the edge of the cemetery. They throw their bag of tea light candles to the ground and flick their cigarette lighter, illuminating our faces in the dark. "Remember, the circle needs to go around every grave."

"We'd better move fast," Neil says. "If someone spots the

candles before we're ready, we might not be able to finish the spell."

Jordan and I lock eyes, and he nods.

"Let's do it, then," I say, reassured by his determined gaze.

"Okay, Tara, you can light the candles, and I'll place them," Wren tells me, handing me the lighter. They turn to the boys. "Jordan and Neil, you do the same going the other direction. You can space them about a foot apart, I think. And Penny, you should keep watch and let us know if anyone's coming."

It's strange to see dreamy Wren taking charge like this, but Bauer and WWG's love story seems to have lit something inside them. They are filled to the brim with it. And maybe I am too. It feels like we're doing more than destroying Magni Viri. We're giving WWG and Bauer back to themselves.

I rip open the pack of tea lights and get my lighter ready. I light one and hand it to Wren, who places it on the ground. Wren moves a foot away, and I follow, handing them another light. We go on like this for what feels like forever, and I watch the circle form on the other side of the cemetery too. It's taking ages, and there are faster ways to do this, but this is how Bauer's journal said the circle was to be made.

The wind blows in the highest treetops, but otherwise the cemetery is still. Nothing moves or breathes here except us. In all this eerie silence, I almost miss the scream of the cicadas.

My body falls into a steady, thoughtless rhythm: pull a candle from the box, light it, hand it to Wren. My tired mind drifts.

Memories that aren't mine play like a movie reel.

A gray-haired man yelling from behind a desk, shaking

his head. Denying me, saying a bastard like me is unworthy of Magni Viri, unworthy of Denfeld Hall. A surge of feeling rushes through my belly: shame and hurt and rage. And I begin to understand this. It's Isabella's memory, of her grandfather. A nameplate on his desk says Ezra Denfeld Snow. Another piece of the puzzle slots into place. Isabella's family members were Magni Viri benefactors, probably descendants of the ones Bauer complained about so bitterly in his journals. Denfeld Hall is named after them.

Then the same man years later, in bed, sickly, dying. I smile down at him, knowing he is the last obstacle in my path. I feel no grief at his loss, only relief and vindication.

He's the reason Isabella joined the faculty at Corbin, I realize. The reason she got herself appointed to Magni Viri leadership. She wanted what the Snows thought she wasn't good enough to have. She wanted what was theirs. And she got it too.

I don't make it far with my reasoning before another memory, stronger than the first two, overtakes me: Darkness and the smell of soil, the Denfeld graveyard, candles in a circle. I stagger into the middle of it, my body suffused with pain, but my head already swimming from the herbs the botanist gave me. It's summer, the height of summer, cicadas screaming in the trees. I lie down on the earth that's still warm from a day of hot sun. I lie still, listening to the cicadas, and I wait to die, knowing that when I rise again, I will take a new form. My mind will go on, but I'll be free of this weak and sickly body. I'll be able to write again. I'll be able to prove myself. I'll get the honor my grandfather thought he could refuse me: to become one of the immortal minds of Magni Viri.

The screams of the cicadas seem to vibrate in my body, their electric pitch a roar in my ears. I will rise like them, I think. I will go into the cool dark belly of the earth, but I will come out again. This body will rot in the earth, but my mind, as part of the cohort of Magni Viri, will live forever.

I squeeze the grass beneath me in my fists, gaze up at the starless sky, into the dark shapes of the trees, and I wait for my next vessel. I wait to be reborn.

"Tara!" someone yells. "What are you—" Their voice breaks off in a terrified cry. I come to, Wren's hair gripped tight in my fist, the flame of my lighter nearly touching their cheek.

"Oh my God," I say, dropping the lighter, backing away from Wren as the others thunder toward us. Wren stares at me, their expression of fear distorted strangely in the light from the candles.

"I'm so sorry," I say. "It was Isabella. She's—she's trying to stop us. I let my mind wander, just for a second, and she took over. Fuck, I'm so sorry."

"It's okay," Wren says. "Just—just—" They take in a rattling breath. "Just stay focused. We're almost done."

The guys reach us, Penny hurrying behind them. "What happened?" Jordan asks, his eyes wide. "Are y'all okay?"

"Isabella," I say. "But it's okay now. Keep going. We need to hurry in case someone heard Wren scream."

"Jesus, I hate that bitch," Neil says with venom. I know he means Isabella, but I can't help but shrink away from him.

We return to our steady rhythm of lighting and placing

candles, moving as fast as we can. This time, I don't let my mind wander. I stay focused, counting the candles as we go. But I can't help but think about Isabella, about what I saw, what I felt. How she lay in this cemetery dying as the poisons took hold. Unafraid, triumphant.

I finally understand why she titled her novella *Cicada*. It had nothing to do with the characters. It was her own rebirth. *She* is the cicada, emerging from the earth after years of waiting. It's her story, a reclaiming of her history and her life. She gave herself the origin story that she thought she deserved.

It's a nasty, bloody one, but it's her own. And then she chose her own death and afterlife too. She never tasted death, not properly. Her body probably wasn't even cold before she took a new one.

"Done!" Wren cheers as we meet Jordan and Neil in the middle of the circle. I look up and see a wide circle of lights wrapping the gravestones in an uneven, wavering embrace of flame.

"Now we call the ghosts?" Penny asks, appearing out of the darkness.

"Now we call the ghosts," Wren and I both answer.

The five of us stand in the middle of the circle of lights, and I wish Azar were here. It feels incomplete without her. But if this works, she'll be drawn here too, even if it's not to help us.

Wren lifts their voice, a soaring alto, and the same music from my initiation night fills the air. It vibrates against my skin, and I feel Isabella respond to it, trying to rise to the surface. But I beat her back, struggling to stay in control. Isabella is stronger than any person I've ever encountered, but right now I have to be stronger.

I lift my voice and weave it with Wren's, and so do Penny and Jordan. Neil joins last, and his voice is surprisingly beautiful, cool and silver as moonlight. Penny puts her hand in mine, and I squeeze it tight, which helps me stay rooted here, keeping Isabella at bay. I put my hand in Neil's too, in case he needs the help. Soon, the five of us are connected, and we feel almost like one organism, with one purpose, with one voice.

I put all my heart into singing, and even though I don't know the meaning of each word, I know the meaning of the song. It is an invocation, an invitation, an awakening.

After a few minutes, the first Magni Viri student, Gabriel, steps up to the circle of lights, his glasses a reflected flicker of flames. Then come Trey and Jessica, and then Dennis. The students come fast after that, crunching through the dead leaves, pouring through the gate and taking their places outside the circle of lights. Some of them are in pajamas, roused from their beds. Others are still in day clothes. Their ghosts must have taken over and made them stop whatever they were doing to come here.

I spot Azar, but if she recognizes us, there is no acknowledgment in her eyes. She stares flatly at the flames at her feet. Quigg stands next to her, his usually animated features strangely vacant.

Soon, every single student is present, surrounding us. They are eerily silent, not joining in our song. It's as if they are entranced by it.

"Okay, everyone is here," Wren whispers to me. "Are you ready?"

Because WWG is housed inside Wren, they can't be the one to perform the ritual. It's up to the rest of us, and I've agreed to take the lead. I nod, though I don't feel ready. My stomach feels like worms and centipedes are crawling around inside.

I feel Isabella's energy humming in my skin. She can sense what's about to happen, like an animal that knows an earthquake is coming—restless, agitated, afraid. But she's trapped, and there's nothing she can do.

"It's time for you to rest," I whisper to her. "Time for you to lie down and sleep for good." But that only makes her pulse all the more furiously. She doesn't want to let go. She wants to fight for life and the chance to write. She won't go willingly into the dark.

And as much as I hate her, as much as she has hurt me, a part of me can't help but admire her for it. It makes me want to cling more tenaciously to my own life.

That is what I'm doing out here in the Magni Viri graveyard. That's what we're all doing. Taking back the lives stolen from us.

I step close to Wren, gripping the silver knife in my right hand. "Are you sure you're comfortable with me doing what we talked about? In case it comes to that, I mean."

"Definitely," they say. "Do whatever it takes."

I nod. "It's time then."

Wren starts a new song, built from John Bauer's words and Walter Weymouth George's music. We're moving on from the invocation, the gathering. We're starting the breaking. I feel it as it starts to happen; the ghosts must too, because the candle flames go tall as pillars, flickering wildly as wind stirs around us, blowing through the leaves and smoke.

But then I hear a commotion in the dark, past the circle of light. Heavy steps run through the leaves, and then Quigg and Azar are shoved aside, knocking over a few candles and extinguishing their flames.

Dr. O'Connor breaks into the circle as the flames go out. "Stop this! Stop it now!" he bellows. "You have no right!"

To my horror, the students follow him, stepping over the candles and entering the circle.

The ghosts are apparently still in charge of their vessels because no one speaks. They move closer and closer to us, drawn in but without any clear purpose.

But O'Connor is nearly upon us, and my attention snaps back to him. "This is unlawful! I'll have you all out on your asses!" he roars. "How dare you!"

We back away, but then I bump into a student—Bernard Cottingham himself, his ragged dressing gown flapping in the wind. He towers over me, his eyes flat and blank. Others stand beside him. We're surrounded.

Wren starts singing again, trying desperately to keep order. O'Connor stalks straight for them, his eyes promising murder. He raises his hand to slap Wren, but then someone barrels into him from the side with a cry. "No, you don't, you bastard!"

Azar looks up from the ground, where she's straddling O'Connor, her bony elbow across his throat. "I'm so sorry. I didn't want to tell him. It was Edgar." Her voice shakes with anger. "I've been trying to get free of his hold since the séance last night. As soon as he got the upper hand, he ran straight to O'Connor, the little snitch!"

I glance around hurriedly, expecting the other students to have woken up too, the way Azar has. But they are as blank and eerie as before. "He pretended to be you when Neil called," I guessed.

"Yep!" Azar growls. "That was the last fucking straw. He thought he had me for good, but his egghead ass was wrong!" She punches a struggling O'Connor in the face and climbs over him to get to us. "Come on," she yells, stepping on O'Connor and grabbing as many of us as she can reach. She sprints away, dragging me with her.

"Penny!" I yell behind me, worried she won't be able to keep up. But Neil puts an arm around her and waves me on.

O'Connor bellows behind us, back on his feet and moving, and then the students—or rather, their ghosts—finally break out of their stupor and move, starting to chase us too.

"Back to the mausoleum," Jordan yells, running straight for the building. He yanks one of the double doors open. The six of us rush inside, and Jordan picks up the abandoned pickax from earlier and uses it to jam the doors closed. It won't hold forever, but it should be enough to buy us some time.

For a moment, we are entombed in darkness and silence, our panicked breaths the only sounds. But then the ghosts come, banging their students' fists on the doors, yanking the handles. They are enraged, like animals in a feeding frenzy.

I turn on my flashlight, angling its light up so I can see everyone. "What the hell happened?"

"O'Connor—broke—the protective circle," Penny says, panting hard.

"Obviously, the ghosts know what we're doing now, and they're trying to stop us," Wren adds.

"Shit," Neil hisses, starting to pace.

"Understatement of the year," Jordan says, one hand closed tight around the pickax's handle, the other braced against the wall. "Neil, stop pacing and help me."

"Let me in there!" O'Connor bellows.

"We can still do the ritual," I say desperately. We have to finish it—there's no way we escape from this otherwise. "We're in here and they're surrounding us. It's not ideal, but we can do it. Can't we?"

"I think we'd better," Penny says. "It's our only way out of this."

"And now we have Azar," I add. "We can do this." I look into my friends' tired, worried, frightened faces, and feel my own determination bolstered. "We can do this. I know we can."

"Okay," Wren says. "Let's go. Everybody, kneel."

Our knees hit the hard floor of the mausoleum. We circle Wren, who sits cross-legged in the center.

Outside, the ghosts have begun to yell. I make out Quigg's voice, screaming obscenities in a way that doesn't sound like him at all. Someone throws themself at the doors, which rattle and groan.

"We gotta hurry," Penny says. "Before they tear the doors down. Do it now, Tara!"

"Let's hold hands," I say. It's not specifically in Bauer's

notes, but it makes me feel more grounded and connected to them. And I need that more than ever because what we're doing now won't just separate us from our ghosts. It won't just release Walter Weymouth George. It will sever the ties that hold us all together—Magni Viri, our present and our past, our living and our dead.

We aren't putting an end to our ghosts. We're saying good-bye to Magni Viri itself.

Forever.

THIRTY-TWO

We resume the chant, drawing WWG to the surface and laying him bare, holding him captive with his own music. It sounds beautiful inside the mausoleum, eerie and echoing, like we've weaved a spell to hide inside. The banging and shouting from outside seems to fade. But I know those doors won't hold them off forever.

I let go of the others' hands and move to the center of the circle, positioning myself in front of Wren. With a trembling hand, I raise the silver knife to the level of their heart. They open their eyes when the tip of the blade presses into their sweater, fear dilating their pupils until they are black, an endless black like an open, yawning grave.

But is it Wren's fear, or Walter's? Because I see more than fear there. There's longing too. A longing for release.

The words I have to speak now weren't in Bauer's journals. But I can imagine him saying them. I can imagine how he might address the man he loved, formal and tender both. "Walter Weymouth George, beloved founder of Magni Viri, by your blood you created us. With your life, you wove ours together," I whisper. "We honor you and we thank you." I grip the knife more tightly, letting it press harder into Wren's chest, just enough for them to feel it. "This knife once separated your spirit from your body. Remember that it offered you peace, an end to suffering. Remember that it offered you rest. Let it do so again."

A horrible keening wail goes up from the mouths of the hosts outside, and the frenzy outside the mausoleum doors increases. Multiple students must hurl their bodies at the doors at once because there's an enormous thud that shakes the foundations of the mausoleum.

"Keep going," Wren whispers. Or is it Walter?

I raise my voice louder. "We want to dissolve the bonds of Magni Viri—of dead to living, of dead to dead, of living to living. We want to unbind what you have bound, Walter. We want to release what your blood has bound."

Boom. Boom. Boom. The doors creak and groan.

"Go faster, Tara!" Neil yells. He, Azar, and Jordan are doing double duty. They're part of our protective circle but have to keep their backs to the doors too, their feet braced against the floor, helping the pickax hold back the crowd.

"We offer you release, Walter. We offer you rest," I say. "Your work is at an end. Follow this blade into the arms of your beloved."

Tears stream down Wren's cheeks, but I know it's not them crying. It's Walt. I can see the man behind the brilliant music, the man who inspired a love so extreme that his lover could not let him go into the dark. And after so many years of living on in students, Walt has learned to fear nothing except that darkness.

In an echo of the vision WWG showed us during the

séance, I cup Wren's cheek and press my lips against theirs, a final kiss from John Bauer to Walter Weymouth George. "Find me, beloved," I whisper, quoting Bauer's letter, "come and find me."

"John," Walt whispers, his eyes filled with longing.

Wren's body goes limp beneath mine, and they slump to the ground, emptied of their ghost.

Walter Weymouth George has passed on.

From outside the doors, O'Connor starts to scream. It's not the angry bellowing of before, but a high-pitched scream of pure terror, the sound of a man about to die.

"Let me in, please let me in!" he weeps. "They're going to kill me!"

In the silence that falls, I can hear his clothes being torn from his body, punches landing on his back. There's a sound like someone slamming his head into the door. O'Connor groans.

I automatically get to my feet, drawn toward his distress.

"No way," Neil says, putting a hand out to stop me. "He deserves this. He's to blame for all of this. He's the *reason* we have to do this."

"He'll die if we don't let him in!" Penny shouts.

I hesitate.

"Tara, let him in!" Penny says when she sees my indecision.

I run to the doors and push past Neil, wrenching the pickax free. I open one door, grab O'Connor by the front of his suit jacket, and yank him inside. Jordan slams the door closed and returns the ax to its place before the ghosts have even realized what's happened.

But once O'Connor is gone, they start screaming in rage. Inside me, Isabella screams along with them.

Neil and Jordan go back to bracing the door, ready for another onslaught.

O'Connor sinks to the floor, shaking and weeping, his nose bleeding. He curls up into a ball in the corner and glares at us. "What have you done? What have you done?" he yells.

"Don't interrupt us again or we'll throw you back out there," Azar says angrily, pushing at him with her foot before she goes back to guarding the door.

O'Connor raises his hands in surrender.

"WWG is gone. The rest should go easily now," I say. "Let's keep going."

We reshape our circle, leaving O'Connor to cower in his corner. The others sing, but I speak directly to the ghosts now.

"Ghosts of Magni Viri, those who were bound by the spilled blood of Walter Weymouth George, those who were given refuge by willing vessels: That time is no more. Your foundation stone has crumbled. You have no claim. Let go of your hosts. Return to your own element," I intone. "You are barred from our bodies, from our minds, from our spirits. You are no longer welcome to share in our being. Magni Viri is at an end. Release us! Release us!" I yell. "Release us and be free!"

Outside, the ghosts scream in agony and fear. Inside me, Isabella writhes and reaches for my mind, clawing for a handhold. "Release me!" I whisper fiercely to her alone. "There's no more Magni Viri to bind us together. There's nothing here for you."

A final memory floods me, not of Isabella fighting with

her grandfather, not of Isabella dying in a circle of candles. Instead, it's Isabella walking the grounds of Denfeld, gazing down into the cemetery, knowing it's where her remains will lie forever, knowing that she will never be moved from this place. Finally, she is home.

She screams and claws at the edges of my mind as her power fades. Even now at the end, she clings to the dream of Magni Viri. But she's growing weaker, diminishing. Sheer force of will can't stand against the undoing of Magni Viri, not when its bonds dissolve around us like dust.

I feel the moment she finally lets go. It's like a ten-pound pack is removed from my shoulders, and I slump forward without the weight, hands pressed to the cold stone floor. She's gone. She's *gone*. My body is my own again.

And then the cries outside trickle into silence. The fists that beat on the doors go quiet. Soon, our classmates' voices can be heard, asking each other what is happening. A few people weep, overwhelmed by the force of the ritual, by the way their ghosts have been torn away.

I look around at my friends, and I can see they've been released too. Everyone looks lighter, their faces clearer.

"No!" O'Connor screams into the quiet, leaping to his feet. "No! We cannot lose these minds! We cannot lose them!"

"Spirits, come to me!" he bellows, a fanatic desperation in his eyes. "I offer you my body, my blood. *I* will be your vessel, not these ungrateful children. Bind yourself to me!"

"No!" I yell, horrified. I try to grab his arm. If a single ghost can do to me what Isabella did, I don't want to imagine what an entire graveyard of them could do to one person.

O'Connor pushes me away as if I'm an irritating pet. He grabs Bauer's silver knife from the ground. With a cry of pain or triumph, he drags the blade across the soft skin of his inner arm. A line of blood opens up and wells, dripping down his arm onto the floor as we look on, frozen in horror. He switches hands and draws a line down his other arm too. Blood pools on the floor beneath him.

"Spirits, I welcome you!" O'Connor cries, lifting his open hands to the heavens. "I welcome you! I, Theodore O'Connor, offer myself to you. Come in, come in!" He laughs, the sound high and wild, echoing through the close confines of the mausoleum. "Come in and—"

His words are cut short by a choking sound. We all have our flashlights on now, watching him. His eyes widen, pupils growing huge. His expression turns confused, and then bewildered. He puts his hands to his head as if it hurts. He grips his hair and squeezes, his expression contorted with pain, fear, and—unmistakably—wonder.

I feel a single, strange moment of jealousy, that he would get to experience all those minds, see the world from two dozen different perspectives, how the entire universe must have come alive to him, glowing and full of possibility.

But then he starts to scream. His body is thrown to the floor and begins to roll and thrash and twitch. All the while he grips his head, screaming in agony.

"What's going on in there?" someone yells from outside. I think it's Quigg. He sounds like himself again. And he must be—his ghost is gone, same as everyone else's. Gone into O'Connor.

I rush to open the mausoleum doors, and the students surge inside. "What's wrong with him?" Quigg demands, going to O'Connor, staring down at him, though not with any warmth. The other students crowd in, trying to see.

"Ruptured brain aneurysm, I'd bet," Neil says without a trace of pity in his voice. He crosses his arms over his chest.

I feel a pang for Meredith, that she died before this could happen, that she had to die for this to happen at all. But maybe knowing Magni Viri is gone, that Isabella can't hurt anyone else—maybe that will give her soul peace.

O'Connor's screams cut off abruptly, and his hands fall to the floor. His open eyes stare at the black ceiling of the mausoleum. He's dead. Devoured by the ghosts.

The ghosts pour out of him. I can feel their cold breath all around us. The other students must too because they start trying to get out. They push and shove to make a way through. Besides my friends and me, Quigg is the only one who stays. He seems puzzled and tired and like he's itching for a drink. He looks between the six of us, a question in his eyes.

"It's . . . over?" he asks.

I nod.

Quigg puts his hands over his eyes and his shoulders tremble like he's struck with grief, but then he lets out a loud, disbelieving laugh. "Jesus Christ," he says. "I'm finally free of the bastard."

As he leaves the mausoleum, I realize I'm not sure whether he means his ghost or O'Connor. Either way, he doesn't look back.

"It's over, everybody!" he yells into the night. "It's finally fucking over!"

The ghosts reach for the remaining six of us, trying to find a porous place they can slip inside. But there's nowhere for them to go. Magni Viri doesn't exist. The bridges between their world and ours have been burned. They're on their own.

And so are we.

For the first time in weeks, my body belongs only to me. My mind doesn't have to share space with Isabella. I'm just Tara Boone again.

Underneath the exhaustion and the horror, I feel a flare of pride. A growing sense of my own power. I survived her. I *defeated* her.

I step out of the mausoleum and into the cold, biting night air, the others following slowly behind me. The older members of Magni Viri mill around, talking in low voices. Many of them shoot looks at me I can't read. Maybe they're angry I took their ghosts from them. Or maybe they're relieved. Maybe they haven't even realized the enormity of what we've done.

I look up at the sky, and though it's still covered in clouds, a few stars shine in between them. They are bright and sharp, and I shiver looking at them.

I'm alive.

My life is my own, and for the first time in a long, long time, I feel worthy of it. I don't need Isabella's genius. I don't *want* it. I have my own thoughts, my own words, my own self.

My friends come outside too and gather around me. Jordan throws an arm over my shoulder, and Penny puts her hand in mine. We all look at each other.

Wren shakes their head, looking a little lost. "It was a beautiful idea, wasn't it?" they say, tears in their eyes. "Magni Viri?"

Azar wraps an arm around their waist. "Yeah, it was," she says.

Neil stares off into the distance, and I see him wipe tears from his face too. I wonder if they're for Meredith or for himself.

"What's going to happen now?" Penny asks. "Will the board try to replace O'Connor? Will they try to fix what we broke? Will they end the program?"

We all shake our heads. It's too soon for questions like this. No one knows what happens next.

"We can fight to keep it together," I say. "It won't be the same as before, without . . . I mean, it'll be different. No ghosts. No cosmic pact. But we'll still be friends. We'll still be together."

"Of course we will," Jordan says. "We don't need Magni Viri for that."

As I huddle close to my friends in the cold air, waiting for whatever comes next, I realize that they're the reason I survived Isabella. I could never be smarter or stronger than her. But I was wiser in one way. And it's the reason I'm standing here. It's the reason I'm free.

She and I both got a shitty deal, family wise. That's one thing we have in common. Isabella built an entire life out of resentment of her roots. She spent her entire life trying to be worthy of the family that rejected her, trying to prove they were wrong not to love her. She spent her afterlife on it too.

But me? I'm going to spend every moment I have creating a life that's worthy of me. And that means finding a new family, one that will love me and sacrifice for me, that will always have my back.

As I look around at my friends, I know it doesn't matter that we're no longer bound by vows and blood and spirits. We're still together, we're still here, and that means we can take the dark and beautiful ruins of Magni Viri and build something new.

EPILOGUE

Fall break starts tomorrow. Wren and I are going to drive up to Pennsylvania with Penny. When we get back to Corbin College next week, everything will be different.

Dr. Hendrix will be in charge of Magni Viri. The school appointed her as interim director after the entire board resigned. If O'Connor's death wasn't reason enough, Quigg's threatening to show Magni Viri's historical documents and occult collection to the administration, the press, and anyone else who might care made up the board members' minds. But mostly I think they no longer deem Magni Viri worth investing in now that the ghosts are untethered and we're just ordinary students. They did us the courtesy of covering up the strange circumstances of O'Connor's demise, and then they left. Magni Viri will have to find new funding to stay alive. Dr. Hendrix says she's excited for the challenge.

Not everyone is a fan of the changes—or of the Magni Viri freshmen who caused them. Some of the students have had to alter their research projects since they're too advanced. There won't be any more Sunday night parties in the graveyard. We will all be a little less brilliant.

So it's probably a good time for us to get out of town for

a while and give the older Magni Viri students a chance to remember what life is like without ghosts in their brains. I'm excited for the long drive with my friends, a change of scenery, and the chance to meet Penny's family. I promised Mr. Hanks and his sister I'd spend Christmas break with them, but for now, I'm ready to flee the embrace of these green and ominous hills.

But before I go, I have some things to do. First, I delete *Cicada* from my computer, as well as any emails I sent about it. Then I take my taped and tattered notebook, filled to the brim with Isabella's midnight scrawls, and I carry it outside.

Fall is nearing its end and the trees are mostly bare, with only a brown leaf here and there trembling in the wind. Winter is coming early this year, Penny says. I missed the chance to see her bats, at least until the spring.

I walk downhill toward the cemetery, savoring the way my boots crunch in the dead leaves, the way the air smells like old books and pipe smoke. I enter the cemetery gate and walk its winding paths through the gravestones. It's colder here because of the ghosts. I can practically sense them shivering in the air, craving a warm body to inhabit.

They'll all eventually fade, I think. They won't be able to linger forever without a living host. For now, they cling to Denfeld Hall and its cemetery. They watch us and pine for us. Quigg told me sometimes they whisper secrets in his ear. But they can't get to us anymore. We'll never belong to them again, and they'll never belong to us.

I find Isabella's grave easily, lonely under its tree. I feel a strange burst of tenderness for her, the sad, clever, unloved little girl who grew into a monster. I kneel in front of her grave marker.

"I brought you this," I say, holding out *Cicada*. "I read it again last night. I'll admit it's brilliant and that it would get me a book deal if I tried to publish it. It might even win me a fancy book prize and turn me into a literary wunderkind. But it's not mine. It's yours."

With a sigh, I lay the notebook on the dead leaves and pine needles that cover her grave. Its pages riffle in the wind as if phantom fingers are thumbing through it. Lily of the valley fills my nose, its springtime scent at odds with the autumn setting.

"I know there is some of me in here too, but not enough of me. It belongs here with you," I say. "It's your masterpiece."

With a hand spade I brought in my bag, I dig a small, book-shaped hole at about the place Isabella's heart should be. I put the notebook inside and cover it with dirt. By the time I'm done, my fingers are numb with cold. I brush the leaves and pine needles back into place.

Then I push myself to my feet and stare down at Isabella's grave. "Rest in peace, Isabella Snow," I say, even though I know she won't.

Her eyes follow me all the way back up the hill to Denfeld, where a white screen with a blinking cursor waits for me to finish what I started.

I have a book of my own to write.

ACKNOWLEDGMENTS

It takes an astonishing number of people to transform a novel from idea to manuscript to published book. I am so grateful for all the smart, hardworking, and generous individuals who contributed to this one, in ways both large and small.

Thank you to Alice Jerman and Clare Vaughn for helping to make my projects a little more human, a little more tender, and, of course, a lot more readable. I've been so honored to have the chance to work on four whole books with the both of you.

Big thanks to my literary agent, Lauren Spieller, who keeps me from getting too lost in the wide world of publishing.

Thank you to everyone on my teams at HarperTeen and Triada US. I am, as always, so appreciative of your excellent work and support.

A special shout-out to my dear friend Philip Brooks and to Professor Kate Holland for helping with my Latin. Thanks also to my authenticity readers for your wisdom and insight. Any mistakes in this book are my own.

I'm endlessly grateful for my writing pals, especially:

Cat—for all the writing sprints and check-ins.

Alder—for the kinship and acceptance I always feel when you read my words.

Cayla—for providing me with an absurd quantity of chocolate Twizzlers to see me through my second round of edits. (They were disgusting and I loved them.)

And finally, thank you to John for walking through so many creepy cemeteries with me. You're my favorite.